Reason to Believe

USA TODAY BESTSELLING AUTHOR

REBECCA YARROS

REASON TO BELIEVE

Editing:

Karen Grove

www.karengrove.com

Copy Editing:

Jenn Wood

Cover:

RBA Designs

❀ Created with Vellum

To Aidan,
My Hulk, my monster,
my zombie apocalypse partner—
Because you held on to your little sister
from the moment the social worker
placed her in our arms
and never let go.

CHAPTER ONE

nox

7 Years Ago

I LEANED INTO THE FRIDGE AND GRABBED A COUPLE OFF-BRAND sodas. Alcohol would have been preferable—finals week had been a bitch, but there was zero chance Mrs. Anders would have been cool with it.

Ryker? Sure. He was twenty-one.

But I was still twenty for another six months. It was the perpetual curse for having skipped second grade—I was in the same class as my friends but always a year younger.

"Hey, Ry, can you hand me Vic's boutonniere?" a light, feminine voice asked from behind me. My pulse leapt in response.

With robotic movements, I grabbed the clear box with the white rose from the second shelf and stood to my full height.

I felt her indrawn breath run through every nerve in my body as I slowly turned around, the sight of her making my fingers flex, my grip denting the sides of the flimsy plastic box.

"Knox." Her eyes widened in surprise, and she finished my name with that breathless hitch that never failed to kick me in the stomach.

"Harper," I answered, somehow forming the word without swallowing my tongue.

"I…I didn't realize you were here." Her long blond hair was up in some kind of soft arrangement that begged for hands to tunnel through it, and her strapless dress—the same blue-green color of her eyes—hugged every damn curve on its way to the floor.

Harper was no longer the little girl who'd followed us around the fire station as we grew up. She was eighteen now. A full-grown woman on her way to her senior prom.

She was also my best friend's little sister.

Little sister. That was exactly how I was supposed to think of her, considering I'd spent most of my teenage years in this very house, but my thoughts were anything but brotherly as I tracked the swell of her breasts rising with every breath she took. Her lips were full and glossed, her skin flawless, and her lashes impossibly long. In the past year, she'd gone from beautiful— she'd always been beautiful—to…gorgeous. *Really* fucking gorgeous.

And I was staring.

Speak.

"Just got back today. I drove in with Ryker." I slid the boutonniere and sodas onto the counter and leaned back against it, drinking in the sight of her.

I wasn't unaware of the affect she'd always had on me. Oh no, I was all too familiar with it, but I'd kept my hands off Harper for three reasons. The first was that I couldn't afford to piss off Ryker—he and our best friend, Bash, were the only family I had left besides Grams. The second reason? I had a social and legal rap sheet about a million miles long in this town that proved I was nowhere near good enough to be anything but her friend. The third? I had every intention of becoming a hotshot firefighter just like our dads had been—like Bash already was—and Harper wanted nothing to do with that life.

Not that I could blame her. It had only been four years since the Legacy Mountain fire burned our town—and our fathers —to ash.

"Right." She flashed a shaky smile and shook her head. "I mean, I knew you were home, I just didn't know you were in our house." She winced, her cheeks turning pink. "Not that you shouldn't be in our house. Of course, you should. You've always pretty much lived here and you're always welcome, you know that. Heck, you have a key. I just didn't realize that you were... you know, here." She finished her babbling and laced her fingers in front of her.

God, I'd missed her. There was no point fighting my smile. I'd adored that about her—the babbling. To everyone else in our tiny hometown of Legacy, Colorado, Harper was cool, confident, and completely empowered. But when we got within ten feet of each other, she got flustered. Had to admit, I liked being able to fluster the belle of our little ball. Half the time, I fucked with her just to *get* her flustered. She was mine in a way no one else was—to fluster, aggravate, protect, and even adore...but never touch.

"You look beautiful."

"Thank you." She smoothed her hands over the high, jeweled waistline of her dress to settle on her hips. "It's prom night."

"I noticed."

She walked forward across the kitchen, reaching past me for the little plastic box. Harper was fucking tiny, a full foot shorter than my six-foot-three height, and even with her wearing heels, I towered over her.

She glanced at the clock on the stove and swallowed hard. "Almost time." Her hand trembled as she slipped off the silver elastic around the box and then popped open the plastic buttons.

Something was off here.

"Why are you nervous?" I asked quietly, knowing Ryker would walk in any second and she'd clam up.

Her gaze flew to mine, those blue-green eyes slaying me like no one else's had in the entire three years I'd been at Boulder. Not that there hadn't been girls—there were always girls—but none of them affected me like Harper, and it was damn unsettling. If she'd been anyone else—

Stop it.

She fumbled the box.

"Harper, why are you nervous?" I repeated.

"I'm not," she blatantly lied, grabbing the boutonniere from the floor before I could. There was still a slight tremble to her hands as she put the box back on the counter, but she straightened her shoulders and tilted her chin, plastering a plastic smile on her face that set my teeth on edge. "It's nice to see you, Knox."

She dismissed me and walked away, heading down the hall.

Let her go.

But I couldn't. Something was obviously bothering her.

Against my better judgment, I followed her down the hall, then leaned against the open doorframe of the downstairs bathroom as she checked her already perfect makeup and looked over the contents of a small purse.

"What, Knox?" she snapped, her gaze meeting mine in the mirror.

"Why are you nervous?" I asked again. "And this time, don't lie."

Her eyes spat fire back at me.

Flustered.

"Is it the guy?" I walked into the bathroom and she retreated, her back bumping against the towel rack in the small space. Then I closed the door and leaned against it. "It's just the two of us, and I promise I won't tell Ry, but please tell me why your hands were shaking out there. Prom night is supposed to be fun."

Her lips pursed. "The way you *had fun* with Angie Crawford afterward?"

I blinked. "How would you know—"

"I'm not an idiot, Knoxville Daniels." Her arms crossed under her breasts.

And there it was—the name no one else dared to call me, but Harper threw around like it was hers. In a way, I guess it was.

"Okay, well, I had a…good time with Angie," I agreed. A very good time, where we'd both ended up naked on the edge of Lake Hawkins— "Wait. Do you think this guy is going to pressure you for sex? Because I'll fucking kill—"

Her hand was across my mouth faster than I could finish. "Shhh! If Ryker hears you, I'll die a virgin."

Wait. What? I was down with that plan.

She glared up at me. "I'm not kidding. It took *forever* to find a guy to take me tonight who wasn't scared of the three of you, and you are not ruining this." She slowly lowered her hand. "It's bad enough that Bash will be there with Emerson, which means I'll have to avoid my best friend all night."

"You're a virgin?"

"Hung up on that fact, are you?"

"Maybe." Hell yes, I was. Harper talked a good game, constantly teasing Emerson that she needed to jump Bash—who was basically gnawing off his arm, waiting for Em's eighteenth birthday. "I guess I thought from the way you talked…"

She arched an eyebrow at me. "That I was experienced?"

"That you were firmly in charge of your sexuality," I

corrected, knowing how quickly Harper could turn a phrase on me.

"Oh, I am. I am firmly in control of what I want, and how I'm going to get it. But Ryker, and Bash, and...you"—she stabbed a finger in my chest—"scared off almost every single guy at Legacy High before you left for college. You three are like the forcefield of death, so I haven't exactly had the opportunity, and now I'm going to my senior prom an unkissed virgin with a guy who is *way* more experienced, according to a quarter of the girls in the senior class, so yeah, maybe I'm a little nervous that I'll be bad at it, and he'll know I'm..." She shook her head.

"A virgin," I repeated, wondering who I had failed to scare away from Harper. The three of us had been pretty damn thorough in a high school that boasted only a couple hundred students. Wait...did she say unkissed?

"Why do you keep saying that word?"

"Because you are." I shrugged.

"Not for long. That is the whole dream date, right? Losing it on prom night?"

I would have believed her bravado if her voice hadn't hitched and her lip hadn't quivered slightly.

"Not to everyone. You're supposed to wait until you're in love. *That's* the dream." And it was what she deserved.

"And you were in love with Angie Crawford?" Was that jealousy in her tone?

"No. And she wasn't my first." Or my second.

Harper's mouth dropped open for a second before she snapped it shut. "How many have there been? Did you love your first?"

That simple question felt loaded, and not only inquisitive, but intimate. "No," I answered truthfully. "I've never been in love." I wasn't capable of it. "And my numbers are nothing to aspire to."

If anything, they were evidence to how irrevocably fucked

up I was, running through girls like water, always looking for something I couldn't find, walking out before someone else had the chance to.

Her posture softened. "Well, at least you're not an unkissed virgin, right?" She forced a little laugh. "You weren't nervous on prom night."

"Harper," I whispered, my stomach twisting, hating everything about how she felt right now. "Do you want this guy to be your first...everything?" I ignored the ache in my chest that screamed for her to deny it.

Her gaze darted to the wall as she offered a little shrug.

"You're not supposed to feel like this." I gently lifted her chin until we locked eyes. She was too damn beautiful for her own good. Too smart, and kind, and fiery, and fucking perfect. Whoever the hell the guy was didn't deserve any part of her. Not that I did either. "Kissing...sex isn't about getting it over with. It's about mutual need, and want, and desire. It's about craving something—someone—so badly that there's no other option than to get your hands on them. If you're lucky, it's about love and using your body to communicate, not just take. If you're this nervous, then don't waste something as precious as your first kiss—your first time—on some guy whose only quality is not being scared of Bash and Ryker."

"Or you," she corrected.

A primal jolt of protectiveness I had no right to feel surged up my spine. "Yeah, well, he should be scared of me. If he does one thing you don't want him to, I'll fucking destroy him—Bash and Ryker be damned. All you have to do is call, and I'll be there to end him."

No one was going to touch her without her wholehearted participation. Shit, I didn't want anyone touching her, period, but that wasn't my call. It didn't matter that every instinct in my body suddenly demanded I lay some kind of claim on the one woman I wasn't allowed to want.

"Show me," she whispered.

"My number?" I reached into my back pocket for my phone.

"No. Show me...the want, the need. Kiss me."

Fuck. Me. Every muscle in my body locked as my attention shifted to her mouth. "Harper—"

"What's one little kiss? You've probably had thousands."

One kiss was *everything* if it was with her.

Logic warred with my instincts, and the selfish asshole I was overpowered every rational thought. I wanted that kiss. I wanted to be the first to feel how soft her lips were, to hear whatever sounds she'd make. I wanted to show her how good a kiss could feel, how it was a complete act all on its own. I wanted to be the man she compared every other guy to after this moment, and that wasn't right.

"Please? I won't tell anyone," she promised. "Just...show me. Because I know you can, and what if I never feel it, and what happens tonight... I just...I trust you." She smiled. "You're Knox."

Oh shit. The want morphed into the kind of need I couldn't deny, not with her looking at me like that. The impossible transformed into the inevitable in less than a heartbeat.

You can't.

"Harper..." I took her face in my hands, my thumbs lightly stroking across her cheekbones. "It's not a good—"

She surged on her toes, slamming a kiss onto my mouth. It was hard, close-lipped, and over before I could react. She pulled back, looking up at me with apprehension and wide eyes.

"You kissed me," I said slowly. She'd given me her first kiss. Me. Not the guy currently on his way to pick her up. Not anyone at school. Me.

Mine.

"I did. And now, I've been kissed." Her shrug was all for show.

"No, you haven't." Fine, I was going to hell, because there

was no stopping this. That quick little peck had been the first trickle of snow that signaled the oncoming avalanche. All I could do was hold on and hope we both survived as I slowly lowered my head toward hers, giving her an eternity to pull away. "Not yet."

She sucked in a breath, and her eyes fluttered shut a second before I kissed her, brushing my lips over hers like we had all the time in the world. She was even softer than I'd imagined.

She sighed, and I kissed her again, lightly sucking on her lower lip and letting my tongue glide over the plump flesh. I'd never taken such care with a girl, measured and savored every single motion and reaction. Then again, I'd never kissed Harper.

"Knox," she whispered, leaning in for more.

I gave it to her, kissing her a little deeper, running my tongue over the seam of her lips. Pure heat shot through me, singeing my nerves, burning the sound of my name on her lips into my memory. She gasped, and I sank inside her mouth with a groan, my fingers sliding back into her hair.

My tongue rubbed along hers, tasting something sweet I couldn't place. She caught on quickly, swirling and stroking as she melted against me. Fuck, this was perfect—damn near divine. I turned us until she was pinned to the bathroom counter and brought our bodies flush.

She moaned, her arms twining around my neck to pull me closer.

Oh God, that was too good. It was *all* too good, too much.

It had to stop.

Her tongue found its way into my mouth, and all thoughts of stopping flew out the window. She explored and stroked, and I sucked her deeper, wanting her to mark me, to lay claim in the way I was desperate to with her.

In some bizarre way, this felt like my first kiss too.

Her nails bit into the back of my neck, and I nearly lost what self-control I had. I wanted those nails raking down my back, leaving tiny red trails on my bare skin. I wanted Harper. Only Harper. I wanted her under me, her thighs around my hips, her back arching as I made her come. My dick throbbed at the thought of how hot she'd be when I slid inside her, how I'd teach her how to move. How she'd teach me how to love.

Taking control of the kiss, I leaned into her, letting her feel exactly how badly I wanted her. She rolled her hips back against mine, and a low rumble sounded from my chest.

The tether of my control frayed, and I took her mouth like I wanted to take her body, with long, sure strokes. Our tongues twisted and tangled, until the kiss turned from a slow, sensual exploration into a wildfire of pure, scorching need. I cradled her head, tilting her for a deeper angle, knowing if I moved my hands in the slightest, they were going up her dress to discover if she was just as molten all over.

She nipped at my lip, sucking it into her mouth, and I couldn't hold back my groan. She was softer than silk, and everything I wanted—and couldn't have.

Ever.

This was madness, and it had to stop.

I slowed the kiss, drawing out every ounce of pleasure from the simple connection of our mouths. Then with one last, lingering caress of my lips, I lifted my head.

"Harper." Her name was a reverent whisper as I leaned my forehead against hers.

"Knoxville." She sighed. Her hands traced my cheeks, her fingers grazing over my finals-week stubble.

"*Now* you've been kissed." It took every ounce of self-restraint I had not to kiss her again.

She nodded slowly, her fingers brushing her swollen lips. "Is it always like that?"

"Like what?" I could hardly think; how was she putting sentences together?

"As necessary as air? Like you'll die if you stop? Like the ache will burn you alive?" She reached for me.

I took two giant steps back, putting my ass against the wall. I had to get out of this bathroom before whatever was left of my control snapped.

"Is it?" she asked again, her eyes glazed.

I should have lied—should have told her that a kiss was just a kiss. But I couldn't. Not when the last few minutes had just thrown my entire world off its fucking axis, not when my gravity shifted from the center of the earth…to her.

"No." It was the most honest and damning word I'd ever spoken. Heavy footsteps sounded above us, coming down the stairs. *Ryker.* My stomach pitched. He was going to kick my ass if he found us like this, and I'd deserve it. "And it can't ever happen again. Not between us."

Even if he busted my lip over what had just happened, it would have been worth it.

Her entire face fell. "What? Why?"

Because you're dangerous. Because you have the power to rip me apart. Because you're everything I've ever wanted and nothing I deserve. Because there's something broken in me that even you can't fix. Because you're Ryker's little sister. Pick one.

"Because it can't," I finally answered and then flat-out fled the small room.

I walked quickly down the hall and found Ryker standing in the kitchen.

"Dude, where did you go?" he asked.

"Bathroom," I answered.

"What's all over your face?"

I swiped my hand over my mouth. Tiny specks of shiny glitter. *Harper's lip gloss.* "Nothing."

Ryker looked at me strangely, but my gaze snapped to the kid coming in from the living room, walking with the kind of fake swagger I normally would have laughed at, but not now.

Vic Donaldson? Was she fucking serious? He'd been a punk as a freshman, and my guess was nothing had changed since I'd graduated. Fucking asshole. Asshole in a *tux*...because he was taking Harper to prom.

My Harper.

Not yours. Well, not his either.

I was in the kid's face in two seconds flat, using every inch of my height to stare him down. "You know who I am?"

He glared up at me but nodded. Good to know my reputation was still intact.

"You see my face?" I pointed just to be sure he was following.

"Yeah, man, I see it," he snapped, but the blood drained from his face.

"Good. Because if you touch her without her express, whole-hearted, sober consent, or if you so much as think of hurting her, this face will be the last thing you see as I put you in the fucking ground. Got it?"

"Whoa." Ryker stepped closer, his forehead puckering.

"Do. You. Fucking. Understand. Me?" White-hot jealousy pumped through my veins.

"Got it," the kid finally said.

"Knox," Harper called out behind me.

I stared Vic down for another few seconds, until he knew I'd carry out my threat, and then I turned around to face Harper. Confusion put two lines between her eyebrows, and her lips were still bee-stung from our kiss.

The same lips Vic was going to try to kiss later.

Nausea rolled through my stomach.

"Why?" Harper asked.

We both knew she wasn't asking why I'd just threatened to murder her date.

"Because you're Ryker's little sister." It was the only answer that would keep her heart intact, keep her safe from me.

Devastation washed over her features so fast I thought I

imagined it before she straightened her spine and forced a smile. "Got it. Vic, shall we?"

"You look hot," the guy said with about as much charm as a drunken frat guy.

"You kids ready? I found the camera!" Mrs. Anders said as she came down the steps.

I anchored my feet next to Ryker in the kitchen, wishing my soda was tequila, while Mrs. Anders took pictures. My jaw clenched as Vic put his hands on Harper's waist and pulled her close. The empty can crumpled in my grip. This was wrong.

With each second, something wild inside me grew louder, meaner, more irate, until it was screaming, clawing at my guts to get out, to be heard, demanding I throw Vic out on his ass and take Harper myself.

Do it.

Maybe Ryker would understand. Maybe he'd wish us well. Maybe the whole reason I could never commit to anyone at school was because I'd just been waiting for…Harper. Ryker was my best friend—my family. He knew I'd never intentionally hurt her.

Intentionally.

Twenty years of friendship was on the line, but this was Harper. *My* Harper. Even if she wasn't mine, I was hers. So what, maybe I wasn't worthy of her, maybe I'd fuck us both up in the end, but maybe I wouldn't. Maybe the chance was worth the risk.

"Knox?" Ryker asked quietly as we watched Harper and Vic.

"Yeah?" I put the crushed can on the counter and prepared to make my move.

"You're my best friend, and I consider you my brother. So, I'm only going to say this once."

"Okay?" My gaze narrowed as Vic tucked Harper in against his chest.

"That list we keep? The one where we all get to name a girl that no one touches?"

"Yeah?" Bash had created it and named Emerson as his girl *years* ago. The penalty for touching a girl on the list? Immediate excommunication from our friendship, not that Ryker or I had cared enough about someone to call dibs though.

"I'm ready to name my choice." My usually laid-back friend's voice went flat.

I looked my best friend in the eye and saw his expression go damn near glacial.

"My girl is Harper." He said the words quietly, with an eerie calm that told me there would be no mercy given.

That instinct-driven wildman inside me who craved Harper more than air roared as Ryker's words sliced through my emotional jugular. Pain like I'd never known shredded my insides, tearing through every cell, until I expected to find myself standing in a puddle of blood and regret.

"Do you understand?" he asked, his brow lowering.

He'd never asked me for anything, not in all the years we'd been friends, but this wasn't a request. It was a demand. A line. An ultimatum.

My gaze found Harper's briefly before she turned for another picture. She was someone I'd never deserve. Hell, Ryker knew me best. If he'd somehow seen what was in my eyes and still didn't think I was good enough for his sister, then I wasn't.

"Knox?" he prompted.

I stood completely still, silently screaming as Harper threw me one last look, Vic ushering her out the door. The screen door slammed with brutal finality, and my heart stuttered, then slowed as the possibility of what could have been bled out right there on the kitchen floor.

She'd never be mine.

"I understand."

CHAPTER TWO

arper

7 YEARS LATER

IN OUR SMALL TOWN OF LEGACY, COLORADO, WE WERE ALL A
little damaged. Usually, it was hidden under the new paint, new
construction, new...everything, but even the smallest scratch
revealed the charred remains underneath. The people, the
buildings, the town—we were all the same on one level or
another—rebuilt, remade.

And not always stronger for it.

"Hey, Lisa," I said into my phone, leaving a third voicemail as
I glanced up at the clock. *Six p.m.* "It's Harper...again. I called
the diner, but Agnes said you'd left after your shift around three.
I hope you don't mind that Cherry dropped James off here, so I

have both of the boys, and I'd love to know when you'll be able to grab them. Give me a call when you get this, okay?" I hung up, letting my shoulders fall, and locked the back door of my preschool. This was one of the only undamaged buildings on Oak Avenue, because I'd had it built last year after finishing my master's.

Lisa was one of those damaged people—too broken to rebuild after the fire. Losing her first husband on that mountain with Dad and the rest of the Legacy Hotshot Crew had fractured her, but then her second had walked out while Liam's little brother was on the way, sending her into a full spiral.

"Miss Anders," Liam called out from the table where he was coloring, his eight-month-old brother, James, sitting at his feet.

"Yes, Liam?" I answered, bending down to his five-year-old height.

"I'm hungry," he said, his giant brown eyes darting to mine, then James's, before swiftly falling back to his picture of Spider-Man.

"You know what, buddy? I am too. How about I grab us a little snack until pizza gets here, and then I'll make a couple calls, okay?" I ruffled his dark-brown hair.

He nodded.

I fetched a few bags of Goldfish crackers out of my desk drawer emergency stash, then paused and grabbed one more. Liam was always hungry, and not in a preschooler way, but in the way no one liked to think about—a way I couldn't *stop* thinking about.

But I'd been assured by the county they had Lisa and her boys on their radar.

I opened three bags and sat down next to him, squeezing my butt into the preschooler-sized seats. He waited for me to hand a cracker to James and pop one in my mouth before taking any of his.

"Spider-Man?" I asked nonchalantly, keeping an eye on

James as he peered up at me with big brown eyes, his chubby fists squeezing one of the teething toys I'd found in his diaper bag. As babies came, he was super freaking adorable.

Liam nodded, savoring another of his own snacks as he colored the red on Spider-Man's suit. When no other kids were around, he treated each bite like it was the best dessert, a far cry from the way he inhaled both snack and lunch in our program.

It was one of the reasons I told Lisa I'd take him full-day for free. As a preschool teacher, I wasn't allowed to have favorites, but…I did, and it was Liam. He was smart and observant, sweet to every other kid in his class, and had a smile I took pride in earning.

Liam slid from his chair to the floor, handing James another cracker, and was immediately rewarded with an incomprehensible babble and a two-tooth grin. "Here you go, buddy." His voice was way too old for five. "He's gotten really good at chewing," he assured me with a nod of his head.

"Well, you're doing a very good job taking care of him." Okay, that just melted my freaking heart.

"Where's my mama?" he asked, breaking it.

We never lie to children. We never lie to children. I repeated my mantra. "I'm not really sure, but I called her," I answered, trying to keep my voice light.

He looked skeptical but pulled James closer and fed him the rest of the Goldfish crackers, one by one.

Where was Lisa? Sure, she'd been late for pickup a time or two, but never without a call.

"You know, you should really keep that door locked after hours," Emerson called as she walked in the front door, her arms full of pizza and two shopping bags.

"My savior!" I said, jumping up to help and grabbing the pizza boxes from my best friend.

She set the bags on the child-size table. "Hey, Harper," she said, hugging me tight. Her winter coat was still chilled from the early April air. "What's going on?"

"Nothing big, but thanks for the help." Next to my brother, Ryker, who couldn't really help when he was called away for fires, Emerson was the most dependable person in my life.

"No, I can see they're very small." She grinned and waved at my little charges. "Lisa's kids?" she guessed, shrugging out of her coat and draping it over one of the undersized chairs, careful not to snag her long brown hair.

Small towns, man. Everyone knew everyone.

"Yeah. This is Liam, and James. His nickname is Jamie." The baby offered up a grin.

"Well, hi there! I'm Emerson." She gave them both a smile and led me a few feet away. "What's going on? Not that I'm not always happy to bring pizza."

"I don't know where Lisa is, and I don't want to have to call Elliot." My chest squeezed tight at the thought.

She nodded slowly, her face falling as she glanced at the boys. "I get that. But if it gets much later, you might have to."

"I know." I just really, *really* didn't want to. I adored Elliot, and always had. She was only a year older than I was and had never been anything but kind to me, but she was also one of Legacy's two social workers, and I didn't want to see these two little guys end up in foster care for the night.

"You hungry, little dude?" Emerson asked Liam as we headed back toward the table.

Liam eyed both the pizza box and the bags but stayed quiet.

"Sorry, Liam's not a people person."

"No offense taken," Emerson answered, grabbing the plates out of the bag. "Honestly, I'm glad you called. Bash is gone for the night, and it feels like forever since I've seen you." She hip-bumped me, and I took the plates, opening the plastic wrap.

"Hey now, not everyone wants to be around your love-fest

twenty-four seven," I teased as she opened both pizza boxes on the table.

"Yeah, yeah." She rolled her eyes. I didn't begrudge her happiness. She and Bash were living a hard-earned happily ever after, and I was nothing but ecstatic for my best friend, but since the hotshot team was moving home slowly in preparation for this first season, they'd been attached to each other at the face. "You could date again, you know. I know you're wicked busy keeping this place running, but there's life out there."

Dating and I didn't go well together. I didn't miss Richard and hadn't missed him in the year since we'd broken up. If I was being honest, he'd just been a placeholder, an attempt to forget...him.

Knox. My hand gripped the plate a little tighter at the thought of him.

"Pepperoni or cheese, Liam?" I asked.

He glanced at Emerson, then the pizza, but didn't move from the floor.

"Okay, how about one of each?" I put a slice of each on a paper plate and set it in front of his chair, sliding Spider-Man out of the way of any cheesy messes.

Liam didn't move toward the plates, but his eyes certainly didn't leave them.

Emerson noticed, looking my way and sighing. Then she dug out a handful of containers from the bag. "Hey, Liam. I brought your brother some food. Do you want to tell me what you think he'd like?"

Liam's eyes lit up and he was all over it, selecting James's food carefully and making sure I was feeding his little brother before he took a bite of the pizza. Then he devoured it.

"That's love," Emerson said, her voice soft as she watched Liam tear into his piece of pepperoni.

"Yeah," I agreed, wiping James's tiny mouth as I sat on the floor in front of him. "He's a great big brother."

"Speaking of Ryker, any news on when he's getting home?" She snagged a piece of cheese.

"Nothing yet. He's still in Wyoming." He'd given his previous crew an extra month before officially switching over to Legacy, and the early-season fire had caught him and his travel plans off guard. A knot formed in my throat. It wasn't that I feared fires— we'd been raised on them—but I was terrified of losing him to one just like we'd lost our father.

And now the next generation was resurrecting the very hotshot team that had taken him—taken them all.

"He'll be back before you know it. You at his place until then?" She held out a fresh slice of pepperoni, and I leaned forward, snagging a bite between feeding James.

"Thanks." I nodded. "They swear they'll be done with the reconstruction from the flood damage in two weeks." Jamie grabbed a chunk of my hair and brought it to his mouth. "No, no," I said gently, smiling as I traded him my hair for the bottle Cherry had packed in his diaper bag. He grabbed onto it with both hands and sucked it down. "How's the clubhouse?"

"Finally finished," Emerson answered. She'd quit her job with the city council to manage the hotshot team. "Good thing too, since I think everyone is slated to move back over the next month. We only have this year to get the team up and certified, and it's going to go fast."

"Bash and Ryker will whip them into shape." I glanced at my phone. It was nearly seven. *Don't call. Not yet.* Maybe Lisa had car trouble, or her phone was dead. There were a million possible answers, but none of them were good.

"Knox too. You're going to have to call her soon," Emerson whispered.

"I know." I avoided the first part of her statement and shifted James into my lap so he'd be more comfortable.

Blue lights flashed in the front windows of the school,

sending shadows dancing across the walls, and we all turned our heads toward the door. My stomach sank.

"Oh no."

Three knocks sounded on the door.

"Go. I'll stay with them," Emerson said, offering Liam a reassuring smile as she reached over for Jamie.

"No. I've got him," Liam countered, sitting on the floor and holding his arms up for his brother.

I gave Emerson a knowing look and handed Jamie to Liam before heading for the door, my chest constricting with every step. It couldn't be good if the cops were here. My hands shook as I opened the door, finding Elliot escorted by two police officers, Bobby and Kaden. They were only a few years older than Ryker.

Elliot's mouth was in a tense line, the skin between her dark eyebrows all puckered up.

"Oh God," I said quietly so the boys wouldn't hear. "Is it Lisa? Is she okay?"

Elliot sucked in a shaky breath. "There's been an accident, Harper. The officers found Lisa's car just off Route 192. It looks like she may have been under the influence—"

"We can't tell you any more than that," Bobby interrupted.

"Is she okay?" A knot threatened to close my throat.

"She didn't make it," Elliot answered, shaking her head.

I tried to stifle my cry, shoving my hand over my mouth.

She was gone.

Lisa was *dead*.

Liam and James were inside.

"You're here for the boys." My chest tightened around my heart like a vise, the beats stuttering.

Elliot nodded.

"They don't have anyone," I whispered. "Lisa's parents are dead, and no one knows where their father is. He was gone long before James was born." Where were they going to go?

"I know," she said softly. "Can we come in?"

I nodded, moving out of the way so they could enter. The officers dwarfed the tiny furniture.

"Hey, Elliot," Emerson said, a solemn look passing between us.

"Emerson." Elliot's smile was forced and shaky.

Suddenly, I was fourteen again, hearing the news that Dad wasn't coming off that mountain. That Emerson, my best friend, lost her father too. Knox's dad. Lawson's mom. Bash's dad. Bishop and River's...the entire Legacy Hotshot team had been devoured by the very monster they'd spent their lives fighting.

I watched in a hush as Elliot gently broke the news to Liam, watched his little face fall into somber lines of confusion and devastation.

Sinking to the floor next to the boys, I pulled Liam under my arm, tucking him in tight and rocking softly. He leaned into me.

God, I remembered that feeling, and I'd been so much older than Liam. How did a five-year-old process this kind of news? His entire world had just been upended, shaken like the worst kind of snow globe.

"That means I'll find somewhere for you to sleep tonight, okay, buddy?" Elliot finished.

His eyes grew huge with shock.

Where were they going to go? Liam hated strangers. Tears burned my eyes as Liam tugged James closer, the baby finishing the bottle like nothing had happened.

"Jamie too?" Liam asked, his voice small but strong. Too strong.

Elliot struggled for words.

Realization hit me like an avalanche, and my heart started to pound.

"Of course, they stay together, right?" I asked her, my eyebrows shooting upward.

Her eyes begged me to understand something I obviously didn't. "It's more complicated than it looks." Then she looked up to the officers. "DSS now has custody of both the Clark boys. You guys can head back to the station."

More *complicated* than it looked? What the hell did that mean?

Bobby and Kaden nodded to me and left, both visibly shaken.

"How exactly is it complicated?" I demanded.

Elliot glanced at Liam and then motioned for me to follow as she walked across the room.

"I've got them," Emerson said, taking Liam's other side.

"I'll be right back," I promised Liam as I stood, noting he moved away from Emerson. Then I followed Elliot, who had stopped near the cubbies, where we could see the boys but hopefully stay out of earshot. "They get to stay together, right?" I folded my arms across my chest.

She cringed. "The Pendridges are in Milwaukee for the week, visiting their new great-grandbaby."

"You're telling me they're the only foster family in Legacy? Besides, the Pendridges are about a hundred years old. How do you expect them to take care of two little kids?"

"They're seventy and still get by," Elliot said. "We haven't had to place a kid with a non-family member in years, and we don't have anyone else. People aren't exactly lining up to foster, Harper." She sighed and rubbed the bridge of her nose. "We'll have to send the boys to Gunnison until the Pendridges get back, and DSS there has already told me they'll have to be split up, at least for the week. They just don't have a family that can take both of them."

My stomach twisted painfully.

"No!" I snapped, then whipped my gaze toward the boys. Liam wasn't looking. He wasn't looking over here, or anywhere really, just rocking James back and forth as Emerson spoke softly to him. "You can't split them up."

At least when Dad died, I'd had Mom. I'd had Ryker. My eyes burned and my vision turned blurry.

"Harper—"

"They have no one," I whispered, my voice breaking as the first tear slipped down my cheek. I shoved it away.

"I know, and it's not fair."

"None of it is fair."

"It's just for the week, or until we can find Nolan."

Their father.

Liam would fall apart if they took James. They couldn't be split apart. I didn't even know if they could thrive with the Pendridges, but at least they were only a week away. They just needed to make it through the week.

But a week had the possibility of breaking them. Every cell in my body screamed to do something, anything, to keep this from happening.

"I'll take them!" The words gushed out of me.

Emerson's head snapped up, her brown eyes going wide as dinner plates.

"What?" Elliot looked at me like I'd lost my mind.

Maybe I had, but if I had the power to help, then I had to.

"I'm background checked already, and I've read about teachers taking kids in cases like this. Just let me take them for the week. We'll figure out what to do once the Pendridges are back."

Elliot glanced at the boys. "Where are you going to put two little boys? They need their own bedroom, and we'd have to come out and do a home study." She lifted her brows. "Tomorrow."

Oh, crap. Right. There were logistics involved here, not just emotion.

Ryker's one-bedroom bachelor pad wasn't big enough—or

the right atmosphere for kids. Emerson had given up her apartment when she moved in with Bash last month.

"I don't…" I shook my head, my mind scrambling for an answer as I looked to Emerson like she'd have it.

She glanced at the boys and then snapped her gaze back to meet mine. "She has a place," she said to Elliot. "It's four bedrooms, almost four thousand square feet, and perfect."

I blinked, wondering what the hell she was talking ab—

"No," I said, my throat nearly closing up. "That's not an option." There was only one house she could possibly be talking about.

Emerson tilted her head. "It is if you want to keep them. It's only a week, right? That house is finished, furnished, and he won't be moving back here for another month. Take it. Take them." She motioned to the boys. "You know he'll say yes."

Knox's house. The one he'd started building seven months ago when the town council agreed to resurrect the Legacy Hotshot Crew. The one that meant he was coming home.

"What's the address?" Elliot asked.

"328 Phoenix Point," Emerson answered.

"The Hotshot neighborhood?" Elliot's eyebrows flew sky high as she penned the address.

"Yep," I answered, keeping my eyes on Liam and James. I could do this. My entire nervous system went bonkers at the knowledge I was going to have to call Knox and ask, but Emerson was right. If I wanted to keep Liam and James together, it was the only option.

"Look, Harper, I'm with you," Elliot said as I pulled out my phone. "I'm willing to do whatever we can to keep the boys together, but are you sure you can actually take them tonight?" Her voice softened.

"I need a second," I told Elliot as I opened my text messages.

Emerson was by my side faster than I could open a new message. "I can call him. You don't have to."

"No, if I'm the one who wants to borrow his house, I'm the

one who should ask." My thumb hesitated over his contact information just like it did every time I thought about texting him but didn't...which was a lot.

"He'll say yes," she promised.

"I know. That's what makes it so hard." At least I could text him, which would cut out the whole heart-stopping-at-the-sound-of-his-voice issue I'd always had.

ME: HEY, I NEED A FAVOR.

Three little dots immediately appeared on my screen. He was texting back.

KNOX: NAME IT.

God, that was so like Knox. Perfect in every way but the ones that really mattered. My stomach dipped and dived while I typed out my request.

ME: I NEED TO BORROW YOUR HOUSE.

Three dots appeared again.

KNOX: CODE IS 1208.

My eyebrows hit the ceiling even as my heart did that annoying melting thing it always did when it came to Knox.

ME: REALLY? YOU DON'T EVEN WANT TO KNOW WHY?

KNOX: DON'T CARE.

ME: WHAT IF I'M THROWING A PARTY?

KNOX: THERE'S A BAR IN THE BASEMENT. NO TIME TO CHAT, JUST USE THE CODE.

HARPER: THANK YOU.

KNOX: DON'T MENTION IT.

He actually meant that, *don't mention it.* There were a lot of things we didn't mention. Ever. Like they never happened.

"It's settled. We'll be at 328 Phoenix Point," I told Elliot as I slid my phone into my back pocket.

"Is it..." She peered up over her notebook with a knowing look.

"Yep," I repeated. Small freaking towns, man.

She whistled. "You sure?"

"Yep." Apparently, that was the only word I was capable of saying.

"I'll accept it," Elliot said. "I wouldn't normally since you're not on title or the lease, but there's nothing normal about what's happening here. The boys have bags in the car that I grabbed from Lisa's place, and you have to sign some papers, but I'll accept it, at least until I can do a home study. Then we'll see what we can work out until the Pendridges get back."

I nodded, my mind swimming, but something inside me unfurled, expanding through my chest until I felt stronger, capable. Determined. Those boys were not being separated or being sent to a stranger's house. Not the same night their mother had been taken from them. Not if I had a single thing to say about it.

"Okay. Let's sign."

CHAPTER THREE

arper

AN EAR-SPLITTING CRY WOKE ME, AND I SLAPPED AT MY PHONE,
trying to shut off the alarm. Why the hell did I set it for 5:45
a.m.?

Oh, wait. That wasn't an alarm...that was James.

Right. Because I'd taken the boys last night.

Holy. Shit.

I fell out of the queen-size guest room bed and scrubbed the
sleep out of my eyes as I stumbled across the hall.

"I'm sorry," Liam apologized in a tiny voice, his wide eyes
darting toward mine as he leaned over the playpen. Emerson
had saved my butt and picked it up, along with some provisions,
while I signed the temporary foster-parent paperwork.

"It's not your fault, bud," I said, running my hands over his dark hair. He leaned into my touch, just like he usually did at school, so maybe there was hope of him not closing me out.

I quickly changed James while he hollered, and then took them down the stairs to the great room.

"This place is big," Liam said, his eyes sweeping the layout.

"It is," I agreed, heading for the kitchen. It was *huge* for a guy who constantly swore he'd never have a family of his own.

"I can make his bottle," Liam said, grabbing the yellow can of formula, half gallon of water, and said bottle before I could object. "I do it all the time. I'm really good at it."

"Okay," I said, struggling to keep my voice level as he carefully measured out the scoops. My first instinct was to tell him not to worry, that I'd take care of it—of them—but he'd lost every bit of certainty in his little five-year-old world, so I understood his basic need to care for James—to keep something normal.

"How about I grab you some cereal while you're doing that?" I offered. "Em picked up some Lucky Charms."

"Yes, please." Intense concentration furrowed his brow as he poured the water, doing his best not to spill.

James chewed on a stray strand of my hair while I fixed the cereal and thanked God that Emerson had helped with all this stuff last night. Once James was happily breakfasting on formula, I turned back to Liam.

"You know, I'm still just Miss Anders," I said as I hoisted him onto the stool at the kitchen bar. "You can even call me Harper if you want."

He nodded but didn't take his eyes off his marshmallow hunt.

I popped a K-cup into the new Keurig and pushed all the set-up buttons. As it brewed, I ran my hand along the dove-gray granite counters. Construction had been completed a month ago, and the builder had outdone themselves. It was traditional without being stuffy, and contemporary without being cold.

The furniture was sturdy and masculine but comfortable with buttery soft leather couches and a television that looked like it belonged in a movie theater. The walls were mostly bare, the décor nonexistent. There were no personal touches, nothing that might give any clues to who Knox was under the surface, because he didn't live here...yet. But within a month, he'd be back in Legacy.

Don't go there. You're here for a week—max—and out.

Speaking of the giant television, I said a silent prayer of thanks that someone had gotten it set up as I popped on a cartoon and put James into the jumping contraption Emerson and I had assembled last night with a glass of wine after the kids were asleep.

"Is *Paw Patrol* okay?" I asked Liam.

He nodded enthusiastically, sinking into the thick cushions of the couch closest to James.

Wait. Was I supposed to let them watch TV this early in the morning? Wasn't I always the one telling parents to lessen screen time? But, for God's sake, it was—I checked my phone—barely six in the morning and I hadn't even had coffee yet. Surely there was a mercy rule when it came to technology and parents going on four hours of sleep.

I doctored the coffee with cream and sugar, then tiptoed through the downstairs like I'd be in trouble if I got caught. Last night had been so hectic with getting the boys down that I hadn't taken the time to really explore. How was it that even the lines of the floor plan reminded me of him? Open spaces welcomed friends and closed-off hallways led to the more personal rooms like the study.

The great room was vaulted to the second story, with windows that ran the height of the room. The view was spectacular, looking out over the valley and up at the peaks above. The scar from the fire ran a wicked, curved line down the closest mountain. There were new pine trees and a few survivors here and there, but they were far outnumbered by the corpses of the trees that had burned that day.

The view was just like Knox. Beautiful to the point of breathlessness with undisguised damage front and center to serve as a warning he'd never be entirely safe. There would always be that part of him that was ready to burn under the right circumstances.

Who would eventually stand here with him? Watch the scar disappear with the growth of new life as the years passed? I knew two things about his hypothetical future wife: she was incredibly lucky, and I already hated her. Maturity was never my strong suit when it came to him.

Venturing into his office, I admired the clean lines of the furniture and a shelf of leather-bound classics, wondering who he'd hired to decorate. He was still living in California, but this place was move-in ready, from the bed linens to the dishes in the cabinet.

It was almost like he wasn't bringing anything with him from California.

My fingers traced the line of his desk as I sipped my coffee, my eyebrows rising as I caught sight of the photo gallery on the opposite wall.

Like a freaking magnet, I gravitated to the only solo picture he had of himself on the wall. My breath hitched at a two-dimensional picture—I had it that bad. Of course, he was decked out in full gear with a devil-may-care smile plastered on his gorgeous face. The sun glinted off his light-brown hair, sweat-soaked from the fire they'd been working, and his helmet held under one arm. Why did he have to be so annoyingly gorgeous? Man, I hoped I didn't gawk like this when he actually got here next month.

What would it be like now that he was moving home? Would he still treat me like an annoying little sister whenever Ryker was around? Being on the same crew would only bring them closer than ever, and it wasn't like either of them had a choice of quitting—not if they wanted the Legacy name on the hotshot crew.

Sixty percent Legacy members—children of the original team—*that* had been the stipulation the town council had made when Bash, Ryker, and Knox submitted a proposal to reestablish the team. The council said the rule was made to assure the support of the surviving family members, but our town wasn't stupid. It was half deterrent and half PR stunt, but they'd demanded sixty percent, and now they were all headed home to put on the patch our fathers had died in.

Nothing like tempting fate in the name of family tradition.

Ugh, my stupid heart ached from looking at his picture, like I was some high-schooler with a crush and a notebook full of signatures with his last name attached to mine. I hated how much I missed him, that I knew the exact number of days since he'd visited last. I loathed the way I felt about him—abhorred the dreams I had where he did way more than just kiss me. I despised the jealousy that threatened to turn my skin green when I saw yet another woman on his Instagram.

But none of those words fit how I actually felt about him.

No, I was head-over-heels in love with that arrogant ass and had been since I was old enough to name the emotion.

But to him...well, I wasn't anything, not even a blip on his sexual radar.

I was his best friend's little sister.

And I hated that most of all.

I left my feelings in the office and closed the door, walking back down the short hallway to the living room, where I found the boys watching TV. Liam's little head kept moving side to side like he was watching a tennis match, and Jamie jumped happily a few feet away.

Maybe if I was quick, I could sneak upstairs and at least put on a bra before they got restless, because the little shelf number in this pajama tank top wasn't doing my D-cup girls any favors.

Right on cue, James started to wail, his shrill cry echoing off the walls in the great room. I scooped him up and cradled him to my chest, rubbing his back, but the cries didn't stop. They only grew louder.

"You're clean. You're dry. You're fed," I whispered, mentally going through the logical reasons a baby would fuss and flinching as the next cry hit a pitch that made nails on a chalkboard seem like a symphony. "Maybe a little walk?"

Liam observed, matching my steps as I paced the halls with James, patting his back, humming, promising I'd buy him everything short of a pony if he'd just stop for a little bit. His tone reached an ear-piercing shriek and somehow stayed there.

An hour later, I promised him the damn pony.

I tried a bottle, burping, a diaper change...anything and everything I could think of, to include singing, which only made him cry harder. Anxiety flooded every cell in my body. What if I couldn't get him to stop? What if he knew I had exactly zero experience with a baby and wanted nothing to do with me? If this went on much longer, I was going to start crying *with* him.

Liam watched me with nervous eyes. "I'm sorry. He does this. He gets really loud. Mom usually lets him cry it—" He blinked quickly and looked away as we made the loop back into the kitchen.

It was the first time he'd mentioned his mother since Elliot's arrival last night.

"It's okay, Liam. He's just a baby and doesn't know how to tell me what's wrong. Don't worry, we'll figure it out. And it's okay to talk about your mom—"

"Maybe he's hungry," he interrupted, reaching for the bottle. He leaned as far as he could onto the counter, and before I could help, knocked over the open box of Lucky Charms, sending the entire bag of cereal spilling in a colorful arc over the dark hardwood floor.

I mentally cursed the cereal company for allowing that to happen. Who the hell designed cereal boxes? Didn't they realize kids would be using them? Couldn't they come up with something a little better than an open plastic bag secured with a tiny cardboard tab?

"I'm sorry!" Liam cried, tears welling.

My heart clenched. "It's okay," I promised, forcing a smile as I bounced James on my hip. The wailing reached an all-new level of misery, and my head exploded in pain as he hit the perfect pitch to bring on a headache.

Maybe I needed to call Cherry, Jamie's usual babysitter. She had to know how to settle him down, right? Or maybe I'd simply lost my fool mind. Convincing Elliot I could absolutely handle bringing the boys home was one thing—the reality was quite another. This was like drinking from a fire hose.

Hello, crash course in parenthood.

I heard the alarm *ding* behind me as the front door opened and nearly cried in relief as the security code was input, silencing the harsh warning tones. Emerson was here. I'd never been so freaking thankful in my life.

"We're in here!" I called out over my shoulder as I heard two sets of steps coming down the hallway from the entry. Maybe Bash had made it home early?

James's little belly heaved, and before my brain could process the action, he vomited. An impossible amount of warm, sticky liquid gushed all over my back. I froze, not even daring to breathe as he wretched again. How could one little baby have *that* much in his stomach?

Oh. My. Gross.

He finished his *Exorcist* routine, and I quickly took stock of the damage. My hair, my back, the floor behind me—it was all covered in splattered puddles of baby vomit.

Liam grimaced. "Eww."

"Eww indeed." I pulled the chubby, now-smiling baby off my miraculously clean chest and held him at arm's length to check him over. Of course, he didn't have a drop on him or his little footy pajamas, and mercifully, he'd stopped crying. "He must not have felt good," I said to Liam, pondering how to get Jamie back to the living room without tracking puke all over the place. "I'm so glad you're here, because I desperately need a shower," I called out to Emerson.

She was going to laugh her ass off at me.

"Oh. My. God," a feminine voice replied. That was *definitely* not Em.

I turned around as James hurled again, this time splashing puke onto my chest. A warm flood rushed down my tank top, filling the shelf bra and soaking through the fabric.

This was officially the grossest moment of my life, and I taught preschool.

"I can't believe you're…married!" a woman shrieked from just inside the kitchen, smacking the guy behind her with an oversized handbag.

My stomach dove for the floor.

That was *not* Bash.

Oh, no, no, *no*.

Fuck. My. Life.

This was a nightmare, it had to be, like the one where I was naked at school without my homework, except worse. So much worse.

I shifted James to my other, non-puke-covered hip and watched the fully made-up brunette supermodel in her immaculate, studded jeans spin, her Louis Vuitton bag knocking my coffee mug off the counter and sending it sailing to the floor.

The mug shattered on the hardwood. Coffee joined the cereal and puke. *Awesome.*

"How dare you!" she shrieked, a fury of angry little stomps as she charged toward him, her finger shaking in rage. "We may have kept it casual, but I'm *not* down with this shit!" She swung her arm, motioning toward me.

I moved sideways, pulling an open-mouthed Liam behind my back.

The room fell silent, and when I looked up, deep brown eyes were locked on mine, wide with a little shock and a touch of amusement. With the hundreds of ways I'd pictured his homecoming... well, I'd never been soaked in baby puke in any of those fantasies.

"Hey, Harper." His voice was soft and deep as the corners of his mouth quirked up slightly.

"Knox." I barely managed a whisper, praying my eyes conveyed the apology I knew he desperately deserved. He'd brought a woman home, and I was a flat tire of a third wheel.

The model started yelling again.

"Months!" She turned panicked eyes on me, and I clutched James a little tighter. "I've been sleeping with your husband for months! And he's never *once* mentioned you." Her gaze swung to Knox. "How could you never mention a *wife*? Or kids?"

Before I could tell her Knox and I were anything but married, she went off on another tirade, this time directed at Knox, stabbing her finger in his direction.

The puke on my boobs started to chill, which only made it that much grosser.

"And if you think I'm going to play side chick in this hot mess, you're sorely mistaken!" She motioned back toward me, and my cheeks flushed with embarrassment.

"Stop, Melinda," Knox warned, putting himself between us.

I could only imagine how I looked in crumpled sleep pants, soaked in vomit, last night's makeup that was probably smeared under my eyes, with my hair a tangled pile of rat's nest. She wasn't far off on the *hot mess* comment.

James, however, thought the whole situation was hilarious,

and giggled while Liam looked around my hip and tried to hush his baby brother.

"How could you *do* this?" she yelled.

"For f—" Knox's gaze caught on Liam, and he stopped himself mid-swear. "God's sake, Melinda, could you give me just a second?"

She folded her arms and glared.

If there was a hole in the floor I could have disappeared into, I would have.

"Holy crap, you're already home," Avery, River's girlfriend, said from the entry hall, carrying—thank you, God—fresh coffee. "Sorry, the door was open, and Emerson asked if I'd drop off some coffee and check on Harper." Her bright-blue eyes bounced between us, and I forced an awkward smile, knowing she was more than aware of my feelings for Knox, thanks to a few glasses of wine after she'd moved here from Alaska with River. "We weren't expecting you for a month."

"That's pretty obvious," Knox replied with a tilt of his head, his gaze swinging to mine. "Did I order a crib with all that new furniture?"

"I'm so sorry, Knox." I sidestepped the puddle of puke to keep Liam in the clear. "I thought we'd be gone before you got here."

"Wait, are you two separated?" Melinda asked.

"Awkward," Avery sang softly.

He held up his finger in Melinda's direction and turned back toward me with a look of annoyance. "Harper, stop saying you're sorry. My home is yours, no questions asked. I can't count how many times you've come home to find me standing in your kitchen. Don't apologize. You asked. I said yes. I'm just a little...surprised by the small people, that's all."

Lowering his finger, he looked back at Avery. "Avery, this is Melinda, she's a *friend* from California, and she needs a ride to

Crested Butte to visit her family. Would you mind driving her over?"

Crested Butte was about twenty minutes up the pass—hold up. Did he say *friend*? Because the way she was looking at him said she felt way more than friendship.

"I can do that," Avery replied, setting one of the takeout coffee cups on the counter. And shooting me a *wtf* look.

"Thanks." Knox turned his attention to Melinda, a muscle ticking in his jaw. "Mel, Avery is my friend River's girl, and she's going to take you to your sister's. And just to set the record straight, Harper isn't my wife or girlfriend, or anything. And she's not a hot mess—she's my best friend's little sister."

Whoomp, there it is. Whatever spark of hope I'd kept alive for the last decade deflated like an untied balloon. That's what it would always come down to. First, foremost, and always, I was Ryker's little sister in Knox's mind. Funny how that hurt worse than his *friend* calling me a hot mess.

"Oh," Melinda said, her gaze darting between us all. "I'm just...I'm sorry. I saw the kids and jumped to conclusions." Her eyes flared with sympathy as she looked my way. "And I didn't mean that *you're* a hot mess. Just the whole Knox-has-a-wife thing would have been a mess."

"It's okay. I'm pretty"—the dripping puke reached my navel —"messy."

She laughed, and I somehow doubted this woman had been messy a day in her life. *Don't be a jealous wench.* "I should have known better. Like this guy would ever settle down." She lifted her bag back onto her shoulder. "I'll be in town for the next week or so. Call me if you get bored." She flashed Knox a smile. "Thanks for the ride."

"Yeah," Knox replied, his voice taking on that crisp, blunt, dismissive tone he used when cutting someone out. *Whoa.* The woman was done in his mind, even if she didn't realize it. I'd seen him slice out countless people when they stepped over whatever imaginary line he'd drawn, and I couldn't help but feel sorry for her. She'd be added to the list of women who had zero clue why they'd been ostracized. "I'll walk you out."

The two disappeared down the hallway, and Avery turned her wide eyes on me. "Holy crap, that was intense. Where is your phone?"

"My phone?" I blinked. "Um. I think it's upstairs on the nightstand."

"Em's been trying to call you for the last hour. Bash got home about an hour ago and told her Knox was already on the way too. I was coming to warn you." She flinched. "Sorry I was too late."

"There's nothing to be sorry for. Thank you for the coffee." I shook my head. "If I'd known he was on his way home, I would have run the other direction."

"I know. You okay?" Concern filled her eyes. "I was going to offer to help out this morning, but if he wants me to drive her..." She glanced back toward the door.

"I'll be fine," I assured her, part of me screaming for her to stay so I'd have a buffer between me and Knox.

"Okay. Fill me in later, or text if you need backup." She waved to the boys and hurried out after Knox and Melinda.

"Is it okay?" Liam whispered.

"Yeah, it's okay, bud." I ruffled his hair with my spare hand. "I think we just surprised Knox."

"And the lady." His nose crinkled.

"Especially the lady," I agreed. "But I'm really glad you're here."

He swallowed, his gaze dropping to the mess on the floor. "I can help clean up."

Before I could reply, Knox walked back in, pushing up the sleeves of his gray sweater to his elbows, and revealing tan, muscular forearms.

His forearms? Get a grip.

Okay, but those hips? The way the jeans hugged him? *Mercy.*

Liam stepped back behind me as Knox took in the spilled cereal, busted ceramic, splattered coffee, and baby vomit all over his floor and sighed before shaking his head. "So, I'm just wondering, did I miss the part of my life where we got married and had a couple of kids? This is all feeling very *Twilight Zone.*"

"Like you even watch *The Twilight Zone.*" I scoffed, shifting my weight as I felt the puke drying in some places on me and turning ice cold in others.

"How would you know? Maybe my tastes have changed."

"After what I just saw, I think it's safe to say they haven't." I cringed at his quirked eyebrow. "Sorry. It's been a long morning. Night. Everything. Now I just got you in a fight with your girlfriend and wrecked your kitchen."

"She's not my girlfriend. Pretty sure you heard that part. It was more of a friends-with-benefits kind of thing that ended weeks ago, but when she heard I was driving home, she asked if she could catch a ride so she could see her sister. I was already on my way when you texted last night. Why don't you hand me Sir Pukes-A-Lot and go take a shower?" He walked forward, flexing his hands in the classic give-me motion.

My jaw dropped. "You're going to watch the kids—including a baby—while I shower?" I'd never seen Knox so much as look in a baby's direction before.

"Relax. I highly doubt I could manage to accidentally maim them in the amount of time it would take you to rinse the puke off." He stared me down, standing a foot away with outstretched arms.

"You wouldn't mind? You don't want to know what's going on first?"

"Of course I do, but you smell. So, hand him over. We'll sort this all out once you're not wearing his breakfast. I don't think the guest bath is stocked yet, so use my shower—first door on the right." He nodded up the stairs.

Maybe this *was The Twilight Zone*. "He could very well ruin your shirt. Just look at me."

He arched an eyebrow, then reached behind his head and pulled his sweater and T-shirt off in one smooth, mouth-watering motion. The guy was all cut lines and hard surfaces, topped off with a cocky grin, which was exactly where I kept my eyes. Looking any lower would have slaughtered my sanity. "There. No shirt to ruin. Hand him over."

When he reached for James, I let him go without another protest. Mostly because I was speechless. Knox shirtless? I was a puddle of decade-old need and idiotic longing.

Knox shirtless with a baby? Boom. Pretty sure I was instantly pregnant.

"What's up, little man?" he asked James, holding him with both hands like a breakable vase. James gave him a toothy grin, and then Knox turned his smile on Liam, who wasn't as easily won over. "Baseball? *Star Wars*? *Evil Dead*? What's your poison?"

"James likes *Paw Patrol*," Liam answered, stepping away from my legs and giving Knox a very judgy once-over.

"Go," Knox urged me. "I've got this."

The promise of a shower was too good to pass up.

"I'll only take a couple minutes, I promise. Liam, this is Knox, and he's my brother's best friend. I've known him since I was a baby. I trust him, so you can too. Will you be okay if I go rinse off?"

He looked at Knox again and nodded solemnly.

I ruffled his hair again and smiled. "Be right back."

I raced for the shower. I may have had my hands full with two boys, but add Knox into the picture and I was seriously in over my foolish little head.

CHAPTER FOUR

K nox

I COULDN'T HELP BUT LAUGH. WHAT THE HELL ELSE WAS I SUPPOSED to do when Harper Anders ran from my kitchen, soaked in puke, after wrangling two kids that most definitely did not belong to me?

He's my brother's best friend. That's how Harper had introduced me.

Damn, I hated when she felt the need to remind me she was Ryker's sister. I was well-fucking-aware of who she was and why I'd never get to touch her again.

The miraculously clean baby immediately gave me a drooling grin. Cute kid. *James*, that's what the other boy called him.

The older boy with the huge brown eyes looked up at me and narrowed his gaze.

"Liam, right?" Time to break that ice. I'd never really been around kids, but they couldn't be that much different than adults, right? Small humans. Just had to talk to them.

"That's my brother. James is mine. Kind of Miss Anders's too, but all mine." Liam glared at me with a healthy dose of skepticism, like I was going to drop the squirming baby.

Territorial. Okay, I could work with a mini-alpha pup. "Cool. I like him. Why don't you show me what he likes to do while Harper showers some of his stink off her?"

Liam tilted his head, clearly judging me. "Can you make him a bottle?"

I had zero idea what to do with a baby and this kid knew it, like he was equipped with some kind of radar that told him I was a complete rookie.

"Can you show me?" I asked. "And do you think maybe we should give him a minute before he upchucks that too?"

Liam sighed and nodded once. "We'll watch *Paw Patrol*...after you put a shirt on." He went up on his tiptoes and retrieved my sweater from the counter.

Okay, then. "All right, but it's going to take me a second to work the TV," I said, setting my clothes on the back of the couch. "It's new." And upgraded from the model I had in California.

"It's already on. Miss Anders took care of us," Liam said, rolling his eyes, but led the way. Guess he'd begrudgingly accepted me into his pack.

"Gotcha. Now I need somewhere to put you down," I told James as I looked over my living room.

The couches were a little smaller than I'd pictured when ordering them with the decorator, but they fit well. The built-in bookcases turned out great too. From what little I'd seen of the house, everything was exactly as our Facetime final walk-through had shown.

But how safe was it for a baby? At what age did they start

sticking shit into power outlets? How fast could they crawl, anyway?

"You're not going to run away on me, are you?" I asked the baby. Harper would murder me if something happened while she was showering.

"He can't *walk* yet. His jumper is there," Liam told me, pointing to something that looked like a baby-torture device.

"And he likes that?" Now it was my turn to be skeptical.

Liam looked at me as if I was quite possibly the stupidest adult on the planet. When it came to kids, I might have agreed with him.

"Right." I threaded James's chubby legs through the holes, and he immediately babbled and jumped, jiggling the whole frame and the toys attached to it. "It doesn't look stable."

"He's *fine.*" Liam stepped in between James and me.

"And on that note, I'm going to clean up our little mess. You cool in here?"

He nodded, and I took off for the kitchen, throwing on my T-shirt but leaving my sweater on the couch. Usually when I walked into this kind of disaster, I'd had a hell of a night to justify it. Dropping down to the cabinet under the sink, I muttered a curse. No paper towels. No cleaning supplies. Nothing.

Because I hadn't moved in yet. Right.

The buyers for my California house had bought the thing completely furnished, so every personal item I owned was in the bed of my truck.

Ten minutes and some ruined kitchen towels later, the floor was as clean as it was going to get until I purchased a mop. Or hired a maid. Yeah, the maid was more likely.

What was Harper doing with two kids? Babysitting? When she texted last night, I figured she'd just needed a place to crash, and I'd thought it would be funny to surprise her this morning since I was already on my way. Hell, maybe part of me had been craving the sight of her.

And fine, maybe that's why I'd insisted Melinda and I get on the road super early this morning…from our separate hotel rooms. The second Melinda had started hinting last month at wanting something more serious, I'd taken the benefits portion of our friendship off the table, so it wasn't like we were together, or ever had been. But I was self-aware enough to know I'd only brought Melinda in—instead of driving her straight to Crested Butte—to help build a much-needed wall between Harper and me. Then she'd lost her mind and I'd… delegated, leaving me alone with Harper.

I lifted James from his jumper and gave his butt a quick whiff to make sure he didn't explode from the other end too. Merciful God, he was still clean. I wasn't even sure how to change a diaper —or where Harper had them. Liam sat on the loveseat, but when I took the sofa, settling the baby under my arm next to me, Liam moved over, sitting on the other side of his brother like I couldn't be trusted with Sir Pukes-A-Lot. He then handed James some kind of chew toy and sat back into the cushions, dishing up the side-eye as I pulled my sweater on. It was like the kid knew I'd only taken it off to fuck with Harper, and he didn't approve.

Guess he wasn't territorial over just his brother.

Get in line, kid.

"So, you're hanging out with Harper?" I asked him, wondering if he knew just what the hell was going on around here, because I didn't.

"She's my teacher, but she brought us here last night."

Well, that sounded ominous. "Okay," I said, noting the way he tensed. "Did you have a bad day yesterday?"

He sucked in a shaky breath and his lip trembled for the smallest of seconds, making me wish I hadn't asked. Whatever it was, this kid was not okay.

"My mama had an accident. She died."

Holy shit.

I froze momentarily, my mind drawing a blank on anything I could say to this kid that wouldn't be too much or not enough. Mom had walked out when I was a few years older than him, and it had cut me to the bone, but she hadn't died. That level of pain didn't come until Dad was killed, and there hadn't been any words that could have helped back then.

"I'm so sorry. You must hurt a whole lot." I don't know how I got the words out around the lump of my own memories in my throat. I'd felt completely abandoned back then. Even Grams hadn't been able to fill the hole, and I'd been sixteen. This kid was, what? Four, maybe five?

He looked up at me with tears swimming in his eyes, pursed his little lips, and nodded. Then he put his arm around James, pulling him from under my arm and against his side even as he swiped at his tears with the back of his other hand like they were a nuisance.

Fuck, my heart broke for this kid. For both of them.

"I don't know exactly what you're going through. No one does, but my dad died," I said quietly. "I was older than you, but I remember how bad it hurt. Kind of makes you feel lost."

Liam nodded again, his lower lip puffed out as he blinked back tears. Fuck, even my eyes were starting to water. I forced that shit back with a hard swallow and cleared my throat.

"It's good that James has you. Then he won't feel so lost."

Liam leaned his cheek on the top of James's nearly bald head and focused on the cartoon. Conversation over.

Where the hell was their dad? Who was their dad? How did Harper end up with them? Where were they going to end up? At least I'd had Grams when Dad died, but it looked like these two were on their own.

Three short knocks sounded at the front door, interrupting the barrage of questions in my head.

"Come in!" I called out, knowing it had to be Bash. I'd texted him on my way in, not realizing what I was walking into.

I heard the door open and shut.

"This wasn't quite what I meant when I said, 'Let's have a planning session.' I didn't think you'd drive in or anything," Bash said as he walked into the great room. A wrinkle formed between his dark eyes, his head tilting to the side as he saw me on the couch with both boys. "Where the hell is Harper? Did you scare her off already?"

Emerson came in beside him, then smacked his chest with the back of her hand even as she stopped short. "Sebastian Vargas, don't swear in front of kids."

"Like they haven't already heard worse if they're sitting with Knox," Bash muttered, and I would have laughed if Emerson hadn't shot him a go-to-hell look. They'd been back together for eight months and engaged for all of six weeks, but it was only a matter of time before there were little Vargas babies running around. My guess was they'd have dark-brown hair like both their parents and stubborn streaks just as wide.

"They have *not* heard worse. I've been on my best behavior, and Harper is scrubbing puke off."

"Hey, Liam," Emerson said with a smile as she sat down next to him. "Remember me from last night?"

He nodded.

"Want to fill me in?" I asked Emerson. "Because I didn't exactly get details from Harper before I sent her off to shower." Which I was *not* thinking about. At all. Not even in the slightest.

"Maybe she's already done. Give me the baby and go find out," Emerson said, wiggling her fingers with an excited glint in her eyes. Bash was in trouble.

I handed over Sir Pukes-A-Lot with the warning of his morning activities, and he babbled, smiling for Emerson. Damn, that kid was cute when he wasn't projectile vomiting his breakfast all over Harper's tits.

Don't even think about that word in combination with Harper.

Yeah, like that was going to happen. Thank God Ryker couldn't read thoughts, or I would have been dead a decade ago.

I told Liam he could trust Bash and Emerson, before sprinting up the steps and knocking on my bedroom door. When she didn't answer, I went in slowly, cracking the door and calling out her name. No answer. I peeked to make sure the bathroom door was shut before I came in fully. The shower was still running full blast, so I sprawled out across the king-size bed as the exhaustion of driving caught up with me.

The decorator had done a good job in here. The furniture was all dark wood, nearly black, which was nice against the light-gray walls. The whole room had a very comfortable yet still guylike feel.

Funny that Harper was the first person to spend the night in this house.

She was also the first person in my shower.

Naked.

About thirty feet away.

Shit. Now my dick was reminding me of the same facts. Like I needed his fucking opinion.

As if on cue, the shower cut off.

"Hey, I'm in here," I warned her loudly. "I just didn't want you to come out...naked or anything." *Liar.*

"Thanks, I'd rather spare us both that embarrassment," she answered through the door.

Embarrassment? She had nothing to be shy over.

I rubbed my hands over my eyes. I'd been in the same house as her for what, twenty minutes? She'd been covered in puke with a baby on her hip, and I still thought she was the most beautiful woman I'd ever seen.

You always want what you can't have.

She opened the bathroom door and came out dressed in

jeans and a blue V-neck shirt, toweling off her long blond hair. "Hey."

I patted the bed next to me in response, but she shook her head and leaned against the doorframe. I hadn't given her much reason to want to be close in the last couple years, so I couldn't blame her there.

"On a scale of one to ten, how pissed are you?" she asked, her hands gripping the towel.

"Not pissed. Confused. Why don't you clue me in on what's going on?" I suggested as I sat up. The altitude was already getting to my head. I needed to chug some water.

She sighed and rested the back of her head against the doorframe. "I don't know where to start."

"You're Liam's teacher," I prodded her.

"Yes," she answered with a soft smile. "He's such a good kid and he's had it so rough."

"Yeah, I caught on to that. His mom died yesterday?" My chest went tight just thinking about his tears.

She nodded. "They're Lisa Clark's kids."

"Shit. She never really did come back from losing Clint. Drugs?" I guessed. Lisa had been the youngest widow from the fire, and her spiral had been deep, hard, and unrecoverable.

"Car accident, but it sounds like she was under the influence of something. The Pendridges are the only foster family in Legacy—"

I blanched. "They've got to be a hundred. How are they going to care for Sir Pukes-A-Lot?"

"James," she corrected with another smile, this one hitting me like a line drive to the stomach. "His name is James—or Jamie—and yeah, that was the same thing I said to Elliot yesterday. Besides, they're on vacation for the week, so it was either watch the boys get shipped to Gunnison and separated, or I take them for the week."

"Just the week?" I could have collapsed in relief. It was one thing to have a few days of child-induced insanity, and quite another for Harper to take on that kind of responsibility on a permanent basis, especially in my house, but... "Then what? Where's their family?"

"Elliot's hoping Nolan—their biological father—will surface for the funeral, or some other family member will step up." She wrapped her arms around herself, and I fought the urge to add mine to hers.

"And where the hell has he been all this time?" I snapped. Fathers weren't supposed to walk away. Women, maybe—I knew that one firsthand—but never a father. Not when his children needed protecting.

"He walked out early in Lisa's pregnancy with James. He didn't want another kid. Honestly, he wasn't around much when it was just Liam." She shook her head. "I've had him in preschool for two years and I've only met Nolan once or twice."

"Fuck." I let out a long breath and ran my hands over my hair, lacing my fingers behind my neck. "I've never wanted kids, but I couldn't imagine walking out on them." I wasn't even responsible enough to own a dog, let alone have kids.

"Because you never would," she said softly, her eyes going liquid.

My chest went tight. That might have been the nicest thing anyone had ever said to me.

She cleared her throat. "Anyway, I'm so sorry about the house. I've been at Ryker's for a couple weeks while they're renovating my apartment. Big flood."

"Yeah, I knew that. Ryker told me. So, you texted me?" She must have been desperate. For the past seven years, our communications had been limited to simple civilities whenever I'd been in town. If I wanted to see her, I made sure it was "accidental." If I wanted to take her lunch, I put the thought in Ryker's head so it was his idea.

She cringed. "I'm seriously so sorry. I couldn't think of

anywhere else, and Emerson suggested here because you weren't supposed to be back for another month. And I'm sorry about Melinda. She seemed...nice, and I can see why you'd like her. And *really* sorry about the puke and the mess—"

"Stop," I interrupted her babble, standing up but not moving toward her. I tried like hell to keep five steps between us at all times. It stopped things like accidental kisses from happening. Or intentional ones. "Harper, this is just a house. Four walls and a roof. You're family. As for Melinda, we were really just friends. We lived on the same street in L.A., and like I said earlier, she asked to come along for the ride so she could visit her sister. I'll say it again—you're family. Family trumps all."

Her smile shook slightly. "Thanks. I'll get that mess cleaned up and we'll be out of your hair."

"I already cleaned it up." I folded my arms across my chest. "And where the hell are you going to take them?"

"You did? Uh, thanks." She was wringing the shit out of that towel. "I...I don't know where we'll go. Elliot is supposed to be here this afternoon to do a quick check that they're in an approved home, and it's not like we have groceries or anything, and it's not even my house." She rubbed her hand over her face and sucked in a deep breath. "What did I do? I had no business taking them, not like this. But I didn't want them getting separated, or going to strangers, not after everything—I still don't. And I know they're not technically hotshot family, but Lisa was one of us, and we take care of our own. That means Liam and James too. We both know what it's like to lose a parent."

She'd said *we.* My heartbeat stuttered.

Fuck. I wasn't going to shove her out with two little kids and nowhere to go. Especially *those* kids. Their mom was a Legacy Fire widow, and their situation hit a little too close to home for me to just wash my hands of it.

It was only a week or so. I could keep my hands to myself for that long. Besides, Ryker wasn't due home for another week or two from what he'd last texted me, which drastically cut that complication.

"What were you going to do before I came home?" I asked.

She met my eyes for a heartbeat before looking away. "Grocery shop this morning and ask the girls for help getting everything else set up so I could pass the home study and get the home approved by Elliot."

"Fine, then we'll do that. We'll get the house approved." I broke my own five-step rule, crossing to her and gently pulling her hand from her face. The towel hit the floor.

"It's not just the house, Knox, it's the *home.*" The pulse in her wrist jumped under my thumb.

"Come on, I'm not that bad. I haven't moved in the kegerater, or the Vegas hookers—"

"Yet," she mumbled.

I caught my laugh before it slipped out and gave her a serious look. "I'm not kidding. It's a week, right?"

"Give or take," she answered quietly. "Funeral is Tuesday, so they're hoping the boys will be with family or placed by Friday."

The word "placed" didn't sit well with me. They were kids, tiny little helpless guys, and baggage was the last thing they needed to be treated like. "You're staying here. All of you. There's plenty of rooms, and the boys could probably use a little bit of stability after yesterday. They don't need to get bounced around."

"Knox, that's really nice of you, but you're a silk sheets kind of guy—and yes, I looked—and they are messy, puking, rambunctious kids."

"One, silk sheets aren't hard to wash. It's a water temperature thing." My thumbs stroked the soft skin of her inner wrist. "And two, no buts." I watched her weighing pros and cons in her mind. Her expressions had always been so easy to read. "Look, Harper, the last I saw of my mom was when I was what, ten?"

"Yeah." She'd know, she'd been there afterward, hugging me with little arms and a heart bigger than her whole body.

"Right. When Dad died, Grams stepped in to raise me. As horrid as that time was...for all of us...I had her. If I hadn't, I have no clue where I would have gone. I would have been as lost as those two boys."

"We would have taken you." She looked up at me, and I sucked in a breath as her turquoise eyes hit me hard enough to knock the wind out of me.

I nodded once, incapable of words until I swallowed back the giant ball of unwelcome warm feelings that comment brought to the surface. "Right. Well, I'm telling you that this is their place for now. We're their people for the week."

Before I could prepare myself, she launched into my arms, hers looping around my neck as her face pressed lightly into my neck. "Thank you, Knox."

My arms slowly closed around her and, unable to stop myself, I held her close as her feet dangled off the ground. She smelled like some kind of fruity shampoo, summer days, and home. She felt like every unspoken dream and ignored fantasy. Damn, I'd forgotten how perfectly she fit in my arms, the way holding her made me feel powerful and terrifyingly vulnerable at the same time.

"Are you sure?" she asked against my throat.

I rubbed my chin across her wet hair, the strands getting caught in my scruff. "I've never been so sure about anything in my life." Those boys weren't getting split up.

We stood there for a second, both absorbing what we'd just decided.

"Knox?" she asked quietly.

"Harper?" I needed to put her down. Needed to step away.

"You're not always an asshole, do you know that?"

I laughed. "Yeah, well, just don't tell anyone."

"I like this version of you." Her arms tightened around my neck, and I flinched.

Like was dangerous. It was everything I'd avoided these last seven years when it came to Harper. Aloof, insolent, cocky. Those had been my weapons. Go figure she'd strip them away in the first half hour we lived under the same roof.

Shit. I lived with Harper Anders.

Separate bedrooms. Separate beds. Separate lives.

One week.

Yeah…I could do this. *Right.*

CHAPTER FIVE

arper

"WHAT'S THE DIFFERENCE?" KNOX ASKED, HOLDING UP TWO different cans of formula in the middle of the baby aisle of McGinty's Groceries.

Was I seriously grocery shopping with Knox Daniels? *Yep, and apparently living with him for the next week.*

Eleven a.m. on a Saturday meant the store was reasonably full, and therefore we'd reasonably be on Legacy's less-than-reasonable gossip radar in the next hour or so. Especially since we'd already seen Mrs. Greevy in the produce aisle. May as well hire a skywriter that we were playing house.

"I have no clue, but this is the one he uses," I answered, taking the one in his left hand and handing it to Liam. "Right?" James reached for my side braid, and I switched him to the other hip, keeping my hair safely out of his surprisingly strong grip.

Liam looked it over like the world's tiniest sommelier and nodded. "He likes those too." He pointed up to the puffs.

"Okay," Knox answered, throwing one of each flavor in the quickly filling cart.

"He's not going to eat all of that in one week," I said, stifling a laugh. Knox just shrugged and tossed in one more.

Diapers and wipes were next. We walked up and down the aisles, stocking the house, letting Liam pick whatever he wanted, but he didn't select anything without prompting. Poor guy was overwhelmed.

"Ooh, look what they have!" I grabbed a box of Bottlecaps candy off the endcap.

"You still eat those things?" Knox asked.

"Processed sugar in soda flavors? What's not to love?" I said, tossing a box in the cart, then turned my attention to Liam. "Now, what do you want to do for dinner tonight?"

He shrugged. Food was definitely a sensitive subject with him.

Knox dropped down to his eye level. "I like hamburgers." His tone didn't slip into what I called kid-talk. He spoke to him like he was an adult, just shorter. "I'm a fan of the big, thick ones with bacon and cheese. What do you say we make those? They're very manly burgers. Only for the biggest of boys."

Liam's eyes narrowed slightly, but he nodded. "And ketchup."

"Absolutely. Why don't you pick out a box or two of cereal?" Knox nodded toward the brightly colored boxes before standing back up. "What else does Sir Pukes-A-Lot need besides paper towels for cleanup?" he asked me.

I rolled my eyes at the nickname and thought through my mental list. "I think we got it all—" My stomach sank as a familiar face came around the corner.

Some days I hated small towns.

"What's wrong?" Knox asked, moving closer and turning slightly, shielding me from view.

"My ex," I said quietly, glancing around his shoulder. "We didn't exactly have an amicable split."

He glanced discreetly and snorted. "Ah, yes. Richard 'the Dick' Stone. What the"—his gaze flickered to Liam—"heck were you thinking? He's eleven years older than you."

"Who I date is none of your business." I had been thinking he was the opposite of Knox and therefore worth a try, but I wasn't about to say that. "He wasn't a…dick," I whispered. "Well, not until the end, at least. Then it got a little ugly, but…well, he was just another episode in the series of Harper-chooses-the-wrong-guy." I shrugged, not bothering to repeat the ugly words Richard had said during the breakup.

"What happened?" Knox's eyes chilled, sending a shiver up my spine.

Ah, there he was, the guy who had made sure none of the boys at Legacy High would come near me with a ten-foot pole. Guess my dating life was about to suffer another hit with him back in town. The problem with being Ryker's little sister was that it came with Bash, Ryker, and Knox all locked and loaded to lose their shit on anyone who hurt me. It was kind of like growing up with nuclear launch codes—with the power came the responsibility not to use it.

I arched a single eyebrow at Knox. "Nothing you need to freak out over. He wanted to get married, and I didn't." I kissed the top of James's head and inhaled the scent only babies seemed to possess. I'd read somewhere it was like a drug to women—the smell of babies. *Truth.*

"And it ended just like that?" He tilted his head.

I swallowed and made sure Liam was still occupied choosing cereal. Richard was getting closer. "I broke up with him because we'd been together for over a year, and I knew that he wasn't it for me. Dad always said that you don't marry the one you can live with, you marry the one you can't live without. And I could definitely live without him." *Because there's only been you, and you're a rather impossible standard to live up to.* I just about smacked myself for that thought. "I was gentle about it, and he...was not. Then he got a little spiteful and basically did his best to block the construction of the new preschool until Greg stepped in from city planning to push it through zoning."

Knox's jaw flexed. I knew that face. That was the face that kept Vic's hands off me on prom night.

"Whatever you're thinking, don't," I whispered as Richard saw us. "It's been a year, and my school is open. No harm. No foul. Let it go. God knows I have."

"Harper, imagine seeing you here," Richard said, carrying his basket. His brown hair was perfectly combed to the side, his teeth unnaturally white, and he was decked in head-to-toe Patagonia, which nearly made me snort because I knew his idea of getting outside was walking from the courthouse to his car.

Knox tensed and his hands curled into fists.

I ignored the pit in my stomach and plastered a fake smile on my face. "Well, there's only one grocery store in town, so the odds are pretty good that it would happen eventually, right?"

He stared at James and blinked in confusion. "Right," he said softly, his gaze moving to see Knox. "Ah, Mr. Daniels. I see you've come to join our new hotshots." He paused, waiting for Knox to fill in the gaping holes in the puzzle before him.

Our? Hardly. Richard had been adamantly against reinstating the crew. He'd argued for hours that the town couldn't take the bad press if something happened again.

"Yep. I'm home," Knox answered, wrapping his arm around my shoulder. I fit perfectly under his arm like always, and maybe it was only for show, but that didn't stop my nerve endings from sizzling to life, or Richard from glaring. "I hear you're a judge now."

"I am. Just elected last November." Richard's chest puffed out like a damn bird.

"Pretty young for that kind of job," Knox said. "Good for you."

"I'll be thirty-seven next month. I'm just flattered that the citizens of Legacy saw fit to trust my judgment." His smile was practiced, polished.

"Running for mayor soon?" Knox said with a veil of sarcasm so thin I knew I was the only one who could pick up on it. He rubbed my arm in absentminded circles, and I nearly purred and leaned in. Did he feel that too? The charge that seemed to run from his fingers, into my skin, and through my veins? He couldn't, or he would have stopped, I was certain.

Knox never touched me, not if he could help it. Not since... well, prom, but that definitely wasn't up for discussion. I wasn't even sure he remembered it, to be honest. He and Ryker had been trashed when I'd gotten home later that night.

"I hadn't given it much thought," Richard said with his politician smile. "But I like to keep my options open."

He'd been salivating over Mayor Davis's seat for *years*.

"Well, I guess I should let you three"—he eyed James again—"get back to your shopping."

"Got 'em!" Liam said, dropping two boxes of cereal into the shopping cart.

Richard's eyes flew to mine. "Are those the Clark boys?"

"We're taking care of them this week until their family can be located." I held James a little tighter and didn't flinch when he decided to yank on my braid.

"Huh," Richard said, raising his eyebrow slightly. "I thought you weren't interested in a family, Harper. I never took you for a foster parent."

Liam took my free hand, and I smiled down at him in reassurance. "Me either," I answered. "But we're figuring it out. Right, Liam?"

"Right," he answered softly.

"Harper always rises to a challenge," Knox said protectively.

Don't poke the bear, I mentally begged him. Richard could be a massive pain in the ass for us both if he wanted to be.

"Oh?" Richard lifted that brow again, and the urge to smack the smug look off his face ran amok in my brain. "Sorry to say that was never my experience while we were together."

"Maybe there wasn't much worth fighting for then," Knox threw back with a shrug and a smile that was pure menace and sexy as sin. He reached for James, and the baby went willingly, running his hands over the scruff on Knox's chin. "We'll catch you later, Richard—we have a new house to stock. Home study and all."

As we walked away, my brain knew that show had all been for Richard's benefit, that Knox wasn't really interested in me, but my heart went all gooey just the same.

Ugh. It was going to hurt like hell when Knox inevitably brought the next Melinda home.

"CRIB IS TOGETHER!" RIVER CALLED OUT FROM THE BOYS' bedroom. Liam had thrown a fit when we suggested he get his own room, so together they went.

"Bed is made!" Avery added.

"Child locks are on every cabinet," Bash said, waving a screwdriver before putting it back into the bag on the counter.

"Food is all stocked and organized according to mealtimes." Emerson closed the pantry door.

"What are we forgetting?" I asked, throwing the lunch dishes into the dishwasher.

"We've got smoke detectors in every room, carbon monoxide alarms on every floor, and I just padlocked the hot tub," Knox said, coming into the kitchen. "I think we've got it,

Harper. Elliot will know they're safe here. I even hid the sex toys under the bed."

"Can you be serious for once in your life?" My heart was jumping all over the place with nerves and picturing...well, *that* wasn't helping.

"I take my toys very seriously." A corner of his mouth lifted into a smirk. "Relax. We've got everything taken care of."

I nodded. "Okay, and with ten minutes to"—the knock at the door startled me and I almost dropped a dish—"spare."

"We'll get it," Bash offered, taking Emerson toward the front door and leaving me alone with Knox.

"We've got this, Harper," Knox promised. "The boys are playing in the living room, Sir Pukes-A-Lot is in fresh clothes after his last upchuck, and I think he honestly likes that giant cage Bash built him."

I put the last dish into the washer and closed it. "It's a playpen, Knox. Not a cage. Oh God, that's Elliot. She's here. Say it again."

"Octagon, playpen, whatever. It's not a cage," he said with a grin that nearly stopped my heart. Ugh. He had to stop that.

"No, not that part."

Confusion puckered his forehead for a heartbeat and then he relaxed, taking my face in his hands. I almost forgot the nausea, the worry, the gut-wrenching fear Elliot would say this wasn't working...all because Knox had the most beautiful eyes I'd ever seen. They were giant pools of warm chocolate highlighted by flecks of toffee and gold. "We've got this."

"Okay," I whispered, believing him, savoring the tiny breath of relief I felt at not having to carry this alone.

"It's Elliot," Bash announced. "Emerson took her into the living room."

Knox's hands fell away like I'd burned him, and that tiny bloom of hope withered a little. Okay, a lot. I blinked. Did he seriously just back up five steps?

"Harper, is there anything else you need?" River asked from the bottom of the steps, Avery right behind him.

I looked over toward the great room. Elliot was talking to Liam, along with Mrs. Dean, the only other social worker in town. "Nope, I think the rest is all on us."

Emerson walked over and hugged me. "This is going to go great. Don't stress. And you really owe me details on how living with Knox is going to go," she ended in a whisper.

I squeezed her back and let her go. "I will."

After wishing us luck, Bash took Emerson's hand and they left, River and Avery following in their wake. "Elliot, you know these two are awesome, right?" River asked before he reached the front door.

I cracked a smile. River and his brother, Bishop, were hotshots too, but while Bishop had graduated just ahead of Bash, Ryker, and Knox, River and I were the same age and had been friends since kindergarten. It was more than nice to have him home.

"Out, River." She shooed him, seeming way older than her twenty-seven years, and out he went.

"In we go," Knox muttered as we entered the great room.

Elliot sat down across from us on the loveseat with Mrs. Dean. We took the couch next to where James played on the floor, and Liam kneeled at his side, pretending to not pay attention to what was going on. "Man, I've always heard you hotshot boys were a family, but I didn't expect them both to be here. Honestly, I didn't expect to see you here, Knox. But I'm glad you are."

"Me too," he answered, leaning forward into his serious pose. "We know this is unorthodox, but we're hoping you'll let the insanity slide just to get these guys to their family. The last thing either of us want is for them to be split up or put with parents who can't keep up with them or clean up gallons of vomit."

"What?" Her pen froze against her clipboard and her forehead puckered.

"Spit up. He means spit up. James doesn't keep a lot down," I corrected.

"Oh, okay. This is going to get a little intrusive. You're background checked, Harper, so at least that's easy, but Knox—"

"I am too," he assured her. "It's all on file at the clubhouse."

"Oh." She smiled with surprise. "That's great news. Makes it way easier. Like I said, I wasn't expecting you to be back already, and I'll need to ask some rather extensive questions."

"Are you both comfortable with that?" Mrs. Dean asked, like she was offering us tea. Silver now streaked her brown hair, but other than that, she looked like I'd always remembered.

"I don't think there's anything about my past Harper doesn't know, and I think I caught up to date on hers a little earlier today." He looked over at me.

"I'm fine with questions. I'll even go first," I answered, mentally preparing to have every single moment of my life exposed in front of Knox.

This was a great idea. Awesome.

Elliot nodded once, then put on her glasses, adjusted her grip on her clipboard, and launched into her questions, writing down notes on my answers as we went.

Mercy, she hadn't been kidding when she said the questions were intrusive.

She asked about my childhood, about the impact of losing Dad in the fire, about how I'd been disciplined. What were my views on adoption? How did I feel about fostering a student? What if this was longer than a week?

That last question drew me up short. "Then we'll handle it like we do everything else in this town. One step at a time."

They both nodded.

Knox leaned back into the cushions, crossing one ankle to his knee in a deceptively relaxed pose. What the social workers didn't see was the way his fingers quickly drummed against his jeans.

This had to be torture for him. He barely let Ryker and Bash in, let alone me, or relative strangers. They asked about the arrests on his record. It wasn't like the entire town hadn't had a front-row seat to Knox's adolescence, but everything he'd done as a teenager—from drag racing down Main Street to putting Sheriff Peterson's patrol car inside the high school gym—had long since been expunged from his record.

Knox might still be an ass when it came to the revolving door that was his bedroom, but he'd kept himself out of handcuffs since he turned eighteen.

"Money isn't an issue between the two of you?" Mrs. Dean asked, jotting down notes.

Knox snorted. "I made enough investing in Sebastian Vargas's tech company that I only firefight for the love of it. I don't have any debt. The house is paid off. The truck is paid off. I'm a fully invested member of Legacy, LLC, which means I'm financially responsible for the success or loss in the new hotshot crew too."

My eyebrows hit the ceiling. I knew Bash had made a killing for the three of them when they'd all gone in together on his apps, but *damn.*

"Okay then, we know your father was killed in the Legacy fire, and you were raised by Agnes, your grandmother," Elliot said. "Do you have any other living relatives? Your mother?"

Knox tensed, his fingers digging into the couch.

I reached across the small space that separated us and put my hand over his, squeezing lightly.

He gave me a tight, closed-lip smile that I knew meant "thank you" and relaxed slightly. Then he turned back to our inquisitors. "It's just Grams and me. The last I saw of my mother was her walking away when I was ten. She hasn't been in the picture since, and she never will be again."

Mrs. Dean nodded, probably remembering when that happened. "And how do you feel that's affected you as an adult?"

"I'd say that it doesn't, but I knew that was a lie the moment I found Harper in my house with the boys."

I held my breath.

"How so?" she asked.

I studied the carved lines of his face, the way his jaw flexed once, twice, and his focus darted toward where the boys played.

"Her leaving gave me a sense of determination to prove myself, and as of today, to keep Liam and James together. I'm thankful every day that I had Grams to raise me after the fire. I'm not going to let anything happen to these boys while they're here. They're…" He took a deep breath and released it slowly. "Well, in a way, Harper and I have been where they are. They're just like us."

My heart ached with a familiar pressure. The years didn't matter. I was still foolishly in love with this man.

They finished up that line of questioning, and Mrs. Dean leveled a no-bullshit stare on us both. "And what exactly is the relationship between the two of you?"

I froze.

"What would you like it to be?" Knox asked.

Mrs. Dean pursed her lips.

"You're obviously not roommates," Elliot jumped in. "Especially since we all know that Harper's been at Ryker's since her place took all that flood damage during the spring melt."

Small. Freaking. Towns.

"*Roommates* isn't an acceptable living situation for us," Mrs. Dean added, her focus zeroed in on Knox. "It's too unstable, and while there are elements of this emergency placement that we'll make exceptions for, Harper not having an official place of residence isn't one of them, since she's the one who will be their primary foster parent."

"So, it looks better for the paperwork if we're dating and she lives here?" Knox asked Elliot.

My head whipped in his direction, and I squeezed his hand, but he kept his attention fully locked on Elliot.

She glanced from Mrs. Dean to me, and then to Knox. "We've always allowed foster parents to live with their partners in the home, provided that they're background checked and pass a home study, but of course stable relationships are preferred," she finished slowly.

"Great. Go with that." He laced his fingers with mine. "That okay with you, Harper?"

My mouth dropped.

"Are you seriously going to tell us you've been dating Harper long distance?" Mrs. Dean asked, looking over the rim of her glasses.

"Are you seriously going to tell me I haven't been?" Knox challenged. "Go ahead, ask me anything about Harper, and I guarantee I can answer it."

"How l—" Mrs. Dean started.

"I think we have enough," Elliot interrupted, coming to her feet. "It's just a week, Maggie."

Mrs. Dean looked at Knox and I, her gaze dropping to our hands, then softening as she looked at the boys. "Just a week."

Knox and I both breathed easier when they told us they were ready for the walk-through of the house. Knox took them on the tour while I made the boys a snack. My hands shook at the possibility that we'd be turned down, but I managed to slice up the banana without cutting myself.

"Okay," Elliot said once they finished, leaning across the kitchen island as Mrs. Dean headed into the great room with Knox. "We're expecting to get some news of their father in the next week, or any remaining family. Until then, you're their official foster mother."

"And Knox?" I asked, fighting the urge to hold my breath.

"He's your very supportive...partner," Elliot said. "You're not married, which of course is always Maggie's ideal, but she hasn't quite kept up with the times and your living arrangements are acceptable to us. It's such a short time period that they'll be here."

My entire body sagged in relief. The boys could stay. They wouldn't be separated. "Thank you, Elliot."

"No, thank you. You did a huge thing stepping up for them."

We both turned when James giggled, and we saw Knox blowing on his neck.

"Well, that's a punch to the ovaries," Elliot whispered, her jaw slack. "Never thought I'd see Knox Daniels with a baby."

I couldn't tear my eyes away from the careful way Knox held James, or the way he easily scooped up Liam in his other arm, who surprisingly let him. They both looked so tiny against Knox's huge frame, so delicate compared to the strength in Knox's body. If he was this good with them after a few hours, what would a week be like?

What would he look like with his own babies?

"He's going to make an amazing father one day," I agreed, slightly breathless. He might swear up and down he'd never have kids, but I knew a natural when I saw it.

"Well, as your friend, and not your social worker? I'd stand in line to help him with that, if I were you." She shot me a knowing look. "You've waited long enough for him to come home."

Stand in line? Hell, I would have stood on my head if it got me Knox. But Knox wasn't exactly the "getting" kind, and though he'd put on one hell of a show, I knew once this week was over, we'd be back to one-word conversations when he came around with Ryker.

"But do me a favor," Elliot whispered.

"What?"

"Put on a good show for Maggie this week, or I'll never hear the end of it."

CHAPTER SIX

K nox

I PUSHED THE BAR UP, BREATHING INTO THE BURN IN MY CHEST AS I lowered it again, only to repeat the motion another dozen times. The altitude was still kicking my ass. It would probably be a full month before I was at the top of my game again.

I'd already partially tuned out Bash, who was spotting me, because if I had to hear any more of the special details he'd put into the house for Emerson, I was going to use my sweat rag as a gag. Not that I wasn't glad they were finally back together and engaged. The only thing worse than listening to them gush about their relationship now that they were living together was watching one slowly wither without the other. Thank God she'd taken him back.

I was genuinely happy for them. We'd all been through our fair share of hell in the last ten years, but they'd gotten a particularly brutal helping.

"Has he told you about the bathtub yet?" River asked as he joined us in the gym at the firehouse, his voice dripping with sarcasm. "You know, Emmy likes the one with the jets."

"Shut up," Bash countered. "I'm not that bad."

"Yeah," I grunted as I pressed the bar up again, "you are. But we're your friends, so we'll refrain from handing you your balls about it."

"Speak for yourself," River said, folding his arms across his chest.

"It's only because we can't. They're in Emerson's purse," I finished.

Bash gave me a go-to-hell glare and took his hands off the bar as I was lowering it. It immediately sank to my chest. "Fuck," I growled.

"Cruel, Bash." River laughed, helping me lift it. "Struggling with three hundred pounds, Knox? You out of shape?"

"Hardly," I answered, sitting up on the bench. "I think I'm adjusting to altitude. Or I'm just delirious from lack of sleep. James was up three times last night." For the second night in a row.

"Damn." Bash whistled.

"Yeah," I said, rubbing my scratchy eyes. "Harper had him twice, and it was a fight to get her to give him to me so she could go back to bed that third time."

Bash's gaze narrowed on me.

"Her own bed, jackass," I clarified.

"Just making sure. Not that I'm against you two." He put his hands up. "I'm just against shit going down behind Ryker's back. You know he's going to go ballistic when he finds out."

"He's never going to find out," I countered. "This will all be over in a few days. He told me he won't be here for another week, if not longer. I swear that guy's a bigger fire junkie than anyone we know."

"True." Bash's jaw flexed. "But rumor going around town is

that you two are *living* together, and you know that's going to get back to him."

"Let me guess." I ran my hand over my hair, my stomach pitching sideways. "Maggie Dean?"

"She told your Grams this morning at the diner." River picked up a set of dumbbells. "Avery heard her, so I'd expect that phone call at any minute."

"Shit." Sneaking by with a little smudge of untruth with Mrs. Dean was one thing. Flat-out lying to Grams was another.

"Yeah, good luck with that phone call." Bash grimaced. "The three of us in this room might know the truth—"

"Seven, if you count Avery, Emerson, and Harper," River added.

"Eight." I shrugged. "Elliot knows. She's just letting it slide."

"Fine," Bash agreed as he headed for the leg press. "Eight people may know the truth, but good luck in fooling the rest of the town while keeping it from Ryker. You might want to give him a call and a heads-up."

"Yeah, no thanks. I'd rather keep my dick attached, and we both know he'd fly home just to cut it off. I'll fill him in once it's over. He'll understand." He had to. *Then why won't you call him?* Because if he didn't take it well—and he wouldn't—I'd be put in the position of deciding to keep my oldest friendship or the boys together until the Pendridges got home. It was better to ask forgiveness than permission, right?

Besides, nothing was going on with Harper. We were just...roommates.

And hell is just a sauna.

"I'm going to shower so I don't stink up the boardroom," I said to the guys and headed out. I chose one of the private stalls and ran the water so hot I nearly scalded my skin as I stood with my back turned to the spray. The end of the stall was frosted glass up to my chest. Gorgeous for the view, but probably shocking for any hiker who wandered too close with a pair of binoculars.

The water beat into my sore muscles as my eyes wandered up the ridgeline. I initially thought Bash had lost his mind, wanting to restart our dad's hotshot crew, that he was a masochist for wanting to rip open a decade-old scar. But the longer I let the thought linger, the more I realized it was impossible to reopen a wound that hadn't ever really healed—not when it was still gaping, festering. Maybe, just maybe, putting on that patch and starting up the crew would help it heal, even if just a little.

But we only had months to get certified—that was part of the rules the council had levied on us, and it felt more and more like they'd set us up to fail. Certifying an entirely new crew in that amount of time was unheard of—it was also why I'd come home a month earlier than the rest of the crew was due to report. Hopefully we'd be able to hit the ground running May first.

About ten minutes later, I jogged up the stairs of the Legacy Hotshot compound. The bottom floor was bedrooms, bathrooms, and the gym, all prepped for the team's arrival in the next couple of weeks. The next level housed the massive kitchen, dining room, gathering room, and the team offices. Bash had spared zero expense when he had the massive compound built, and though he fronted most of the cost, Ryker and I had thrown our money in too. It was part ours, and there was something to be said for that.

"Thank God," River said as I walked into the conference room. "He was telling me about the granite Emerson put in the kitchen. I'll leave you three to it. I'm going on a run with Bishop." He gave us a wave and walked off.

Three?

"Ry, Knox just walked in," Bash said.

"Nice to hear you're alive," Ryker's voice boomed from Bash's phone on the glass tabletop.

Fuck.

Bash lifted his eyebrows at me.

I shook my head. "Good to hear your voice, brother. You coming home any time soon?" Guilt ate at me, souring my stomach.

"We've almost got her contained, so probably early next week." He sounded tired.

"It will be nice to have you back," Bash replied, his gaze meeting mine.

Fuck, I hated that the pressure in my chest eased up a little. Harper would be long gone by the time he got home.

Part of you hates that too.

"Bring us up to speed," I said, leaning back in my chair.

Bash pointed up to the dry erase board that had been strategically lined out with the names of all the Legacy Hotshots in different colors. "We only have until June fifteenth to get every single one of those names here and qualified. I'm not worried about the veterans, but we've got rookies out the ass to fulfill the council's sixty-percent stipulation. Qualifying them as individuals is the first hurdle."

"We've got the Maldonados, and they're already qualified," I stated. Bishop was a few years older than us and one of the meanest assholes I'd ever met. He cared about one person in the world, and that was River, his little brother.

"Yep, they're good," Ryker agreed.

"What about Indie?" I asked, seeing her name in blue.

"She's due down in a couple weeks. She promised her Montana crew she'd stay as long as possible. Same with Lawson. The non-Legacy members will be here next week, so get ready for the influx." Bash tapped the list of names on the right.

"What about Braxton Rose?" His name was in blue too.

"He's still in Chicago but promises he'll get back by the deadline. He's not certified in wildland, though. Only structure. And he's pretty pissed that his sister put her name down."

"She's only eighteen, of course he's pissed," Ryker said. "Don't blame him. I don't want Harper near firefighters, let alone becoming one. He has every right to be angry."

Bash glanced my way before raising his eyebrows at the speakerphone. "You know, Harpy is twenty-six, Ry. You're going to have to give her a little freedom with her dating life now that you're moving back full-time."

Where the rest of us had moved to join other crews, Ryker had only operated seasonally, spending the rest of his year here in Legacy.

"She can have as much freedom as she wants. Hell, I put up with Richard 'the Dick' Stone for a year. He may have been a pretentious asshole, but at least I knew he wasn't going to get called away in the middle of the night for a fire and never return. My sister isn't going to live like my mom did."

And there it was. Reason number three billion and six I wasn't ever going to be good enough for Harper. I rubbed the bridge of my nose.

"What about Cohen?" Ryker asked.

Spencer Cohen was the lone survivor of the Legacy Hotshot Crew, and he'd never forgiven himself for it. Instead of being burned alive in a deployment shelter, he'd been driving Bash off the mountain.

He'd also reluctantly agreed to be the crew's superintendent since none of us had the experience or desire, getting us to the sixty percent the council demanded. That magic number had required Emerson joining on too, if only as our manager. Not that she'd ever see a flame.

"Next week," Bash answered.

"Big week," Ryker noted.

"Big year. We've got one season to get this team off the ground and certified, or this has all been for nothing. I've pulled every string in my arsenal of favors, and it looks like August is going to be our month to be evaluated for certification. We fuck that up and we're done."

We'd bet everything we had on this new crew. Our money, our old jobs, homes, and parents' legacies. If we failed, it would all have been for nothing.

"Guess we'd better not fuck it up," I said as my phone rang. I answered it with a swipe of my thumb. "Hey, Grams."

"Knox Daniels, you have some explaining to do."

LIAM WAS QUIET AS WE WALKED INTO THE HOUSE THE NEXT DAY, his cheeks streaked with tears. The somber set of his face seemed almost criminal on such a little guy. No kid should have to go through what he just did.

I held the mudroom door open for Harper, and she thanked me softly as she squeezed past with James on her hip.

"Can I take this off?" Liam asked from the kitchen, and I walked in to see him tugging at his tie.

It was black, just like his suit, and matched what the rest of us had on.

Harper bit her lower lip, and I knew she was close to crying again. She'd held off most of the service, but the second Liam started, she'd understandably joined. Jamie babbled and rubbed his eyes with both fists. It was a blessing and a curse he'd never remember any of this.

"Sure you can." I dropped to a knee so I was at his eye level. "Make you a deal," I said to Harper. "You take Sir Pukes-A-Lot and I'll take this young man." It wasn't that I didn't like Jamie. He was cute, but after the third diaper I'd put on backward yesterday, I was shamelessly taking the kid who could speak.

She gave me a sad smile. "Deal."

"Can I help?" I asked Liam.

He nodded.

As Harper took James to the living room, I undid Liam's tie and unbuttoned his suit coat. "Is that better?"

He nodded, looking away. He hadn't cried since we left the gravesite, but I didn't know enough about kids to figure out if that was a good or bad thing. The not talking about it had to be bad—even I wasn't that naïve.

"Hungry?" It was three, but after living with the boys for four days, I had yet to figure out if there was a rhythm to their hunger. It seemed if we were offering food, they weren't hungry, and if we weren't, they were starving.

Liam shook his head and fidgeted with his belt.

If I had just buried my only known relative and had no idea what the future held for me, I wouldn't have been interested in talking either. Hell, I had no clue what to say to the kid. All I had was what I wished someone had said to me that day.

"It's okay, you know," I said, helping him with the buckle. "If you want to talk, or don't want to talk, it's okay."

His sad brown eyes met mine, and that lump grew in my throat.

"If you want to cry, or yell, or scream, that's okay too. You get to feel however you want."

"Did you cry when your dad died?" he asked quietly.

"Absolutely." My throat worked, but the lump didn't move. "But my dad died with a bunch of his friends, so there were a ton of cameras and people around, and sometimes..." I swallowed hard. "Sometimes it felt like I had to pretend to be okay when I wasn't. But you don't have to pretend, okay? You get to feel however you want."

He nodded.

"Why don't you go upstairs and get out of the monkey suit? I think Harper put your new clothes in the dresser." I stood, and he took his tie from my hand, then walked away, his footsteps heavy on the stairs.

I grabbed a bottle of iced tea from the refrigerator, then took out one for Harper too, putting them on the counter. It was almost funny how quickly I'd gotten used to always grabbing two of something—taking care of her when I could. After today, I definitely wished the teas were the Long Island versions, but that could wait until the boys were in bed.

"He didn't come," Harper said from behind me.

"Who?" I turned toward her, untwisting the cap before handing her the bottle of tea. They'd only been here four days and the sound of James jumping in the living room seemed almost normal now.

"Thanks." She took a sip and hopped onto the counter, her legs and feet bare under her black dress. "Nolan. I talked to Elliot just after the service, and she said she's left messages for him on the number listed in Lisa's phone."

"Maybe he didn't get them." I tugged at the knot in my tie, loosening it. That was the only answer I could find acceptable for putting your kids through something like this without being there for them. Then again, the guy had walked out, which didn't exactly give me the impression he gave a damn.

"His dad did. He lives in Reno. Guess that's where Nolan ended up, because the second time Elliot called, the guy said he'd told him."

"And?" My grip on my bottle tightened.

"And he didn't show up. And his dad doesn't…" She glanced behind her, no doubt making sure Liam wasn't in hearing range. "He's not interested in parenting."

I smoothed my hand over my jaw, keeping my vicious thoughts to myself. The last thing Liam needed was to hear me lose my shit over his family.

"I don't understand someone who wouldn't want their grandkids, or their sons," she whispered. Her eyes widened and filled with regret. "Oh, shit. Knox. I didn't think."

I waved it off. "Don't worry. You haven't said anything about my mother that I haven't thought at some point. Hell, I've said a lot worse, and besides, I had Grams."

"I never understood it back then either. I can't think of a single person in the world who wouldn't have wanted you." She played with her bottle as her cheeks flushed. "I don't know what to say to Liam."

"There's nothing we can say. Nothing that's going to fix this for them, at least. I just keep saying what I think I needed back then, and that's probably wrong too."

Liam's little steps made their way into the kitchen, where he stood in a pair of jeans and the new *Paw Patrol* shirt we'd bought yesterday when we went suit shopping.

"I have a question," he stated simply, his gaze bouncing between Harper and me.

"What's up?" I crossed the floor to stand beside Harper. *So much for five steps away.*

"What happens to us?" he asked. His eyes nailed me to the floor, wide, innocent, and expecting an answer I didn't have to give. Words failed me.

"Tonight, we're going to have dinner, and then you'll take a bath, get to bed, and we'll go to school tomorrow after we drop James off at Cherry's. How does that sound?" Harper's hand gripped the fabric of my coat behind my back.

Thank God for Harper.

He nodded slowly. "Like normal."

"Like normal, except you'll wake up here," she assured him.

Don't ask what comes after that, I mentally begged. Harper was so calm, her voice reassuring and at odds with the death grip she had at my back. I didn't know what to tell him.

So, I kept my mouth shut.

"Okay." Liam looked at us both in turn and then slowly nodded. "Can we go to my house tomorrow? I really want my special blanket. I know I'm big, but I miss it."

"How about I call Elliot, and we'll see if we can make that happen?" Harper offered.

He nodded again and headed off to where James jumped.

"I hate this," Harper whispered, releasing my coat as she slid off the counter. "I don't know what's going to happen to them. I don't even know if I can get them their stuff, or tell them where they'll wake up next week." Her shoulders slumped.

"It's not fair." Knowing I was crossing the line yet again, I pulled her close, tucking her against my side. She didn't wrap her arms around me, but she didn't push me away either. Her head turned, and she rested her cheek against my chest.

I tried to ignore how easy it felt to hold her, how my heart seemed to stop, then gallop. *She's off-limits.*

"I'm so sorry I dragged you into this," she whispered.

I dropped my chin to rest on the top of her head, avoiding where she had her hair piled in some kind of knot. "Harper, there is nowhere else I would rather be."

Her breath hitched, and we both fell silent.

Before I could ask myself what the hell I was doing holding Harper, the moment burst like the fragile bubble it was. Harper's phone rang at the same time James let out a bellow.

"Baby," I declared.

"Phone," she answered, and we split apart, each taking our declared target. James was in the middle of a double-fisted eye-rub as I walked into the great room.

"I think he's tired," Liam said from where he sat on the ground next to him.

Shit, he'd done that before and I'd missed it. "I think you're right." A quick glance at my watch told me it was 3:30. At least James was on schedule, if the last four days were any indication. I lifted him from the jumper, and he looked around for a moment before settling his gaze on me.

Liam stood, anxiety tightening the lines on his face.

"Nap time for this guy," I declared. "How about you, Liam? I know you're big and naps aren't cool, but maybe you wanted to keep James company?"

"Yeah. Good idea." Liam softened with visible relief. If I'd lost everyone except my little brother, I'd want to keep my eye on him too. "But just so he's not scared."

"Of course," I said with an exaggerated nod to the alpha pup.

It took me ten minutes and one wasted diaper—I still had trouble figuring out how hard to pull the paper tabs before they broke off in my hand—but I got them both down. Not bad for a guy who'd never changed diapers before this week—and never would again.

"You know, I don't understand how those diapers can hold everything they do if they just seem to rip apart. It defies logic," I told Harper when I found her staring out the window. "Harper?"

She turned, her phone clutched in her hand, those turquoise eyes of hers torn between sadness and utter panic. "That was Elliot. The Pendridges are back early. Something about racing back to beat a snowstorm. They want to come over to meet the boys tonight so they will be ready to move tomorrow."

Wait. What?

Shock. Sadness. Relief. Worry. Absolute terror. Every emotion slammed through me like a freight train, so fast I couldn't grasp onto one before the next one hit. *That's good. It's supposed to be good.*

Except it wasn't.

And the look on Harper's face said the same thing.

The boys were supposed to be with family. They were supposed to stay in a routine. They were supposed to be ours for a few more days. This wasn't the plan. Then again, nothing in their life was going according to plan at the moment.

"Okay," I said slowly, testing out my mouth's ability to form words. "Then I guess we'd better get ready."

~

"HE GETS A LITTLE TESTY IN THE EVENING AND SOMETIMES AFTER he eats," Harper said over the sound of wailing as she walked the floor with James. "I was thinking we should ask the pediatrician about switching his formula. Of course, you can do that…"

The Pendridges sat on the couch across from where I sat with Liam, watching with soft smiles as Harper paced. They were exactly like I remembered, calm, kind, and straight out of a fifties TV show. They were also older.

"Of course. That shouldn't be a problem," Mrs. Pendridge answered, placating Harper more than James. Her tone was level, but a flash of panic ran through her eyes.

Her husband took her hand and ran his thumb across her skin. "So, Knox, are you all done with California?" Mr. Pendridge asked.

"Yes, sir. Well, almost. I still have to close on my place out there, but they're overnighting the paperwork."

Liam's eyes darted nervously between the adults in the room. Elliot had perched herself on the arm of the sofa, and she tried to give him a reassuring smile.

"No need to 'sir' me. It's just Ben," Mr. Pendridge said, like he was letting me into the big boys' club.

James continued to express his displeasure, and Harper made bigger circles, cradling him against her chest.

"I've known you all of my life, Mr. Pendridge. I'm not sure I could ever call you 'Ben.'"

"Fair enough." He chuckled.

"I'm so sorry," Harper apologized. "It's just a really tough time of night for him."

Mrs. Pendridge slowly rose to her feet. "Nonsense. You don't need to apologize for a baby. Why don't you let me hold him?"

Harper's grip tightened slightly on James. If I didn't know her so well, I would have missed it. Her eyes flew to mine, like I had all the answers. Spoiler alert: I didn't. I was so out of my depth here, we may as well have been swimming over the Mariana Trench. I tried to give her a reassuring smile, but it might have come out more as a grimace.

Liam leaned forward as Harper transferred James to Mrs. Pendridge's arms. I put my arm around his shoulder and tucked him into my side.

Mrs. Pendridge made the same motions Harper had, shifting James in her arms frequently. Not that I blamed her. The kid was heavy.

Harper looked lost for a second, then folded her arms across her chest like she was trying to contain herself. "So, you guys have horses, right?" she asked.

"Not anymore. We actually sold the ranch last month. We were hoping one of the kids would want to take it over, but they're all happily settled where they landed. We downsized into something much more manageable."

"Downsized?" I asked.

"We bought one of those little condos that just went up on the east side of town," Mrs. Pendridge said over James's loudest wail yet. "There's a park right down the block," she told Liam.

He didn't respond.

Condo. Apartment. No yard. No space for Liam to run around in, or for James to learn to walk in. My tidy little vision of the boys happy on the Pendridge ranch went up in smoke, leaving behind something way harder to swallow.

As she neared me on her rotation, James reached out with a particularly ear-piercing shriek. I locked every muscle in my body to keep from taking him.

He squirmed his way out of her grip, lunging for the floor.

I shot to my feet, catching him by the back of his pajamas right before certain impact with the end table. *Thank fuck.*

"Oh God!" Mrs. Pendridge gasped as the adults rushed toward us.

James's eyes widened with shock as I cradled him to my chest, and then he let loose. Holy shit, the kid's lungs were unparalleled.

"You dropped him!" Liam accused in a shout, scurrying off the couch to stand at my side.

I couldn't argue with Liam's assessment, or his anger.

"I'm so sorry, I just didn't expect..." She covered her mouth.

"It's okay," her husband said in hushed tones, hugging her.

"He's fine, really," Harper reassured her while shooting me a look to reaffirm what she'd just declared.

James protested when I held him far enough away to make sure that there were no bumps, bruises, or sites of impact, then pulled him against my chest and nodded to Harper.

"We can't do this," Mrs. Pendridge's cry was muffled in her husband's shirt.

"Betty..."

"No!" She stepped out of his arms. "I know we said we were up to the challenge, but look at us, Ben. We have no business taking on something like this."

I stopped rocking back and forth, my hand paralyzed on Jamie's back. What the hell did that mean?

"Why don't we step outside?" Elliot offered, ushering them out. "I'll be right back," she threw over her shoulder.

"How could you?" Liam yelled, his face turning red. It took me a second to realize he was yelling at Harper and me.

"What's up, bud?" I asked, trying like hell to hear over the sound of James going for a new decibel level in my ear.

"They're old! And she dropped Jamie! You can't give us to them!" His whole little body shook.

Harper dropped to her knees in front of him. "Liam, we don't get a say. There are rules about kids and who they can live with."

He glared at her. "They let us stay here."

"That's because they knew it was temporary. The Pendridges

are the only foster parents we have in Legacy. We"—she motioned back at me—"aren't qualified, aren't allowed to keep you for the long term."

"It won't be long! My dad will come. He'll want us!" he shouted with a child's certainty.

My gaze hit the ceiling as I blinked furiously, trying to beat back the excruciating sting as the knot in my throat swelled to painful proportions. James went quiet against my chest, resting his head on my shoulder.

She'll come back for me! Maybe she left you, but she wants me! How many times had I thrown that in Dad's face in the first few months after she bailed? How long did it take me to realize it wasn't true?

"Liam, all I want for you is to be happy and loved. I promise," Harper pleaded for understanding as he backed away from her.

The door opened and Elliot came back in, her mouth in a straight, tight line. "We may have a problem."

James lived up to his nickname and vomited all over me.

"Ah, good. I was wondering when it was going to get exciting around here," I muttered, patting the baby's back.

Fighting fires was tame compared to this.

CHAPTER SEVEN

K nox

"Well, you've certainly gotten yourself into a pickle this time," Grams said as she slid a cup of coffee across the counter of her diner, The Chatterbox. A town staple on Main Street downtown, The Chatterbox was a hub of food, friends, and gossip, just as Grams liked.

She tucked a strand of hot-pink hair behind her ear and greeted a couple by name as they walked in the door.

"Poor girl," she muttered as she gave them a little wave. "She thinks they're destined for the wall. Watch, she'll choose the table closest to it."

I swiveled on my stool a few degrees and snorted as she did exactly what Grams predicted. "How did you know?"

"They've been together about a year, and she's bringing him in at least once a week. Shea, table fourteen looks a little low on coffee," she whispered to the waitress closest to me.

The longer I'd been gone from Legacy, the harder it was to recognize people. The wall, though? That never changed. Sure, names got added, but the meaning was the same. It ran the back length of the diner and was pretty much the precursor to Facebook. For the last forty years, couples had carved their names into the wood, declaring their love. Part of it had been annihilated by the fire almost eleven years ago, but that hadn't stopped Grams from rebuilding with the scraps that had survived. It was sappy and more than a little outdated, but when I saw Bash and Emerson's names carved together, even I could admit it had its charm. Well, until some jilted wife came in with a pocketknife, or in Amity Gunderson's case, an actual mini torch.

Nothing quite said your relationship status had changed like an angry ex-lover with a tiny blowtorch. I could still see the burn marks from here.

"Now stop avoiding my question, Knox." She quirked an eyebrow at me.

"You didn't ask a question."

"You know what I meant! What are you going to do about those babies? About Harper?" She stared me down like I was eleven again.

"There's nothing I can do about either. Those boys are under the control of the county. I don't get to make choices for them. And as for Harper…" I sighed and took a long swallow of my coffee, hoping she'd let it drop.

"And what? You can't fight for them?"

Of course she didn't let it drop. She was now the eighth person to know the truth about Harper and me, but she had yet to give me her opinion on the matter.

"Grams, there are bigger forces at work here." Forces like the county…and Ryker. "And we both know it's only a matter of time before I do something to piss Harper off anyways." I excelled at that. We were just in this little bubble of time where we were working together toward the same goal. Hell, it had been five days since I'd walked into my ready-made family, and we hadn't killed each other yet, or even gotten into a fight, which was a miracle. *Probably because you're both too exhausted to fight.*

She leaned over and smacked the side of my head lightly. "Maybe that will knock some of the sense back into you. That girl has been moon-eyed over you since she was eight, and let me tell you, you could do a hell of a lot worse than Harper Anders."

More than a few heads turned toward us. This would be all over town in the next hour. "You don't think I know that?" I whispered in hopes she'd take the hint. "Harper is...Harper."

"Oh, you mean beautiful, smart, kind, good with kids, and—"

"And Ryker's little sister."

Grams tilted her head. "You're telling me that's what's keeping you from—"

Mrs. Paulson leaned close enough to smell my coffee, and Grams shot her a glare. You had to be fucking kidding me. That was why I'd moved to California. The busybodies, lack of privacy, and the town's need to weigh in on *everything.*

"Besides, I'm not exactly the marrying type," I told Grams. Marriage meant trust and faith, and I was pretty damned spectacular at shoving people away who got too close. I was never going to put myself in a position to get decimated by a woman the way Dad had been.

The bell chimed, and the subject of our conversation walked in. Her hair was down, curling just beneath her breasts in long blond waves, and she looked every bit the preschool teacher in a blue skirt and white sweater set.

I wanted to peel it off her body.

Awesome, now "Hot for Teacher" was going to be stuck in my head all damn day.

She glanced around the diner until her worried eyes found mine.

I was off my stool and striding toward her before she could say a word. There was a panic in her eyes I'd only seen once before—the day they'd evacuated us for the Legacy Mountain Fire.

"Harper?" My hands landed on her shoulders. *Five fucking steps. Is that too much to ask?* My conscience rolled its eyes.

"We have to get to the courthouse. Elliot just called. They're about to decide where to place the boys." She looked up at me with complete trust, like I could make this all better, like I was someone worthy of that kind of faith.

I wasn't, but in that second, I wanted to be.

"I don't understand. She just told us last night that the Pendridges didn't want to foster. Aren't they out of options?" I dropped my hands before I did something stupid, like pull her closer.

"I don't know—"

"Are you two talking about the Clark boys?" Mrs. Paulson asked.

We looked around the diner to find that ninety-five percent of the eyes were on us.

"They are," Grams confirmed, coming around the counter.

"I overheard Judge Sanderbilt saying that they were going to have to separate them and ship them to Gunnison, or worse— out of the county." Mrs. Paulson shook her head. "Such a shame."

Okay, at this moment, living in a small town was pretty phenomenal from the standpoint of available information but shitty in our lack of ability to care for the boys.

Damn it, they couldn't separate them.

"They can't separate them! Liam can't handle that!" Harper voiced my very thoughts, glanced around us, no doubt noting we had everyone's attention, then grabbed my hand and marched back toward the kitchen, hauling me behind her.

"I've only been waiting twenty years to see that," Mrs. Paulson muttered. "Pay up."

I swung my head toward Grams, but she was too busy handing over cash to Mrs. Paulson.

Seriously?

The kitchen door swung open, and I followed Harper to the back office.

I flipped the light switch as the door shut behind us.

"What are we going to do?" she asked, folding her arms under her breasts and staring up at me with raised eyebrows.

That was one of the reasons Harper had always intrigued me. She never took anything lying down. *Except when you walked away from her on prom night.*

I sat back on the edge of the wooden desk and gripped the trim. "What would you like to do?"

She started pacing, making sharp, fast turns in the small space. "What I want…I can't tell you what I want, because then you'll feel obligated to go along with it. And you'll say you're not obligated, but we both know you are. That's how you always are with me, doing things you don't want to do so that you can be the good guy—"

"I'm not the good guy." Anything but, and there was an entire diner out there who could testify to that.

"Kind of like that little kiss we don't talk about, not that you even remember it. I'm always forcing you into things you don't want, and this can't be one of those times because it's not just our lives we're messing around with—"

"I'm sorry, you think I don't remember that kiss?" The same fucking kiss that haunted my dreams so frequently I could reenact it right now without missing a single detail? What the actual hell?

"You were drunk off your ass later that night, and anyway, no time to debate that." She waved me off. "I know you don't like me—"

"Don't like you?" My voice rose. Was she even living on the same planet?

"And I'm just Ryker's annoying little sister, or your little sister, whatever." She threw her hands out.

"My... I do not see you as a damn sister!"

"Will you shut up and let me finish?" She spun and put her fists on her hips as if I were the one who'd just insulted *her*. "The point is that I can't tell you what I want. You have to tell me first. Otherwise, I'll just think you're telling me what I want to hear because you're my brother's best friend and you feel obligated to help me for Ryker's sake."

If it weren't for that shot of fear in her eyes, or the ticking time bomb we were sitting on, I would have shown her exactly what I wanted. On this fucking desk. But she was right—this wasn't about us right now.

It was about the two little boys who slept down the hall at my house. The ones who depended on us to keep their world as routine as it could be considering it had just turned topsy turvy on them.

"They can't separate them," I said softly.

"I agree." Her voice dropped to match mine in tone.

Liam would have a full-on meltdown if he was separated from James, and no one else knew all of Jamie's little quirks. If they took them to Gunnison, or out of the county, they'd be with strangers, split up, and miles away from anyone they knew. But without the Pendridges to foster them...

"Let's keep them." I blurted out before I thought about the ramifications, or the time commitment, or anything that would scare me off like the selfish asshole I generally was. "Let's go fight to keep them. We can make it work until they figure out what's going on with their dad, or whatever. If Elliot agreed to us keeping them for the week, I can't see why they wouldn't let us do it a little longer. I can't live with myself knowing we allowed them to be separated and shipped off to strangers."

Harper was in my arms before I finished the last word. I gave myself that moment, tunneling one hand through her hair and splaying my other over her back as I held her tight. Seeing as this was my second hug this week, I had to assume all I had to do to get some affection from Harper was offer her kids.

"We have to go," she said, breaking our embrace and heading for the door.

I beat her to it, holding it open for her. Three women fell back on their asses as the door swung open, and there were at least ten of the diner patrons in the kitchen, relaxing against the various counters, pretending they hadn't been listening.

Fucking. Small. Towns.

"Okay, will someone at least tell me what time they're on the docket for?" I asked the small crowd.

"One p.m.," Grams called out. "You have ten minutes. Let's go. Harper, I called over to the school and told Summer Weston that you'd be gone the rest of the afternoon."

"Thank you!" Harper answered as we wove through the crowd.

Grams met us at the kitchen door. She'd ditched her Chatterbox apron, revealing her slacks and Tardis T-shirt. "Let's go."

"You're coming too?" A rush of relief hit me. Grams was a force to be reckoned with in the town. She controlled more information than the mayor.

"We all are!" Mrs. Paulson answered from behind us.

"Seriously?" I whispered to Harper.

"You're going to need all the support you can get," Mr. Madera added, following us through the doors. "You didn't pull Judge Sanderbilt."

"Oh no." Harper stopped so suddenly I had to brace my hands on her arms to keep from mowing her over.

Grams took a deep breath and fidgeted with her wedding set that hung from her necklace. Grandpa had been dead twenty-four years, but she never took it off.

"Please tell me we didn't…" My fist clenched.

"You pulled Judge Stone."

"And you're sure about this?" Elliot asked as we stood outside the courtroom.

The small crowd of spectators hung back, giving us a shred of privacy.

"Absolutely," I answered. "Those boys have already been through hell. If we can make it even a little easier on them, then we're in."

"You'll let us, right?" Harper asked.

"Let you what?" Mrs. Dean asked as she came out of the courtroom with a woman about our age with red hair and a black skirt suit.

"Oh, good, you're both here. Maggie, Knox and Harper have agreed to foster the boys. We won't have to send them out of the county," Elliot told her.

"Really?" Mrs. Dean's eyebrows shot up. "I mean, you've taken excellent care of them for these past few days, but you're talking about a much larger commitment. Plus, you'll have to go through the training—"

"We understand. We just want to know if we'd be allowed to do it for longer than an emergency placement," Harper rushed.

"Faith?" Elliot asked the other woman.

Faith glanced at her watch. "We have exactly three minutes," she said with a deep southern drawl. "I'm Faith Simmons, and I've been appointed as the boys' guardian ad litem. That means that while Mr. Baxter will be representing the best interest of DSS, I represent the best interest of Liam and James."

The vise that had gripped my chest for the last few days eased up just a little. The boys had someone legally in their corner.

"I'm Knox Daniels, and this is Harper Anders." We both reached out and shook her hand. "We'd really like to continue fostering the boys until you can find their father." This wasn't forever. We were just a bandage on a hemorrhaging wound.

"For how long?" she asked, her sweet tone at odds with her careful appraisal of us.

"As long as it takes," Harper answered. "We know you're trying to find Nolan, and that reunification with the biological family is always the first priority. We just want to give them somewhere stable and safe while DSS is facilitating that. I'm Liam's preschool teacher, so I know him incredibly well, and we've gotten to know James in the past few days. We adore the boys, and we'll do whatever it takes to keep them together." Her chin rose a good inch as she met Faith's stare.

A small smile crossed the lawyer's face, as if she recognized another woman who wouldn't back down. "Okay, well, we'd better get in there. Let's see how this goes." We followed her to the double doors that led to the courtroom. "By the way, you guys are a super cute couple. How long have you been together?"

Oh, shit.

"We've known each other our entire lives," Harper answered smoothly. "I can't honestly remember a time in my life where I wasn't following Knox around."

"Well, if that's not just the sweetest thing! Thank you," she said as I held the door open and the ladies swept through. "Oh, and turn off your phones. This judge is a real stickler for that."

As long as it takes. That was probably, what? Another month at most? How hard could it be to locate Nolan Clark? A month was doable. I just had to keep my mind and hands off Harper.

Ryker was going to be pissed.

The courtroom was an all too familiar sight. The single aisle split it in two, with long wooden benches and huge windows that let in natural light. It was beautiful, now that I was twenty-seven. Maybe a little too grand, too John Grisham for such a small town, but definitely a piece of art. It had been terrifying at sixteen, when I'd parked the sheriff's car in the gym. Not much better at seventeen, when I'd stolen the goats from the McPherson ranch and left them to graze in Principal Montoya's office. This was one of the only buildings that hadn't burned to the ground.

Harper took my hand, sending a jolt of awareness up my spine. Her fingers trembled almost imperceptivity, and I wrapped mine around hers as we walked down the carpeted aisle.

"You two sit here." Faith motioned to the first row of spectator seats as she walked through the swinging wooden gate that housed four different tables. Elliot sat at the front table with Mrs. Dean and Evan Baxter, who was easily edging toward retirement.

"Scoot," Grams ordered, and I did so.

She edged past me, sitting on my left while Harper took the spot to my right. I turned off my phone and looked around the room to see at least thirty people filling the other benches. I was half tempted to check Facebook to see if someone had created an event or something.

"Full house," River muttered as he squeezed into the bench behind us with Bash and Emerson. Harper's hand fell away from mine.

"Emerson!" Harper turned and hugged her. "What are you doing here?"

"Let me see if I can get this right." She looked up at the ceiling in thought. "Mrs. Paulson called Mrs. Greevy, who then called River, who then told Bash, who told me. Avery's on the way."

"Holy game of telephone." Harper leaned back. "I'm glad you're all here."

"Quick," Bash handed me a wad of fabric. A tie.

"Thanks," I said quickly as I flipped up the collar of my button-down shirt and tied the fastest knot in my life.

"All rise, the Honorable Judge Stone presiding," the bailiff called out. Apparently, Tommy Shreiner still held the job.

We stood as Richard walked in, his robes doing nothing to cover his ego. He climbed up to the bench, and we got the all-clear to sit.

He surveyed the courtroom and leaned toward his microphone. "Am I missing something? Since when does a family court matter warrant a higher attendance than town council meetings?"

Mr. Baxter stood up, pushing his spectacles to the top of his nose. "Our apologies. The town heard that we were lacking foster parents for the minors—Liam and James Clark—and came to show their support and even volunteer so the boys won't have to be separated. They're the children of a Legacy Fire widow, Your Honor." He finished with an apologetic shrug.

Baxter may as well have brought God himself down by invoking Lisa's status as a Legacy widow. Exceptions were always made in this town. Period.

Richard sighed. "They can stay while placement is determined, but anything else isn't for public dissemination." His eyes swept the room, locking on to Harper, then me. He looked away quickly. "Mr. Monroe, are you ready?" he asked the other lawyer.

"Yes, Your Honor." The forty-something man stood, adjusting his tie. "I'm representing the interests of Nolan Clark until such time as he can make his wishes known."

"Noted," Richard said. "Mr. Baxter?"

"Sir, our circumstances have changed as of this morning. We will no longer need to send the boys outside Legacy, as suitable foster parents have stepped forward to take responsibility for the boys."

"I see." Richard shuffled a file on his bench. "And who might they be?"

"Harper Anders and Knox Daniels." Elliot stood tall as Mrs. Dean joined her.

"And you find them to be acceptable foster parents?" His tone indicated he certainly didn't.

My stomach pitched. Were all my mistakes about to bite me in the ass?

Harper's hand found mine, interlacing our fingers, and I gave it a reassuring squeeze.

"We do. They passed a home study, and their home is more than appropriate. They both have suitable employment that allows for the care of the boys, and they're willing to take the required classes to be certified foster parents."

"Is that so?" Richard turned his icy stare on Harper, and my skin prickled, heat racing through my veins.

Keep control. Losing my temper had never gone well for me in this room.

"It is, Your Honor. They've been caring for the boys since their mother's death, and we feel it's in the boys' best interest to stay in their routine, and within their community."

"And what do you think, Ms. Simmons?"

Faith stood. "Your Honor, I have no objections to the boys remaining in the care of Ms. Anders and Mr. Daniels. Having only received the case this morning, I haven't had time to interview the boys, but for now, staying in their community, with people who care for them daily, as Ms. Anders does as Liam's teacher, is in their best interest." She sat, her back straight, and threw us a smile.

I exhaled in relief.

"Well, I'm not sure it is in their best interest," Richard stated.

My blood turned to ice.

"I'm sorry?" Mr. Baxter questioned. "You disagree?"

"I do." Richard looked straight at Harper, who had gone stiff next to me. "As I know the prospective foster mother quite well, I can say that she has never expressed interest in motherhood, or in any form of long-term commitment. Add to it that the *couple* isn't in any way committed to each other, and I'm not sure how we can, in good conscience, leave these already-traumatized boys in their unstable care."

Don't slaughter the judge. I repeated the phrase in my head until I could breathe through the white-hot rage flooding my muscles with adrenaline. No one got to attack Harper. Ever.

A murmur went through the courtroom, and Emerson's hand reached forward to rest on Harper's shoulder.

"With all due respect, Your Honor," Mr. Baxter said, breaking the pin-drop silence, "it's the responsibility of DSS to certify the worthiness of foster parents, and our team finds them more than appropriate."

"Really?" Richard arched a snotty brow. "An unmarried couple living in an *arrangement* that over half our town wouldn't approve of."

I jolted forward, only to find a hand on each of my shoulders, keeping me in my seat. Bash and River.

An arrangement? For fuck's sake, he made it sound like we were in the middle of some torrid affair. Even if we were, that was none of his damn business.

"We find them acceptable," Mr. Baxter said slowly, enunciating each word.

"As the judge presiding over this case, I don't see how it would serve the boys' best interest to be kept in an uncertain, unstable situation. There is no legal commitment between the parties in question. That might not disqualify them from being foster parents, but it certainly doesn't make them the right parents for this case."

Grams hands fidgeted with the clasp of her necklace.

"Because they're not married," Elliot clarified.

"Because they're not bound to each other in any way. They

could break up tomorrow, which, given the parties in question, is highly likely. That's not a stable environment for these boys."

Cool metal landed in my open palm, and I looked down to see Grams closing my fist. "Do what it takes, Knox. Don't you let those boys get separated." Her command was only loud enough for me to hear.

I didn't need to see what she'd given me. I already knew.

"Knox?" Harper's eyes were wide with fear and anger that, for once, wasn't aimed at me.

"How far are you willing to go for them?" I whispered.

The skin between her eyebrows puckered. "As far as it takes. He's not going to ruin those boys just because he's pissed at me."

"Your Honor, I understand your burden, but the status of their relationship is a private one," Evan urged.

Hell yeah, it was. Small town or not, this was out of line.

I knew how to stop it.

I knew how to keep the boys.

I didn't know what Harper would say.

My heart pounded, blood roaring through my head as I opened Harper's hand.

"I'm not the one who insisted this case be a town event, counselor," Judge Stone droned on.

I slid the ring home.

Before I could look, or be swayed by her reaction, I stood. "Your Honor, if I could speak, we can solve this issue right now." *Your Dick-headedness.*

He didn't even answer, simply tilted his head and stared me down like I was beneath him.

I grinned. This was the only chance I'd ever have to say this, and damn if I wasn't going to revel in it. "We haven't spread the news yet, but Harper and I are engaged."

The courtroom erupted in murmured excitement.

"I'm sorry?" Richard exclaimed, his eyes bigger than his gavel.

I looked down to Harper, her attention glued to my grand-mother's engagement ring. I slipped the wedding band and Grams's chain into my pants pocket and waited while my stomach tied itself into knots.

Slowly, Harper brought her gaze to mine. That look cut through the thousand layers of bullshit and armor I'd piled on since her prom night. Those wide, blinking eyes and parted lips made this moment as true as it could possibly be...without being real.

"What do you say, Harper Evelyn Anders? Want to stand up here and say you're going to marry me?" I whispered. My stomach careened as she stared a second longer. Was this what it felt like to really propose? A chaotic, gut-churning fear she was going to say no wrapped its spiny claws around my heart and squeezed.

The confusion in her eyes softened as she stood up, leaned against my side, and lifted her hand, letting the light catch the antique diamond-encrusted band that housed a perfect one-carat solitaire. "I'm going to marry Knox Daniels," she said to me before turning her radiant smile loose on the courtroom.

"Like I said, we're engaged."

Ryker was going to fucking kill me.

CHAPTER EIGHT

arper

Holy. Shit.

I was engaged to Knox Daniels.

Cue montage of childhood fantasy coming to life. Except it wasn't real. It was for the sake of keeping the boys together.

It's not real. It's just for the boys. Then why did my heart feel like it was ready to sprout wings and launch into the sunset?

Cheers erupted all around us, and Richard banged his gavel like a petulant toddler. *This is what happens when candidates run unopposed.*

"Settle down! This is a serious matter!"

The room fell silent as Judge Sanderbilt walked down the aisle past us. He shook his head, opened the wooden gate, and approached the bench. Richard leaned down, his dark-brown hair contrasting to the wispy silver that marked Sanderbilt's years of experience.

This could go either way. Sanderbilt was a good judge, kind, reasonable, and more than fair, but Knox had stood on the defendant side of his courtroom too often to be forgotten.

Knox's hand intertwined with mine, warm and firm. Steady. He flaked out on every woman he'd ever known, with two exceptions: the pink-haired woman on his left, and me. For us, he was rock solid.

Richard sighed and stood. "Everyone with the exception of counsel, DSS, and the prospective foster parents needs to leave. Now. This hearing is now closed to the public."

A groan went through the courtroom, but they all stood and shuffled toward the exit.

"What the hell?" Emerson whispered excitedly as she yanked me into an awkward hug over the back of the bench.

"Just so we can keep the boys," I assured her in the same whisper, but hugged her tighter. "It's not real. It's not real." I said it once to her, and once to myself.

She pulled back and took my face in her hands, seeing too much like she always did. "Smile. Act like it's real, even if it's just to keep those boys together."

"I can do that." My smile shook.

"Okay, then wipe the shocked look off your face, and you know…just act like you're in love with the guy you've been in love with for the last twenty years or so. Should be a piece of cake."

I tossed a glance toward Knox to see if he'd heard her, but he was locked in what looked like an overly intense discussion with Bash.

"And after?" God, how long could we keep this up? Until my mother planned a wedding? It would break her heart.

"We'll deal with that later. One bite at a time." She smiled as she picked up my hand, grinning down at the diamond. "But, wow."

"Yeah," I agreed. "Wow." The whole thing was wow. Before I could beg her to stay with me for the sake of my sanity, she headed out with Bash and River.

A few heartbeats later, the courtroom was empty, save us, the lawyers, DSS, Judge Sanderbilt, and Richard.

"Why don't you two kids come up here?" Sanderbilt motioned with a smile. "There's no need to be so damn formal."

Oh my God, I was about to lie to a judge. Well, two of them, but I didn't care so much about what Richard thought.

Hand in hand, we walked through the wooden gate until we stood between the first two tables. I returned Judge Sanderbilt's smile, determined to keep my eyes off Richard.

"Richard, for Christ's sake, get off your high horse and get down here." Sanderbilt rubbed his forehead.

A quick glance told me the court recorder wasn't recording.

"I'm the presiding judge in this courtroom," Richard snapped.

Judge Sanderbilt's face dropped all pretense of civility. "You will get down here, or you will recuse yourself, as you should have done the moment you realized it was your ex petitioning to be the boys' foster parent. This is Legacy, son, not L.A., or wherever the hell you learned to practice law."

"Chicago," Richard muttered as he climbed down from the bench.

"Same difference," Sanderbilt said with an eyeroll. "Now, there's no need to stand on formality. We're all here to determine where to place the boys in their best interest, not get into a pissing contest."

I blinked. Had he always been this awesome?

"They're not really engaged," Richard accused, folding his arms across his robes. "If they're willing to lie in order to keep the boys, that definitely makes them unsuitable."

Knox tensed next to me, which, in my experience, meant nothing good was coming next. I swept my thumb over his, hoping he'd remember to check his temper for our endgame. "I asked Harper if she'd stand with me. If she'd marry me. She said yes. Not sure about you, but where I come from, that means we're engaged. So does the giant rock on her hand."

"We're from the same place," Richard spat.

"You moved here after law school, but I'm born and bred Legacy, and we don't put little kids at risk over vendettas." Knox's grip tightened.

"They wouldn't be at risk," Richard argued. "They'd be placed with certified, trained foster parents, which you aren't. I might not like you, Daniels, but I wouldn't move those kids if I didn't have a damn good reason. I know your history, your pattern, and I won't let you disrupt those kids' futures when you decide to kick them out because you're done playing daddy, which you will."

"You don't know the first thing about me," Knox argued.

It was on the tip of my tongue to bite back in Knox's defense, but Richard turned to me next. I found myself tugged up against Knox from hip to shoulder.

"You're really engaged to him?" Richard asked, pure challenge in his eyes.

"I am." I wiggled the ring. Maybe he was right and Knox would eventually walk out as always, but the boys needed me to take that chance.

"Prove it." His gaze narrowed.

"That's enough." Sanderbilt rubbed the skin between his eyes. "Stone, you may have been elected, but you're nowhere near ready for a responsibility like this if you can't at least pretend impartiality. I'm going to give you one chance, and if you blow it, I'll be *forcing* you to recuse yourself. Just because Ms. Anders didn't want to commit or have children previously doesn't mean she isn't entitled to change her mind in the future."

Just because I didn't want to have kids with you. That's what I wanted to say, but I kept my lips pressed tightly together.

Richard flushed cherry red. We were going to be in for quite an explosion if he didn't breathe in the next ten seconds. Not sure he could contain his own pressure…or his ego.

"If we weren't engaged, why would she be on the title to my house?" Knox asked.

My head snapped toward his so hard I thought I'd hear an audible *snap.* I was on his *what?*

Knox nodded as everyone gaped at him. "It's true. Pull the title. She's been on it from the moment I purchased the land as part of my estate planning."

Relax your face. I couldn't let them see my shock.

"If I'd known that, the fostering thing would have been way simpler in the beginning," Elliot mumbled.

"Sorry," Knox told her. "After the town council approved the hotshot crew, and I realized I'd be moving home, I did the responsible thing and met with an attorney regarding my will and my property in Legacy. Yes, Richard, I'm capable of being responsible."

"That's Judge Stone while we're in this courtroom." Richard shifted his weight but didn't look appeased.

What the hell would it take to convince this guy we weren't lying when we…well…*were?*

"Is your only concern that they're not stable as a couple?" Sanderbilt asked.

"It is," Richard answered, sparing me a quick glance. "The Clark boys' entire life has been disrupted, and while I agree that leaving them where they are will lessen the trauma they endure now, I'm looking at the long term. It could be months before we locate their father or find a suitable pre-adoptive home. Though Harper and Knox have been living together for all of five days, they're not married, and not proven to be stable. I'd rather uproot the boys now than devastate them in a month when this all crumbles." He motioned between Knox and me.

Damn it, he was being almost reasonable. Thoughtful, even. I squeezed Knox's hand, and he held mine tighter.

"What would it take for you to agree to let the boys stay here in Legacy with them?" Sanderbilt asked, losing the earlier annoyance in his tone.

"It would take being a stable, married couple. Not that single women can't foster, and Harper, I know you're physically capable. But these boys are in this position because they lost their mother—their sole caretaker. They need the reassurance that it won't happen again while they're in this limbo. They need two stable foster parents."

Judge Sanderbilt looked at Knox, then at me. "You two kids didn't have a date or anything planned, right? You don't mind doing a little paperwork now so the boys can stay with you?"

A date? Knox and I had never even been on a date. Not that they knew that.

"We'll do whatever paperwork you want," Knox answered.

Judge Sanderbilt clapped his hands. "Excellent. Problem solved. Midge!" he called over to the court reporter.

"Sir?" The middle-aged redhead looked up over her glasses.

"Go down the hall to the clerk and recorder and grab a license. We can take care of this right now."

We were going to get the fostering license. Relief flooded my veins and nearly took out my knees. I honestly didn't care what had made Richard change his mind as long as it was changed.

Knox shot a grin at me, and I couldn't help but echo it. Butterflies took flight in my stomach. I couldn't remember the last time he'd looked this happy.

"Sure!" She jumped up with a legal pad and headed our direction. "Full legal names?"

"Harper Evelyn Anders," I said clearly, making sure she spelled it correctly.

"Knoxville Matthew Daniels," Knox added, and then Midge shot out of the courtroom like someone lit her skirt on fire.

"You're sure this will satisfy you?" Sanderbilt asked Richard.

Richard nodded, his face tense.

"So, kids, we can do it here. Super simple. This will just be the legal stuff, and then you can do a big celebration with your families whenever you feel like it. You willing to do that?"

"We can do a barbecue with the crew this weekend or something," Knox suggested with a shrug.

I'd never really thought about celebrating a foster placement, but the boys deserved to meet everyone and know they were wanted.

"Yeah, I'm good with that," I answered.

"Invite your mom too?" he suggested.

"Good idea." At some point, she was going to have to know what was going on. Living in Crested Butte wasn't far enough away to escape Legacy gossip.

The legal minds stepped to the side, talking among themselves while Knox and I discussed the important details of our life, like where we would pick up dinner tonight. Since Legacy had all of five options, the choice was pretty simple.

Takeout Italian from Pizzano's, it was.

Midge came back in, her heels clicking rapidly on the floor as she hurried down the aisle. "Here we go!" she said, waving a white paper above her head.

"Excellent." Sanderbilt took it for a thorough examination. "Okay, kids, why don't you make sure your names are spelled correctly. Richard and I both think it would be best for all involved if I take over this portion of the legalities, and then he'll finish up the placement decree."

Judge Sanderbilt handed me the fostering license and turned around to grab a set of robes from Midge.

The paper was thick in my hand, that good, expensive stuff that felt—

What the fuck?

I blinked, then read the heading again.

One more time.

Nope, it was still there, in big bold letters: Marriage License.

My mouth did its best fish impression, and Knox snatched the license, reading it himself. His brows rose and his wide, brown eyes sought out mine, but that was his only visible reaction.

"What do we do?" I whispered. My stomach sank. Faking an engagement to Knox was one thing. Actually marrying him was quite another. The guy didn't even like me in that way. I was just his best friend's little sister, and now he was holding a marriage license in his hand because I'd put him in this position.

"Whatever it takes, right?" His lips flattened into a tight line.

"That's a marriage license, Knoxville." Guilt tasted like sour day-old socks in my mouth.

His lips parted as our eyes locked. "God, it's been ages since you've called me that."

"Sorry. It just slipped out." I fidgeted with the diamond on my left hand.

"No, it's good. Say it again." The request came out slow, the deep, sandpaper-rough words sliding across my skin and leaving goosebumps in their wake. Knox was a natural seducer, but his voice was far and away his best weapon.

Or maybe it was just his mouth in general. Then again, that kiss had been eons ago. Maybe I'd glorified it into something it wasn't. Maybe he'd been right back then and we didn't have chemistry. Maybe the crackling tension between us was all in my head.

"Harper," he whispered, stepping closer, until I had to crane my neck to look up at him. It seemed unfair that he got hotter as the years went by.

"Knoxville," I answered. "What are we going to do?"

His jaw flexed. "You going to make me ask you twice in one day?" His thumb brushed over the ring on my left hand.

"Whatever it takes?" I asked, so quietly I barely heard the words myself. That tiny part of me that still held out hope for Knox's love cried out, begging me not to do this, to win him fair and square. To hear his declaration of love, not his promise of loyalty.

I wanted this to be real, but it wasn't about me. It was about Liam and James.

"Whatever it takes," Knox agreed with a single nod.

He didn't want this—not really. I knew it in my bones, but it was the only way to keep the boys together. Besides, we could always annul it once Nolan showed up. *Not could, will. You will annul it.* My throat tightened.

"You kids ready?" Sanderbilt asked.

"Are we ready?" Knox asked me, lifting one brow.

"We're ready," I answered, not taking my eyes from his.

Judge Sanderbilt started the ceremony in a blur, and before I could take a proper breath, Knox let go of my right hand and pulled a ring from his pocket, handing it to the judge. This was happening fast. So fast. Earth-tilting fast.

"You keep a ring in your pocket?" Judge Sanderbilt asked with a puckered brow.

"Long story." Knox took my hand back, and my equilibrium restored.

"I don't have one for you," I apologized, like I should have known we'd need one or something.

"We'll get one later," he assured me with a gentle squeeze. "Don't worry about that now."

Yeah, just worry instead that I was forcing the guy I'd always loved into marrying me when he in no way felt the same. *Awesome.*

"Repeat after me," Sanderbilt urged.

Hands bound, eyes locked, I repeated the words to Knox.

"I, Harper, take thee, Knoxville, to be my wedded husband; to have and to hold from this day forward, for better, for worse, for richer, for poorer, in sickness and in health, to love, cherish, honor and ob—I'm not saying that." I glanced at Sanderbilt, then back to Knox.

Knox full-out laughed, and my heart thundered. "I think we can work around it."

Judge Sanderbilt chuckled, and we kept going.

I cleared my throat. "To love, cherish, honor, and obey only when I feel so inclined, till death do us part." *Or we annul it.*

Then it was Knox's turn. His voice dropped lower, the words layered with so much feeling that I almost believed him.

"I Knoxville, take thee, Harper, to be my wedded wife; to have and to hold from this day forward, for better, for worse, for richer, for poorer, in sickness and in health, to love, cherish, honor, and to obey your every single whim, till death do us part."

Now I was the one laughing.

He slid the band onto my finger alongside the engagement ring, and my laughter died. Knox was marrying me. He was promising to love me. Promising to cherish and honor me. My heart clenched.

I so wanted to believe the lie.

Hell, I wanted to live in the lie.

I loved him, and not in the little girl crush kind of way. I loved every part of Knox, from his grin to his scowl. I loved his humor and his anger. I loved his intensity and his general recklessness. I was under no illusions about who he was and loved him for every flaw, not just in spite of them.

Knox's thumbs brushed over my fingers, and I felt the small touch in every cell of my body.

"I tell you now to love faithfully," Judge Sanderbilt continued. "To cling to each other through the best and worst—whatever may come. And in moments when you falter, remember the love you share, and what has brought you here this day. And now, the good part. By the power vested in me by the State of Colorado, I now pronounce you husband and wife. Go ahead and kiss your bride."

Oh. God.

Knox's eyes flared at the same moment, as if the total implications of what we'd just done finally hit him. He swallowed. Then a slow smile spread across his face as he tugged me closer.

My breath stalled in my chest as the moment froze.

Knox cradled my face, and then he took a second to look at me. A slight smile softened his sculpted lips, and his eyes danced with something that looked a lot like adoration.

My lips parted slightly as he lowered his head and kissed me.

His lips were soft, the kiss delicate. Chaste without being prudish. Sensual without being sexual. It was the most perfect wedding kiss in the history of wedding kisses, and it was over before I could even sigh.

Electricity zinged through me, just as it had years ago. It wasn't in my head—our chemistry really was that reactive.

His eyes darkened as he pulled away, dropping to my lips before taking my hand. I didn't remember walking, but we made it to the table where our license waited.

I heard congratulations somewhere in the roar that filled my ears, which only intensified when I saw Knox's firm scroll on the signature line.

"You sign it Daniels if you're taking his name, or Anders if you're keeping yours," Midge told me quietly when Knox turned to talk to Elliot.

Harper Daniels. How many times had I signed that in a high school notebook? Scrawled it on pages I'd thrown away, or hidden beneath my mattress? Signing my name as his was every dream, the perfect ending to the fairy tale I thought I'd have.

But this was a lie.

A beautiful, heroic lie.

He'd been forced to marry me by his own honor code, but I wasn't taking his name. That felt like flat-out stealing from him.

I signed my name as Anders and Midge nodded, then took the license to be filed. April thirteenth was officially my wedding day.

Richard ruled that the boys would remain in our home. *Our* home. Elliot assured us the placement paperwork would be delivered tomorrow, and we were free to go back to our days.

Our days.

Like nothing momentous had just happened. As if we'd stopped in for a cup of coffee and then discussed the Broncos.

Knox squeezed my hand and guided me toward the double doors. "You ready for this, wife?"

"Wife." I almost skidded to a stop in a cartoonlike flurry of arms and legs.

"Yeah, wife," he repeated with a nod, his jaw flexing again.

"We really need to talk about what just happened," I said, gripping the sleeve of his shirt so hard I certainly left wrinkles.

He nodded, his muscles tensing beneath my hand. "Yeah, I figured we could handle that at home. Unless you want to sit for a second?" He motioned to the benches in the back of the courtroom.

"No, home is good. Home is perfect." Because there were no prying eyes there, and he'd just referred to his house as *home*, where I lived with him. Kind of.

"Okay, then let's get out of here." He held the door open for me, and we walked into the crowded, noisy hallway. Half of Legacy was out here.

"Oh my God!"

"Seriously, you two!"

"Let me see the ring!"

They were still here. They were *all* still here.

Emerson pulled me into a hug. "You guys are keeping the boys?"

"We are!"

"And you're *engaged*!" Avery squealed, reaching for my hand.

"You're fucking *what*?" a familiar voice roared, and I let go of the girls to see a sharp pair of blue eyes the same shade as mine gawking at me in surprise.

"Ryker!" Relief hit me like a freight train, and I jumped at him, clasping him in a hug. "I didn't know you were here! When did you get home?"

He hugged me tight for a second, then set me back on my feet, holding me at shoulder's length. "About ten minutes ago, when I pulled into town and was told to get to the courthouse because my sister is *engaged* to my best friend." His stare turned glacial as he looked over my head, his hands slipping from my shoulders.

"Not exactly," I said, sidestepping so I stood in front of Knox. Ryker was going to lose his shit.

"Oh, thank God." Ryker sighed, his shoulders falling slack.

Knox picked me up by the waist and moved me to the side before facing Ryker head-on. "I'm married to her."

Ryker swung.

CHAPTER NINE

K nox

I RAN MY TONGUE OVER THE SPLIT IN MY BOTTOM LIP AND PEELED the aluminum casing off the champagne bottle. It was the only thing I could find at Legacy Liquor that had been over ten dollars a bottle. If I'd known the way this day had been headed, I would have ordered something better to celebrate with.

Not that we were really...*really* married. It was all just for show, but if we were, Harper deserved a hell of a lot more than a thrown-together ceremony with her ex standing as one of her witnesses. She hadn't even gotten to do the whole wedding dress thing.

Just another way I fucked things up when it came to her.

Holy shit, Harper Anders...Daniels, was my wife. I had a wife. A wife that was Harper. Married. Legally bound to each other. Wife. Harper.

Maybe if I said it in a different language a few times it would all feel real, even though it wasn't. What a mind fuck.

Harper's footsteps sounded on the staircase, and I opened a cabinet, looking for wineglasses.

"How did it go?" I asked her, examining the higher shelves.

"They're down. Liam seems relieved that they're staying, so that's progress, right? Way easier than handling that call with Mom."

GUILT SETTLED HARD IN MY GUT. THAT COURTHOUSE FARCE definitely wasn't what Mrs. Anders had in mind for her only daughter, and I was certainly not the son she'd envisioned at the end of Harper's aisle. But at least she knew the truth. Guess that made nine people.

Shit, ten with Ryker.

"I'm glad Liam feels relieved. He was so mad at us yesterday." We were going to have to get that trust back, but how was I supposed to get a five-year-old to trust me when I didn't even trust myself? I was just winging it over here.

"He was scared, and in his defense, Mrs. Pendridge did almost drop Jamie."

"I just about lost it," I admitted, putting two wineglasses on the counter. "How did things go with your mom anyway?"

She flushed. "She's...um...shocked, but weirdly excited for us. I still feel horrible about lying to her. I mean, I told her the basics, that we'd done it for the boys, but she still thinks..." She somehow managed an even pinker shade to her cheeks.

"That we're together?" I asked softly. Guess she didn't know the truth, so we were back to ten.

She nodded. "I hate lying to her, and I'll come clean once the boys are settled, but we both know she'd tell the entire county that we'd duped Richard if she knew the truth. It just sucks.

What are those?" She leaned a hip against the counter, and her lips turned up in a little smirk.

"What?"

She shrugged. "Knox Daniels owns wineglasses. Just figured you were still a Solo cup kind of guy."

I grabbed my chest. "You wound me. I've matured."

She put her hands on the counter and boosted herself up, sitting so her feet dangled beneath the granite. Her skirt brushed against her knees, which was a crazy, sexy combination of flirty, classy, and insanely hot.

"Still have that Han Solo cup?" She tilted her head slightly.

"Okay, I've matured in most areas. And that's a collector's item."

"Uh huh," she teased as I poured the champagne into the glasses. "We're celebrating?"

I handed her one of the glasses and lifted mine. "It's not every day you get shotgun married while your friends and family wait outside to beat the hell out of you."

"True." She winced, her gaze dropping to my split lip. "So, what do we drink to?"

My feet took me closer to her while my brain begged me to back the fuck up. But Harper was like gravity—she didn't mean to draw me to her. My nearness was the simple result of her existence.

"We drink to our win today. To those boys upstairs." I clinked our glasses, but Harper didn't drink. She pushed her mass of blond hair back behind her shoulder, then ran her finger around the rim of the glass.

"Harper."

She slowly brought her eyes to mine, and it was all I could do to keep a straight thought. I could stare in those blue-green eyes for an eternity, that's how captivating they were, how intricately the colors wove together.

"I didn't mean for this to happen," she said softly, her gaze dropping to my lip.

"I know." I set my glass on the counter and moved to stand in front of her.

"I put you in a shitty position, and I'm sorry, Knox. This wasn't what I wanted for you—finally coming home and not just worrying about getting the crew up and running but having a wife and two kids that you didn't exactly want in your house. It's like a bad reality TV show around here."

I put my hands on either side of her knees and locked my grip on the edge of the counter, wishing I'd had shackles installed to keep my hands off her. She was at the perfect height to kiss. Hell, she was always perfect to kiss.

Which I had done just six hours ago... Which I would probably never get to do again.

"I told you to use the house."

She rolled her eyes. "That is *not* what I mean, and you know it. After that night..." She shook her head and took in a deep breath, like she needed fortitude. "You've made it perfectly clear over the last few years that you don't want me around, and now I've pretty much scammed you into marrying me. That doesn't mean I'm not incredibly grateful that you've been ridiculously nice about it all, and I know we can get it annulled as soon—"

Scammed? Annulled? *Over my dead body.* The thought sent my brain into short circuit.

"I never said I didn't want you around." *Danger, Will Robinson.* I hadn't said it then, and I wasn't saying it now because I never lied to Harper. Ever. I always wanted her around. That was the problem.

Her lips parted, and my chest actually fucking ached. Wanting her was an indescribable mix of pain and pleasure I'd lived with so long it had become part of my marrow. It was as if that ache just grew cells that multiplied with the same longing, and being here in Legacy, with Harper in my house, my kitchen, my *life*, was intensifying it to the point of pain.

"You never said you *did*," she whispered.

"I don't say a lot of things when it comes to you." Didn't she know? Couldn't she tell the way I'd kissed her that night? Did she think I kissed everyone like that?

She smiled slowly and reached her hand toward my face, her thumb delicately brushing across the split in my lower lip that had been Ryker's wedding present. "And things that have to do with this?" Her fingers grazed my chin.

That tiny touch was a lick of flame to the walls of ice I'd built around my control when it came to her—control I needed to keep a firm grip on. I was scared to nod, to move in the slightest, for fear she'd take her hand away. Fear wasn't an emotion that visited frequently. It never struck when I was on a fire, when I knew there was every reasonable expectation I wouldn't make it out. Never felt an ounce of it driving on snowy mountain roads, or climbing, skiing…anything, really.

But Harper? I was terrified.

Terrified she'd finally realize how much that kiss meant to me, that she'd know she was the standard I measured every woman against. Scared shitless she'd find out I was too much of a coward to lose her brother's friendship, to cut away another piece of my already tiny family. Utterly afraid she'd know and then reject me, and I'd lose the possibility of her too. Because the fantasy of Harper may have been an ache, but it was a hell of a lot better than the finality of a no.

"You ever going to let me in, Knoxville Daniels?" she whispered.

She took a blowtorch to my defenses. My answer was on the tip of my tongue when the doorbell sounded, shattering the moment. "Any guesses on who that could be?" I asked instead, stepping back to give her space.

"Any one of the few thousand people in Legacy," she

answered as she landed on her feet. "Apparently we're the talk of the town."

"Oh, we're definitely half of the gossip at the Chatterbox." We made our way to the door, and I kept five feet away.

"You think only half? I'd definitely give us three quarters. I hear they're taking bets on how long we'll last."

"We should outlast them all and then see if we get the money." I smiled back at her, then opened the door. Every muscle in my body went rigid.

Ryker had the nerve to look mad as hell as he shifted the weight of a duffel bag on his shoulder.

"Oh, come on," Harper snapped from behind me. "What are you doing here, Ry?"

"Unless you've come to say you're sorry for that bullshit you pulled at the courthouse, you can turn around and leave, because as I told you this afternoon, as my best friend, you're entitled to that one punch, but you're not getting another one in." We were pretty equally matched. I had two inches on him, but he had twenty pounds on me, and the last time we'd truly thrown down, we both walked away with black eyes, bloodied noses, and busted lips after Bash had interfered. We'd been in fifth grade, so the odds were that we'd do a little more damage at this size.

His blue eyes—so much like Harper's—narrowed. "Hell no, I'm not apologizing!"

I slammed the door in his pretty little Ken-doll face.

"Knox!" Harper gasped.

Calm as I could manage, I stepped away from the door. Ryker had done enough damage to our friendship today, I didn't need to completely destroy it. Did I deserve the punch? Maybe. But he sure as hell didn't let me explain before he threw it.

Harper pushed past me and opened the door. "Say you're sorry!"

"No!" he retorted.

I leaned against the wall, hooking one ankle over the other, waiting to see how this would play out. I'd never had a brother —Ryker and Bash were the closest things I had—but I wasn't stupid enough to get in the middle of a sibling squall. It wasn't like Ryker would ever put his hands on Harper, but I'd step in if his words got sharp. She was mine to protect, now, too.

It's not real.

"Ryker Bradford Anders, if you don't say sorry this very minute, I'm going to throw the deadbolt and go to bed. You were an asshole today. Now apologize." She used her no-bullshit tone that probably sent preschoolers scurrying for their seats.

Tense silence stretched between them for a minute, maybe two.

With a sigh, Harper pushed the door shut, but just before it closed, Ryker called out, "Fine! I'm sorry! Happy now?"

She swung it open and tilted her head. "What was that?"

"Damn, Harpy. I'm sorry I hit Knox, okay?" He said it like he was guessing the answer to a question. He wasn't actually sorry. I knew him better than that. "Now can I come in?"

She looked over her shoulder at me, and I nodded, respecting her all the more for it. She hadn't just let him in, she'd asked my opinion.

"Okay, then," she said, opening the door wide enough for Ryker to walk in, then shutting it behind him. "And no yelling. The kids are asleep."

"The kids are asleep," he muttered. "I leave you alone for three weeks and you join the cast of *Full House*. Got a beer?" he asked me unapologetically, looking just as livid as he had at the courthouse.

I scoffed. "Nope, but we have some champagne. Care to toast with us?" Fine, that was uncalled for, but I was still pretty pissed about the right hook.

His eyes narrowed. "Not really."

"Okay, then no champagne for you!" Harper joked, coming

to stand at my side. "But seriously, what do you want, because I'm not sure if you noticed, but it's our wedding night." She wiggled her eyebrows, and Ryker's glacial glare transferred from her to me.

Holy shit, he was going to charge at me if she kept up that teasing.

"Hey, I didn't say that." I put my hands in the air like he was arresting me.

"Right." His grip flexed on his duffel bag, whitening his knuckles.

"Seriously, Ry, what do you want?" Harper crossed her arms and delivered a glare of her own. "And what are you carrying?"

"My stuff, and I want to know what the hell is going on!" he snapped, his gaze flicking between Harper and me. If the veins on his neck were any indication, he was going to blow a gasket soon.

"I told you earlier, we did it to keep the boys," Harper answered with a shrug. As if marrying me was the simplest thing in the world. "And you're absolutely out of your mind if you think I'm doing your laundry."

"I don't need you to do my laundry. And that's all you told me. I got a five-second explanation that doesn't even *begin* to cover how ludicrous this situation is." He ripped his hand over his blond hair. "Look, I think you taking the kids is pretty amazing, Harpy, but you kind of skipped the part of how the fuck you ended up *here*." He whipped his gaze toward me. "How did you let this happen?"

My eyes narrowed. "First off, she was here when I *got* here because she asked to borrow the house. I was already on my way. Second, watch your tone."

He blinked. "Watch my tone?"

"Stop it," Harper lectured, stepping in between us. "Ry, I told you. I brought the boys here because I didn't have anywhere else to bring them. Knox got here, and the home study happened, and it just rolled from there."

"I get why you're here," he said, his tone softening. "But I don't get why *you* stayed." He glared at me. "Why didn't you just move into my place?"

It was my turn to blink. "I guess it didn't occur to me." Really, that would have been the simplest solution, but if I was being honest with myself, I hadn't wanted to leave Harper...or the boys.

"It honestly worked out for the best," Harper answered. "Richard was only going to place them with a family with *two* foster parents. If Knox had moved into your place—which is an asinine suggestion anyway, this is *his* house—the boys would have been split up and sent elsewhere."

Ryker's focus shifted between us, as if he was weighing her words. His grip tightened on his bag. "And that's how you ended up *married?*"

"Richard was being a dick—as usual—and he said we weren't stable, and the boys need stable. So Sanderbilt suggested we become stable." Harper shrugged.

"By getting married." He said each word slowly, as if they could change meaning mid-verbalization.

"Pretty much," I answered. "It was get married or watch the boys get shipped off to separate homes in a town they don't know with people who don't know them."

"And that's all that's happening between the two of you?" His stare bore into me like he was trying to see under my skin.

"That's all," I repeated.

Harper's shoulders dropped slightly, and I wanted to punch Ryker in the face for barging in before Harper and I had the chance to hash this shit out ourselves. But there had been enough punching between us today. "It all happened pretty fast." She spun the diamond engagement ring around on her finger. "I honestly thought we were getting a fostering license and then *boom*, we're getting married."

That ring fit her perfectly and looked spectacular on her hand. *Stop it.* What the hell was wrong with me?

"So you two aren't sleeping together..." He looked back and forth between us.

Harper's mouth dropped open.

"That's none of your fucking business," I snapped. "None of this is, we're just filling you in as a courtesy." I pushed off the wall, standing to my full height.

He could call me out on the carpet all day long for my tendency to bed hop, but he didn't get to know about Harper's sex life. That was way overstepping the brotherly bounds.

Harper's sex life? You're the one married to her, you moron.

"Awesome, then you won't mind me moving in." He dropped his bag on the floor.

"No chance!"

"Hell no!"

Harper and I answered at the same time.

"Get out," she growled, and he backed up a step, his blue eyes flaring slightly.

I took mercy on him.

"And that's my cue to walk you out before Harper commits a murder that will make us ineligible to foster anyway." I picked up his bag.

"Harpy..." Ryker pleaded, his face stricken with concern that tripled the guilt in my chest.

"I'm not kidding," she responded. "Get out of this house. I'm a full-grown woman, and as honorable as your intentions may seem to you, they're sure as hell a piece of misogynistic assholery. You don't own me. You don't tell me what to do. I'm not your ward until you choose a suitable husband for me. My honor isn't yours to defend or watch over. It's *mine*. You don't get a say in who I sleep with. Not now, not ever. So get the hell out before I—"

"Jesus, Harper, before you what? Yell some more? I'm just trying to look after you, because I know him—" He threw a pointed finger in my direction.

Awesome.

"Before I call our mother!"

Ryker's head snapped back like she'd hit him. "Oh, come on!"

"Get. Out. Or I get my phone." She folded her arms across her chest and stood her ground.

The two faced off in a staring battle, and my money was on the aqua-eyed blonde. If looks could kill, Ryker would be a puddle of goo, with an *I'm melting* voice-over.

"How about I walk you out?" I offered him a chance to retreat.

Punch or not, he was my best friend.

"Yeah, that sounds good," he agreed quietly, withdrawing with as much dignity as possible when your little sister laid you out with a single threat.

I opened the door, and he walked through. The April air had that crisp chill that signified one thing.

"Snow?" Ryker asked, apparently thinking the same thing as he checked out the starless sky.

"Has to be," I answered, walking him to his truck. He opened the door and threw the duffel bag into the cab.

I couldn't believe the ass had actually thought he'd move in.

"So, are we going to be civil?" I asked, addressing the two-ton elephant in the room.

He turned, shoving his hands in his pockets. At least he wasn't planning an immediate swing at me again.

"You married my sister." To his credit, he kept his voice low and even.

"I did." There was no denying that fact, or the little jump to my heartbeat at the thought.

"But you're not..." His eyebrows jumped sky-high.

"No. I'm not." He really knew how to suck the joy out of a guy's night.

"And you're not going to..." His eyes narrowed.

"For fuck's sake, Ry. She has her own bedroom. I married her because she said she'd do anything to keep the kids from being separated. This was *anything*, and unless you want to be the one who gets those boys removed, you'll keep that reasoning to yourself. To everyone else, this marriage is legit, and it has to stay that way until they find Nolan Clark or permanency for James and Liam. Regardless of what you think, I'm not some jackass who married Harper to get in her pants...which, oddly enough, is pretty much the history of marriage in the world." *Just not mine.* "At least you know this one is for a much larger purpose."

Conflicting emotions raged across his face. "It's just that I know you, Knox. The second the new-and-shiny wears off, you'll split to the next challenge. You're not the guy who sticks around and sees things through. You're restless in a way that makes you a kickass firefighter and a pretty horrid boyfriend—"

"Yeah, I got it." I backed away. "If it's okay with you, I'd rather not stand here in my own driveway and get every single one of my flaws flung in my face by someone who is supposed to be my best friend. Because I did the first fucking decent thing I've ever done in my life today, okay?"

I wasn't good enough for Harper. Point taken. It wasn't like he needed to beat me over the head with that fact. He'd told me seven years ago, and I'd gotten the message loud and clear. So damn clear that it altered every interaction I had with Harper from that day. I could have him as my best friend or shoot my shot with Harper, but not both.

"Man." He rubbed his hands over his face and let out a monster sigh of exasperation, his breath visible in the rapidly chilling air. "That's not what I'm doing here. I swear. You *are* my best friend. You and Bash are the only brothers I'll ever have, but Harper is my sister. Even if some miracle happens and you do stick around, or worse"—he grimaced—"you two become a *thing*, I don't want her sitting home like my mom did for countless nights while our dads were off on fires. I don't want Harper getting that phone call that turns her into a widow before she's had a chance to go gray. It's not fair. Just promise me this thing is temporary."

Logically, I knew it was, that she'd be gone the second the boys were, but I wasn't promising him anything.

"You have more than made your point." *I don't want her with you.* That was pretty much what that boiled down to. Somehow the physical punch had hurt a hell of a lot less than this conversation.

"Look, I'm just saying that she'd better be able to get an annulment when this thing is over. Understand me?"

Loud and fucking clear.

"Welcome home, Ryker." Without waiting for him to hurl the next well-meaning insult, I turned and headed back to my house. The 4000-square-foot, perfect fucking house I'd had built. The house I'd designed, choosing everything I thought Harper might like, knowing she'd live in it after I inevitably died in some fire like Dad.

Except she was living in it *now*.

"Knox!" Ryker called out.

"I'll see you at the clubhouse tomorrow," I called back, walking through my front door and shutting it a little harder than I had to.

She'd better be able to get an annulment meant *don't touch my sister.* Fuck, maybe I should have moved him in. At least he would have been a physical barrier between me and my waning self-control. The boys kept us busy, but that didn't mean I wasn't well aware she was sleeping just across the hall every night.

"How did that go?" Harper asked softly, holding our champagne where the foyer ended and the great room began.

"About as well as I expected." I walked over and took the glass she offered. "He's pissed, and with good reason."

"Did you mean it?"

"Mean what?" I asked, damn well knowing exactly what she meant.

"When you said that we're only married to keep the boys." Her gaze dropped to her glass as she ran her finger over the rim.

"That's pretty much what happened today, isn't it?" I tried to keep my tone neutral, clinical even.

"Right." She glanced away. "Sorry, the champagne and the ring and...everything just threw me, I guess." She shook her head. "So, what do we do about the future?" She lifted those eyes to me, and I knew I was fucked. Standing here, having her...but not, was killer.

Which future? The one with Harper? The one for the boys? The one with my best friend on our hotshot crew? It was impossible to have all three, and two of those were a choice.

"We do what's best for the boys. We make sure everyone in this town knows we're married and happy." Instead of married and dying of sexual frustration. I'd leave that part out of any inquiries.

"Happy," she said to her glass.

"If we want to keep them here until they can officially find their dad, or whatever the next step is for them, we have to put on that front." The words tasted like sand, gritty and impossible to wash out.

"Front," she repeated, her eyes going dim. "Fake it." She nodded her head, as if coming to some kind of conclusion, then forced a smile at me. "Okay. I can do that. For the boys. Let's lay down some ground rules."

Her chipper tone grated on my raw nerves like broken glass over an exposed artery.

"I don't have to fake it—being around you. That's the easiest part of this," I tried to reassure her. "It's not about you."

"Oh, I know that, because you kissed me today like it wasn't exactly a chore, or maybe you're just that good at faking it. Then again, the second Ryker walked through that door, you went back to cool and aloof toward me without skipping a heartbeat. Whatever this is, it's about *you*. So, about those ground rules."

Man, I wished the champagne in my glass was tequila.

"What would you like?" I asked, instead of chugging the alcohol and searching for more.

"If we're faking this marriage, then can I assume you won't be sleeping with anyone local?" She lifted her brows.

"I'm sorry?" She may as well have tossed the rest of her champagne in my face.

"Well, I know your history, and your"—she waved her empty hand at me—"general appetite. It's not like you didn't show up here last weekend with someone. I just want to make sure it's not anyone I'd have to deal with gossip about, because that would be detrimental to the faking it goal." She headed toward the kitchen, and I followed.

Gravity.

"Appetite? What, like I'm a general danger to the female population of Legacy?" I set my glass on the counter and then put the island between us.

"Oh, I'm sure the Legacy girls are currently mourning your loss after the news of our marriage. Ring or not, some would be all too willing to oblige you, especially now that the crew will be officially back in a couple weeks. You guys will be like rock stars around here. How many news teams have asked for interviews? Seventeen? Eighteen?" Her glass hit the counter, sending some of the champagne sloshing over the edges.

I liked it better when angry Harper was aimed at angry Ryker.

"I have no clue. Emerson handles all that. And are you seriously telling me that your first concern is that I can't keep my dick in my pants?"

She folded her arms. "What's the longest you've gone? Because I have no clue how long it will take to settle Liam and James. I'd like to know your timeline, so I know what our shelf life is here." Her face was all kinds of smiling and kind, but those eyes gave her away. They were about as warm as the snowstorm building outside.

"Three months," I answered without thinking. They were the months after I'd kissed her the first time, the ones I'd spent trying figure out just how serious Ryker had been about putting her name on that list.

Really damn serious, as it had turned out.

She blinked once. Twice. "Three months. That's your limit. Good to know." She came around the island, and I stepped in front of her, blocking her exit.

I wanted to kiss that fake-ass, serene smile off her face, but I kept my hands to myself.

"I didn't say that was my limit," I explained. "I said that was the longest I'd gone in the past. While we're on the subject, what's your longest dry spell? What's your shelf life?" I'd been home enough to know the guys around here asked her out like it was a rite of passage to get turned down. All except the fire-fighters—both structure and wildland—stayed far away from her.

Ryker had seen to that years ago.

She stepped to the right.

I matched the movement.

"That's not important," she sang, scrunching her nose. "I'm not the one the town will be watching. You are. You may have been gone for the better part of a decade, but it's not like you don't visit, or people don't remember what you were like. Small towns have longer memories than Facebook screenshots." Her smile slipped.

"Nope. Don't put this all on me. You want the details of my sex life, then I get yours. That seems fair." I shrugged, folding my arms across my suddenly tense chest.

"Fine. About a year." She glared up at me, and damn, it was hot. I loved that she always stood her ground, never backed down. Maybe that trait was a bit of a pain in the ass right now, but she was Harper.

"Huh." My forehead puckered.

"What is that supposed to mean?" Gone was the glacial nonchalance. Her eyes were spitting fire at me now.

"Nothing." I shrugged. It really meant nothing. I just liked pushing her buttons.

"You know, not all of us see sex as just a physical need. Some of us require a level of emotion to let someone that close, so forgive me if I'm not out at the bar picking someone up, someone from LFD, for a one-night stand." Her cheeks pinkened.

That hadn't been what she'd said seven years ago. Oh no, then it had been about her inability to lose her virginity, let alone her first kiss. *Vic-fucking-Donaldson had been good enough though, right?*

"And there was an emotional connection with Vic Donaldson?"

"What? Vic? Are you out of your mind?" She sent me a look that said I was.

"You seemed pretty sure that he was the one on prom night, remember?"

Her eyes popped wide. "So you *do* remember that night." A slow smile lifted her lips, and I cursed my temper. Some things were better left unsaid.

"And don't think I didn't notice your little jab that you'd go home with someone on the structure side. That was a low blow." The rivalry between the Legacy Fire Department and the Legacy Hotshots wasn't just well known, it was legendary. Well, at least for a small town.

"Oh, you'd rather I pick someone on the crew? Because I know Bishop's home, and I can't think of one good reason I wouldn't climb that man like a tree." She smiled.

"I sure as hell can!" I snapped, raising my voice.

"Oh, and what is that?" She fisted her hands on her hips.

"Because you're not emotionally connected to him, and you're married to *me!*" My voice echoed off the bare walls, and I cringed, hoping I hadn't woken the boys. For fuck's sake, it was the first night of our "marriage" and I was already losing my temper. She would have been so much better off choosing someone else's house, someone else's last name.

But she took yours.

"Oh, that's right." She tapped thoughtfully on her chin. "So, ground rule number one means neither of us will be having sex outside of our marriage, even as fake as it is."

That last part stung unexpectedly.

"I wasn't going to in the first place." I advanced on her, my skin prickling with heat. Her back hit the counter, and I caged her in. So much for five feet. "But since you brought it up, no. We won't. I would never do that to you, Harper—or myself. You think I could fuck another woman knowing you're here at home? Even if you're down the hall and not in my bed, there's no chance." *Because no one compares to you, and I would know it the whole time.* "Even if it's just for...now." I swallowed back the bitter taste that came with that word. "Those vows mean something to me. I'm not going to break them."

I might not be able to keep her—that had been made apparent—but I sure as hell wasn't going to do anything to fuck it up while she was mine, even if it was just a technicality.

Her gaze dropped to my mouth and her tongue skimmed her lower lip, reminding me I'd had those same lips under mine just a few hours ago. Kissing Harper was a religious experience that had ruined me for casual sex years ago. I'd spent years chasing that high I'd felt on prom night, only to realize today, with that bare touch of a kiss, it only existed with her.

"What about having sex *within* our marriage?" she asked softly. My entire body went tight, and my heart thundered in my ears. All of that beautiful hope lingered in her eyes, the glimmer of a future I could have if Ryker wasn't my best friend.

But he was.

He and Bash were the only family I had besides Grams.

Fuck, she smelled good, and her lips were close enough to kiss if I just ducked my head—

"That's not going to happen either," I replied slowly, trying to match her soft tone and praying my regret came through in more than just my words. In another life, maybe, but not this one.

Watching that hope die in her eyes was right up there with the moment I'd let her walk away on prom night. It fucking *hurt*. Anger, I could have handled. Even some snarky comment would have been easy. But her quiet acceptance, the sadness that permeated the air between us, was heavy enough to push the breath from my lungs.

"Okay. Any other ground rules we need covered?" she asked, as though I hadn't just squashed any chance we'd had. Not that there'd ever really been one.

"I think we can give those a break for tonight." I backed away, and she sidestepped out of my arms.

"Right. Then we can pick this back up tomorrow. Or the next day, or whenever." She lifted her glass and drained the contents, chugging the champagne like a freshman sorority girl. "Night, Knox."

She left the kitchen without waiting for my reply, leaving me alone with both Ryker's and Harper's words ringing in my ears, and a dull, throbbing ache in my chest where I used to think I had the possibility of a heart.

"Night, Harper," I whispered to myself.

Then I slammed back the champagne, toasting myself to the biggest irony of my life. Me, the proverbial bachelor, had just married the one girl in the world I'd always wanted, dreamed about, blatantly fantasized about, and I *still* couldn't lay a hand on her.

This house was about to get interesting.

CHAPTER TEN

arper

"All soy for you, my dude," I said to Jamie, balancing him on my hip as we walked out of the pediatrician's office, Liam at my side. It had been a week since our courthouse wedding, and it felt like things were settling into a new, chaotic normal.

"So he'll stop puking?" Liam asked.

"That's the hope. His tummy isn't a fan of milk." I walked the boys to the car and got them all buckled in.

My mother called before I could pull out of the parking lot.

"Well, if it isn't Mrs. Daniels!" She came through the speakers loud and clear as my phone connected to the car.

"Anders, still, Mom," I assured her, just like I had when she'd blown a gasket after our wedding.

"Hmmm. When are you bringing your new husband over for dinner?"

I cringed. That was the last thing I wanted to do—haul Knox into a room with my mom so she could guilt him about what we'd done. It didn't matter that I'd told her it was for the boys, she'd still gotten all teary-eyed and called it our "first" wedding.

She didn't quite understand there wasn't going to be a second one.

"Maybe next week? Or the week after? Weekends are easier."

"How about brunch? I'll invite Ryker over too. We can chat wedding details, since I'm assuming you're going to have a church ceremony this summer, right? June might be too soon, but we could probably swing something for July."

My stomach sank and my hands tightened on the wheel as I turned onto Apple Blossom Avenue, heading out of Legacy Proper and up into the mountains. We'd gotten about six inches of snow yesterday, but the roads were already clear.

Colorado weather was weird like that.

"Mom, I thought we talked about this." I kept my voice even and firm, knowing she'd ride that runaway wedding-planning train all the way to the altar if I let her.

Was I lying to my mother? Yes.

Did I feel like absolute crap about it? Also yes.

But would she accidentally let it slip that we were faking this whole thing? Probably, and that wasn't a chance we could take.

"Yes, I know, you rushed it just so you could keep those beautiful boys safe, but we really need to start planning a celebration. You're my only daughter, Harper. And I still can't get over that you kept your relationship a secret this whole time!"

Guilt train arriving right on time, platform number seven.

"I know, it's just not the time." I glanced in the mirror to see Liam looking out the window.

"Well, let's talk at brunch about what the right time will be. I'm not going to have you living with Knox without having been properly married, young lady."

"We are properly married, and you didn't have a problem when I lived with Richard for a few months."

She scoffed. "I mean in a church, and you know it. And as for Richard, I only didn't put up a fight about that one because I knew you'd discover what an ass he is."

"Mom! The boys can hear you!"

Liam laughed, and I almost asked Mom to say it again so I could hear the sweet sound from him.

"Well, darn. Sorry about that, boys. Grandma doesn't mean to swear, it just slipped out."

Grandma. Oh shit. She was in deep.

"Besides, everyone knew you were just biding your time for Knox to come home. You know, why don't you come over for dinner tonight? I can throw a few things on."

"We would love to, but we're headed to the clubhouse for dinner with the crew." I'd never been more thankful for an excuse in my life. One look at Knox and I together and Mom would know this was all a ruse. Then *everyone* would know.

"Oh, I used to love those. I'm so glad those boys are carrying on the tradition." I could almost hear the smile in her voice.

We passed Phoenix Point and turned onto the new road, taking us into what used to be the Parson land but was now property of Legacy, LLC, which Bash, Knox, and Ryker all managed.

Official hotshot territory, once they got certified.

"Me too. Everyone is getting into town, and it's almost unreal that it's happening." We climbed higher, the evening sun hitting us in staccato bursts as we passed through the mature pine trees. This side of the mountain had survived the fire.

"It feels like the rebuild is complete. Like we're finally recovered."

"You could always start dating, you know. That might make me believe you." The subject of her dating wasn't one I pushed, but one I brought up every few months just so she knew we were cool with it. Dad had been her everything, but she deserved happiness.

"Harper, once you love someone like that and lose them… there's just no point trying to date because no one lives up to that standard. Your dad set my bar so high that it wouldn't be fair to any man to try to reach it. Even if they were perfect, they wouldn't be…him."

"I know. I just want you to be happy." We approached the tall gate that led to the clubhouse, and it opened as we came closer.

"Then let me help you plan your wedding," she requested, her tone dripping sugar.

"Mom." I groaned.

"I always knew you two would eventually figure out why you were always at each other's throats. Everyone else knew years ago."

I pulled into the empty spot next to Knox's truck and rested my forehead on the steering wheel. "That's not what happened."

"Then tell me all about it at brunch. I'll make reservations! Bye, love!" She hung up, and I gave up on trying to get out of dinner. Knox and I were just going to have to suffer through it and let her down gently.

There wouldn't be a big church wedding. No white dress. No bouquet. No happy bridesmaids or groomsmen in tuxes. No reception. No cake.

Definitely no wedding night. Knox had made that embarrassingly clear, and he'd kept a chunk of distance between us ever since.

The phone rang again, and I hit the button on my steering wheel to answer it.

"Yep."

"So, were you thinking of coming inside, or were you in prime nap position?" Knox's deep, sandpaper-rough voice made me sigh yet again and lift my head.

He stood outside my window with one eyebrow raised.

I rolled down the window, and he leaned down, his hands on the top of the doorframe. "Sorry, I was dealing with my mother."

"Ah, how is Mrs. Anders?" He smiled like we hadn't been in a silent stalemate for the last week. Which we had. Not that we weren't pleasant with each other, but there was a tense awkwardness that hadn't been there before.

Well, it had existed the summer after I'd kissed him the first time, but not since then. It was back in full force now.

"She's wondering why we haven't started plans to turn me into Mrs. Daniels, and she'd like to discuss those plans at brunch."

"Did you tell her you're already Mrs. Daniels?"

Not exactly.

"I told her we were already married, but she insists it's not good enough because we weren't married in a church, so while we may be legally married, she's pretty sure we're still living in sin. Just...you know..."

"Without the sin?" he supplied, the corners of his mouth lifting, but the smile didn't reach his eyes.

"Yep, that." I sighed. "What are we going to do?"

"Well, I thought we'd start by you getting out of the car, and then heading into dinner so I can introduce you to the other crewmembers who have shown up this week." He reached for my door handle.

"You know what I mean."

He sighed and his jaw flexed. "I guess we go to brunch, Harper. She's your mom. Of course she wants a big, fancy, white-dress wedding with all the trimmings for her only daughter. Did you think she wouldn't? I'm just surprised she supports you being married to me at all."

"What are you talking about? My mom thinks you're fantastic." I left out the whole *biding my time* comment.

"Yeah, well, she's always been blind to my flaws. Look, I'm

not nervous, but if you are, just remind her that Adeline is getting certified to babysit so we won't be able to make it happen for a couple weeks. Not sure the boys would be down for sitting through a wedding planning session." He opened my door and walked around to the other side of the car, unbuckling James from his rear-facing car seat. "Hey, Sir Pukes-A-Lot! I missed you all day! Well, maybe not the puke, but definitely that grin. Did you go around sharing that with Cherry today?"

I rolled my eyes but couldn't help the smile. Just when I was certain I could guard myself against Knox, he said something like that, and I went spinning back into the torturous infatuation that had pretty much been my default state since childhood. He might be keeping his distance from me, but he was all-in for the boys.

Grabbing the huge vat of salad that occupied my passenger seat, I got out of the car while Knox helped Liam out.

"And how was your day?" Knox asked.

"My mom wasn't home," Liam answered with a little shrug. "But Elliot got my blanket."

My heart crumpled all over again.

Knox's eyes shot up to mine and I mouthed, "Later."

He gave me a quick nod and looked back at Liam. "I'm sorry, bud."

Liam shrugged again.

Knox and I shared a *wtf are we supposed to do* look. We were both out of our depth here, which was why Liam was starting counseling next week.

"Well, you know, one of the new guys, McCoy, he has little boys about your age. How would you like to meet him?" Knox asked Liam.

"Yeah, that's good," he responded quietly, like he was on autopilot.

"Okay, then let's get you inside." With the diaper bag on his shoulder, James in one of his arms, and Liam's hand in the other, Knox led us into the clubhouse through its large glass front door.

How domestic we were, Knox with the kids, me bringing in a dish for the potluck. Had this been how my mother saw her life? My father carefully holding us as we went to yet another party with our second family, the hotshot crew?

But her life had been perfect up until the fire.

Mine was currently a very large lie.

Warmth blasted us as we entered the clubhouse, and I couldn't help but glance around in awe, just like the first time I'd seen the compound. With high, vaulted ceilings and floor-to-ceiling windows at the back of the building that showcased the valley, it felt like a modern piece of art.

It was the perfect place for a fresh start, but with the picture of our dads on the wall, it also felt like coming home. We were miles away from the original clubhouse, but this one still had that same feeling of community and purpose, with more than a few upgrades.

Liam kicked off his snow boots and put them on the mat next to the door that already had a few small pairs.

"Oh, thank God you're here," Emerson said, skipping barefoot out of Bash's office. "There are so many people, and I'm having the damndest time remembering names. Wanna put that in the kitchen?"

"I've got these two, go ahead," Knox said, leading the boys toward the windows, where I saw two kids playing with tablets on the sectional couch.

Emerson took the salad from my hands and marched off toward the kitchen. I untied my snow boots and toed them off, then went after her.

She slid the bowl onto the island with the rest of the food, then checked on something baking in the oven that smelled heavenly.

"Brownies?" I asked.

"Of course," she answered. "Okay, so about half the crew is here, thank God, because I'm not sure I could remember everyone if they all showed up at once. The rest are due in next week, so maybe we could do flash cards or something?"

Of course, Emerson's solution was flash cards. Anything she could study, file away in her brain, and master quickly was right up her alley. She'd quit her job at the mayor's office to help manage the crew, so this was her baby too.

"Stop stressing out," I said, eyeing the huge spread that was lined up on the stainless-steel islands that ran the center of the kitchen. Lasagna, fried chicken, mashed potatoes, garlic bread, veggies, and at least two different casseroles took up only the first half. "We'll do it just the way I do with a new class every year. Get to know each family and their needs and strengths on an individual level."

She leaned against the counter, letting her shoulders drop. "I feel like I've been managing this transition for so long, and some days it felt like it would never get here, but now it's time for it to happen. The houses are built, the legacies are coming home, or here. The new crewmembers are showing up." Her forehead crinkled. "I just want it all to go smoothly."

"Em, you're doing great, and if something goes wrong, then it goes wrong. Not everything can be perfect or planned for, and that's okay. We've got new dynamics, rookies, and these guys to support while they get the crew up and running for certification. All we can do is care for the families just like our moms did." I shoulder bumped her. "Don't be so hard on yourself."

"What if it's all for nothing?" she asked softly. "What if everything comes together and we still can't make it happen?"

A knot formed in my belly. The guys would leave and seek out jobs at other crews. "Then at least we'll know we gave it our all. Now, put away your color-coded to-do list and let's just enjoy our new family, shall we?"

"Who said anything about a new family?" Ryker asked, coming into the kitchen with a Team Phoenix shirt on. We weren't a crew yet, not until we were certified, so team it was.

"We're talking about the newbies," Emerson answered.

"I wasn't talking to you, jackass," I threw back.

"Harpy, come on, are you still pissed?" He tilted his head, which usually worked on the women he got into spats with, but I wasn't one of his girls, I was his freaking sister, and I didn't find him cute in the least.

"About what, Ry? Maybe you showing up on my wedding night, questioning my sex life with my husband? Or you splitting his lip right after we said our vows? Not even giving us a chance to explain? Acting like I'm some kind of possession for you to bequeath to whom you see fit? Would you like me to continue?" I folded my arms across my chest.

He put his hands up and backed away slowly. "Still pissed. Got it."

"And will be. For a really long time." I stared him down so he knew I meant every word. Decking Knox had been bad enough, but showing up at our house like he could lay down the law had put me over the edge. And fine, maybe I blamed him for Knox putting up a solid wall of awkwardness between us.

"For how long?" he asked from the doorway.

"Really long!" I snapped.

"Got it." He nodded slowly, then turned and left.

"Questioning your sex life?" Emerson prompted, taking the brownies out of the oven and setting them on a trivet to cool.

"He said he was going to move in with us to make sure we weren't sleeping together. He brought a duffel bag, and no, I'm not kidding."

Emerson pulled two Cokes out of the fridge, and we popped the tops.

"So, you're really not going to take advantage of the fact that you're married to the guy you've been in love with since you a kid?" She lifted her dark brows at me.

"Knox drew a line. I told you he's never seen me that way. I'm just Ryker's little sister, and now I've got him knee-deep in this with the boys. He's stuck. I'm like a ten-billion-gallon vat of quicksand and I've got him trapped. Super sexy," I finished with a tone of heavy sarcasm.

"I've seen the way he looks at you." She cocked her head to the side. "Pretty sure the entire town has seen the way he looks at you."

"He doesn't look at me."

"Yeah, okay." She rolled her eyes. "That's why it was so easy to convince two judges that you guys had already been engaged and were down for a ten-minute marriage ceremony." She gave me a thumbs-up.

"I'm serious. He doesn't. And maybe I fooled myself into thinking he did once or twice...okay, maybe more than once, but I'm telling you that he doesn't feel that way about me. He sees me as his best friend's little sister. And he promised he wouldn't sleep with anyone else while we're...doing this, but that's just because he would never hurt me—or piss off Ryker. I'm pretty sure I could walk around naked, and he'd just smile and offer me a robe in case I was cold."

She took my hand. "Harper, he looks at you like you're the Christmas present he can't wait to open. All this hope, and longing, and curiosity mixed with anticipation and the knowledge that he can't unwrap you. I highly doubt he sees you as a sister, but your brother *is* his best friend. You're in a tough spot." She grimaced, wrinkling her nose.

"Living with Knox is a special kind of torture. Look but don't touch. Fantasize but don't act on it. Watch him snuggle that baby but remember you're not having *his* babies. This is all pretend." I eyed the brownies and debated shoving my face into the pan to inhale the chocolate. "The sexual frustration over here is at redline headed for complete meltdown, and that's assuming I don't give in and start walking around the house naked to test the robe theory."

"Harper, he's here," she reminded me, gently shaking my shoulders. "He could have moved into Ryker's or gone back to California until May, but he chose to stay. With you. Just give it some time. There have been few things I've been certain about with that group of guys, but you and Knox? That was always an inevitability. Hell, you two just ended up married. Married, Harper!" She shook me again, grinning with excitement.

"So backward." I glanced at the rings on my left hand. Agnes told us to keep them, but I knew it was only a matter of time before I was handing them back.

"You say backward, I say fate." She shrugged. "Now, let's get you introduced. If we stay in here one more minute, I'm eating all of those brownies."

She grabbed my hand, pulling me out of the kitchen and into a newly gathered crowd.

There were River and Avery, who came in with trays of ribs River claimed were the best south of Alaska. Bishop followed, silent and observant as always, nodding his head as Avery's teenaged sister, Adeline, ceaselessly chatted at him.

In addition to Bash, Ryker, and Knox, there were the McCoys—Miles and his wife, Jessica, who had moved from Oregon and had the cutest twins, Noah and Gavin. Those two were currently running around with Liam, who was miraculously smiling.

Braxton Rose was home, mostly to keep his little sister, Taylor, safe on the crew. She was barely out of high school, and he was pretty pissed about the council's sixty-percent decree, but he'd come.

Derek Chandler and Indigo Marshall rounded out the last of the legacies who had already made it home. We were still missing Lawson Woods and Spencer Cohen, but they were due to arrive early next week.

None of the other new guys were married, just McCoy, which didn't surprise me. Most wives weren't keen on uprooting their families so their husbands could take up the mantle of a hotshot crew that had been wiped out in its entirety.

Call it superstition or common sense. Either way, I understood.

After making sure Jessica McCoy felt welcomed, I found myself at the window, looking out over the snow-covered mountains. The sun had set behind the peak, leaving that pale streak of blue against the black outline of the terrain.

Dad was buried just beyond that ridgeline with rest of his crew.

Maybe this was what he would have wanted, to see Ryker take up his patch. Then again, maybe his opinion would have changed if he'd seen the fallout after the fire.

"You're Harper, right?" a deep voice asked, jolting me from my thoughts. One of the new guys smiled down at me. He was a little shorter than Knox, but built. Raven-black hair and crystal-blue eyes made him almost too Disney prince, except that bump on his nose told a history of having been broken, and the scar on his chin gave him just enough of a flaw to make him human.

"I am," I answered, offering a smile in return. "You must be one of the new guys."

"I am," he repeated. "Chance Thornton, out of Arizona. I've read all about your father's crew, so this is pretty much a dream come true. I'm honored to have been selected for it."

"Chance, huh? Perfect firefighter name." I ignored the hero worship in his voice over my father. I'd heard it far too many times, especially in the years after, when the news crews came, the documentaries were made, and the books were written by people who had never even known our fathers.

"I guess I don't like to play it safe." He smiled, but his tone deepened as he winked.

I blinked. *Oh shit.* Was he…hitting on me?

"Apparently you like to have your ass kicked too," Knox said, coming up behind me. "Because that's what's going to happen if you use that line on my wife again."

My wife. My heart jolted.

"Oh man. I'm sorry." Chance put up his hands and backed up a few steps quickly. "I didn't know. Hell, I thought you were one of the single guys, Daniels."

"Nope. Taken. By Harper." His voice dropped to a soft tone that felt all the more menacing for its softness.

"Got it. Sorry, Mrs. Daniels. My bad." He gave me a wink and quickly disappeared into the crowd.

"Seriously?" I asked Knox, taking James off his hands.

James snuggled down, resting his head on my shoulder.

"He's tuckered out," Knox said, running his hand over James's baby-soft hair.

"Seems like it." I rubbed small circles on his tiny back. "Did you need to scare the new guy so badly? It's not his fault he's not up to date on the current Legacy gossip."

"We're not gossip. We're married, and it's better he learn that today than piss me off later. Now, let's go, Mrs. Daniels, it's time to eat with half of our new crew." He wrapped his arm around my shoulder and led me to the table where everyone was sitting down to dinner.

It was the most he'd touched me since our wedding, and a tiny pinprick of guilt reared its head that I hadn't told him I'd kept my own name.

Then again, since he'd kept his heart, it only seemed fair I keep a portion of mine when he already owned the rest of it. The fact was, no matter how many times Knox made it clear he didn't want me in that way, I still loved him.

I had a feeling that fact would never change.

CHAPTER ELEVEN

nox

"Bottle, bottle, bottle... Where is the fu—" I stopped mid-freakout as Liam appeared in my line of sight. "Fudge and bottles?" I finished, well aware my cover-up was lame. Eventually, I was going to slip up and teach Liam his first curse words. It was inevitable.

He pointed wordlessly to the diaper bag on the counter.

"Gotcha." I opened the bag and found the bottles perfectly packed inside with formula, three extra outfits, and a slew of bibs. It was Friday, my morning to take the boys to school and daycare, but Harper had pre-packed the diaper bag like the early-morning hero she was.

"Man, she's good. I should marry that woman," I muttered.

"You already did!" Liam called back, already having run to the living room.

Right. I did. Had it already been three weeks? In some ways

it seemed like it had been only a few hours and in others, three weeks was forever. We'd fallen into an easy rhythm between getting the boys where they needed to be and getting ourselves to work.

We were surprisingly good partners. Courteous, thoughtful of each other, both willing to pitch in on chores or whatever needed to get done. It was like we'd been roommates for years, the very definition of platonic.

Fucking *platonic*.

Gone was the subtle flirting, the high-strung moments packed with enough sexual tension to send a fault line into a full-blown earthquake. Now her smiles were...friendly or reserved for the kids. She'd flipped a switch from flirty to just friends.

Well, I'd forced the flip, but that wasn't the point. I fucking missed her real smiles and quick, stolen glances when she didn't think I was looking.

I threw a few extra containers of baby food into the bag—mostly to feel like I'd done something—and grabbed a stainless-steel coffee mug.

"Push." The note on the Keurig was in Harper's handwriting and pointed to the "brew" button. I slid the cup under the dispenser, pushed the brew button, and waited.

The dark, rich scent of coffee filled the kitchen, and it wasn't just any coffee. Oh, no, that beautiful, deep, soul-stirring smell could only be from one place.

I threw open the cabinet above the machine and my jaw fell slack.

Black Velvet Coffee.

Harper had remembered from the last time I'd visited, and she'd ordered it for me. She'd taken that time, kept that memory, filed the information away for no other reason than to make me happy.

I'd had women give me ties, cuff links, all the guy shit girls thought we wanted. Hell, I'd been given blow jobs as a birthday present on more than one occasion.

But the coffee meant more than all of that because there was no occasion, no reason to do something nice other than the fact that she was Harper and that's just what she did. Maybe we were platonic, but she cared.

I screwed the lid onto the cup and put it next to the diaper bag, feeling lighter than I had since telling her our marriage would be in name only.

"You boys ready to roll?" I walked into the living room to find James bouncing happily as Liam tied his shoes. He stuck his tongue out every time he did it, as if it needed that precise position to be successful in his shoe-tying endeavors.

"Almost. Done." Liam said each word carefully as he pulled the laces into a perfect bow.

"You got it!" We high-fived and I reached for James. "Okay, if we leave now, we can stop by—" Well. Shit. Literally. Jamie reeked. "Never mind. Clean pants for you, and then we'll go."

Thank God I didn't have a typical nine-to-five or I would have been screwed trying to figure out how to actually get two kids out of the house on time. Harper didn't seem to have a problem with it. She even managed to get out early, but it didn't matter how early I started, we always seemed to walk out five minutes late.

Five minutes later, Jamie was clean, and we were on our way with a pit stop at the pantry to snag a little box off the highest shelf.

"I've got the bag!" Liam said as I strapped James into his car seat.

"One, two, chest buckle, scoot it up," I muttered, remembering exactly what Harper demonstrated that first day. Kids were a hell of a lot easier than babies, that was for sure. Half my time went to trying to keep James alive.

"Good job," Liam said, leaning over from his booster seat.

"Glad you approve. You click in, and we'll take off." I walked around the end of the truck, pushed the step stool Liam used to get in the truck to the side, and shut his door after checking that he'd clipped in.

Independence was important to the alpha pup, and I got that on a purely experiential level. If you could depend on yourself, you didn't need to worry about what anyone else would—or wouldn't—do for you. The step stool was a small thing that made him feel a little more self-sufficient, and I didn't mind in the least. Kind of like moving the snacks to the lower drawers in the kitchen so he'd always feel like he had access to the food. The first time Harper walked in on him standing on the kitchen counters, reaching for the granola bars, she'd hooked him up.

As long as the kid wasn't asking to drive, I was up for just about anything to make him feel a little more in control of a situation he had almost no say in. They'd been with us for three weeks now, and there was no sign of their father. *More like sperm donor.*

We pulled out of the driveway, headed through the hotshot neighborhood, and started down Apple Blossom Avenue toward Legacy, making one small detour before reaching Little Legacies.

I helped Liam down and got James, before walking the boys with their bags into the preschool. Parents who would have usually ignored me waved on their way out, smiling like I was allowed admittance into their club because I now cared for miniature humans as well.

Well, except Ethan Coulter, but that guy was always going to be a self-righteous douche, if history was any indication.

"When are you going to stop playing with fires and get a grown-up job, Daniels?" Ethan asked as his son ran toward Liam's classroom.

Liam hung up his bag in his cubby and took off his Legacy Wildland Fire jacket.

Sue me, I liked that we had matching jackets.

"Right about the time you realize there's more to life than money, Coulter." James ran his hand over my light beard, and I made a few monster noises to get a giggle.

"Right. Welcome home and all that. I heard you somehow landed Harper Anders. Not sure how you managed that in less than a week. What did you do? Shotgun wedding?" He lifted his eyebrows, and I more than got his meaning. "Not that I blame you."

Liam put his hand in mine, buffering my instant need to crush Coulter to a pulp. A few years ago, I would have, consequences be damned.

"How's Kim?" I asked pointedly. Coulter married our class prom queen in a flurry of small-town excitement, but I knew he was found most nights at Wicked, the local bar. And he wasn't alone.

"Fine, thanks." His eyes narrowed. "Have a good day and all that." He nodded in our direction and walked away.

He had definitely been one aspect of Legacy I'd been happy to leave behind.

"That's Blake's dad." Liam hung up his jacket carefully. That was one thing about having a kid who hadn't owned much in his life; man, did he take care of what he did have.

"Yeah? I went to school with him. Is Blake nice?" Talk about a name that was pretty much invented to be printed on a Harvard acceptance letter.

"Nope. He's kinda spoiled and mean." Liam shrugged.

Go figure.

"Liam, honey, let's go, you're going to be late!" Harper said as we walked into the class. She ran her hand through his hair, and he leaned in a little. That kid might not want to depend on anyone, but, man, did he have a huge soft spot for Harper.

We were pretty similar in that way.

"Bye, Knox!" Liam said loudly and hurried to his desk.

"How did the morning go?" Harper asked, stepping just outside the classroom with me. Not sure how a preschool teacher managed to look hot all buttoned up like she was, but she did. Then again, I probably would have found Harper attractive in a potato sack, let alone black pants that hugged her curves and a pink knit top that looked like it had been sewn with her body in mind. She took James and kissed his forehead. "Mmm, he smells good."

"I splashed a little cologne on him," I joked. "Nothing big, just a little Axe. He wasn't quite ready for Old Spice."

"Ha, ha. Very funny. He always smells good." She took another sniff at Little Man's head, closing her eyes in bliss. As much as I'd never imagined myself with kids, Harper was in her element, and it looked good on her.

"Morning was great, thanks to finding my favorite coffee." My voice dropped a little.

Her smile was instant and a little shy. "I'm so glad you like it. I thought you might need a little pick-me-up."

"It was a great surprise. Perfect." Just like she was. Her hair was down and currently in possession of James. "Thank you."

Her cheeks flushed, and she cleared her throat. "So, did you get into it with Ethan? I saw you talking to him."

"That guy hates me. Always has." I stuffed my hands in my pockets.

"You slept with his girlfriend before the homecoming game." She arched a brow my direction.

"Hey, they were on a break, and she was more than willing. Trust me." I shrugged. It wasn't my fault Coulter couldn't keep his woman happy.

She scoffed. "I have no doubt. Just play nice. This isn't your sandbox anymore; it's Liam's, and he already has a hard enough time fitting in."

My hackles rose.

"What do you mean?" I glanced over her shoulder and saw

Liam sitting alone at his table, organizing pencils while his classmates gathered near Blake.

"I mean, kids are kids. Liam hasn't always had the new back-packs, or new shoes, or the stuff that some of those kids value. They aren't always welcoming to him." She followed my gaze and sighed. "Kids can be jerks."

"Whatever, my kid is way cooler than that Gap model wannabe over there licking the dry erase board." I nodded toward Blake.

Her eyes widened momentarily and then she stifled a laugh, kissing James again. "Okay, get out of here." She handed James back over. "Thanks for handling this morning so I could leave early for the staff meeting."

"Thanks for marrying me," I said with a shameless grin.

Shit, I was flirting.

She blinked. "Bye, Knox. I'll see you at home." She turned back to her class, and I moved quickly, slipping the awkward box free of my jacket pocket and putting it in her hand. "Bottle-caps!" Her smile lit up the freaking world.

"See you at home, Mrs. Daniels," I called back over my shoulder. That was officially my favorite nickname for her. Ever. "Let's get you to Cherry's, Little Man."

James let out a squeal as I blew a raspberry into his neck and carried him out of the preschool.

Not a bad way to start a day.

MONDAY FUCKING SUCKED.

"What do you mean he's not here yet?" Good thing Bash's office was soundproof because the other crewmembers didn't need to hear this shit.

Bash tied his running shoes. "I mean, he told me he owed his old crew one more day and he's giving it to them. He's coming."

"It's already the second of May. He'd better show, because he agreed to be our Supe, and if he doesn't show, our whole charter with the town is fucked." All our work, the money, the begging we'd done to the town council, it would all be for nothing if Spencer Cohen didn't show up.

He was the only surviving member of the original Legacy Hotshots.

"He will. He bought a house and everything. He will come."

I ran my hands over my head and rested them on top, interlacing my fingers. "It's not like I can blame the guy. I know it's painful as hell for him to come back here and put this patch on."

"Yeah, but we can't do it without him, and he knows that. None of us have the experience to be superintendent. He'll come."

"For the patch?"

"No. Because the last thing he said to my father was promising to get me off the mountain. To keep me safe. There's no way he's not showing up now that we're headed back up."

What a fucking guilt trip. Spencer had taken the truck down with Bash kicking and screaming not to leave his father, and they'd lived.

Every other crew member had been found in their deployment shelters, arranged in their site just how they'd practiced hundreds of times.

"I guess we'd better get out there," I said.

A few minutes later, we stood at the head of the great room, where all but one of the new Legacy crew waited.

Most of the crew were seasoned wildland firefighters. The others...well, we had to get them in shape and ready for certification.

"Glad to see everyone made it in today," Bash said, zipping up his fleece. "Most of you know me. For those who don't, I'm Sebastian Vargas, and this is Knox Daniels. Spencer Cohen will be our Supe, but Knox here is going to be in charge of keeping you all in shape."

The fuck I was.

Pretty sure my face said as much as Bash slapped me on the back.

"You saying you're not the most in-shape asshole out here?" he asked with more than a little challenge in his tone.

"Well. Yeah. Of course I am." Hell yeah, I was. I ran every day, lifted at night, and ate like a GNC ad most of the time. Lately, I'd put in extra sessions at my home gym, but that was honestly to keep my hands busy and off Harper.

"Then they're yours." Bash left me standing at the head of the crowd.

Everyone looked at me with expectant faces, and I cleared my throat. "Okay. Well, then." What was I going to do with them? Seventeen faces stared at me like I was supposed to know what the hell I was doing. Ten of them, I'd known for most my life, but the other seven were virtual strangers. An idea struck. "For those of you who are legacies, welcome home. For you newbies, we're going for a little tour. On foot. Hope you're hydrated."

We ran.

I chose the worn path up Legacy Mountain, keeping us well below the tree line. My lungs burned for the first mile, but then adjusted as usual. I'd babied myself on the treadmill too much lately. There was simply no simulating these rocky turns and dramatic elevation changes.

Two miles in, Bash jogged up next to me, giving me the evil eye. "I'm regretting giving you this position."

"Only because you're too out of shape to keep up. Emerson's turned you soft." My breath was even and steady, but many of the guys behind us couldn't say the same. The newbies had all been here for a week, so they'd had a little time to adjust to the elevation, but I knew I was going to have to slow them down before one or more of them dropped from altitude sickness. It would take a full month to get them acclimated.

"What, and Harper hasn't made you soft? Or was that not a little cupcake on your desk with a 'good luck today' note?"

"Stay the fuck out of my office, and you better not have touched my cupcake." I'd kill him if that little bite of red velvet wasn't there when I got back.

"What is this I hear about cupcakes?" Ryker asked, coming up on my right.

"His wife brought him a little first full-crew day present," Bash teased.

"I hate when you call her that," he muttered.

"Well, that's what she is," Bash countered.

"Wait." Ryker's head snapped in my direction. "Harper brought you a cupcake and didn't leave me one? What the actual hell?" The guy looked crestfallen.

I kept my mouth shut. Harper was a sore subject between us, and I wasn't sure we'd found any common ground to declare a truce yet.

"She's still pissed at you," Bash told him.

"Figured that out. She can be as pissed as she wants, I only have her best interest at heart," Ryker answered like the egotistical ass he was.

"Bullshit," I muttered as we rounded another curve.

"Excuse me?" Ryker snapped.

"Here we fucking go." Bash sent us both a stern look that we ignored.

I glanced back and noted we were about ten feet in front of the next guys, Bishop and River Maldonado, who were lost in their own conversation. "Look, Ry, I get why you wouldn't want her with me. But you have to let go of the idea that you can control her. She's a full-grown woman."

"I'm well aware of what she is. And damn right I don't want her with you, but I also don't want her hating me. She's my sister, which is nothing either of you two would understand. She's my responsibility."

I snorted. The idea Harper would ever think of herself as a responsibility was laughable. She was more of an adult than the three of us put together.

"Technically, she's Knox's responsibility. Legally and all that," Bash interjected with a smirk and a quick glance my way.

"She's not Knox's anything," Ryker snapped.

My hands curled into fists. "And I'm out of here. Bash, do me a favor and stop at that little grove right before the descent? I want to check on stragglers." I kept my focus solely on Bash because I was ready to throw down with Ryker.

Usually he was the most easygoing in our friendship, so why was he such an immovable asshole when it came to Harper?

"You got it," Bash answered, and I turned around, running back through the line. I passed the Maldonado brothers with a nod, noting they were keeping up just fine. Then again, they'd been home for months, so they were more than adjusted. Plus, Bishop pretty much lived in the gym and hauled his little brother along.

Indigo Marshall was next in line, running with sure strides as her braided, jet-black ponytail swung behind her. Her trademark dark-blue eyes were hidden behind her sunglasses.

"How's it going, Indie?" I fell into pace next to her.

"You're taking it easy on us," she remarked, peering over her glasses at me. "I know you guys can run twice this fast."

She could outrun all of us.

"But can the rest of them?" I asked, motioning toward the back of the line. "There are two rookies behind you, plus seven transfers that came from low altitude. Not everyone has been running at the same elevation."

"Their lack of training is on them. Are we going to be able to qualify them? You know I love the idea of wearing my dad's patch, but I gave up my spot on my Montana crew for this, so I bet everything on you guys getting us off the ground."

No pressure, or anything.

"We will if you're willing to step up and help. You've been on that crew for, what? Two years?" The gravel path crunched beneath my feet as we climbed steadily.

"Three. And don't get me wrong, I'd rather be here. I'll help in any way I can. I know I'm not your most experienced firefighter, and that I'm not exactly someone who the guys are going to take seriously—"

"Because you're a girl?"

She nodded, her mouth going tense.

"That's a load of shit, Indie. You're young. What? Twenty-three now, right?"

"Yeah. I just had my birthday in February."

We turned at the fork in the path, heading higher up the mountain.

"You're not the youngest here either. None of these guys will give you any shit because you're a woman or I'll toss them. You understand? Hell, you're outrunning most of them. Speaking of which, I need to check on the others."

She nodded again, and I ran down the line. Derek Chandler ran twenty feet behind Indie and was currently staring at her ass. Kid was nineteen and the spitting image of his father, who probably would have smacked him upside the back of the head if he'd seen the way he was ogling his crewmate.

Guess that was my job now.

Lawson Woods noticed too. He was another Legacy kid, just a couple years younger than I was. Graduated with Harper, if I remembered correctly, and he'd been smart enough to keep his hands off her.

"You'd better keep your eyes on the trail, the fuel, or the sky, kid, because if you put them on Indie's ass one more time, I'm going to knock them out of your head. Understand?"

Lawson practically growled at the kid as he passed him on the left.

"Yes, sir." Derek paled as I ran by.

I gave Lawson a nod of thanks, and he returned it, glaring at Derek.

The transfers were keeping pace, and I reminded them to drink water as I passed them. Chance led the pack, wearing the same cocky smirk he'd used on Harper.

Asshat.

Wait. Where was… *Well, shit.*

At least a quarter mile back, Braxton Rose was running with his sister, Taylor. Kind of. I picked up the pace to get to them.

"You can do it," he told her in the same big-brother tone Ryker used with Harper.

"I'm. Not. Sure." Her words were punctuated with gasping breaths. The girl was struggling, and her face was red with exertion.

"Just breathe in through your nose, out through your mouth, and push through. Keep moving," he urged.

"My nose isn't the damned problem, Brax! I'm out of shape! Didn't you notice that?" She fell out of the run and started to walk, her chest heaving as she fought to catch her breath.

"Don't stop, Taylor," Braxton pleaded. His brown eyes widened when he saw me. "Knox, I can get her up to speed, I promise."

I slowed to a walk next to Taylor, who was gulping for breath but still pushing up the hill. She was eighteen, our youngest legacy, and if she hadn't signed up, we wouldn't have a crew. We needed every single legacy left.

"Brax, why don't you run up ahead? The transfers are about a quarter mile up, and Lawson is beyond them. I'll take care of Taylor."

"I'm not leaving her." He shook his head.

Great, it was Ryker Junior.

"You *are* leaving her. Now. Get up that mountain and join the crew. I'm not going to cut Taylor, and you know it. Go." I pointed up the mountain.

"I'm okay," Taylor told him, bending over slightly. "Please go."

He grimaced but did it, breaking into a run to catch the others.

"I volunteered. So he would. Come back," she told me with uneven breaths. "I knew you'd. Need him. For the numbers."

"We do. We need you too. Put your hands on top of your head." I did the same. "Like this."

She did, and the sound she let out was too self-deprecating to be a laugh. "Yeah, okay. What part of this"—she motioned to her body as she caught her breath—"do you need? I was raised by a hotshot and my brother is a structure guy...or he was until I guilted him into coming back to join you guys. I know how in shape you have to be. We both know I'm going to hold you back. I'll be the reason we fail." The wind picked up, blowing a hunk of red hair across her face. She whipped it away with a groan. "Even my hair is sweating."

She looked miserable, but I ignored the stab of guilt in my conscience that I'd done this to her. We had to get every member qualified, and if that meant running the mountain every day, we'd do it.

"Are you done?" I asked with a shrug.

"What?" She blinked at me, her arms falling to her sides.

"I'm asking if you're done setting yourself up to fail." I took my water bottle off my belt and handed it to her, noticing hers was empty.

"I can't take that. You won't have any."

I pushed it toward her. "If you drop of dehydration, we're short a crewmember. Make no mistake about it, Taylor Rose, you are a crewmember."

She took a drink and handed it back. "Thank you."

"Do you want to do this? I don't mean do you want Braxton to do this, or if we need you for the sixty-percent rule. I mean, do *you* want to be a hotshot?"

She nodded, watching the path rise above us as we took the steepest part of the trail step by step.

"You're going to have to speak louder, especially around those guys up there." I motioned up the path, where we couldn't see the rest of the crew anymore.

"Yes, I do." She nodded again. "I really do. I love the science of it, the way the fire moves with the wind and fuel. I love the thought of outsmarting it, using fire itself to burn out and control it. To save towns and homes because ours burned. I guess I want to save a kid from being me." She shrugged, still looking at the path.

"I get that. It's the same reason I agreed to foster Liam and James. I didn't want them growing up like me either. Not that I didn't have a great dad, and a fantastic gran, but I understand wanting to protect someone else."

We walked in silence for a hundred yards or so while her breathing evened out. "Emerson…she had to order XL pants for me." She tugged on the khaki fabric at her hips. "That's the biggest size they make."

"And if they didn't, we would have had some custom-made. We're not losing you over a dress size, Taylor. Besides, you know it's about strength and endurance. And you made it two miles, uphill, before walking. That's an incredible feat. You have to focus on that. Are you in certification shape? Probably not."

Her shoulders fell.

"Stop. Some of those guys up there aren't either. You're not alone. We have *months*, Taylor. Months to get you up to standard, and you've already kicked ass doing it by yourself. Next week, it will be three miles. The week after that? Four. You. Are. Not. Alone. You have the entire crew to help. The only question is: do you want to get there?"

She nodded, her head down as we turned the last corner, where the path leveled off about halfway toward the tree line. We were probably around ten thousand feet or so.

"And you're going to. Know how I'm sure?" I grinned.

"No."

"Look up ahead." I pointed to where the rest of the crew waited, all resting in the grove I'd asked Bash to stop at.

"Okay?" She followed my line of sight.

"One, your crew is waiting for you. They didn't leave you behind. Two, you didn't stop moving. Maybe you didn't run the whole way, but you sure as hell didn't stop. You didn't quit. You pushed forward, and you covered the same distance they did." That told me everything I needed to know.

She swallowed. "They're going to think I don't belong here," she whispered as we walked toward where the transfers now stood, most holding their hands on their head just like Taylor had. One of the guys was puking off to the side.

"You belong here more than they do. Don't you ever forget that. You're a Rose. This crew is in your blood. Now, before we get up there where everyone can hear...I can help you, but I'm probably not the best person for the job. What do you say I hook you up with Indie?"

"Indigo Marshall?" She slowed and shot me a more than skeptical look.

"Yep. She's our only other woman, since Emerson is in the managerial position. She's also one of the best hotshots out here, and she's going to be able to tell you exactly what you'll need to be able to do."

"She's terrifying," Taylor whispered, her eyes widening as she watched Indie stretching by one of the trees.

"She's fierce." I cocked my head to the side. "And fine, a little terrifying too. But I have a feeling you'd be more comfortable pairing up with her than say...Chandler over there."

"He's a dick," she blurted. "Anyone but him. He's been an ass since kindergarten."

I filed that information away. "See? Indie is your best bet."

Braxton saw us and jumped up from his seat against a tree.

"Plus, no overbearing older brother," I added.

"Now that might be the best reason." A smile curved her lips.

"I'll tell Indie that you might need a little help," I said quietly as Braxton approached. Then I left the two and headed over to where Bash and Ryker waited with the rest of the legacies.

There were two clearly defined groups up here—transfers and legacies. *That's an issue.*

"She going to be okay?" Ryker asked, motioning toward Taylor.

"Yeah."

After I gathered the crew, we took a narrow but well-worn path down the mountainside into a flat stretch of bare land. The trees here were either saplings or carcasses, with the exception of one or two lucky pines, but even those bore the scars of being singed.

I led the crew to the center of the small glade, and then faced them. "Bash, Ryker, Indie, Lawson, River, Bishop, Derek, Braxton, and Taylor, come up here."

The transfers shifted their weight, watching the legacies move to stand behind me.

I looked over the transfers. "Everyone standing with me has a blood-given right to be on this crew." I glanced at Taylor. "And I know you've heard the stories and read the reports, but seeing it is different. Almost eleven years ago, the Legacy Mountain fire started on the back of this peak. The crew dug a line, but the winds shifted." I looked over to Bash.

He nodded and took over. "Weather reports had indicated the winds would pick up, but no one forecasted seventy-mile-an-hour gusts or the change in direction. The line held at first, it gave the town time to evacuate. But when those gusts hit…" He shook his head. "The fire jumped across the treetops. It was the most terrifying and devastating thing I've ever seen." His jaw tensed, and I knew that was the most he was going to say. Hell, it was almost more than he'd ever said about that day.

Unlike the rest of us, he'd been there, seeking out his dad to see if there was anything he could do to help.

A moment of unintentional silence was broken by the sound of someone walking out of the grove of trees behind us.

Spencer.

He looked anything but happy to see us.

"The fuel was dry," he said, running his hand over his trim beard. The guy was only thirty-two—just five years older than me—but there was a weariness about him, like his soul had aged far faster than his body. "We were in the middle of a drought, and the trees went up like matchsticks. Vargas's son drove up and found the crew." He came to a stop, standing between Bash and me but not looking at either of us. "There was a healthy amount of yelling between father and son, and Vargas told me to get Bash off the mountain. We were just there"—he pointed to the trail we'd just come from—"heading down to the south ridge to cut another line in hopes that they could head the fire off there, but the fire came to meet them instead."

His jaw tensed, and he curved the bill of his baseball hat as he cleared his throat. "This"—he motioned to the small area of the glade we occupied—"is where they deployed their shelters. This is where they found all eighteen of them." He fell silent.

I'd been up here hundreds of times. It was where I felt most at peace on days I missed him too much to take a full breath, where Harper found me two days after the funeral, where she'd sat silently for hours next to me on a fallen, burned-out tree because I hadn't been ready to leave—to let go of him.

This was the place I'd come that night seven years ago after realizing while she might never be mine—not really—I'd always belong to her.

"They're all buried together farther down the path in Aspen Grove." My voice sounded a hell of a lot stronger than I felt. "But this is where I feel them the most. I wanted you to see it," I told the transfers. "To stand here and understand what we lost that day, and why we have to rebuild it. This isn't just a job to us. It's true that we're legacies, that this is our home, but it's yours now too. From now on, we're one crew. Whether you're here by blood or by choice, we're all Legacy now."

Silence stretched, broken only by the gentle whistle of the wind through the trees and the chirping of birds.

"Good speech," Bash muttered.

"It was the best I could come up with on short notice, after you threw the whole training job on me," I whispered in answer.

"I'd give it an eight," Ryker added. "But ten with Spencer's dramatic entrance."

"For fuck's sake," Spencer mumbled, rolling his eyes. "For anyone who hasn't been a pain in my ass since they were born, I'm Spencer Cohen. Yes, I'm the only surviving member of the original Legacy crew, and your new superintendent. I hope you were listening, because that's the only time I'll tell that story. Fire is all I know, and damn, does she know me well. Listen, do what I tell you, always guard your brothers"—he sent a look toward Indie and Taylor—"and sisters, and I'll bring you home alive." He glanced between the groupings and narrowed his eyes. "Now, every transfer pick a legacy—whichever one you want, as long as it isn't me. You'll have dinner with them within the next week. We'll switch it up until you all get good and cozy with one another."

I folded my arms across my chest and watched as each transfer picked a legacy. *Good, this should help team cohesion and really build— Oh, hell no.*

Chance grinned at me.

"Seriously?" I asked.

"So, what are your wife's favorite flowers? I'd hate to show up empty-handed." That little glint in his eyes was going to get his ass kicked.

I knew his type. It wasn't about Harper as much as it was about getting under my skin and trying to establish the dominance he didn't have.

"Oh, she's a big fan of Lily of the None-of-your-fucking-business. Dinner's at seven, dessert is on you, and if you so much as smile at Harper, I'll smoke your ass on runs every morning until you'll wish you'd never seen her."

"Yeah, that's never going to happen," he said with a laugh as he left to join the other crewmembers hiking up to the trail. "The wishing I'd never seen her part, that is," he called back with a wink.

Yep, he was itching to get his ass kicked.

"Trouble with the newbie?" Ryker asked, clapping my back.

"He hit on Harper at dinner the other night."

"Tell him he doesn't have a shot in hell." Ryker sent a glare in Chance's direction. It was nice to have that hatred focused elsewhere, even if it was just for a minute.

"Already done."

"At least that's one thing we agree on." That glare turned on me as he backed away, whispering, "Not that you have a shot either."

Well, so much for that minute. At least he wasn't broadcasting that our marriage was fake, but that was probably because he was smitten with Liam and James.

"What the hell did you do to piss off Anders?" Spencer asked as he hiked beside me up the hill toward the trail. The terrain was steep, decomposed granite slipping beneath my shoes slightly as we made our way up the incline.

"Married his sister."

"Harper? No shit, really?" His eyebrows rose in surprise.

"Why so surprised? Everyone else seems to think it was inevitable." Everyone but Ryker.

"You got back into town about a heartbeat ago, and now you're married? I think it's a pretty fair reaction to be surprised." We reached the trail and turned to look back over the clearing as the rest of the crew passed by, heading down the mountain.

"Speaking of getting back into town, what was with you walking out of the trees back there? I thought you told Bash you owed your old crew one more day before you showed up?"

He folded his arms over his chest, his eyes scanning the now-empty glade. "I did owe my crew one more day. Just not the one Bash assumed, and I wasn't exactly expecting you guys to haul everyone up here." The sound he made was too heavy to be called a sigh. "I haven't been here since it happened. The last memory I have of them is alive and breathing, joking and working. I didn't want to replace that with charred terrain and burn marks."

"Understandable." The ground had been black when I'd come up after the funeral, the locations where the shelters deployed clearly defined. I'd spent hours wondering which mark had been my father. What his last thoughts had been as the flames made him fuel for the fire he'd spent his life fighting. But grass had grown over the mutilated remains of the grove as the healing process took over. "It looks...better now. Eleven years is a good time for a forest to begin a recovery."

"What about a man?" he asked, watching the breeze sway the branches of the aspens. Spencer had been notoriously quiet after the fire. He didn't give interviews, didn't pose for cameras, or write a memoir. He avoided the media like the plague and sought out fires with a ferocity that could almost be called a death wish.

"I think it's a good time for a man to start recovery too." I clapped my hand on his shoulder as Harper's face crossed my mind, laughing with Liam as James sat perched on her hip in the kitchen. Maybe there was hope for us all to find a little happiness. "Take your day, Supe. Just don't forget that there's a whole new Legacy crew who needs you. Including me."

I left him standing at the edge of the trail and joined my crew. We were all haunted by our parents, our personal ghosts, but Spencer had it worse.

He *was* one.

CHAPTER TWELVE

arper

"WHAT DO YOU MEAN THEY'RE NOT HERE?" MOM'S FACE FELL. "I bought them toys and coloring books, and I really wanted to spend some time with them." Her shoulders drooped, rustling her cream silk blouse. Her hair was up in a simple chignon, and she rounded out her accessories with a single strand of black pearls. Perfect for the country club she belonged to in Crested Butte, where she now lived.

I'd pushed her brunch for weeks, and now it was time to pay the piper on a Saturday morning.

"We thought it was best to leave them with a babysitter for brunch," I explained in the club's foyer as she brushed a piece of dirt from my arm. "Avery's little sister Adeline is certified, and Elliot did all the checks, so she's home with the boys."

Mom used her fingernail, scraping at something on the

light-green fabric of my ballet sweater, which went great with the black pencil skirt and black equestrian boots I'd chosen for brunch. I'd debated heels but changed just in case we were forced to flee from my mother. "I just wanted to get to know them a little better. After all, they're going to be family."

"Mom, stop. That's…" I glanced down at the whitish spot and sighed. James left his mark. "That's puke. You have to remember that we're only their foster parents. They're not ours. We don't really get a say in what happens to them. Right now, Elliot is still locating their father."

"So you're not keeping them?" Her hand flew to her chest.

"It's not our choice. Nothing about what happens with their future is our choice. We just get to take care of them for now. The goal is to reunify them with their dad." Wherever the hell he was.

"Well, it would have been nice to have them for brunch. They could have gone swimming or something." She waved toward the window with a view of the pool.

It was barely sixty-eight degrees outside, definitely not pool weather, but I knew she meant well, so I just nodded and prayed that Knox finished parking the truck soon.

"It's too cold for swimming, Mom," Ryker said over my right shoulder. He passed by me with a quick squeeze of my arm before going to our mother.

Considering I'd barely spoken a word to him in the last two weeks, this was going to get interesting.

"Hi, honey," she answered as he kissed her cheek. "I'm so glad you could make it. Oh! Knox! Great, now the whole family is here! Or it would be if you'd brought those boys." She *tsked* before turning to the hostess.

Knox adjusted his bright-blue tie and pulled the cuffs of his shirt down to his wrist as he rolled his shoulders in his suit coat. My whole body clenched. *Hot damn*, the man was gorgeous.

He'd shaved his customary scruff, leaving nothing but smooth, touchable skin. My fingers curled into my palms.

Screw sexual frustration, I was at the level of sexual *agony*. He'd walked down the hall in nothing but a towel this morning when he heard James crying, and I'd been in a drooling stupor ever since.

The definition of irony? I was married to the man. *Married*, and yet I couldn't even enjoy the honeymoon.

His throat moved, drawing all my attention. How could a neck be that sexy? It was perfect for running my tongue over it. *I bet he tastes better than candy.* Running my thumb over the inside of my wedding band, I—

"Wait, what?" I blinked as Knox waved his hand in front of my face.

"Earth to Harper. Our table is ready. You okay?" He lightly took my arms, stroking over my biceps with his thumbs. "You get enough sleep last night?"

"Yeah, just thinking about dessert," I lied. Kind of. Maybe if I laid out naked on our kitchen island, he'd break down and—

"Let's go, you two," Ryker called back, already following Mom and the hostess.

"Seriously, you seem distracted." Knox's forehead puckered.

Distracted by deep brown eyes and curved lips, definitely.

"We have to go," I managed to say with a tight smile. "They're waiting."

"Let them wait. Are you okay?"

Ugh, why did he have to be so freaking considerate all the time? Why couldn't he be an ass like he was to everyone else? Even after we shared that kiss prom night, he'd never been cruel, just distant. It made it impossible to hate him.

"I'm fine," I promised. "If you survive brunch, I have a present for you in the car."

"You got me a present?" His eyes lit up like Liam with a new toy.

I fought my smile. "Don't get too excited. I'm not even sure it's something you want." I'd almost given it to him on the drive over but didn't want to start the morning off awkward.

"I'll love it. I promise." His lips curved.

That *smile*. It sent electricity to my thighs, telling them to part and ditch the panties while they were at it. It wasn't just that he was beautiful—that was just genetics. Knox really meant it—he'd love whatever I gave him. Under all those yards of muscle, witty mind, and pretty eyes was the skinny ten-year-old I knew who just wanted to be loved and still didn't realize he'd *always* been loved.

By me.

"Can I show you to your table? The rest of your party is already seated," the hostess asked in that polite, distant way that belonged in tourist towns like this, where it was impossible to know everyone.

"Yes, thank you," I answered. His hand found my lower back as we walked through the fully seated dining room, and I almost took off at a dead run just to break the contact. It was too much. I wanted that hand on my bare skin.

One morning without the kids and I was back to eighteen, attacking him in Mom's powder room. It had barely been a month of living with Knox and I was ready to crawl out of my skin. How was I going to survive...however long this would be?

"Absolutely not," Mom chastised Ryker. "Let your sister sit next to her husband."

I didn't miss the glare Ryker sent in Knox's direction. Half of me felt guilty for what this was doing to their friendship, and the other half wanted to smack Ryker across the back of his head and remind him this was none of his business.

We took our seats, Knox sitting across from Ryker at the square table, and made it halfway through brunch before Mom started in.

"So, I was thinking, if July is too soon, maybe we'd do September?"

My mimosa caught in my throat, and I started coughing, trying desperately to keep my lips shut so I didn't spew orange liquid all over the pristine tablecloth.

"For what?" Ryker asked.

"Harper, are you okay?" Knox questioned at the same time.

I nodded, managing to swallow the watered-down alcohol and immediately wishing it was pure vodka.

"Their wedding, of course," Mom said with a pageant-worthy smile. "I'm just so excited to get this going with you guys. Of course, Pastor Hopkins said he'd officiate, and we have access to the chapel whenever you want."

"Uh, Mrs. Anders—" Knox started softly.

"I know it's a good forty-minute drive, but I was thinking of having the reception here, if you two like it." She ran him right over. "It's got plenty of room, and I'm sure we could see if we could rent out the lodge, since it would be the off-season. No one wants guests drinking and driving."

I threw back the rest of my mimosa and sought out the waitress with my eyes so I could beg for another one or two.

"Their *what*?" Ryker snapped.

Knox gave him a nearly imperceptible shake of his head.

"Their wedding!" Mom answered with the same tone. "Honestly, Ryker, you think it's okay that your sister, your *baby* sister, got married in a rushed ceremony at the courthouse with only a few social workers and her ex-boyfriend as witnesses?"

My hand found Knox's under the table, and he wrapped his fingers around mine, somehow calm when I was ready to bolt.

"Of course, I don't!" Ryker hissed.

"Here we go," I muttered, and Knox squeezed my hand.

"Exactly! So, we're going to make sure they get married properly. The entire town's been waiting on these two to carve their names into the wall—"

"Kill me now," I whispered to Knox, turning my head toward him. That wall was a hell of a lot more permanent than the ring on my finger. I squeezed my eyes shut.

"And I refuse to believe that was their real wedding if I wasn't even in the same room," Mom finished.

"It's okay." Knox leaned forward and pressed a kiss to my forehead.

"It wasn't r— Oh no, don't you kiss her," Ryker growled.

Knox turned abruptly. "I've had enough, Ry. Just be glad your mom is sitting here."

I snagged our waitress's attention and lifted my empty glass. "I will give you anything you want if you bring me another one of these." There was not enough alcohol in the world for this. I'd planned on dealing with Mom, gently but firmly clarifying this marriage was on paper only, while begging for discretion, but I didn't realize I'd have to handle Ryker at the same time.

"Ryker, what has gotten into you?" Mom asked. "Of course Knox is going to kiss his wife. I would hope there's more of that going on," she said to me with a wink.

Heat rushed my cheeks.

"Not a f—" Knox took a deep breath, and I stroked the side of his hand with my fingers. "Not a word, Ry. I mean it."

This had gotten out of control. "Mom, you know we only got married for the boys, right?" I said with a wobbly smile.

"Of course you did. I think what you two did was just so honorable. Giving up your dream wedding so that you could make sure those boys didn't get separated..." She shook her head, and her eyes took on that watery sheen we avoided at all costs. "I'm just so proud of you both. I mean, I always knew we'd end up here. It's not like we couldn't see the way you two looked at each other, right, Ryker?"

His jaw dropped, the same as Knox's.

"Oh, come on." She sipped her mimosa. "I'm not an idiot. I'm glad you two finally stopped dancing around each other and took the plunge. A very sudden plunge, but at least now you can cut through all that sexual tension that winds you two up tighter than tornadoes. Seriously."

"My mother just said sexual tension," I whispered as she ordered another mimosa.

"You looked at me?" Knox answered, his attention locked on me.

Slowly, I turned to meet his gaze. He wasn't teasing or mocking me. There was honest bewilderment in his eyes. "You looked at *me*?" I countered.

"Really, kids?" Mom sighed. "Always have. Both of you. I just can't believe it took you this long to figure it all out."

"And that's my cue to go." Ryker stood up. "Mom, thank you so much for inviting me. I'll be over tomorrow to fix that sink, so make a list and I'll knock everything out at once." He leaned over and kissed her on the cheek.

"Are you sure you have to go?" she asked, two lines appearing between her eyebrows.

"Very." He looked over at me. "Harpy, be careful, okay?"

I nodded. "I love you, Ryker."

His lips flattened, but he nodded. "I love you too. I can't with you right now," he finished at Knox and walked off, leaving the three of us sitting at the table.

Knox rolled his head back and sighed.

"Don't worry about him. It's hard to lose your best friend to your sister. Once he realizes nothing will change between you, he'll be fine," Mom assured us.

The problem was, everything had changed, and if they went downhill any faster, they'd take the entire crew down with them. If either of them walked away, the crew wouldn't have the needed sixty percent legacies to satisfy the town council.

We made small talk for the rest of brunch, avoided the wedding talk like the plague, and when Knox tried to pay the bill, the waitress told us Ryker had beaten him to it.

Man, I loved that jerk. Well, both of those jerks.

"So you looked at me, huh?" We were almost home when Knox spoke, breaking me out of my endless cycle of thoughts that were mostly about him.

I rolled my eyes when I saw his grin was a mile wide. Okay, he was done being all privately distant and back to flirty. I could handle flirty.

"Shut up. You looked at me too."

"Every day," he said softly. He spared me a glance before putting his eyes back on the curvy mountain road. "I lived for the moments I saw you. I could never explain it, especially when I was younger, but just having you in the room brought on this crazy rush of emotions. Kind of like a kaleidoscope—they were always different, but I *felt*, and back then, I didn't feel much. Ryker kept me sane, but you made me…feel."

My pulse jumped. "What did you feel?" I asked, bold only because he kept his eyes on the road.

He ran his tongue over his lower lip. "Happy. You made me happy, and then peaceful, then alive. No matter how shitty everything got when my mom walked out, you were this bright spot of color, like a stargazer lily in the middle of a dead field. It was the same when Dad died."

"Like a friend?" I asked quietly.

"No." His hands tightened on the wheel as he pulled onto the road that would bring us into Legacy. "I mean, sure, when we were kids, but later…"

"What else was there?" My voice dropped, like if I spoke too loudly, he'd realize what I was asking and not answer.

"Don't ask me that." He shook his head.

"Why?"

"Because there are things I can't say to you and keep…" He turned into our little subdivision. "Keep things the way they are. Keep my word."

His word. To Ryker? Was my brother so big he even fit between us when he wasn't in the truck, or the neighborhood?

We pulled into the driveway and Knox killed the engine.

"Wait," I blurted as he reached for the handle. "I wanted to give you your present." If he didn't like it, I'd rather know now, when I didn't have to act all chipper for the kids.

He turned toward me as I fished the little box out of my purse. The velvet was soft under my fingers as I opened the lid and removed the smooth, hard metal, enclosing it in my fist.

Then I turned toward him, thankful the console was down between us, separating the bench seating. *Just do it.*

"Okay, so I know we have to pull this off publicly for the sake of the boys, and that's been tough on you, especially with the tension between you and Ry." I sighed and looked at my closed fist. "And I thought this would help with the whole public part."

Without watching his expression, I reached for his hand and dropped the present into his palm.

The platinum band matched mine in tone, but that was where the similarity ended. His ring was smooth, wide, and beveled only for the ridge that ran along the center of the band, making it dimensional yet simple. Understated.

His fist closed around the band. "You bought me a ring?"

It was the gravel in his voice that finally brought my eyes to his. "We're married," I said with a shrug.

His fist got even tighter. "We are."

"I figured if we were going to make it believable, you should probably have one." My nerves got the best of me, and I fidgeted with my hair, tucking the mass behind my ears. "Read it," I encouraged.

His fist opened instantly, and he lifted the ring between his fingers, his eyes narrowing to read the inscription. "As necessary as air."

That's what he was to me—what he'd always been.

My heartbeat sped to a gallop. "Do you like it?"

"Will you put it on?" His voice dropped lower.

My fingers trembled slightly as I took the ring from him and then aimed for his left hand. The metal was warm from his hand, and it slid on easily, only needing a little push to make it over his second knuckle. Then it was home.

My ring was on Knox's hand, the platinum a direct contrast to his tan skin, a giant, flashing neon sign that told everyone he was mine.

"It should be the right size. Your gram helped me with that." I babbled as he sat silently, staring at the ring. "But if it's not, then we can take it back, or get you one of those silicone ones, they're probably safer for the field anyway, right? Or, you know, you don't have to wear one at all. It's not like everyone in this town doesn't know we're married and have an opinion on the matter." Okay, it was time to get out of this truck before I became a total idiot.

"Like the ache will burn you alive," he said softly, spinning the ring on his finger.

He remembered.

I inhaled sharply. "What?" I finally managed to ask in a whisper.

"You asked me if that was what a kiss always felt like. *As necessary as air.*" Our eyes locked. "Then you said, *like you'll die if you stop. Like the ache will burn you alive.*"

My mouth popped open. "You...you recall the exact words?"

He smiled, and it was the saddest, most beautiful thing I'd ever seen. "I remember everything, Harper. The shade of your dress, the feel of your hair in my hands, how fucking soft your lips were. I remember the feel of you against me as I backed you against the counter and how badly I wanted to take more, even though you weren't mine to take. I still dream about it, that's how well I remember it."

My nerve endings fired with electricity at every word he

spoke, until I was certain I was going to physically combust if I didn't get the hell out of this truck. I wanted him too much, loved him beyond any form of measurement, and needed...air. Now. I reached for the door, and felt Knox's light grip my other wrist.

"Kissing you is the only time I've ever felt like that."

"Knox," I whispered.

"Fuck it." He tugged, and I went, our mouths colliding. His tongue swept past my lips, and I groaned as my fingers burrowed through his hair. *Yes, thank you, God, yes.* He gripped my waist and lifted me over the console, never breaking the kiss. My skirt slid up my thighs as I straddled him in the driver's seat.

The kiss was ravenous, desperate, and sent me skyrocketing into Lustville so fast I was ready to take him in any way I could get him. In the truck. Against the garage door. On the porch. Wherever he wanted, whenever.

Holy *shit* could he kiss. He teased the curves of my mouth like he was learning it all over again, sliding his tongue along mine, then sucking mine past his lips to do the same. He took enough to make me dizzy, then backed off until I demanded more.

His phone rang once, then twice, but he didn't answer it. There was just sweet silence and the sound of tech hitting the floor.

He tasted like the sweet orange juice he'd had at brunch. I bit his lip gently, and he groaned, moving one hand to the back of my head and sliding the other down to my ass, squeezing. "God, Harper," he moaned.

The sound of my name on his lips was an aphrodisiac.

"Say it again," I begged against his mouth.

"Harper," he obliged.

Then he kissed me deep and hard, tangling our tongues, until the moment became the eternity in which I existed. There was nothing outside this kiss—nothing before, and nothing after.

I was going to live in every second he gave me.

He broke our kiss, and I almost screamed in frustration, but then he tugged my hair gently, exposing my neck to his lips.

My thighs clenched with each kiss he set to the delicate skin, and I knew he felt it because his grip tightened on my ass in kind. I groaned when his mouth reached the high, straight neckline of my sweater.

"Stupid clothes," I muttered.

He laughed, and the sound was so damn sexy all the muscles in my core constricted.

I kissed his jaw, tracing my tongue down his neck, and he stopped laughing. His skin was smooth, and he smelled divine— cologne and Knox. Every time his breath caught, it made me bolder, until I had his tie off and the top three buttons of his shirt undone.

His hands slid up my thighs, under my skirt, until he met the smooth skin of my ass, and his fingers brushed the straps of my thong. Score one for not wearing the full-coverage ones I'd debated this morning.

"Holy shit," he moaned as I rocked forward, finding him hard under my hips.

"You want me." It wasn't as much a statement as it was a revelation.

One of his hands cupped my cheek tenderly, at odds with the other that had a firm grip under my skirt.

"I have always wanted you. I will always want you. You are in my fucking bones, Harper. Wanting you is part of who I am." He didn't give me a chance to respond with anything but my tongue as he fused our mouths.

I kissed him with everything I had, hoping he understood what that meant to me. Tears pricked my eyes, the emotions looking for somewhere to escape, but I blinked them away.

There was no way I was going to be that stereotypical hysterical, sobbing girl if this was the only time I got to touch him.

Grateful the windows were tinted, I took his hand and guided it to my breast. He ripped his mouth from mine and pulled back just enough to see the contrast of his hand—his wedding ring—against my green sweater.

Then he brushed my nipple with his thumb, and it tightened, pressing against the fabric.

"Fuck. I want…" He ran his tongue over his bottom lip as his gaze darted to either side of us.

I pushed the console up so the front seat was one long, soft, leather bench.

His eyes seemed even darker, deeper as he arched an eyebrow. With one smooth motion, he flipped me. My back hit the leather, and he rose above me.

"We have an entire house, and you want to make out in the car like teenagers," he muttered against my neck.

"We should have made out in the car when we were teenagers," I answered.

He shook his head slowly. "I would have pushed you too fast. I was too young, too desperate to get my hands on you." He lifted my sweater to just above the silk of my bra and hissed. "Damn. I'm still too desperate." He lowered one of the cups and covered my exposed nipple with his mouth.

"Knox!" My back arched as his tongue licked and flicked before he sucked at the raised flesh. *Magical freaking mouth.*

My hips rocked up on their own accord, and he lowered himself between my spread thighs. I had one knee bent against the back of the seat, and the other foot braced on the floor of the truck, using it for leverage as I ground against him, seeking friction, pressure, anything that would soothe the spiraling ache low in my stomach.

"Please," I begged him. The raw need I'd had coursing

through my veins since seeing him shirtless this morning spiked to nearly painful.

He released my breast and turned his attention to the other, making me squirm until his erection settled exactly where I needed it. He groaned when I rocked against him, seeking relief and finding an even hotter fire instead.

"Fuck. Harper. You. *God.* Stop." Each word came out like its own battle.

His hands shifted to my hips, pinning them still against the seat.

"I don't want to." I couldn't. Any second now, his stupid promise to my brother was going to come roaring between us, and this would end. I wasn't waiting another seven years to touch him. My lips found his, and after a long, drugging kiss, I sucked on his lower lip, releasing it with a flick of my tongue. "Don't make me beg."

Because I would, shamelessly. There was nothing I wouldn't do for Knox.

I saw the moment he decided, felt the give in his muscles, the way he tugged my hips closer to his instead of holding me at a distance.

"No begging," he told me as he shifted and slid his hands up my inner thighs. "So soft." His thumb swept across the juncture of my thighs, lightly pressing in on the thin silk. "So wet I can see it. Fuck, Harper, you want me too."

"Always." I ran my hands through his hair, needing to touch him in any way I could. I was so far past *want* that it existed on a different planet. I was a puddle of primal, urgent *need*.

His thumb slipped under the fabric, stroking through my core until he swirled around my clit. My thighs locked, and I cried out, the sensation overwhelming and yet not enough.

When I opened my eyes, I found him watching me, those dark eyes measuring my reactions and shifting his thumb accordingly, but never quite touching me where I needed.

"You're scorching hot, you know that?" He lowered his mouth to mine, brushing a kiss across my lips. "Would you burn me alive if I sank inside you right now?"

The sheer imagery—imagining Knox naked, sliding inside me—was almost enough to make me come. My entire body jolted, my fingernails biting into the skin of his neck.

"Yeah, I bet you would. I bet we'd set the entire world on fire, but I'll settle for watching you burn." He finally stroked my clit, and I moaned.

He covered the sound with his mouth, kissing me with a new sense of urgency as his thumb stroked me higher, wound me so tight I thought I might die from the tension.

My muscles clenched, and I rocked against his hand. "I," I gasped as he pressed lightly. "I need—"

He slid one of his fingers inside me, and I whimpered. He'd known exactly what I needed without being told. A second joined it, stroking deep, sending incredible bursts of pleasure through every nerve in my body as he curled those fingers within me. I felt it in my toes, my fingers, even my lips before it coiled tight within my belly.

There was a wildness in his eyes, a barely leashed hunger I ached to let loose, to drive him as out of control as I already was. He looked down, watching his fingers slide in and out of me, and I spiraled to the edge, my body tensing with pleasure.

"You're so damn tight, Harper. God, I can feel you coming. Burn for me, baby." His mouth covered mine, as I toppled over the edge of the highest cliff I'd ever reached.

My body arched against his, pulsed around his fingers as white-hot pleasure took me in waves, each stronger than the last as he dragged out every single ounce of bliss I had within me, and when I thought it was over, he used that thumb to kick back a series of aftershocks that left me limp as they finally receded.

Our eyes locked as our foreheads rested against each other,

our breathing ragged, his body impossibly hard, rigid above me. I felt like worked-over clay, soft and ready to be molded however he wanted.

My hands shifted to his face as he pulled back slightly, his jaw flexing.

"As necessary as air," I told him between breaths. "That's how it feels between us." My hands stroked down his chest and over his lean waist. It would only take a zip and tug, and he could be inside me for real. I could make him burn just as bright.

He stilled my hands with his and shook his head, the muscles in his cheeks popping before he found words. "No. I'm not fucking you in my truck."

"I don't care where you *fuck* me."

"That *mouth*." That earned me a very tense, shaky smile. "I care, and the first time I slide inside you and fulfill every single fantasy I've ever had isn't going to be outside our house in broad daylight. It's going to be in a bed. A very big bed. My bed, preferably. And I'm going to have hours to make you come again and again. That isn't happening until we have this—what we are together—figured out, because I refuse to feel anything but you. Only you, Harper. No guilt, no lies, just what we are together. No. Fucking. Truck."

What we are together. If my heart could have orgasmed, it would have. Was he saying there was a real chance for us? That we might be more than paper?

A buzzing sound caught me off guard.

"Fucking seriously?" He leaned over and grabbed his phone off the floor. "River's called three times," he told me before answering it. "What do you want?"

He immediately tensed, looking over my head and out the window as River's muffled voice came through the phone.

I was suddenly, awkwardly aware of how nearly naked I was.

"Well, fuck. Yeah. Okay. Give me fifteen."

He was leaving. Disappointment tasted more than a little

bitter on my tongue. Not that I expected him to carry me upstairs and fulfill that hours-and-hours promise right now, but running off was pretty much the opposite of what I was going for.

He hung up the phone, then tenderly adjusted my bra so my breasts fell back into the cups.

"You're leaving," I said slowly.

His hands tugged my sweater down to cover my torso, and he nodded. "Yep. Spencer activated the alert roster. That was the first call I ignored. Happy Saturday." He lifted my hips, and I kept them elevated as he smoothed my skirt down over my thighs.

"And River?"

"Well, Adeline called him when she saw us pull in, thinking she'd need a ride home."

"Oh. My. God." The first time I'd ever made out in a car, and I didn't even want to think about where this was headed.

"Yeah, he's parked at the end of the driveway." He sighed and shifted backward, helping me sit up.

"Good thing it's a long driveway." We locked eyes and started laughing. What else was there to do? "What now?"

His face fell a little, squashing a lot of the hope that had taken up residence in my chest.

"Now we get Adeline home and I go to the clubhouse. Everything else…we'll figure out." He stroked my cheek and glanced at his hand. "Thank you for my present. I've never had anything this perfect."

Testing my new freedom, I leaned up and kissed him, letting my lips linger for a second. "Remind me to buy you stuff more often."

"Ready to do the walk-of-shame with me?" He popped the door handle.

"Any time, any place."

CHAPTER THIRTEEN

K nox

A HALF HOUR LATER, I WALKED INTO THE CLUBHOUSE TO FIND every other member of our crew lounged on the couches in the great room. Thank God my dick had finally realized playtime was over, but my brain wouldn't get the message.

I'd kissed Harper. *Touched* Harper. My tongue had been in her mouth, my fingers inside her sweet little body, and she'd given me a glimpse of heaven. We'd been just as explosive as I knew we would be seven years ago, and I wasn't sure if I felt vindicated or terrified.

Everything I'd told her was the truth. She was in my bones, my soul, every fucking piece of me. That didn't mean I was worthy of her, or even right for her, it was simply fact, and now she knew it.

"Took you long enough," Bash called out.

I glanced at the clock. "We have one-hour recall, and I'm

within ten minutes of that, so fuck right off. I'm getting a drink."
I told that last part to Spencer, who nodded from behind his
clipboard.

Ryker stood in the kitchen, and I blatantly ignored him,
throwing open the refrigerator door and scanning the contents.
I pulled out a bottle of water and shut the door, twisting the top
off before facing my best friend.

I could still taste Harper in my mouth, sweet and more
intoxicating than any alcohol I'd ever consumed. My shirt
smelled like her perfume, my fingers still felt warm with the
memory of being inside her.

I was more than a shitty friend.

I was also wearing Harper's wedding ring, and damn it, I
wanted to.

Gulping down half the bottle, I turned to see Ryker leaned
against the wall, watching me with narrowed eyes.

"What?" I snapped, setting the bottle on the counter.

"Those had better not be my sister's fingernail marks in the
back of your fucking neck." His tone was low, steady, and
dripped with threat.

And I had fucking *had* it with him.

"Would you rather they be from someone else?" I rolled up
my shirtsleeves, wishing I'd taken the time to get out of my
dress clothes like he had. This shit was uncomfortable.

"Are you kidding me? You've been married to her for less
than a month, and you're cheating on her?" he roared, stepping
forward to the opposite side of the stainless-steel island.

"Whoa, guys." Bash filled the doorway.

I put my hand out to deter him. This was between Ryker
and me.

"Hell no, I'm not cheating on her. I wouldn't ever do that. Do
you have any clue what she means to me?"

"Besides the satisfaction of winning a chase you've been on
for years?"

My hands clenched on the cool steel of the island. "She's not a goddamn chase."

"Tell that to the countless other women you've fucked. Or do you forget that I know you better than anyone else on the planet?"

"Nope, out," I heard Spencer say, and spared a glance to see both he and Bash had their backs to us, guarding us from prying eyes, but not prying ears.

"You are my best friend, Ryker. I don't want to hurt you. I don't want to break my promise, but right now, you're not my number-one consideration anymore. Harper is." I wasn't even sure when that had changed, but it had.

"She's my *only* consideration! You don't think I know how she feels about you? The stupid infatuation that just won't die? That ruins every relationship she tries to have? You are wrong for her on every level. You won't settle down, and she wants a family and a damn tire swing in the backyard. She's had two serious boyfriends, and you bounce from girl to girl like a pinball in the machine. You risk your life every time you step out on the line, and she shouldn't have to take a phone call like that."

"What exactly do you object to about me? The fact that I'm a manwhore, or that I'm a firefighter just like you?" I folded my arms across my chest.

"Yes to all." His palms slammed down on the island.

Well shit, that hurt.

"So, I'm good enough to be your best friend, just not good enough to be with your sister." Because that's what it came down to every single time.

"Correct!"

Bash spun. "Fuck you, Ryker, that's too far."

"This doesn't involve you, Bash, unless you want him fucking your sister."

"I don't have a sister, asshole."

"Exactly. Neither of you do. I have been responsible for Harper since the day she was born, since my dad put her into my arms and said that she was mine to protect, and I'm not going to fuck that up because you happen to be my friend."

"Yeah, well, it's okay, because we're not friends anymore." I didn't realize how true the words were until I'd already spoken them.

He blinked, his features going completely blank.

"Knox," Bash warned softly.

"You want to draw lines like this, then that's what it means. Because I'm done putting your happiness above Harper's, and you should be too. I've never lied to you, Ryker. Not once in our entire lives. You do know me. You know every little thing about me, to include how I felt about Harper the night you put her on the list. You can't trust me to settle down enough to restart this crew with you, trust me enough to save your ass in a fire, and then tell me I don't cut it when it comes to Harper. That's not fair."

"Are those her fingernail marks?" he asked again.

"Let it go before you put us into territory we can't come back from."

"How would you feel if I went after your girl on the list, Knox? If the tables were turned, how would you handle it?"

"If you think my grandmother will let you fuck her, feel free to try, but she's got some pretty high standards."

Spencer turned, matching Bash. From the corner of my eye, I saw Bash shake his head to keep Spencer quiet.

"Are those her fingernail marks?" He seethed.

"You already know the fucking answer! Yes, they're hers."

He flew across the island, but this wasn't the courthouse. This time, I expected the assault. As he slid to land on his feet, I ducked the punch he threw. Ryker was a big asshole, but I was faster. I swept his feet out from under him with my right leg and took him to the ground. His back hit the tile floor, and he struggled for a second to get air into his lungs.

Served him right to get the air knocked out of him. Maybe it would deflate his head a little.

With my hand on his chest, I leaned over the guy who was supposed to be my best friend.

"I will never lie to you, so don't ask questions you don't want the answer to. You think all her relationships are fucked up because of me? You think I'm a manwhore? Guess what, asshole, they're linked. You sealed our fates the moment you hit me with that ultimatum."

He glared, still sucking in air in tiny amounts.

"Yeah, that's right. You're the selfish one here, Ry. She can't have a good relationship for the same reason I don't ever seem to last more than a couple months with a girl. Because I know Harper's the only one I could ever even attempt to commit to, so why the fuck would I torture another woman and drag something out that won't last? So I break it off, and I stay the fuck away from your sister because that's what *you* demanded, and you and Bash are the only brothers I have, and I'll be damned if I'm going to lose the only family I have left. You want to know why your sister is miserable? Look in the fucking mirror."

He shook his head, his breaths coming in even.

"I'm sorry I'm not good enough for Harper. You're right about that. I don't deserve a single word from her lips. But no one on this Earth is good enough for her."

"She's my sister!" he managed to growl.

"She's my wife!"

That brought us both up short. I'd never said it like that, never thrown it in his face that I'd gone against the pact we'd made years ago. I'd never let myself feel that primal possessiveness that came with the title of husband.

"She's my wife," I said again, softer. "And that makes her my family. She and those boys. They are the ones I owe my allegiance to. You are my best friend, and yeah, I want your blessing to see where this thing is headed with Harper, but I don't need it. She doesn't either, believe me. Stop acting like you're her father, or like you're the only one who lost your dad on that mountain. Harper isn't your responsibility anymore, she's mine."

I stood slowly, ready for him to attack me again, but he simply laid his head back on the tile and closed his eyes, his muscles sagging in defeat.

"Do you love her?"

"What?" A vise gripped my chest.

"Do. You. Love. Her?" he repeated.

Did I? I'd never loved anyone that I knew of. Grams, sure. My dad, absolutely. But romantically? I wasn't even sure what that felt like. I wanted Harper. I needed her. But did I love her?

"I…" My forehead puckered. "I don't know?"

Ryker blew out a breath. "Well, you'd sure as hell know if you did, so you don't. But I do. So you might be married to her, but you're still the worst thing for her, Knox. That's not going to change just because you don't like hearing it. She'll tie herself into knots trying to keep you happy, which is something you don't know how to be. You'll ruin her because you're not capable of loving someone the way she is. Now who is the selfish one?"

I swallowed back my first impulse, which was to tell him that he was wrong…because he wasn't. I didn't know how to be happy, how to be in a healthy, stable relationship, how to give a woman my heart and then trust that she wouldn't walk out like Mom did. I only knew that if I had a chance at anything resembling love, Harper was the only reason.

Bash and Spencer parted as I walked past them. When I reached the living room, everyone there was actively not looking at me. They also actively didn't look at Ryker when he joined us, choosing the opposite side of the room from where I stood.

Spencer cleared his throat. "Okay, well, I was going to have us clear some lines for a few hours, but I'm not sure I should hand out chainsaws and axes today, for fear the entire crew won't come back alive. So, how about we do some shelter drills. Everyone get dressed and meet me in the gym with your packs."

Three hours later, my anger still simmered, but the physical activity had drained my need to punch the shit out of Ryker. Besides, I didn't want to upset Harper.

We drilled shelter deployment, teaching the rookies how to effectively get under their protective shelters in case a fire came for us the way it had our fathers. I noticed with more than a little pride that Indie had taken Taylor under her wing, helping her get settled.

We left the clubhouse after Spencer told us to be back bright and early Monday morning, when we'd spend the day cutting line. Fire season was coming fast, and though most of us weren't rookies, we needed to work as a solid team.

I drove home without music, letting my thoughts fill the silence.

Had I ruined our friendship? Would I feel the same if I had a sister? Was he being a protective older brother or an asshole? My heart hurt, the anger giving way to the pain of potentially losing Ryker. My life wouldn't look the same without him, but I was done putting his ultimatum above Harper.

I pulled into the driveway and hit the garage door opener, then laughed, closing it again when I saw Liam's new bike and a few other toys occupying my spot. Headlights came up the drive as I got out of my truck, and by the size and shape of the vehicle...yep, it was Ryker.

Fantastic.

Harper came out of the front door with James on her hip, all smiles. "Hey, you're home!" Her face fell as Ryker put his truck in park but didn't kill the engine.

He got down and walked to where I stood as a barrier between him and Harper.

"Ry?" Harper asked.

"I just need a second with him," he told her.

"It's okay." I gave her what I hoped was a reassuring smile. She nodded slowly, but her mouth was a straight line as she headed back inside, shutting the door behind her. "What do you need? Because I don't know how much more I can take today."

He stuck his thumbs in his pockets and sighed. "I'll think about what you said."

"What?" I would have been less shocked if he'd announced he was moving to China.

"You made some pretty valid points." He finally looked at me and shrugged. "I don't know what will happen, or where my head will land, but I will think about what you said."

"And stop trying to beat the shit out of me?" I prodded.

"Maybe." He gave me a little half smile. "Tell my sister I love her. See you Monday."

He was halfway to his truck before I found my voice.

"We're having Chance over for dinner tomorrow. He couldn't make it tonight. Why don't you come too? I know she'd love to have you. Plus, it would keep me from slaughtering him."

Take the olive branch.

He paused for so long that I nearly gave up hope, never turning around.

"I'll bring steaks."

Relief hit me with such strength I almost fell to my knees. "Sounds good. See you at five."

He put up his hand in a wave and walked the rest of the way to his truck. I watched him pull out of the driveway with an odd mix of sadness and hope warring for priority in my head.

I chose hope and walked inside to see my wife.

CHAPTER FOURTEEN

arper

"HARPER! COME QUICK!"

I dropped the pan of brownies on the counter and threw the oven mitts on the island as I ran out of the kitchen to the great room.

"What's wrong?" I skidded to a halt on the hardwood.

"Look!" Knox said, his phone up to face as he took video.

I followed his line of sight and laughed. James had pulled up to stand and was grinning like a madman as he pounded on the coffee table with his hands.

"No way!" Keeping my footsteps soft, I walked onto the carpet, scared to startle him.

"He's standing!" Liam came in behind me and raced over to his brother. "Are you a big boy? You're standing like one!"

James bounced, his giggle utterly contagious, before falling back on his butt with a loud thump. He clapped his hands together and crawled over again, pulling himself to stand.

"He's amazing, right? That's got to be some kind of world record. I know he's bound for the Olympics," Knox said, tucking his phone into the back pocket of his jeans. His long-sleeved shirt was pushed up to his elbows, revealing the tanned skin of his forearms. How was it fair that he'd seen me practically naked yesterday, and I was still drooling over forearm porn?

"I'm not sure they have a baby-standing event, but if they do, James is definitely a contender," I answered.

He came over, a look in his eyes I couldn't quite define, but I liked it. It was the same one he'd had since he came home last night. Before we'd had a chance to talk, he had to run out again for a busted pipe at the Chatterbox, and I'd been asleep by the time he made it back.

"You have chocolate on your face." He brushed a finger at the corner of my mouth.

"I have a thing for brownie mix," I answered with a shrug.

"I have a thing for you," he whispered before ducking his head and kissing it clean.

Boom, I was high, my heart fluttering in the way I thought only happened in teenage rom-coms. He kissed my lips next, a soft brush of lips that left me leaning forward for more.

"Can we talk?"

My eyes flew open. "Is this about you and my brother last night?"

He nodded.

I looked to see that Liam and James were happy in the middle of the living room and stepped back into the kitchen with Knox, where we could see if the kids got into trouble, or if James decided to start running or something.

It was crazy how fast he developed, and we'd only had him a little over a month. What would he be doing in another month? Or two? Three? Would they still be here? That happy, glowy feeling Knox gave me plummeted at the thought of them leaving.

"Okay, what's up?" I hopped up onto the counter with my back to the boys.

He put his hands on my knees, and they spread slightly, like my body recognized what the man was capable of and was more than willing for a second round.

I definitely was.

"Okay, so yesterday…"

"Which part of yesterday? The part where my mother wouldn't accept that we're not married in the real sense of the word? The part where Ryker stormed out?" I dropped my voice so the kids wouldn't hear. "The part where you gave me the best orgasm of my life?"

His grip tightened, and the way his eyes dropped to my lips started a low-level hum in my belly. "Kind of all of it, but mostly the way Ryker and I got into it at work and said a few things we probably shouldn't have."

"Okay." Crap. Ryker was driving me nuts with his super-protective bullshit, but he was my brother. That was sacred no matter how much I loved Knox.

"He saw some nail marks on the back of my neck and put two and two together." No regret showed in his eyes, which was a huge relief.

"Well, shit. Sorry about that."

"I'm not." His hands slid to my thighs, tugging me closer so my knees flanked his hips. "I'm not sorry about a single damn thing that happened yesterday. Are you?"

My breath caught. "No, of course not. I've been trying to get my hands on you since I was sixteen…even though I still haven't really managed that. Don't smile at me like that, not when we have kids in the other room and company coming in an hour," which included Bash, Emerson, Ryker, and the new guy.

He glanced over my shoulder, no doubt checking on the

boys. "So, after we had…a moment at work—don't worry, there was no blood—he came over to say that he's thinking about what I said to him."

"Which was?"

"A lot."

"Got it." A lot was bro-code for *not telling you*, and I was cool with that. They were best friends, and if I wanted any chance of being with Knox, I had to make sure I didn't cost them that bond.

"So as much as I want nothing more than to carry you upstairs, strip you naked, and make you come about twelve different ways to start with, I can't." His grip tightened on me.

"Okay." A thousand different reasons went through my head, and none of them came to the conclusion that it really was.

Maybe he didn't regret what happened yesterday, but he wasn't looking to repeat it either. *It's prom night all over again.* As usual, I'd fallen into the trap that was Knox, lured by kisses and even the barest sliver of a chance he'd be mine. Even married, he belonged to my brother.

Think about the boys. They were why we were doing this. Wanting Knox was unfortunate, but it wasn't like I'd never *not* wanted him. We were simply returning to the status quo, but I wasn't sure I was capable.

"Harper."

"Yep?" Using my hands, I pushed back on the granite so our bodies weren't so close, but I couldn't close my knees with him between them.

"It's not because I don't want to." He used those eyes on me, all liquid and soft enough to drown in.

Problem was, I'd been drowning so long I feared death was imminent from lack of oxygen and too many shots to the heart.

"Yeah, okay. Got it. I need to change really quick, if you'll just move."

"No. Not until you understand."

I looked pointedly at his hands, which were still on my thighs, and then lifted a single eyebrow at him.

He picked them up and stepped back, leaving me enough room to get down, which I did.

"Harper!"

I walked right past him, blinking back tears of my own stupidity.

"We're not done," he said, coming up behind me.

I went up the first three steps and turned, bringing me eye level with him. "Just let me get it straight. You want me. You've always wanted me. You had no problem kissing me yesterday, or today, but because of a conversation you had with my brother, it won't be happening again, but it's not because you don't want me."

"Yes. No. Kind of." He shook his head.

"Then I think our conversation is done. I'm going to change into something clean. If that's okay with you, or you could call Ryker and ask his permission." Without waiting for his response, I went upstairs, into the guest room that was across the hall from Knox's.

Stupid fucking men.

I shut my door a little harder than necessary and ripped my shirt off. It found the hamper, and my yoga pants came off next, joining it. I never was a clean baker.

"Harper." Knox knocked at the door. "I'm coming in."

"Whatever," I said, rifling through my things that hung in the walk-in closet. I heard him open and shut the door.

Blue...green...did it even matter what color shirt I wore? Maybe I'd let Ryker and Knox decide, since they were all about making my choices for me.

The purple blouse with the lace overlay would be just fine.

"I would have followed you faster, but I had to put James in his prison."

I refused to laugh, but a snort escaped. "It's a playpen."

"You say playpen, I say baby prison. Will you please come out here and talk to me?"

"Sure." I walked out of the closet and tossed the blouse onto the bed next to where Knox sat.

His jaw dropped as I walked past in my underwear.

"Holy fucking shit, Harper." My name came out as a groan.

"What? It's not like you didn't see it yesterday, and you're the one insisting that we talk. Besides, since you're not touching it again, who really cares?" I shrugged, then opened the dresser drawer that held my jeans.

I chose the softest pair and shut the drawer.

"I didn't say I was never touching you," he argued in a strangled voice.

I turned to see him gripping fistfuls of the mint-green comforter on my queen-size bed. "You know what? I don't care. I'm so sick of feeling like I have to chase you. It's exhausting, honestly."

"Because you want me to touch you." A slight smirk lifted his lips.

"You know I do!" I snapped.

He was off the bed before I could blink, and I found my back against the wall with Knox pressed against my front. My jeans hit the floor and my body melted, just like it always did when he was close.

"What?" I glared up at him, trying to ignore the way my nerve endings sizzled, my traitorous nipples hardened.

"You don't have to chase me. You caught me seven years ago, you just didn't know it. Hell, you caught me when I was ten years old. You've always been the only person I could ever see myself having a life with."

"You make zero sense, Knoxville. If you want someone, if you love someone, you don't let them walk away. You fight for it. You fight for them."

"In your world, maybe. In mine, people leave. They walk out and never come back, not even when your dad dies."

"I'm not your mom." My heart hurt for him, for his inability to trust, no matter how long he'd known me, how many times I'd stood by him.

"I know that. You're nothing like her. You're honest, and kind, and strong. God, you're the strongest woman I know. There are so few people in this world that I..."

Love. Say it. I knew he was capable. He showed it in every way possible to the people he cared about, whether or not that was how he defined it.

"...consider mine. And I can't afford to lose anyone. Not you, but also..." He sighed.

"Not Ryker," I whispered.

He nodded. "Besides Grams, he and Bash were all I had. And you, of course."

"And me," I echoed.

"Always you. But I can't just turn my back on him when he thinks I violated our most sacred vow to each other. You're his name on this list."

"What list?" My eyes narrowed.

"The one where we get to choose one girl the other two aren't allowed to sleep with." His forehead wrinkled. "Which, when I say that aloud, sounds pretty stupid."

"Try prehistoric," I snapped.

"Yeah, well, we were teenagers, and I think Bash just wanted to make sure we didn't get near Emerson."

"So he licked her like one of my preschoolers with a snack he doesn't want to share?"

His eyes trailed from mine, past my lips, to the rise of my breasts. "Something like that."

"And you're saying Ryker...what? Licked *me*? Because that's gross." Gross and infuriating.

"Not exactly. Prom night, after we kissed, Ryker saw the way

I watched you, how hard it was for me to see you with that other guy. Right before you walked out the door with him, Ry put you as his name on the list. He knew it was the only way I was guaranteed not to go after you."

My stomach turned over.

"Why would he do that?" I whispered. How could he be so cruel to Knox? To me?

"Because he knew that I wasn't good enough for you. Hell, I'm still not."

"Knox—"

"Just hear me out. You were the one who asked me to let you in." He winced. "There's something broken inside of me, something that won't let me..."

"Commit," I supplied.

He nodded. "Something like that. He knew it then, that I would eventually crush you the way I do everyone else, and even if I managed not to, he knew I wanted to be a hotshot. He didn't do it to hurt you, he did it to protect you from me. Because this"—he splayed his hand in the hollow of my lower back and tugged me closer—"this attraction, our chemistry, is pretty obvious. I just never realized everyone else knew until I came back. He knew how close I was to punching Vic in the face every time I saw him that summer, how excruciating it was to know he'd touched you. Ry knew it without me ever having to say a word."

I looped my arms around his neck, running my fingers down the back where my nails had marred his perfect skin. "I never let Vic touch me."

His eyes widened. "What?"

"How could I, when all I could think about was you? God, you pretty much ruined my sex life for years. Every year, if I'm being honest. I couldn't figure out why I didn't feel the same urgency when someone kissed me. Why it was good but not"—I rose against him, rubbing my lace-cupped breasts against his chest and caressing his growing hardness with my belly—"this. I thought I made it up, glorified it in my memory."

"But you didn't." His hand swept down to cup my ass over my lace boy-cut panties. "We're just that good together."

I nodded.

"You ruined me for anyone else with that one kiss." He brushed his mouth over mine.

"So, what do we do? Let Ryker keep us apart another seven years? That's assuming you want to...not be apart." *Smooth, Harper. Super smooth.*

His lips turned up at the corners. "We are married, you know."

"Yeah, I heard. Apparently, it's the latest gossip around town."

"I'm not saying seven years. I'm not even saying seven months. I'm just asking that we give him a chance to come around. If he doesn't, that's on him. I'm not walking away from you." He kissed me gently. "I'm not saying I won't kiss you." His hands gripped my ass and lifted me in an insanely sexy display of strength. I hooked my legs around his waist as he leaned me back against the wall. "I'm not saying I won't touch you." One of those hands slid from my ass to between my thighs, sending tendrils of need straight through me. "I'll make you come as many times as you want, Harper. God, I can't think of anything better."

"I can." I wiggled, which both moved his hand and rocked my hips against his erection.

"Yeah, that." He leaned his forehead against mine. "Just give me a little time so I don't lose my best friend because of what I feel for his sister."

I was helpless against that admission. He could have asked me to wait ten years and I would have—that was the power Knox had over me. "And if he never comes around?"

"Then he's not who I know he is, and that's not going to stop me—stop us—from seeing where this leads."

He meant what he said. I saw it in his eyes, felt it in the way he held me. But that didn't mean he wouldn't decide differently when Ryker forced his hand.

"You scare me," I admitted. "This is everything I've ever wanted, and if you say that you're willing to try and then you change your mind, I'm not sure I can handle that."

He kissed me gently. "Then I'm just going to have keep giving you reasons to believe in me. I can do that. I won't give you the opportunity to doubt me, not ever." He set me down and backed away. "Now please get some clothes on before I doubt my own restraint."

"One question first. Who was your girl for the list?" I tried not to let jealousy seep into my voice, but it was an epic fail.

A slow smile spread across his face. "She's beautiful, inside and out. Loyal, hard-working, tough as nails, and one of the most phenomenal women I've ever met." He paused, and I tilted my head in exasperation. "And she's the only other woman to wear that ring." He pointed to my left hand and walked out, leaving me staring at a closed door.

His grandmother.

I let my head fall back and sighed up at the ceiling. Ugh, instead of guarding my heart, now I loved him even more.

Dressing quickly, I headed downstairs to get ready for dinner and nearly got run over in the hallway by Liam as he ran by me in some kind of vest.

"He's gonna get me!" he squealed.

"You bet I am!" Knox came sprinting out of the office, wearing a bigger size of the same gear and carrying a plastic gun. He paused to kiss me and then took off after Liam. As I heard Knox whining that Liam had killed him with a chest shot, I checked on James, happy to see he wasn't wearing a laser-tag vest too.

Two hours later, the kids were down to bed, and the adults cleaned up dinner. It had gone well, considering Ryker had barely spoken and spent most of his time watching Knox and me watch each other.

Talk about awkward.

"I could get used to this." Emerson took a sip of her wine and watched from the living room as the guys loaded the dishwasher. Even Chance was helping.

"Definitely qualifies as porn." Especially with Knox's sleeves rolled up like that.

"How are things going in that area?" Em asked, raising her eyebrows.

I watched Knox and *wanted* plain and simple. What was it about being so close to what you wanted but so far from having it that made you desperate? I'd never been like this over a guy.

"It's kind of like being in a bakery with your favorite dessert, but it's locked up behind the window, so you can look at it, but that's it. And you're trapped there. Forever. And the dessert is naked. And it's Knox."

"Yikes."

"Oh, and maybe you get to lick the dessert, just get a little taste, and it's so damn good. I mean like…earth-shattering good. And all you want to do is eat the fucking dessert, but you can't. Because your brother locked the display case, and you can't figure out why he won't just give you the damn key."

Emerson's side-eye turned into a full, head-on, wide-eyed head turn. "So, it's going well, then?"

"Did you ever just want to jump Bash? Like, push him down, rip his clothes off, and climb on? Because I seriously feel like this horny, desperate woman who's on the verge of losing her mind over sex. Sex, Emerson. I. Want. Sex."

"Okay, well, yeah, especially when we were in the will-we, won't-we phase. It was tough." She gave her fiancé a dreamy look that I flat-out envied. They'd always been like that, though.

"What did you do about it?"

"I pretty much locked him in his office and did exactly that. But as complicated as Bash and I were, you and Knox take the cake."

"I want the cake."

Knox winked at me and went back to his conversation with Ryker. At least they were talking.

"I can see that." Emerson tried her best not to smile but failed.

"Don't laugh at me."

"I'm not, I promise. I was just thinking about when Bash came home, and you said that I couldn't settle for less than the kind of chemistry…oh, what were your words? *Scratching, clawing, biting need to rip someone's clothes off*, I believe. Now you've got it."

"What if he doesn't want the cake?" My voice dropped to a whisper.

"Trust me, he wants the cake. He's wanted the cake since you filled out your jeans. That's never been an issue."

"Did I hear you say you wanted some cake, Harper?" Chance asked as he came into the living room. "I can grab you some."

"Only if you want Knox to kick your ass from here to the Utah border," Emerson answered, then full-on laughed.

"What was that?" Knox came in and gave Chance a look that sent him to the other side of the living room.

"They were talking about wanting cake, so I offered to get some," Chance answered with a shrug.

Emerson laughed even harder.

"Stop!" I told her, but she was almost crying.

"Oh, come on, Chance is offering you cake. Don't you want some? I bet it's really good cake." She managed a straight face.

"I don't want his cake," I muttered.

Knox's eyes narrowed on me.

"I want *his* cake." I said it quietly, but he heard me.

Something must have clicked, because he immediately turned to Chance. "Don't ever offer my wife cake again. Ever. Or you'll never have cake again with anyone."

"You guys are so fucking weird. I will see you at work tomorrow. Harper, thank you so much for having me over for dinner. Your brownies are seriously amazing."

"She makes fantastic cake too." Emerson giggled.

"No cake!" Knox snapped at Chance, who put his hands up and backed away, darn near running for the door. "Bash, get in here and take your fiancée home. I think she's had a little too much wine."

"Oh, come on, Knox. You're no fun. You used to be fun. I'm just trying to hook your wife up with some dessert. Geeze." Em looked my way. "How much wine did I drink?"

"I think you put away a full bottle."

"Really? Whoa. Yeah, no more." She put her glass down on the coffee table. "Sebastian Vargas!"

"Emerson?" Bash answered, coming into the living room.

"Take me home. I want cake." She threw Knox a look. "One of us should be getting cake, don't you think?"

"For fuck's sake," Knox said to the ceiling.

"Em, we don't have any cake at home. Did you want me to stop at the store?" Bash offered, pulling her to her feet. "I think the closest you're getting are the Pop-Tarts you bought last week."

"Trust me, you have just the cake she's looking for," I told him. "Just get her home."

"Yeah, okay." He walked forward and picked her up, putting her over his shoulder. "Let's get home."

"Night!" I waved at my friend as she tried to prop herself up.

"Get the cake!" she called back, giggling.

I couldn't wait to tell her about this in the morning.

Knox leaned over me, putting one arm on each side of the armchair I sat in. "So, apparently you're in the mood for dessert?" His voice rasped over me like the finest grit sandpaper, smooth but gritty enough to ruffle my nerves.

"Yes, please."

"You're not getting any of Chance's, that's for damn certain."

My fingers tangled in the opening of his button-down shirt. "I don't want Chance's."

"You're fucking killing me, you know that?" He groaned.

"Good."

He grinned, and I felt it in every cell in my body.

Someone cleared their throat, and Knox stiffened. "Totally forgot he was here."

"I didn't," Ryker answered. "Harpy, walk me to my car?"

Knox helped me to my feet, and I headed toward Ryker, who was conveniently looking anywhere but at us.

"Let's go, big brother." I hooked my arm through his, and we walked out to his truck. "Okay, give it to me."

"Give what to you?" he asked just outside our front door.

"The lecture you have prepared about how bad Knox is for me, and how you don't want me with a fireman, and how he's just going to hurt me." I folded my arms to ward off the early-May chill.

He rubbed his hands over his face. "You already know all that, so you don't need me telling you."

"Then what else do you have in your anti-Knox arsenal?"

"Nothing. He's my best friend. He's a great guy. Smart, brave, loyal to the bone, you name it."

"Okay?"

"He's also reckless as fuck during fires, fearless, unattached, and emotionally unavailable to every woman he's ever tried to have a relationship with. His mom really screwed with his head, Harpy. That's the kind of damage you might not be able to undo."

"Maybe I want to try. Maybe he needs someone to try, to

prove to him that it's possible to stay even when it's easy to leave."

"You really want to spend your life paying for another woman's sins? Even if you do get through to him, he's a hotshot. You always told me that wasn't what you wanted. You wanted a guy with a desk job, remember? That's why you ended up with tricky Dicky."

"Richard," I corrected him. "And yeah, I did, but that was when I was sixteen. Are you telling me that you've carried that around with you since then? That you're making us miserable because of something I said when I couldn't even parallel park?"

"You still can't parallel park."

"Stop joking, Ry. I love him. I have always loved him."

He grasped my shoulders like we were kids again. "What happens when he can't love you back?" There was no malice in his eyes, just deep sadness. "I've known him my whole life. I'm not warning you because I want to be a dick, or to control your life. I just want you happy, and loved, and adored. Knox can probably give you most of that for a while, but long term? What are you going to do when he isn't capable of returning all that love in your heart?"

I sucked in a stuttered breath. He wasn't being mean, or even sarcastic. He was genuinely worried, and as the person who probably knew Knox the best, I had to give my brother the benefit of really thinking about my answer.

It was the same discussion I'd had with myself when my building manager called today to tell me the reconstruction was finally done from the flood damage in my apartment. I could leave—it was big enough to take the boys, but I didn't want to. I wanted to stay here and fight for what I had with Knox.

"Then I guess I'm going to have to love enough for the both of us until he won't let me anymore. And yeah, I might get hurt, but I'm going into this with my eyes wide open. I know him. I know what he's like, what he does. I know even he doesn't think he can love, but I know he can. He already does. He loves his gram. He loves you and Bash. If he doesn't love me, then it will have to be okay, because the only thing worse than losing him would be to never have him in the first place."

Ryker studied me for a moment, then pulled me in for a hug. "I love you so much, Harpy. I just want you to know that you deserve to be with someone who loves as deep and strong as you do."

I nodded. "I know." *And it's Knox.*

"Fire season officially starts next week. We're still B level until we certify, but it's still dangerous."

"I know." I squeezed him. "But I also know that you're good at what you do, and so is Knox."

"So was Dad, and you see what Mom is like now."

"I know." This time, my answer was a whisper. "I promise you that I'll be careful with Knox as long as you are too, okay? Bring him home to me."

Ryker kissed the top of my head. "I'm still not sure about this."

"I am."

He let me go, and after his taillights faded from our drive-way, I walked back into the house.

"Well, that was fun."

"Look who woke up with a brownie craving," Knox said from where he sat with Liam at the kitchen island, spoon-deep in a brownie.

I shook my head as I ruffled Liam's hair. Then I grabbed my own brownie and sat next to my boys as Liam laughed. May as well enjoy the only dessert I'd be getting tonight.

"Everything okay?" Knox asked.

"I think it might be." And for the first time, I believed it.

CHAPTER FIFTEEN

K nox

JUNE EIGHTH. THREE WEEKS PAST THE OFFICIAL START OF FIRE season, and we were still waiting on our initial classification. Not that fires listened to any calendar or checked to see if their appearance would be convenient. Fires came when they damn well wanted to and devoured everything in their path until they either ran out of fuel or into us.

And we were nowhere near ready.

We'd gotten the rookies qualified in most of the courses and made sure the experienced firefighters were up on theirs too. The mobilization checklist had been done, and even the preparedness review had been completed by another Colorado crew. Talk about a whirlwind of training and paperwork.

"Bash, get out of my seat," Emerson ordered as she walked into the conference room armed with a cup of coffee, an armful of files, and a look that said she was serious.

"I was hoping you'd sit on my lap," he said with a grin.

She raised an eyebrow, and he moved from the end of the table. She might let him get away with murder at home, but as the manager of our crew, she didn't take his shit at the office. Well, unless Bash's office door was closed, in which case you didn't knock unless the building was on fire.

Spencer sat at the head of our table, with Ryker, me, and Bash on one side, and Miles McCoy and Bishop Maldonado on the other.

"Do you want to start, Spence?" Emerson handed us all files and set the remainder of the pile at her now-empty seat.

"Absolutely," he answered, opening his file. We all did the same.

"Okay." She walked over to the white board in a skirt and heels.

Bash could never stomach putting her in danger, the same way both Ryker and I had told Harper there was no way she was volunteering. Fuck, just the thought of her being in the way of a wildfire was enough to nauseate me.

"Classification came back this morning, and they have us as Type Two after last week's review."

A series of unhappy grunts rose from the table.

"Boys, you can be pissy all you want, but until you can cut two thousand feet of line an hour, you're not going to even touch Type One," Emerson answered with a shrug. "We knew we weren't going to qualify as Type One until the end of season anyway. It's not like we have any incident stats to give them, because we haven't been in a fire yet. That was just preliminary. Chill."

A slight snort escaped me. Man, I adored her. She was no-nonsense, smart as hell, and had stuck by Bash's side, no matter what.

"Thoughts?" Spencer asked, leaning back in his seat and giving us a once-over.

This was a test, and we all knew it.

"We're not split into efficient squads." I looked at the list of names on the white board. "Problem is, we're still feeling each other out, and we've got two real rookies. Three, if you count that Rose is coming from structure. He's never cut line before."

This time the grunts came in affirmation.

"Agreed," Bishop said, his tone low as always. The guy didn't speak much, but he was the second most-experienced fire-fighter we had after Spencer, and he knew his shit. "We have to split into three squads. Two would have been preferable as a first year, but we need to get one rookie on each squad, not just to cover for their segments but to train them up. I know Braxton wants to hover over his sister, but that's not doing him, her, or us any good."

"He's going to fight like hell," Ryker mused. "If Harper was on our crew, especially as a first year, there's no way I would want her on another squad. I'd want her right next to me where I could watch after her." His glance met mine before he quickly looked away.

"Which means you wouldn't be cutting line as efficiently," Bishop countered.

Everyone nodded.

Spencer sighed and rubbed his hands over his close-cut beard. "Okay, I agree with Bishop. Three is going to be the way to go, at least until we get the rookies trained up. Knox, how are we on physical requirements?"

I opened my notebook and put it on top of Emerson's file. "All the legacies are up to standard—"

"Was there any doubt?" Bash interrupted with a grin.

"And so are the transfers."

"Damn straight," Miles said with a nod. As the senior fire-fighter in that group, he'd taken over a role we all appreciated as we worked to integrate everyone.

"So, our issue is stemming from the rookies. Derek Chandler is quick on the run—"

"All-state track," Ryker supplied.

"But his push-ups are way beneath minimum."

"What about Taylor?" Spencer asked, and the table fell silent as I thumbed to her name in my book.

"She's coming along. Her mile run is at twelve minutes, which she couldn't do last month, and she's jogging the trail with the crew and not falling out."

"How are we going to handle that?" Spencer asked me.

"I've got her working out with Indie, and she's come a long way. She's about halfway there with her sit-ups, and her push-ups are actually approaching a good range—better than Derek's."

A rumble of laughter sounded from the table.

"We've got until September eighth," Emerson said, thumbing through her planner. "That's when the IHC certification team arrives. I'm shocked they agreed to come out, considering we won't even have a full season under our belts."

"We're Legacy," Spencer answered, his voice gruff. "No one is going to deny Legacy the chance to rise. Your dads paid for that chance, but that doesn't mean we can't blow it. Don't blow it."

No pressure or anything.

"Okay." I drummed my fingers over Taylor's page in my readiness binder. "Then we'll get her up to standard by then. We don't have a choice. If we lose Taylor, we fall beneath the sixty percent minimum, and the town council will revoke our charter. Doesn't mean we can't still certify as something else, but if we want our dads' patches, then getting her ready is a team effort. I hear anyone say shit to her, or behind her back, and I'll kick them off the mountain myself."

"Agreed." Spencer leaned forward, going through the file of reports. "Everything looks good so far, plans, vehicles, facilities —Bash, you, Ryker, and Knox put together a hell of a facility."

All three of us nodded at each other and then Spencer, a small smile quirking up my lips. Bash flat-out grinned. Putting Legacy, LLC together had been a labor of love, and a hell of a lot of sweat. It had been over eighteen months of design, construction, and purchases before we even approached the town to ask for the Legacy name.

"Okay, bring in Taylor and Braxton," Spencer said to Bishop.

Bishop rose, the fucking giant that he was, and stalked out.

A few minutes later, Taylor and Braxton Rose walked in and stood at the end of the table, both sweating.

"Sorry it took so long. I was on the treadmill," Taylor apologized, her eyes on the table.

"Taylor." Spencer's voice demanded her attention, and she gave it. "Don't apologize for working your ass off on behalf of this crew. Ever. I wish half these guys had your work ethic."

She nodded quickly but looked back at the table. We were going to have to find a way to get that girl out of her shell.

"What can we do for you guys?" Braxton asked.

"We're going to split the crew into three squads," Spencer announced. "We need to work better in smaller groups and increase our line-cutting time. We're just not getting enough chains cut in an hour."

"Okay," Braxton said. "How many more feet do we need?"

"*Chains*, Structure," Bash said with a smile. "Learn the lingo. Sixty-six feet to a chain, thirty chains an hour in grass, six chains an hour in brush."

Braxton rolled his eyes. "Fucking wildland."

"Welcome to real firefighting, son!" Miles laughed, bringing the rest of the table with him.

"Point is, we're splitting you and Taylor into different squads," Spencer informed them, cool as a cucumber.

"What? No. Absolutely-fucking-not." Braxton paled.

"Really?" Taylor answered at the same time, her eyes brighter than I'd seen them.

Brax snapped his head toward his little sister. "You want to be separated? You made me come back here, and now you want to be on a different squad? No. Mom would roll over in her—"

"Grave?" Taylor snapped, crossing her arms.

Well, this just got interesting.

"Taylor," Braxton warned.

"Guess what, Brax? Mom was a hotshot. Not dad. She did it on her own, without a husband or a brother hovering over her during every training, every qualification test, every time she needed to run. What did I have for breakfast?"

"A banana protein shake," he answered. "I know because I made it for you."

"Exactly. You're hovering. You are an experienced firefighter, Brax. Maybe not in wildland, but you know what you're doing. They need you to go do it, not hover over me to see if the grip on my Pulaski is right."

He backed up a step. "You really want to be on different squads? Because I, what...smother you?" His eyes widened.

"You don't smother me, you just make it really hard to be anything but your chubby little sister."

Holy shit, a pin could have dropped in the conference room and we would have heard it. I glanced at Spencer, wondering if we should let the siblings have some privacy, but he sent me a subtle headshake. Guess he wanted to see how they'd interact under fire. Literally.

"You're not...chubby," Braxton countered.

Agreed.

"Then stop treating me like I am! Like I can't possibly make it up the hill without you pacing me. Like I can't cut a line without you asking if I need a break. Without watching to make sure that I'm under my shelter before you deploy yours when we're in a drill. You have to let me do this on my own, Brax, or I'm not going to know that I can."

His jaw flexed.

Ryker leaned forward.

"You're my little sister. I couldn't survive if something happened to you, and I didn't do everything I could to save you. To help you."

Ryker nodded.

"And I get that. I feel the same way about you. But you have to let me make some mistakes and grow, or I'll never be able to do this on my own. Is that what you want? For me to be utterly dependent on you?"

Ryker frowned. *Interesting.*

"No, I don't..." He looked around the table and then shook his head.

"One day, you're going to get married and have kids—your own family. You're not going to have time to supervise my breakfast, and you know what? You're going to be thankful that I'm not helpless. That I can succeed, so that you can too. But you have to let me, Brax."

He swallowed and studied his sister's face for a very long minute. It was an eleven on the awkward scale for those of us watching.

Finally, Brax nodded. "Okay. Same crew. Different squads. I can live with that." He turned to Spencer. "Do it."

Then he walked out of the conference room, the door shutting softly behind him.

"I'm so sorry you had to see that," Taylor said quietly. Her eyes glanced over all of us before she met Spencer's. "Thank you."

"We're proud to have you, Taylor."

She nodded with a forced half smile and left the conference room.

Ryker sagged in his seat, and we shared a look.

It had been a month since he'd told me he was thinking about my relationship with Harper.

One. Fucking. Month.

I was trying—God, I was trying—but my patience was short, my dick constantly hard, and my life otherwise perfect. Living with Harper was everything I'd never known I was missing. She made my house warm in a way that made me anxious to get home at night. The boys were thriving, and for the first time in my life, I saw a future I wanted. A future I would fight for.

But that future also had to include Ryker, not only as my best friend but as Harper's brother, and he was basically just waiting for me to fuck everything up. Not that I hadn't in the past. He'd had a front-row seat to every girl I'd walked out on, every relationship I'd quit the minute some chick went all doe-eyed. What he didn't understand was that none of those women were Harper.

Harper was impossible to walk away from.

"Now that's settled," Spencer said, "everyone but Bishop out. I'm going to hack us up into three squads."

A grin spread across my face as we shuffled out. Bishop would be an amazing assistant superintendent.

We headed for the kitchen.

"Spencer would be an idiot not to choose Bishop," Bash said as he dug into the refrigerator.

"Agreed. He's the best of us. Most levelheaded too." Ryker motioned toward me across the island. "You going to share?"

"You going to let me date Harper?" I held out the second coffee cake muffin Harper had sent me in with this morning.

"Nope."

I scoffed and took a giant bite out of the second muffin, then set it next to the already chewed-on first. He snorted as I swallowed. "Then I guess it's a good thing I'm already married to her, huh?"

He shook his head, but there was a hint of a smile that he might be finally coming around.

Good thing too, because I was on the verge of telling him to fuck off and letting him deal with the fallout. If I had any family outside Bash and Ry, I might have already done it.

Spencer called us all to the great room after about an hour, and we gathered on the large, leather couches.

"Listen up. We're going to run three squads. To tell you the breakdown, I'd like to introduce you to your new assistant superintendent: Bishop Maldonado. This guy has a decade of wildland firefighting under his belt, eight of those being a hotshot. He's also a scary motherfucker, so I figure maybe you'd listen to him."

A raucous round of applause went up, and Bishop just nodded and made a motion for us to settle down.

"Yeah, yeah. I'm honored. I won't let you down. All that." Then he launched into the breakdown. Miles McCoy and Ward Hammond—both transfers from California—would be our senior firefighters, and good guys from what time I'd spent with both. Applause all around.

Then Bishop announced the three squad leaders.

"Sebastian Vargas, Ryker Anders, and Knox Daniels."

A distant hum filled my head. I'd been a firefighter ever since I graduated college five years ago. I knew fire. I knew how and when to set the smaller ones to put the larger ones out. But I'd never been a leader.

As they broke down the names on each squad, the buzzing only grew louder. I would be responsible for five other people's lives.

Eight if I counted Harper, Liam, and James—the little family we'd glued together through paperwork and good intentions.

Hell, I'd been a dad for two months and both the kids were still alive.

I could do this.

I *would* do this.

"Daniels." Five days later, I answered the phone with a groggy voice and a clouded head.

"It's Spencer. We've got a fire near Pagosa. You've got an hour—it's go time."

I listened carefully for the details.

"Yeah, I'll be there," I said when he finished. Usually this was when the adrenaline hit, the rush to get out there and get going. Instead, a deeper, heavier feeling settled in my stomach. I hung up, clicked on the light, and swung my feet over the side of my bed as the clock blinked 4:25 a.m. at me. Then I rolled my neck and scrolled through my contacts, calling each of my squad members to report.

Six minutes after I started, they were all notified. At least they'd all answered, so I wouldn't have to track them down.

I showered quickly, brushed my teeth, and got dressed within fifteen minutes. Then I knocked softly on Harper's door, knowing she was dead asleep, and opened the door. The light fell across where she slept, curled on her side.

I hated that she slept in here, that I couldn't wrap my arms around her while we drifted off, couldn't wake up with her skin all warm under my hands—which was exactly why we *didn't* sleep in the same room.

My self-control was great, but I wasn't a saint.

"Harper?" I asked softly, walking over to the bed. I crouched down so we were eye level and stroked my fingers across her soft cheek. Her hair was pulled off her face in a loose bun, exposing the line of her neck. My chest clenched. God, she was beautiful. "Harper, baby. Wake up."

"Hmmmm?" The skin between her eyebrows puckered, and then her eyelashes fluttered open, as she blinked herself awake. "Knox?" She leaned into my touch.

"Hey, we have a fire down south in Pagosa. We're getting called in."

She shot up, letting the covers fall to her waist. Thank you, merciful Lord, she slept in a tank top. "Right now?"

"I have to be in within the hour. I'm just going to check my gear over and then take off. You sleep." I pressed a kiss to her forehead. "I'll let you know when I'm headed back."

"Oh, the hell with that," she said, throwing the covers off completely. "Go get your gear together, I'll get coffee going. I'm not going back to sleep, you idiot. Not if you're leaving for a fire."

I smiled like a besotted fool. Because I was one. Especially if I was thinking the word *besotted*.

"Stop smiling and get your gear." She swatted my stomach. "Go."

I headed downstairs into the storage room I'd had built for this reason alone. Then I ripped apart my pack, assuring I had everything I needed. If I lived alone, I would have trusted it was still loaded from when I'd stocked it, but living with kids taught me they got into things you never thought about.

Like your line pack.

I repacked, threw in an extra cell phone battery, and locked the room on my way out. Harper shouldn't have to worry about the boys getting into that stuff while I was gone.

A gnawing ache sawed its way through my chest as I walked toward the kitchen. I was going to miss them—not just Harper, but the boys too. The smell of coffee greeted me as I put my line pack on the counter. Harper was up on the counter in her tank top and boxer shorts, reaching for one of the travel mugs I'd put on the top shelf.

"Be careful." I moved to stand behind her just in case.

"Give me one second," she drew out the words as she reached up on her tiptoes. "Got it!" She lifted the black mug like a trophy and turned neatly on the smooth counter.

My gaze traveled up the smooth, toned length of her legs,

but my hands skipped right to her hips and gripped the curves, flexing slightly.

She smiled down at me, and I tried to memorize everything about the moment as I brought her down from the counter.

"What are you thinking about?" she asked as her toes touched the hardwood.

"This is the moment I'm going to think about while I'm on the line." I let my hands rise to her waist, tracing the slope lightly.

"Not when you kissed me in the truck?" Her smile widened.

"That too," I admitted. "But this is better. You're still all flushed from bed, pj's and everything, and there's a little line right here"—I ran my finger down the mark that ran across her cheekbone—"from your pillow."

"So basically, I'm a mess?"

"Never a mess, and only someone who lives with you gets to see you like this."

She smiled, stepped out of my arms, and headed for the Keurig. A second later, the familiar hiss filled the kitchen.

"Give that just a second," she said, then sipped her own coffee as she walked over to the island. "Okay, I know you like to carry the hydration pouch, so I grabbed you the travel packs of Gatorade for your line pack. There's a few extra blueberry protein bars, energy bites, and that gel stuff you and Ryker swear by."

She handed me a Ziploc bag, and I stared at the contents, trying to find words.

"What's wrong? You like the blueberry ones, right? They didn't have lemon, and I know you like those too, but I had to order them. I was hoping they'd get here before you guys got called out, but— Knox? What's wrong?"

"You packed for me," I said to the bag.

"Well, just a few things I found while I was out shopping. I saw that you didn't have anything in your prep room. We should really set something up so it's easy to grab and go on mornings like this."

She said *we*.

"Hey." Her hands covered mine, and I finally looked at her. Those wide, turquoise eyes stared up at me with amusement and a touch of concern. "You okay?"

"You packed for me," I repeated. "No one has ever packed for me."

"Benefits of having a wife." She shrugged. "It's no big deal."

But it was. No one had taken care of me in that way since Mom walked out. Grams had been busy teaching me to be self-sufficient, and Dad had just been plain busy. And yet, here was Harper, up at four thirty in the morning, making coffee and handing me snacks.

Damn, that feeling was back in my chest, light and heavy all at the same time, sweet and sharp like a cliché.

"Is this the same pack you give Ryker?"

"Nope." Her forehead puckered. "I've actually never seen him off for a fire. I haven't seen anyone off since...since Dad."

"Well, it's a really big deal. Thank you." My voice sounded like I'd been smoking for the last fourteen years straight.

"You're welcome. How big is it?" She crossed her arms around her ribs.

"It's up at five thousand acres. Pushed through a chunk last night."

She flinched and I cursed inwardly. This moment right here was exactly why Ryker didn't want me with her.

"Look, Harper, I've never done this before—left someone at home. I don't know how much you want to know, or what info you'd rather me leave out so you can sleep while I'm gone. I don't know the rules, but I'll play by any you want to make."

"No rules," she answered, her chin rising. "I want it all. It might be tough, but I'd rather know. Don't ever keep me in the dark."

"I can do that. We're only Type Two, so you know we'll be mostly doing mop-up and that kind of stuff. Don't worry too much." Any position near a fire was dangerous, and she knew that, but hopefully downplaying it would make her feel better anyway.

"Of course I'll worry," she whispered.

I wrapped my arms around her, pulled her close, and rested my chin on the top of her head. "I know. I'll keep my phone on as much as possible, so you can text. And make sure the boys know I just went to work for a few days. I don't want them thinking I ghosted them."

"They'd never think that." Her fingers scrunched in the thick material of my fleece at my back. "You're so good to them, and they adore you. I'll make sure they know you'll be back."

I held her a few seconds longer and then let go, knowing it was time. "Walk me out?" I slung my line pack over my shoulder and grabbed my duffel bag.

"Of course." She slipped my travel mug into the side pocket of my pack, took my free hand, and walked with me through the mudroom to the garage.

"You have everything you need?" I asked, wondering if the boys had left anything they deemed vital in my truck.

"I'm supposed to ask you that," she teased.

I took one look at her and smiled. "Yeah, I think I do." Then I kissed her, soft and lingering, wishing I could bottle the feeling she gave me for the days ahead. "See you later, Mrs. Daniels."

Her smile faded, but she nodded. "See you later, Mr. Daniels."

I tore myself away and walked down the few steps to the garage, pausing to hit the opener before throwing my bags in the back of the cab.

It was just a fire, right? Just like every other time I'd packed my bags and taken off with a crew. Had Dad felt differently on those two fires? The one he was on when Mom left? Did he smile at her in their kitchen and kiss her goodbye? Had he known when he left that she wouldn't be there when he got back? That she'd leave me with Grams at the diner and never come home?

Had he felt differently the day he died?

The cool pre-dawn air flooded the room through the open garage door, and I saw Harper shiver on the steps.

"Get back in there and get warm," I suggested, but I knew she wouldn't budge. She was the girl who stayed through send-off, the one with open arms when you came home. She wouldn't leave like my mom. "Try not to worry, really."

Her mouth tensed, and before I knew it, she was across the garage floor and in my arms. I lifted her easily, my hands curving under her perfectly shaped ass, and her ankles locked around my back.

Then her mouth was on mine in a hard, closed-lip kiss, which I eagerly returned.

"I'm always going to worry," she said with another kiss before grasping my face in her hands and looking me in the eyes. "I've been in love with you since I was eight years old, Knoxville, and worried about you just as long. That's not going to change."

The world stopped turning. My breath—my very heartbeat —stilled as I felt some piece I hadn't realized I was missing click into place.

"Which part?" I managed to ask. "The worrying?"

"Neither," she promised. "I love you."

When my words failed, I kissed her, turning so her back was against the truck, careful to make sure I didn't jab a door handle into her spine. Then I let go of all reason and gave everything to Harper.

My tongue sank into her mouth, and I groaned. I'd never take this for granted—her taste in my mouth, her curves in my hands. Her hands cradled the back of my head as the kiss went on, neither of us willing to pull away and say our goodbyes.

I poured all of my messy, unlabeled emotions into the caress of my lips, the stroke of my tongue, hoping she understood what I didn't know how to say. Praying she knew what she meant to me when I couldn't put words to it.

Finally, we pulled apart with a softer, shorter kiss, and I rested my forehead against hers. It was past time to get going.

"Just tell me you'll come home. Don't promise me—I know you can't. Just tell me, and I'll believe you," she pleaded. A streak of panic went through her eyes, and my stomach sank with the knowledge that the last person she'd sent away to a fire hadn't come back.

"I *promise*"—I emphasized the word—"that I will do everything in my power to come home to you, Harper. Believe that." As the words escaped, I felt their truth. There was nothing I wouldn't do to feel her in my arms again, even if that was defy death. "I *promise*, do you understand?"

"You never promise." Her brow furrowed.

She was right. I didn't. Not since our dads died and I realized it didn't matter what your best intentions were, fate was a bitch who did whatever she wanted.

"I've never had a reason to, never had you waiting." *Please wait. Please don't let me come home to an empty house.*

"I'll be waiting," she promised, as if she'd known how badly I needed the words.

I kissed her once more and carried her back to the steps so her bare feet wouldn't freeze on the concrete.

"Take care of our boys."

"Take care of yourself."

I somehow managed to drive away.

She loved me. Harper Evelyn Anders—Daniels—loved me. I couldn't figure out why. It wasn't like I'd done anything to deserve it. Hell, I'd kissed her, then all but ignored her for almost seven years. She was everything I wasn't but always wanted to be—open, emotionally honest, brave, and so damn trusting. And she'd just trusted me with her heart. I knew it was because I was leaving for a fire, that she had the now-or-never mentality due to our past, but I was keeping it all the same. She couldn't take it back now.

That feeling in my chest hadn't just returned, it overwhelmed my senses, screaming at me with a ferocious need to be acknowledged—declared.

Oh shit.

For the first time, I wondered if I was in love with Harper.

CHAPTER SIXTEEN

arper

"Hey, babe, how are things at home?"

Knox's voice came through the phone, and I sagged against the wall in relief. He'd been gone for almost a week and a half, called away to another fire—this one in Utah—as soon as the first one was over. In the scheme of things, nine days was nothing, but for some reason the seconds had slowed down to tiny bites of infinity as I waited for him.

"It's so good to hear your voice," I told him. "We're good here. Boys are asleep. They miss you."

"I miss them too. I miss you most of all." His voice softened. "I'm so sorry I didn't get a chance to do anything but text. The service is shit out in the middle of nowhere."

"I know, don't worry. Are you coming home soon?" *Please say yes.*

He sighed, and my heart dropped.

"I wish. This one is wrapping up, but they're talking about sending us up north next. I'll let you know as soon as I do." He sounded just as weary as I felt.

"I understand," and I did. At least my brain did. My heart was stomping her foot like a pissed-off preschooler. "I didn't want to talk about this over the phone, but—"

"Everything okay?" he interrupted, his voice sharpening.

"We're okay. Elliot called yesterday, and there's still no sign of Nolan. We've had the boys for two and a half months, and she's worried about concurrent planning. That means they want us to declare if we're pre-adoptive. If we're not interested in adopting them, they'll have to start thinking about moving them to a family who is, so that the boys are settled for every possible outcome, just in case they never find Nolan." My throat constricted and a riot of emotions assaulted me, just like they had when Elliot had brought up the topic.

I loved the boys. I loved Knox. I loved our life exactly how it was right now—well, fine, maybe not *now*, but the way it was when he was home. Could I see that lasting forever? Absolutely. But would Knox?

Logically, none of it made sense, but my heart screamed at me to grab this family we'd somehow built and hold it together.

Seconds ticked by. The sound of his breathing was the only reason I knew he was still on the line.

"Knox?"

"What do you want to do?" he asked slowly.

"Nope. I'm not going first. You'll just change your answer to match what you think I want. Let's just sit on it and talk when you get back? We have time."

It was a huge decision. It meant permanently tying ourselves to a deal that had been struck with only temporary in mind. It was life, and love, and parenting, and implied things about our marriage that we hadn't talked about. Hell, we'd been married for over two months and still hadn't slept together.

How was that for ridiculous?

"Okay. Let's think about it, then both write down our thoughts and read each other's at the same time so no one goes first," Knox suggested.

"I like that." Then we'd both know the truth of how the other felt.

"Good—" The sound of the crew calling out to Knox came across the phone. "Shit. Baby, I have to go. Take care of our boys."

"Take care of you. Knox?"

"Yeah?"

"Be careful. I love you." I said it just because I could, because it felt so good to finally give myself permission. Because I knew he wasn't ready to love me, but he desperately needed me to love him. Because saying it made me feel stronger, invincible. Then I hung up before he felt pressured to say anything back.

Because I didn't need him to love me back. Not yet, at least.

Not yet.

A WEEK LATER, I SIGNED THE LAST PAYROLL CHECK FOR THE period and glanced at the clock. Megan had taken my Tuesday class we shared so I could get admin work done, but I'd already finished and it was only 9:30 a.m.

I'd also sent an email to my building manager asking about subletting my apartment. We weren't a hot tourist destination, but the ski towns around us were, so maybe my space would be a good moneymaker on Airbnb or something.

"What do I do now?" I muttered to myself, opening my planner to see what else was on my to-do list.

"Take the day off," Clara answered, leaning far enough back from her receptionist desk to look into my office.

"Your hearing is frightening."

"I'm serious. Take the day off. Go home and relax. Enjoy some kid-free time. Do all the things moms are dying to do but can't get done with little ones underfoot."

"You mean laundry? Cleaning?" Man, the thought of a perfectly mopped kitchen floor sounded fantastic. There was so much I couldn't get done lately, or the minute it *did* get done, I had all of five minutes to enjoy it before the boys wrecked something and we were onto the next mess. Cleaning while they were home felt like brushing my teeth while eating Oreos—completely pointless.

"Whatever you want. Just get some sanity. I'll lock up this afternoon." She gave me the stare that had no-doubt intimidated her sons, who were both older than I was.

"Okay," I agreed. "But if anything changes, call me."

"Off you go."

I grabbed my cell phone off the charger, shoving it into my purse as Clara shooed me out the door.

By the time I pulled into our driveway, I'd made a mental list of everything I could get done today if I worked quickly. Laundry, sweeping, mopping...the house was going to be clean just in case Knox made it home, instead of the current toddler-bomb mess our living room had become. Heck, maybe there was even time to get some grocery shopping done all on my own. I hit the garage door opener—

Knox.

His truck was parked on his side of the garage.

I blinked. He was home?

I pulled my car in and killed the ignition, rifling through my purse to find my phone. I had a text alert. *Shit, my phone is on silent.*

KNOX: JUST GETTING HOME. I DIDN'T WANT TO TELL YOU IN

CASE PLANS CHANGED, BUT WE'RE HERE. I'LL GET CLEANED UP AND
BRING YOU LUNCH. I'VE MISSED YOU.

He was home. My heart flew as I jumped out of my car,
barely remembering to shut the door before I ran into the
house, reading the second text message he'd sent a few minutes
after the first.

KNOX: AND DON'T BELIEVE ANYTHING RYKER SAYS. I WAS
PERFECTLY SAFE AND IT'S JUST A SCRATCH.

Wait. *What?*

"Knox!" I called his name in the mudroom, the kitchen, and
the living room. No answer.

Was he hurt? Panic surged through my veins. I needed to see
him *now*. The urge clawed at me, raking giant furrows through
the calm facade I'd maintained the last ten days. I needed to feel
his heartbeat, to know he'd made it through unharmed—needed
to see this *scratch*. After the nightmares I'd had every night he'd
been gone, my very soul demanded it.

I kicked off my heels and ran up the stairs, calling his name
again.

His bedroom door was open, and I knocked on the doorframe as I pushed it open a little farther. "Knox?"

No answer. I stuck my head just inside his room. "It's just
me. I got your—"

Oh. God. Yes.

My jaw slackened as I caught sight of him through the open
bathroom door, standing in the shower. The glass enclosure
gave me the best possible view of his muscled back as he leaned
forward against the stone wall, bracing himself with his hands
as water ran down his head, neck, back, and sculpted ass from
the rain-style showerhead above him.

He was so beautiful, so perfectly carved.

Heat overtook the panic, warming every inch of my skin.

I meant to walk out, to give him some time alone to finish

his shower, but instead of backing away, my feet carried me forward.

My toes crossed the threshold of his huge bathroom by the time he turned around, running his hands over his hair. "Hey, I'm home," I managed in a strangled voice, immediately jerking my eyes to the ceiling. "I called your name, but you didn't answer, and I just wanted to see you. You know. Make sure you weren't dead or anything."

I counted to five, and when he still didn't respond, I glanced quickly at his face—*only his face*—and found him staring at me.

My breath caught at the longing in his eyes, the need and heat that echoed my own. It felt like years since I'd seen him, instead of sixteen days. For charged seconds, we stood there, simply breathing the same steamed air, the tension building until I knew something was going to break if it released.

I just prayed it wasn't my heart.

And if it was, then so be it. I was already in too deep to get out unscathed.

"Harper." He said my name like I was deliverance from whatever hell he'd been in, elevating my pulse to the quickened thrum of a hummingbird's wings.

His eyes darkened as I walked toward him, never once leaving mine as I opened the shower door and stepped inside, closing the glass door behind me.

"You're okay?" I ran my hands over his beard-stubbled cheeks, uncaring that the steady stream of warm water quickly soaked my favorite blue shirt dress.

He sighed, leaning into my touch. "I am now."

"I missed you." My confession came as a whisper I barely heard above the sound of rushing water.

A primal, almost predatory gleam came into his eyes as he looked down at my lips. Then my back was against the stone wall and Knox's mouth was on mine. He tasted like his spearmint toothpaste, the cool flavor contrasting with the sinful heat of his tongue as it rubbed against mine.

My hands made their way up his arms, skimming the ridges of his muscles until I reached his shoulders. Water warmed my hands as they laced behind his neck.

He tilted his head slightly to kiss me deeper, and I surrendered my every thought to Knox—his mouth, his hands, the hard planes of his stomach where our bodies met.

I let my fingers roam down the sides of his ribs, and he hissed.

Jerking my mouth from his, I looked down to see the stripe of an angry, raw wound that stretched from just beneath his armpit to a few inches above his waist. Purple and blue bruises smudged the edges of the injury, and most of his skin had been scraped away—but not burned.

"Knox, what—" My fingers hovered over the abused ribs.

"It's nothing," he interrupted, brushing his lips over mine.

"It's not nothing!"

"I'm fine, Harper. It's a scratch." The corners of his mouth lifted into a smile.

"Does it hurt?" What a stupid question. Of course it hurt.

"Only when you stop touching me." He took my hands and put them back on his body, just below the wound.

"Knox," I whispered. "You're hurt."

"It's nothing to worry about." He kissed me, and I melted. His fingers covered mine, tracing the thick layers of muscle that framed his abs. He was hard everywhere, cut in roped lines from his hours at the gym, his skin slick and soft to the touch. "See? I'm perfectly fine."

He was home. He was mine. My hands abandoned his as I stroked the unmarred skin of his hips, the contours of his lower back as he kissed me senseless.

"I missed you every single day." Knox tugged my lower lip with his teeth.

I palmed his ass.

He sucked in a breath, grasping both my hands in his and pinning them above my head. "Behave," he begged against my jaw. "I'm hanging by a thread here, Harper."

"So let go."

He attacked my neck with open-mouthed kisses, sucking lightly on the areas he knew would get me squirming. One of his hands ran down my arm to my ribs, skirting the edges of my breast to lightly squeeze my waist.

"Knox." I moaned when that hand slid under the drenched fabric of my dress to run up my thigh.

His mouth found mine again as he freed my wrists, then tugged at the belt tied at my waist. His kiss had an edge to it I'd never felt before, not just hungry but ravenous.

For me.

I pushed my belly forward, feeling him hard and heavy where he rose against me. Then I kissed him harder, tangling my fingers in his hair as that familiar tension sparked in my core.

His fingers were amazingly quick with the water-slicked buttons of my dress, freeing them one by one until the fabric fell open, revealing the matching white lace bra and panty set I'd thankfully chosen this morning.

The starved look in his eyes as he gazed down the length of my body was worth every single penny I'd spent on the lingerie. His breathing accelerated, and I shrugged my shoulders, letting the heavy fabric of my dress fall down my arms. It dropped to the stone floor with every single one of my inhibitions.

He retreated a step, rolling his head back so the shower drenched his hair as his chest shuddered with an indrawn breath. Then he opened his eyes, and I saw that cool, incredibly sexy determination he applied to almost every facet of his life replace the battle that usually raged when he looked at me.

His muscled arms wrapped around me, and his hands

cradled my ass as he lifted me to eye level. "Say yes," he growled, his gaze clashing with mine.

It was a question phrased as an order, and I knew if I said no, he'd put me down and walk away without a single complaint. I also knew there was no way I was ever going to say no. I'd been saying yes since I was eighteen—he'd just been too stubborn to hear it.

Secure in his hold, I reached behind me and opened the clasp on my bra, then took it off as his eyes seemed to smolder, his jaw flexing.

"Harper," he warned as I leaned closer, whimpering in relief as my hardened nipples met the slick skin of his chest.

I kissed my way up his neck, grazing my lips across the sensitive spot just behind his flexing jaw muscle before I ran my tongue along the shell of his ear.

"Yes, Knoxville. I'm saying yes."

He adjusted his grip on my ass, and I locked my ankles around his waist, careful not to touch his injury and all too aware of his erection nudging the lace between my thighs. God, I couldn't wait to actually look at him, to stroke him with my hands, my mouth, feel him inside me.

My inner muscles clenched in agreement.

He slammed down the shower's handle, stopping the flow of water, then clasped the back of my neck and kissed me. It wasn't just the wild caress we'd shared before but pure, slow, blatant seduction.

Water dripped from my hair and down my back in cool streams as he carried me out of the bathroom, drugging me with expert kisses at every step.

He lowered us to his bed, and I gasped as the silk of his sheets rubbed against my skin with sensuous friction.

"You might ruin your sheets," I warned him as he rose above me. "Cold water, remember?"

"Don't care as long as I get to ruin *you*," he answered, dragging my lace panties down my legs until he tossed them over his shoulder.

I knew he would ruin me—I'd always known. After he kissed me that night, I'd compared every kiss to his. Every mouth. Every tongue. Every smile.

"Fuck. Harper," he groaned as he looked his fill. I left my hands at my sides, ignoring the instinct to cover my imperfections in front of this physically exquisite man.

This was Knox, and I didn't need to hide.

His fingers trailed from my throat, down the space between my breasts, across the hollow just under my rib cage, and stretched to nearly span my waist. I'd never been a tall girl, always the shortest in the room, and Knox made me feel not just petite but delicate under his hands.

"If you only knew how many times I fantasized about this," he admitted as he caressed my thighs. "Even when I shouldn't have. God, you were just sixteen the first time I wanted to kiss you. And after I finally did, I'd lay in bed and imagine you like this, all smooth skin and curves."

"And does the reality measure up?"

His eyebrow rose at the question, and a slow smile spread across his beautiful face. "Surpasses every dream. You are fucking gorgeous, Harper."

My heart skipped, and I shifted my thighs wider when he nudged them apart so he could kneel between them. My skin felt so hot that I wondered how long it would take for those droplets of water to sizzle and steam right off me.

A drop trickled down Knox's chest, and I followed it with my eyes, losing my breath when I took in the full sight of him kneeling naked before me. The muscles of his abs flexed and rippled as he moved, and the hard, full length of him rising toward those abs sent my muscles clenching again.

"How does the reality measure up?" he asked with a smirk, catching me ogling him.

"You're perfect." I sat up and teased the lines of his stomach.

"Only in your eyes."

I brushed the head of his erection, and he hissed.

"Later," he promised, gripping my ass and tipping me back to the bed. "I've been imagining your taste for seven fucking years."

He slid down the bed and lifted my hips simultaneously.

I moaned when he licked a long line up my center.

My hands fisted in his hair when he flicked at my clit, the tension in my belly coiling tighter. And as he learned every curve and fold of me with his tongue, I lost all sense of reason. It felt so damn good, the pleasure swamping me, filling my limbs, building higher and higher.

"Sweet," he mumbled against my core, sending vibrations right to that spot that was ready to unravel.

He thrust his tongue inside me, and my back arched as I cried out. He pinned my hips with his hands, holding me still while he took his time devouring me, teasing me one second and pushing me to the edge in the next.

"God, Knox!" I begged as he mercilessly drove me insane.

"What do you need, love?"

The endearment nearly sent me into full-on orgasm.

"More."

"Like this?" He slipped one finger inside me, rubbing along my walls until he found the spot that sent me into a full arch.

"Yes!"

He added another finger and licked my clit, dragging his tongue roughly along the sensitive nerves.

I felt like a piece of glass cracking at the edges, ready to shatter.

Then he sucked with his lips and stroked with his fingers, and I broke apart, screaming his name as I came.

Wave after wave took me under, and Knox stroked me through the aftershocks, pushing me higher with a press of his tongue that skyrocketed me into another orgasm that suspended me in that sharp, sweet pleasure even longer.

My thighs quivered as he finally retreated, licking his lower lip in a way that almost sent me into a third.

"Holy. Shit," I said through gasping breaths. "Your tongue is magical."

He grinned, sliding up my body to kiss me deep. I tasted myself and moaned at the eroticism of it, raising my knees so his erection brushed my entrance.

Then he was the one moaning as his tip sank into me a fraction of an inch.

"You sure?" he asked, bracing himself on his elbows above me. His eyes searched mine for any sign that I didn't want him, but there was none to find.

"I'm sure," I promised.

He pushed another inch and slammed his eyes shut. "You feel so. Fucking. Good." Then his eyes popped open. "Condom."

I nodded in agreement, and he pulled out, leaning to the side to open the bedside table drawer. Not that I'd object to taking him bare—it would be a first for me, but I wasn't going to saddle him with the potential of a pregnancy when our future wasn't exactly decided.

He ripped open the condom and rolled it over his erection, then settled back between my thighs.

Then he cupped the back of my head and kissed me, his tongue swirling around mine as he slowly pushed into me, stretching my orgasm-sensitive walls with every inch he claimed.

"Harper." He sighed once he was completely inside me.

He rested his forehead on mine for a moment, until I shifted my hips beneath him, letting him know I was fine.

"Fuck. Hold still. Just a second."

I swirled my hips and he groaned, the sound long and low.

Knowing I could push him to the edge of his control was intoxicating, and I was more than drunk on him.

"Damn it. I'm serious. I've wanted this for too long for it to be over in twenty seconds, which, if you continue that, is about what you're going to get." He squeezed my hip, his fingers digging into my skin for a second before he released me, as if he was scared of hurting me.

"Okay," I agreed, running my hands through his hair before I rocked under him, forcing him out an inch only to bring him back in.

"I want more." The muscles on his face strained as he fought for control.

"More later," I promised, realizing what was holding him back. "This isn't the only time for us, Knox. You can have me any way you want, as many times as you want later. But God, please start now."

The muscles in his shoulders relaxed, and so did the tension in his jaw.

"Any way I want," he repeated.

I kissed him in response, and he finally started moving inside me. His slow, sure thrusts sent pleasure through my entire body like waves on the beach, receding only to come back again and again.

It wasn't long before I had my ankles wrapped around his hips, meeting his powerful thrusts. Our breaths mingled between kisses and groans as he quickened the pace, his hips swinging into mine with such delicious pressure I could almost taste my approaching orgasm.

As if he'd sensed the shift, the tensing of my thighs, he slid one hand down my belly to rub his thumb over my clit in light circles.

"Right there," he whispered against my mouth. "I want to feel you come around me."

One press of that thumb and a crazy-deep thrust, and I did.

My body locked, squeezing down on him as the edges of my vision blurred, the pleasure blinding me as I came again.

"I love you," I whispered as I crested.

He watched me with wide eyes and held me tighter. Then he let go of his carefully held restraint, thrusting faster and harder until he shouted my name into my neck.

I held him close, stroking my hands down his spine as he pulsed within me, his breathing ragged.

After a few seconds, he rolled us to the side, holding me with one hand spanning my back and the other at the base of my head. Then he looked at me with such tender eyes that my heart ached.

"I was wrong," he said softly.

"What about?" It took supreme concentration not to tense in his arms, not to question what we had done, or how I stacked up against the other women he'd taken to bed.

He cupped my cheek, brushing his thumb across my skin.

"You're the one who's ruined *me*."

CHAPTER SEVENTEEN

K nox

"YOU GOING TO TELL ME WHAT HAPPENED?" HARPER ASKED AS SHE slathered antibiotic ointment on the scrape along my side. I would have been all for keeping her in bed the rest of the day, but it was almost time to pick up the boys.

"Tree fell." I shrugged. "No big deal." Shit hurt like hell, but I'd had way worse through the years.

She paused, then reached for the gauze I'd left on the bathroom counter. "A tree fell," she said slowly.

"A tree fell," I repeated as she wrapped the wound. No good could come from telling her what had gone down out there. It would only make her worry more.

Her lips pursed, but she only nodded as she used medical tape to secure the bandage. "All done."

"Thank you." I tucked her hair behind her ear, my stomach

dipping at the unease in her eyes. "Don't worry. It will be healed up in a week or so."

"I'm always going to worry."

And that was exactly why Ryker had lost his shit on me yesterday. When I'd spotted the adolescent, burned-out pine tip in Chandler's direction, I hadn't thought—I'd simply moved, shoving the kid out of the way and getting grazed by the tree in the process.

Ryker could fuck off. Chandler was alive and I was scratched up. Seemed like a pretty good deal to me considering our performance had been barely above a "clusterfuck" rating.

Harper and I finished getting dressed and headed to the preschool in my truck. Mrs. Greevy shocked the crap out of me when she waved as we waited at the stoplight on Main Street.

"That woman hates me," I muttered, giving her a wave and an awkward smile.

"She hated you *years ago*," Harper qualified. "She wouldn't dare hate you now, especially with how hard you're working on the crew. People grow up." Harper waved back, and we continued on our way when the light turned green.

The sun flashed on my wedding ring as I turned the corner toward the preschool. How blissfully normal it all seemed. *This could be your life.*

My heart tumbled and raced.

I could come home to Harper after every fire. Fall asleep with her in my arms. Wake up to her scent in my lungs and her soft curves in my hands. With her at my side, the thought of an instant family wasn't oppressive or terrifying, it was...warm and welcome. And the boys? I was wild about them.

But kids...man, kids were easy to fuck up, and I was anything but a sure bet in the stability department. *Harper won't let you screw them up.*

But was I really ready to say forever? What if I fucked it up? What if I had more of my mom's runaway genes and less of my dad's loyal and steadfast ones? What if I said yes only to break their little hearts in a few months when I did something to piss Harper off—which was inevitable—and she got sick of my inconsistent ass?

I hadn't lied this morning—she'd ruined me. Everything about sleeping with Harper transcended sex into an entirely new level that had to be...making love. Maybe I'd been inside her body, but she'd been in my soul, every emotion heightening the physical act to what I could only describe as stunning.

And terrifying.

There would never be another woman who compared to the blonde curled up next to me, the console of my truck raised so she could lay her head on my shoulder as she fumbled with her phone, scrolling through her playlists. There would only ever be her, even if I screwed this up and she walked away. Only ever her in my head, my heart, my dreams.

That sweet, warm pressure expanded in my chest until it nearly burned.

Oh shit. I was in love with Harper.

I felt it the second my heart had cracked open when she'd told me she loved me again while I was inside her, but there was no denying it now. I'd seen the truth in her eyes, the way she'd stripped herself emotionally bare for me, never thinking to protect herself from the hurt we could cause each other.

I was in love with Harper. The thought repeated in my head like the echo in a canyon, coming back around to hit me from another angle. Harper, who I'd wanted for the better part of a decade. Harper, who had seen my worst sides. Harper, who was legally my wife because she was brave enough to put herself on the line for the boys—our boys.

She was fearless in a way that humbled me.

Oblivious to the epiphany that was currently rocking me to my core, she changed the song streaming from her phone to my speakers, pulling me from thoughts. "I was thinking we might have Ryker over for dinner."

Ryker. *Fuck my life.* My stomach twisted but settled quickly. Ryker was going to have to get over his shit. I just didn't necessarily need him getting over it at my dining room table.

"We might want to wait a day or two." My grip tightened on the steering wheel.

Harper cocked her head at me and waited for me to explain.

"He's a little pissed at me right now," I admitted, watching her eyes narrow in my peripheral vision.

"Does this have anything to do with the giant gash down your side?"

"Scrape," I muttered. "And maybe." I kissed the back of Harper's hand. "It's just work stuff." But it wasn't. Ryker wasn't pissed at me for stepping in and protecting Chandler. He was pissed at me because Harper would suffer the consequences if I'd misjudged, and that was entirely personal.

We pulled into the parking lot and then held hands as we walked into the school with the throng of other parents picking up their kids. I nodded to them as they greeted me by name. Everyone seemed happy the crew had made it back from our first real test.

Not that it was a real test. Working at Type 2 after years of being a hotshot was a big step backward, not in workload as much as state of mind. But we had to prove ourselves, so Type 2 it was.

"There he is," Harper said, pointing down the hall where Liam was loading his backpack carefully with art, his back to us.

"Let's surprise him." We made our way to him as he zipped his bag, and I slipped behind him, a wide grin spreading across my face. I'd missed him in the weeks I'd been gone, and I hadn't even realized just how much until this moment.

"What do you have there?" Harper asked, crouching to his level as I waited.

"I made Knox a picture!" He hefted the little bag to his shoulder and Harper helped him get his other arm through the strap. "It has trees and fire, but not a lot of fire, just a little."

"I bet he'll love it," she told him, zipping up his windbreaker even though he could do it himself. She did that for the people around her, tiny gestures that let everyone know they were cared for.

"I can't wait to give it to him!" He bounced a little.

"You could give it to him now," she suggested, nodding toward where I stood.

He turned, his brows scrunched until he saw me. Then his eyes flew as wide as his smile. "Knox! You're home!"

He jumped, and I caught him, my hands slipping down the slick material of his windbreaker slightly as I lifted him into a hug. He tucked in tight, his little frame bending around mine, his hair smelling like the strawberry shampoo Harper kept in the Iron Man bottle. I breathed in deep, savoring the absolute peace of the moment.

"Yeah, I'm home." I met Harper's eyes, and she gave me a watery smile.

"I missed you," he admitted, his hold tightening to almost strangulation on my neck.

"Well, I missed you more. Trust me." And I did. My heart cracked again, flooding my senses with an even sweeter feeling, and I squeezed Liam in a bear hug in reaction.

I'd fallen for him too, and Sir Pukes-A-Lot, who rested his tiny, kissable head on my shoulder when we picked him up ten minutes later from Cherry's. He hadn't made a single sound as I'd lifted him into my arms, simply looked at me, and then laid his head down, melting into my chest.

Damn it, I loved three people I had no guarantee of keeping.

As if sensing the damning thought, James picked up his head, plopped both his hands on my cheeks, and began to babble, his eyes bright as he drooled through his soliloquy.

"Oh really? What else happened while I was gone?" I asked him as we walked out of Cherry's, his diaper bag slung over my shoulder and Liam's hand tucked in mine.

Harper said goodbye to her friend and came out after us, reaching the truck as I got James strapped in to the soundtrack of Liam filling me in on every detail of the last couple weeks. He buckled his own seat belt across his booster and didn't pause once to criticize how I handled James as I caught up on which kids were staying for the summer session and who he wouldn't see until kindergarten in the fall.

My little alpha pup had become quite the talker.

I grinned at the thought and kissed Harper quickly as she buckled in beside me. Normal...everything was domestically, exquisitely normal, and it was perfect.

"You need more carrots," Liam lectured Ryker two days later as we sat in the dining room. "They're good for your eyes." He glanced meaningfully at the bowl, and Ryker dished another spoonful of carrots onto his plate.

Tonight was going to be a disaster, but Harper had insisted on inviting Ryker over for dinner. Honestly, who the hell was I to tell a sister she couldn't catch up with her brother? If he was still pissed at me, hopefully he'd keep it confined to the clubhouse.

As for me, I was keeping my eyes on my plate and off that slight dip in Harper's neckline. And off the long line of her neck and the curve of her lips. I definitely wasn't thinking about the way I'd kissed her just before Ryker had rung the doorbell, or the soft little whimper of protest she'd made when I stopped.

Nope. Not thinking about any of that.

"Bossy, this one," Ryker muttered with a grin as he passed the bowl to Harper.

"You should see him when it's broccoli." I winked across the table at Liam. "It's a whole other story."

"Broccoli tastes like hot feet," Liam explained, his eyebrows rising at me as though he was an expert on the subject.

Ryker laughed, cutting the tension in the room by half and reminding me why the guy was my best friend. "Well, I brought pie for dessert, if you eat all those carrots and the chicken Knox tortured to death on the grill." His eyes darted to Harper. "I mean, if Harper says it's okay."

"It's fine. Just eat what you can, Liam." She rolled her eyes at her brother. "And Knox grills just fine."

"So protective." I smothered a laugh.

Liam's eyes narrowed. "What kind of pie?"

"Apple," Ryker answered. "The kind with the crumble top."

Liam nodded thoughtfully, then forked in the bites of chicken Harper had cut up for him while James made a mess of his heavily steamed carrots. He'd smeared the squished vegetable all over his face, and his tiny fists were the same shade of orange. Bath time was going to be fun tonight.

"So…" Ryker glanced between Harper and I, his brow furrowing for a moment. I held my breath and sent up a silent prayer that he'd choose a safe topic. "How are the fostering classes going?"

My shoulders dipped in relief.

"Fine," Harper answered. "They've mostly been virtual, and we're almost done, since we did everything backward with the home study and such." She glanced at the boys. "They can get kind of heavy though. The topics…" She winced.

"There's a lot of information to process," I filled in. "The classes are focused on all different age groups, not just the little guys, and some of the stuff kids go through is…" *Fucking horrifying.* "A lot."

Ryker's eyes drifted toward the boys, and he nodded, getting the unspoken message. "And when do you meet with Elliot again?"

"Tomorrow," Harper answered, her gaze briefly meeting mine as color rose in her cheeks.

The two of us had an appointment tonight regarding that very meeting. It was time to figure out just what the hell we were doing.

Silence descended as we ate in an almost awkward silence that was only broken by James's squeals of excitement as he pulverized another carrot.

"So how is the crew coming along?" Harper asked.

Ryker sighed. "For the most part, I think we're getting there, but we haven't really gelled yet." He looked across the table at me. "What do you think?"

"I think we've got some rookies with sh—" I winced. "Crappy shelter deployment times, and we're not cutting line as effectively as we could be. There's still a pretty big divide between the legacies and the transplants."

Ryker nodded in agreement. "But I have a feeling we're going to get a chance to work those issues with the way the weather is looking."

It was hot, dry, and our snowpack was low. Add in the winds forecasted over the next week and that made for a high probability I wouldn't be home next week.

"I swear, it's like the fires just kept coming this year," Harper murmured, stabbing her chicken. "There was no real off-season, even before you guys came back to Legacy. You didn't get a break."

"That's because we didn't." I forked a bite of potatoes. "We went from one crew to another, one fire to the next. Hell, you were seasonal, Ryker, and you were still out there in April with your old crew."

"Remember that December fire on the front range?" Ryker asked, shaking his head. "Fire season used to be five months long and now, it seems we're fighting year-round, and I have to say, it's pretty da—"

"Ryker!" Harper snapped.

"Darn," he corrected, "exhausting."

That was something we could both agree on.

"I mean, you've got to be tired too," Ryker continued, concern lowering his brows as he looked at Harper. "He was gone for weeks." He pointed his fork at me. "And chances are we'll be gone in another few days if the forecasts hold true. You're basically doing this on your own."

And *boom*, so much for safe topics.

Harper shrugged off his comment, and that sickly sweet smile she saddled on him was anything but sincere. "Well, I knew what I was getting into, dear brother." Her nose wrinkled.

Mayday. I shot Ryker a look that said as much. Harper was going to eat him alive if he went down this path.

"But did you?" Ryker challenged, leaning back in his seat. "I imagine it's different watching Mom send Dad off versus being the one left behind with the kids now."

I debated kicking him under the table.

"It's not like I fell apart while Knox was gone." Harper arched an eyebrow at him. "As you can see, both kids are alive and healthy. My business is thriving. The house is still standing."

"I'm done!" Liam announced, showing off his plate like a trophy.

"Wish I could be done," I muttered to myself, then turned to Liam. "Go ahead and take your plate to the counter, little man. We'll be here for a second." *After we navigate this mine field.*

"I didn't say you couldn't handle it," Ryker said softly, but there was a bite in his tone. "I just never wanted you to *have* to."

I gritted my teeth and kept my mouth shut. The only problem with falling in love with Harper was navigating this very tricky dynamic. Every instinct told me to defend her, to insert myself into their narrative and tell Ryker to mind his own damn business. But experience had taught me that Harper had claws when she chose to use them and didn't need me stepping in on her relationship with her own brother.

"Even if I wasn't with Knox, I'd be doing it on my own." She leaned back in her chair, looking toward the kitchen, no doubt to make sure Liam was out of earshot. "I was the one who took the boys in, remember? Knox was the one who stepped up so we could keep them together. If anyone's life has been upended, it's his, not mine."

"That's not what I meant—" Ryker started, the tips of his ears turning red.

"No, you meant, aren't you miserable now that you've chosen the life our mother did? Right?"

Oh, he was going *down*. I set my silverware on the plate and gave up any pretense of eating. James smacked his hands on the top of his high chair, delighted at the sound he made.

"Fine." His shoulders rose in an exaggerated shrug. "You caught me. I'm worried. Everyone at this table knows it's only going to get more hectic from here now that it's about to be July. And who knows when we'll actually be around. Sue me if I'm concerned that my sister is going to be stressed out."

Harper sighed and shook her head. "Ry, don't you think I was already stressed out? I'm always on edge when *you're* on a fire. I hold my breath until you tell me you've made it home. Are you considering giving up firefighting so I don't have to stress out as much?"

His mouth opened, then shut. "I mean…" He looked at me for help, and I just shook my head. This was between the two of them. "Of course not. But I'm your brother, not your husband."

"At least you admit that he's my husband." She flashed him a genuine smile. "But seriously, stop trying to save me from something I clearly want." Her eyes met mine, and my chest went warm. "Is it a little harder when Knox is out there? Sure. Do I worry about both of you? Absolutely. But I always have, even when neither of you lived here." She tore her gaze from mine. "And between us, I'm stronger than our mother because I grew up knowing exactly what could go wrong. I'm not over here with blinders on, Ryker."

His jaw flexed, and my stomach sank at the apologetic look he sent my way as he started to speak. "And you know just how reckless he is with his own safety?"

"Ryker," I warned.

Harper's eyebrows knit. "You're all reckless. What are you talking about?"

Ryker's laugh was anything but comical. "Have you seen the souvenir he brought home from the last fire?" He cringed. "Don't answer that. I don't want to know."

"If you're talking about his side—"

"You're an asshole," I said across the table, then gave James one of my carrots since he'd murdered all the ones on his tray.

"I'm honest," he countered.

"What is he talking about?" Harper demanded.

Ryker's gaze clashed with mine, and the nonverbal warning I sent went unheeded.

"We were clearing out an area for hotspots, and one of his guys wasn't paying attention to his surroundings. A charred tree almost took him out, so your husband here threw himself in between Chandler and the thousand pounds of pine hellbent on turning him into a corpse."

I shook my head at Ryker, even as I felt Harper's attention pivot toward me.

"Is that true?" she whispered.

I closed my eyes and blew out a breath, then opened them to face my wife. "That's about how it went down," I said softly, like my tone could change the words. "Chandler is nineteen, and we're working on his situational awareness. I acted before I thought it through, but it turned out just fine. We both cleared it."

She sucked in a breath, then gave me a shaky smile and leaned over the corner of the table, taking my face between her palms. "You saved him."

"Anyone else would have done the same." This was the kind of shit that happened out there. None of us were looking for accolades, but it felt damn good to have her smile at me like that —like I was someone worthy of her praise.

She kissed me, soft and quick, and when she drew away, I cupped the back of her neck, pulling her in for another one. I was done giving a fuck what Ryker thought. Harper was mine, and I was hers, and that was all that mattered.

She smiled into my kiss, then pulled away. "I'll get James washed up."

"We'll take care of the dishes."

Ryker and I were silent as we carried the dishes to the kitchen and started washing up. James's high-chair tray looked like a crime scene.

"I didn't know he could eat chicken," Ryker said, scrubbing the tray as I loaded the dishwasher.

Take the olive branch.

"You just have to shred it really small," I answered, sliding another plate into place.

He sighed. "You're good at this. The kid stuff."

"Harper makes it impossible to suck at it," I answered, looking over the counter to where Liam was building a Hot Wheels track. *Keep the peace. Keep the peace. Keep the—*

Fuck it.

"You would have done the same fucking thing," I whispered, putting the glasses onto the top rack.

"I'm sorry?" His hand paused mid-scrub.

I turned and stared my best friend down. "That fire in Oregon two summers ago? You did the same thing. If I recall correctly, Bash told me you got a concussion from that falling branch because you covered him."

"That was different." He looked away.

"Exactly how was that different?" I scoffed. "Because it was you? Because it was Bash? If any other crewmember had stepped in for Chandler, you would have been proud, and you sure as hell wouldn't have ratted out crew business to his wife."

"Any other crew member doesn't come home to Harper!" He jerked his head toward the tray and started scrubbing with a vengeance. "Look, you asked me to be cool with whatever is going on with you two, and I'm trying."

"Good, because you don't get a say." I shrugged.

He blatantly ignored me. "But from the moment you started up with my sister, you gave up being just any other crew member, Knox. You're right. If I'd been there, I would have done the same damn thing. I would have shoved Chandler out of the way and let the consequences fall where they may. But I don't have someone waiting for me to come home. You do."

"Jesus, man, she'd be devastated if something happened to you," I argued.

"It's not the same and you know it. We both know she's in love with you. I did everything in my power to keep her heart safe, but"—he gestured to the room around us—"here we are. It's always been my job to protect her, and now that means I need to protect you too."

"Ry, if I start acting like someone else, start hesitating in a fire, I'll be way more dangerous to myself and everyone around me." Out there, I couldn't afford to think about her when shit went wrong, couldn't afford the seconds that could be lost over indecision.

"Yeah," he whispered, his shoulders falling. "I know that too. Doesn't mean it's not frustrating as hell to watch."

We finished the dishes in relative quiet, and the tension between us seemed to wash itself away, sliding down the drain with the remains of dinner.

He was scared for his sister.

I understood.

That was as close to a détente as we were going to get.

After pie, Ryker said his goodbyes and headed back to his place. Harper and I got the boys ready for bed in what had become our usual routine.

I leaned on the doorframe, listening to her read to Liam and let myself fall into the moment, into the possibility this could be our forever. Elliot needed an answer tomorrow, but I was so wrapped up in the present that I couldn't imagine any other tomorrow besides the one right in front of me.

I loved Harper, but that didn't mean we'd make it, which was why I'd kept that to myself. I loved the boys, but that didn't mean I was the right guy to raise them. And telling Harper either of those feelings right now would only unfairly influence what she chose tonight.

Once the lights were out, Harper and I headed downstairs to the office, ignoring the piles of discarded toys in the living room and forsaking the nightly cleanup we tried to keep on top of.

She tucked her hair behind her ears and shifted her weight nervously on bare feet as I pulled out two of everything—pens, sheets of paper, and envelopes. My heart launched into my throat as I pushed one set across the desk.

"I can't believe we're even thinking about doing this," she whispered, picking up the pen and paper.

"It's a little..." There was no right word for whatever this was.

"Sudden? Soon? Rushed? Completely insane?" She stared at me with wide eyes.

"I was going to say 'intense,' but I guess any of those work too." My throat went tight. Was she going to back out? I couldn't blame her.

"I mean, we've only been together for what? A couple months?" She bit her lower lip, panic creeping into her eyes.

"Almost three. Depends on how you count. I mean, are we

going by when I got home? Or when we got married? Or when we kissed in the truck?" I rubbed my hand across the back of my neck. "I've known you your whole life, so it's not like we're strangers."

"We're not exactly…stable." She looked at the pen in her hand like it was going to turn into a snake at any second and bite her.

"Who is?" I countered.

She arched a brow at me. "Anyone who got married because they love each other, for a start."

I shrugged. "It's never bothered me to go against societal norms." *And I love you.*

"If we do this, we're promising these kids that we'll stick together, no matter what."

"You're not getting an argument out of me." I shook my head. "Nothing about this is normal. They should have been put with experienced foster parents. They should have been put in a home where the parents know what the hell they're doing and don't have to google every baby question. They should have been with a perfect, committed couple who are ready to take on the day-in, day-out challenges of bringing up kids, and let's face it, we're…"

"A hot mess?" she supplied.

There was no arguing that point, so I nodded. "We're…what they ended up with because they got caught in a perfect storm." Agreeing to adopt them would be illogical and more than a little selfish. It would also be a gamble emotionally for us, planning our future around something we had no control over.

She took a deep breath and nodded. "You're right." Her smile was shaky as she put the paper on the desk. "You ready?"

Hell no, I wasn't ready, but I knew what I was going to write. "Let's do this."

We turned away from each other, each writing our answers

on the opposite corners of the desk before folding our papers and putting them in the envelopes.

I walked around to stand next to her, envelope in hand, and gently kissed her forehead. What was on these papers could change everything in a heartbeat. She leaned into me, her empty hand fisting in my shirt as we took a moment to simply breathe.

"Ready?" I asked.

She nodded, and we switched envelopes. "We could have just folded the papers," she muttered. "The envelopes are a little dramatic."

A smile tugged at my lips, even as my chest tightened like a vise. I flipped open the top of her envelope, and she grabbed ahold of my wrist. "Harper?" The tears in her eyes nearly took me out at the knees.

"Whatever you wrote in here won't change the way I feel about you." She released me with a soft stroke of her thumb over the top of my hand. "No matter what."

"I know." I tried to swallow past the boulder in my throat and failed. "That's why I wrote what I did."

Eyes locked, we both fumbled with our envelopes, only breaking our stare once we had the papers unsheathed.

I read her words.

Then I read them again, my pulse kicking up with every word until it raced.

Slowly, I lowered the paper and found her already looking at me, her lips parted and her eyes wide. "Really?" she whispered.

"Really."

"So, we're doing this?" A slow smile spread across her face, and my heart stopped dead in its tracks. I'd never seen her look more beautiful or been so sure about something in my life.

"We're doing this."

She was in my arms in a heartbeat.

CHAPTER EIGHTEEN

arper

A GROAN TUMBLED PAST MY LIPS AS KNOX SLID DEEPER INSIDE ME, and he covered my mouth with his hand. It had been a few weeks since making our decision, we were officially the pre-adoptive home for the boys, and I was still way more than officially in love with Knox.

"Shhh," he whispered with a grin, never breaking his pace—slow, hard, and deep. Sweat gathered on our skin, and my breaths were sharp and uneven, but his were steady. The man was an absolute machine. "We wouldn't want to wake anyone up."

The cold metal of the dryer bit into the backs of my thighs with every thrust, but I didn't care. It was one of those rare occasions where Liam napped with James on a Saturday, and I was more than happy to take advantage of the situation and Knox.

The best part about the laundry room? The door locked.

Pleasure built and spiraled tight in my stomach as he replaced his hand with his mouth, kissing me deep. I was never going to get my fill of him. I'd had him in my bed—or his—for weeks now, and the need for him never lessened, never got stale. It was simple cause and effect; he walked in the door, and I wanted to climb him like a tree.

"You feel so fucking good," he said against my mouth, pulling my ass closer to the edge of the dryer. Then he hit a different angle and I think I moaned in answer. Words were beyond me. Every roll of his hips felt better than the last. All I wanted was more.

My fingers gripped his hair as my ankles locked at the small of his back. He'd taken my leverage—or I'd given it. Either way, all I could do was hold on as he took me higher and harder.

"Knoxville." I swiveled my hips and nipped at his lower lip.

His eyes flared and his breath caught. "I love the way you say my name." He left one hand on my hip, pulling me into every thrust, and tunneled his fingers through the base of my ponytail with the other.

"Knoxville," I repeated, just pushing him toward the edge of his control.

His chest rumbled and a growling sound passed from his lips to mine as his rhythm faltered and his hips rocked faster.

I loved when he rode this edge between control and chaos, the moment where I knew I drove him just as wild as he did me. I loved it even more when that tether on his control snapped.

Like right now.

Every stroke reverberated through me, sending little jolts of electricity throughout my body. I swore I felt him in my toes.

"Harper." My name came out like a plea as we strained against each other. "I want you with me." He slid his fingers between us and stroked my clit. All conscious thought stopped. There were only his hands, his body, his mouth on mine, and the sweet, tight coil of bliss that rose within me.

Then it broke, the pleasure so sweet I could taste it as it barreled through me in waves, cresting over me as I cried out. Knox's mouth swallowed the sound as he shuddered against me, finding his own release.

We stayed there, locked together as we came down, his forehead resting on mine. Our breathing steadied. My thighs stopped shaking.

He grinned at me as he lifted his head, his gaze running down my body and catching on the pink lace that lay underneath my breasts. "I didn't even get your bra entirely off."

I laughed, my head falling to his shoulder. "You're still wearing your socks."

"Guilty." He slid out of me, gripped my hips, and lifted me off the dryer, setting me down on the pile of clothes we'd rushed to discard moments earlier. Thankfully, he held onto my hips when my knees threatened to buckle. "I was in too much of a hurry to get inside you."

My lips parted, and I tugged his head down for another kiss.

Then my phone rang, the sound muffled from somewhere in the pile of clothes beneath us.

We both dropped to the laundry room floor, fumbling through fabric as the ringtone sounded again. Knox reached under the folding table. "Found it."

I grimaced at the caller ID and immediately wished I had more clothes on as I swiped to answer it. "Hey, Mom."

Shit, where's my underwear?

"Hi, darling! I was just here at the bakery and wanted to see when you were open to schedule a cake testing."

Knox pushed the little lace thong into my hand, and I stood, shimmying quickly into the underwear like my mother could actually see me naked or something.

"Cake tasting?" I echoed as Knox disposed of the condom.

That ass was going to be the death of me.

He caught me staring and leaned in, his lips brushing my temple. "I'll take my time later, I promise. No socks," he whispered.

I covered the mouthpiece of the phone with one hand and pointed to it with the other. My mother would be mortified if she knew what I'd just been doing.

"Yes, Harper. Cake tasting. I swear, you haven't put any thought into this wedding, have you?" Mom asked.

"We're not having a wedding, Mom. We're already married, remember?" I squeezed the phone between my cheek and shoulder as I yanked my shorts up my thighs.

My mother sighed loud enough to be heard in China. "Really, Harper, how many times are we going to go round and round about this? I've already spoken to the club, and they have the third week in September open."

"I don't even know if Knox will be here." I raised my eyebrows at him, looking for a little support. Just because the man was married to me didn't mean he wanted a wedding, as disjointed as that sounded in my own head. "That's still in the middle of fire season."

Knox had somehow managed to get fully dressed in the time it took me to grab my shirt. There was nothing fair about how fast guys could get their clothes back on. He took the phone and hit the speakerphone button. "What's this I hear about cake?"

"Knox!" I could practically see my mother smile.

"Hey, Mrs. Anders." He put the phone on the very dryer he'd just fucked me on and helped me back into my shirt.

"I was just telling my daughter that we need to get you guys in for a cake tasting. Oh, and she said she wasn't sure you'd be home in September. Would you rather we schedule something for October? Hopefully fire season has died down by then."

I shook my head and begged him with my eyes for a little assistance here.

"We can make October work for the wedding," he said with a smile that lit up his eyes.

"What?" I squawked. Was he really encouraging this behavior?

"October sounds great." He wrapped his arms around my waist and pulled me against him. "Cake sounds great. Whatever Harper wants is great."

My jaw hit the floor.

"Perfect! It's going to be fabulous! I'll make arrangements with the bakery for this week. Wednesday night?"

"Sounds amazing, and if I'm not here, I trust Harper to make the right decision." His smile was positively giddy.

"Mom, I love you, but I have to go." I reached for the phone.

"Love you, bye!"

I ended the call and then stared up at Knox, incredulous. "Stop encouraging her!"

He smacked a kiss on my mouth and then walked out of the laundry room. "Let's have a wedding. What would it hurt? It makes your mom happy, and there's cake. It's a win-win in my book."

I strode after him. "Because a wedding—a big, flashy, poufy-dress wedding, is…" I shook my head, pausing at the threshold of the kitchen.

"It's what?" He turned around and leveled a look on me I couldn't even start to interpret. "It's real?"

"Y-yes!" I stammered.

The man had the audacity to *laugh*. "Mrs. Daniels, I'm not sure how much realer you'd like it to get. We're already married, remember?" He pointed to his ring. "We have two kids upstairs. What else could you want to make it any more *real*?"

I wanted him to love me. I wanted to feel like we'd chosen to spend our lives together instead of fumbling our way through curveballs. My mouth snapped shut because that was the last thing I was going to say. But maybe having a wedding—a real one, with all of our friends and family—would mean that it wasn't all about the boys. It would mean he really wanted me for me.

He cocked his head to the side as if listening for something, then held up his finger. "Scratch that. We have one kid upstairs and one kid on his way down." He was already headed for the stairs when he glanced back. "I like chocolate, by the way."

"We are so not done with this conversation," I called after him.

"Vanilla is fine too," he replied as he turned the corner.

I rolled my eyes. This was so *not* about the cake.

"Here you go," I said to Liam, handing him another slice of pizza.

"Thanks!" He took the pepperoni and ran off to join the other kids in the yard. The sprinkler was on full blast, and the McCoy kids, Noah and Gavin, were already soaked from running through a billion times.

"Thank you so much for having us over." Jessica McCoy watched the boys with a wistful sigh. "They were going stir crazy."

"No problem." I settled back into the lawn chair next to Emerson and Avery. I'd spent the morning ordering serviceable, new furniture for my apartment since most of it had been ruined in the flood. Turning it into a cozy Airbnb kept me a little distracted from Knox's absence, but not completely.

"I'm going stir crazy, and I'm an adult with a full-time job," Avery remarked, adjusting her hat. "And it's only been a week."

A collective sigh went up.

Fires in the heat of late July were never easy, and this one proved to be no different. The guys had been in California, on the same fire, without cell service for long enough to make even the most experienced spouse a little antsy.

"Have you heard from them?" Jessica asked Emerson.

"Spencer checks in from the sat phone every night, but that's it." Her nose wrinkled. "Not going to lie, every time that phone rings, I hope he's going to let Bash update me, but there are zero perks of being the manager here. Whiny, I know." She shrugged.

I glanced at the baby monitor. James was still asleep, but I had a spot all ready for him in the shade if he ever decided to wake up and join us. He must have been going through a growth spurt, because the kid was down for his second nap of the day.

"I get it. I'd kill to hear from River." Avery sent Em a sad smile.

"Containment?" I asked.

"Fifteen percent," Jessica answered. "It's eating up acres like they're matchsticks."

Liam waved, having scarfed down his pizza, and I waved back, assuring him I was watching as he raced through the sprinkler.

"I've never seen him smile so much. He's like a whole different kid," Em remarked, watching Liam. "You've done an amazing job, Harper."

A smile tugged at my lips. "He's amazing. I just get to help him along."

"He really is thriving," Em noted. "So is James. Are we still on for the fourteenth?"

"We are." I nodded. "Seems kind of silly to throw a first birthday party, I know. It's not like he'll remember it, but it's really more for the pictures and cake anyway."

Cake. As if Knox had been clairvoyant, he'd missed our cake-tasting appointment last week. Emerson had gone with me, and I'd chosen chocolate after taking a long look at their refund policy for the deposit.

"It will be fun to celebrate!" Avery said. "Besides, maybe the guys will actually be here."

We all laughed at that.

My eyes drifted to my cell phone, just like they did every few minutes, hoping to see a text or a call from Knox. I knew better, and he'd call when he could, but I couldn't seem to stop looking. It was a sick little addiction that gave me zero payoff.

"Mom! Come run!" Gavin shouted from the sprinkler.

Jessica tilted her head to the side and then stood, kicking off her shoes. "You know what? I think I will." She took off, fully clothed.

"That looks like an excellent idea," Avery agreed, bouncing out of her seat and running for the sprinkler.

"Spill it," Emerson demanded once they were out of earshot.

"I have no idea what you're talking about," I blatantly lied.

"I get it, we have a lot to whine about with the guys gone, but there's something...off about you." She gestured at my face. "What's bugging you? Is it something to do with the boys?"

"No." I shook my head. "They're fine. Everything is fine."

Her eyes narrowed. "Are you regretting the chocolate cake choice?"

"Regretting the cake," I muttered, then flinched. Someday I would learn how to keep my mouth shut around my best friend. Today was not that day.

"Girl." She peered over her sunglasses at me. "You're marrying Knox. *The* Knox. The guy you've been in love with since you were a kid! And not just once, but *twice*."

"The guy I've loved," I repeated. "But I can't help but feel like Knox got swept up on this high-powered train and never got a chance to throw the brakes. Or maybe he had the chance, but he was scared it would hurt the boys."

She scoffed. "Trust me, that man wants to marry you...again. I've never known Knox to do a single thing he didn't want to. Besides, he is head over heels in love with you."

"That is"—I shook my head—"not true."

Emerson's face fell and sympathy filled her eyes. "You don't mean that. You know he loves you."

"He's never once said it." God, how desperate was I? The guy had given me his house, his name—which I hadn't even taken—and everything I'd asked for, and here I was, whining about some words.

"I'm pretty sure he's never said those words to *anyone*," Emerson said softly. "Except maybe his grams. But I've seen the way he looks at you, and I've heard the way he talks about you at the clubhouse. The man loves you."

I swallowed back the knot in my throat and forced a nod, even as my heart ached. It wasn't like I didn't know about his hang-ups, but knowing and experiencing it were two different things.

"And even if he hasn't said it yet, you guys have all the time in the world. He'll get there." Em reached over and gave my hand a squeeze. "You'll get him there, especially with the dress you bought last week. I'm so glad you went with the strapless one. It looks *fantastic* on you!"

My phone rang and we both jumped.

Knox.

I snatched it off the side table, my shoulders dropping when I saw Elliot's name flash across the screen. I shook my head at Emerson and swiped to answer the call. "Hey, Elliot."

"Hi, Harper!"

"Well, you sound chipper. What has you calling on a Sunday afternoon?" I shifted in my seat, watching Liam leap across the streaming water.

"You're not going to believe it."

"Try me." There was pretty much nothing that surprised me these days, our life was that odd.

"We finally got ahold of Nolan!"

I went numb, and the phone slipped out of my hand.

CHAPTER NINETEEN

K nox

"Babe, can you say that again?" I plugged an ear with my finger and concentrated on the garbled sound of Harper's voice coming through the phone. "I've only got one bar."

We'd been in California over two weeks, sweltering in the now early-August heat, and this was the first location we'd been able to climb up for cell phone service, which meant there were fifteen other loud guys up here, all trying to do the same thing.

I turned south, facing miles of pristine wilderness that had been saved from the fire by a change in weather four days ago. Had to admit, sometimes it was hard to see it as anything but fuel ready to go up at the slightest provocation.

"I said, they found Nolan," she repeated, her voice breaking.

"Nolan." I blinked and wiped the back of my hand across my forehead. Filthy. My hand was filthy, my face was filthy, my clothes were weeks past smelling like anything but smoke. "Is that..." My previously ravenous stomach turned nauseous.

"The boys' father." She came in crackled at the end, but I got the point.

"The boys'...father." *Holy shit.* Wait, what did that mean for the boys? And why the hell was it so hard to breathe? I looked down, half expecting to see my chest cracked open or my guts spilled out all over the ground, but there was nothing but ash since we were standing in the black.

"He's on his way here. At least he was about a week ago," she continued.

"And now?" A week ago? I pivoted, facing the line of flames that continued to march its way down the next ridge toward a line a hotshot crew out of Washington had dug earlier today. Not that it was going to help. I'd seen the weather reports, and I had zero doubt this fire would shift west in the next few hours.

But I wasn't a hotshot anymore, so my opinion on the matter was worth shit.

"I'm not sure if he's here yet." Her voice caught, and I could hear the stutter in her breath, like she was trying to rein in her emotions.

"Harper, baby." Damn it. I wasn't there. I couldn't hold her. Couldn't even talk this out with her considering the lack of service up here.

She sucked in a deep breath. "He's getting an apartment, and once he's settled, Elliot said they'd start everything up on their end to begin visitation since they already have a court date next week. It's so fast...just so fast."

"But, they don't go right back to him, do they?" Were they going to be gone by the time I got home? Sweat dripped off my forehead, stinging my eyes.

"No. I guess because he left them when Lisa was pregnant or something, and now since they're in the system, they have to do their due diligence before..." Her voice drifted off.

The silence was heavy, the weight drowning the perfect, picket-fence future I'd been imagining for our family. *Not your family.* I tugged at my collar, trying to get some air.

Nolan was coming back. He wanted his sons. Of course he wanted them. Any guy in his right mind would want James and Liam. So why hadn't he?

"We're supposed to be happy, right?" I managed to get out.

"Right," she whispered. "We're doing exactly what we said we'd do—keep the boys safe and together until their father was found."

"Then why do I feel..." There were no words for this. It was like someone had clamped a vise around my chest and started the slow turns that pressed the oxygen from my lungs.

"Like throwing something?" Harper offered, her voice rising into a forced laugh. "Because that's how I feel. Like throwing something just to hear it shatter."

"Yeah. Exactly." I squeezed my eyes shut and tried to think of the positives. Kids belonged with their parents. "Is Liam happy?"

"Like a kid before Christmas," she answered, and this time her little chuckle was genuine. "Elliot told them when she visited on Wednesday. He's been asking every morning if today is the day his dad is coming."

"Good. That's good." I forced a smile, forcing the ugly, vicious wave of jealousy to take a back seat to the greater good. I wasn't Liam's dad. Not really. "Did Elliot say what to tell Liam if Nolan doesn't actually show up?"

Harper sucked in a breath.

"Come on, you and I both know that's a possibility." The guy didn't exactly have a great track record.

"I guess we'll just have to cross that bridge when we get there."

"Are you okay?" I asked Harper as Ryker stepped into my field of vision.

"No," she softly admitted. "We told them we're willing to adopt the boys. I love them, Knox. I don't want to lose them. And I know this is for the best, but it feels like gravity just reversed and I'm scrambling, trying to figure out which way is up. But I'm putting on a good show for the boys."

"I'm sure you are, babe." Of course she was. I'd never expect anything less of her. But she was going through this alone—had been going through it for the last week without me.

"Is that my sister?" Ryker asked.

"Yeah."

"Don't worry, Harpy," he shouted into the phone. "I'm keeping your husband's dumb ass alive!" He flashed me a grin.

"I'm fucking fine. Keep yourself alive," I muttered.

Harper laughed, and the sound cut through the confusing, intense emotions that battered me from every side, and gave me a glimpse of sunlight. "Tell him I love him," she ordered.

"She loves you," I told Ryker.

"I'm impossible not to love," he quipped, slapping me on the shoulder. His face fell as he studied mine. "Everything okay?"

"Yeah, I'll fill you in back at camp."

Concern flickered through his eyes, but he nodded and took off down the hillside.

"I hate to even think of asking this," Harper started.

I looked out over the burning forest and the giant plume of smoke that filled the sky with ash and soot, dreading the rest of that question. "I don't know. I wish I did."

"I didn't even get the question out," she teased.

"Babe, you have no idea how many times I've asked when I'm coming home to you. Bash is keeping tabs and taking bets on how long it'll be before Spencer kills me." He'd already threatened to remove my head a few times. Fine, I was whipped. I missed my wife.

She sighed, long and loud. "What's containment at?" Shit, she was breaking up again.

"Thirty-five percent, and you know they're just using us to mop up around here. It's frustrating as hell to watch other crews do the work we're supposed to be doing." Until we were certified, we were on glorified cleanup detail, taking out hot spots one by one.

"I miss you." The longing in her voice sliced through me.

"I miss you too." I glanced around our group and saw that most everyone was wrapping up their calls, which made sense since the sun was setting.

"Stay safe and bring Ryker home alive if you can." I could barely make out her words. They were coming out like machine-gun fire.

"Kiss the boys for me."

"I will," she promised. "I love you—"

The line went dead, and my phone beeped, displaying the dropped call icon.

I love you. The three words I hadn't said to her. They were always there, right on the tip of my tongue, but a strangling, paralyzing fear kept my mouth shut. Those words, more than any other in our entire language, were powerful.

Saying them was tantamount to forking over a piece of yourself into the keeping of someone else...someone who could leave whenever they damn well wanted to. There was no contract there, no promise the receiver of those words wouldn't walk away. Once said, those words were theirs to do whatever they wanted to with.

But you're married, I thought as I hiked back down the hill, slipping on debris in places. Wasn't that supposed to be more sacred than the three words of doom?

Not really, the other half of me argued. We'd found ourselves in a shotgun situation and we'd taken the leap for the sake of the boys, not each other. Maybe that's why I wasn't fighting her mom's October plans. Maybe I wanted Harper in a white dress. Maybe I wanted the flowers, the photographer, the cake. Maybe

I needed them to assure myself I wasn't walking into a relationship just like my parents', doomed to fail.

And now the very reason Harper and I were married was...

I muttered a curse and kicked a burned-out tree limb on the edge of camp as Ryker and Bash came toward me.

"What the fuck happened?" Ryker asked, his brow furrowed. "Is Harper okay?"

"She's fine," I assured him through gritted teeth. "It's all fucking fine."

"Sounds like it," Bash muttered, stripping off his helmet and shaking out his hair.

"It's...the boys."

"Are they okay?" Ryker stepped forward, panic etching the lines of his face. As much as he'd been against Harper and my relationship, the guy was a sucker for the boys.

I told them the news and watched their faces fall.

"What the fuck?" Ryker barked.

"Yeah," I said softly, trying to process it all and failing.

"So, you're telling me the guy walked out on his family," Bash seethed, "didn't even bother coming back when Lisa died, and has *now* decided to show up?"

"Pretty much." I managed to nod.

"Can you tell him to fuck off?" Ryker snapped. "Where the hell has he been for the last four months while you and Harper have been raising them?"

"I don't think that's an option." Happy. I was supposed to be happy. Our job was to reunify families, right? So why the hell did I want to rip every tree in this forest to shreds? Why was I so pissed off at a guy I barely even knew? Rage and sorrow flooded my system, along with the one emotion I fucking hated —impotence. The bullshit about all these emotions was that I couldn't do *anything*. "It's not my right to question where he's been or what he was thinking. I don't get to determine if he's legit or if he's going to take off running after a week. None of it is in our hands. And I'm not even there." My posture deflated. "She's dealing with this all on her own."

Ryker's weight shifted, the ground crunching beneath him, but he stayed silent.

Bash glanced between the two of us and put his hand on my shoulder. "Harper's strong."

"She shouldn't have to be." I shook my head and looked over at Ryker. "I'm sorry."

He sighed. "This is not your fault, man. Harper knew what she was signing up for when she took the boys that first night—"

"Well, if it isn't Legacy."

All three of us turned to see Cameron Patel, the supe for the Washington crew, striding our way, four of his buddies behind him, all just as soot-stained as we were.

"Shit," Ryker muttered, moving forward so the three of us stood in a line.

Bash shifted his shoulders back, tucking his helmet under one arm.

"If it isn't the Pratt River crew," I said, without bothering to force a smile. Cameron was an egotistical asshole and had been since we'd served on the same crew six years ago.

"You guys seriously doing this?" Cameron asked, gesturing to the camp just behind us, where our vehicles and the rest of the Legacy crew was throwing together some dinner.

"Looks like it." My chin rose slightly. "You guys still making shitty calls and cutting lines that won't mean shit in the morning?"

"For fuck's sake," Bash muttered, low enough so Cameron couldn't hear him. "Don't pick a fight."

Cameron doled out a shit-eating grin. "You have something to say about our line?" The other guys on his crew stepped forward.

"It's pretty to look at." Ryker shrugged. "But Knox is saying what we both know. She's shifting west, not northeast."

At least I wasn't the only one who thought so.

Cameron's smile fell. "Well, why don't you leave that judgment up to the men with the hotshot patches, and you kids keep mopping shit up like the good little crew you are."

The guys at his side scoffed in assent.

"We'll see how it stands in the morning." Ryker folded his arms across his chest.

"Shocked you'd take his side, Anders." Cameron motioned toward me. "Seeing as he's almost gotten both of us killed plenty of times. You sure you want to sign up with him?"

Fine. That was true. But it had been *years*.

"Didn't you hear?" Ryker slung his arm over my shoulders. "He's my brother-in-law. I'll take my chances with him."

The sound of approaching footsteps behind us registered, but I didn't take my eyes off Cameron. He'd never been one to pull a punch.

"You guys are fools." Cameron shook his head. "Resurrecting a dead crew is a bullshit call. Your dads died as heroes. They deserve to retire that patch, and trying to put it on is bad luck. It's not yours. It was never yours."

"Don't ever tell me what my father deserved." My fists clenched, but I left them loose at my sides.

I felt a hand on my shoulder a second before Spencer stepped past me, positioning himself between us.

Cameron's eyes flared.

"Let's get one thing clear before September. Just because something's never been done doesn't make it bad luck. It's *my* fucking patch." His voice was low, barely over a whisper, but it carried. "*My* fucking crew." He took one step forward. "And they were *my* fucking friends. You don't get to decide how we honor them."

The muscle in Cameron's jaw ticked, but he took a step backward. "I meant no offense, Cohen."

"Yeah, well, I damn well took it as one." He turned around, then paused, pivoting back slightly. "And the line you cut today *is* shit. Twenty bucks says the fire shifts west tonight."

Cameron's eyes narrowed.

"Don't worry, you can pay up when we see you in September." Spencer gave him a single nod and then turned back toward us, leveling a stare on me as the Pratt River crew walked away. "Are you hellbent on fucking us over, Daniels?" he asked quietly. "Because pissing off Cameron Patel is the first way to do it."

"He's an asshole." And why the hell would we be seeing him in September?

"He is." Spencer grimaced. "But that asshole is on the certification team."

I winced.

"Yeah, it's like that." Spencer gave my shoulder a hit as he walked by, headed back toward camp.

"We'll be fine," Bishop's booming voice sounded from behind us, and we all turned around, finding what looked like the entire Legacy crew standing at our backs. "And the line they cut *is* shit."

At least we all agreed on that.

CHAPTER TWENTY

nox

MY EYES FLEW OPEN AS I STARTLED AWAKE, MY HEART RACING
from the dream Harper's alarm clock had just pulled me out of.
Sweat beaded on my forehead. I could still feel the scalding heat
of the flames, smell my skin as it burned off my bones.

I was home. I'd been home for two days. There was no fire.
Ground. Five senses. Now.

Scent. I took a deep breath, and the subtle scent of Harper's
shampoo filled my lungs. *Sound.* Her muttered curse reached my
ears as she leaned over the wide expanse of empty bed,
fumbling for her phone. *Sight.* Steady morning light filled our
bedroom—there was no flickering of flames, or orange, smoky
nothingness. *Feel.* She rolled back into my arms after shutting
off the alarm, snuggling her curves against me and settling right
where she belonged—her ass pressed into my dick and the

smooth skin of her back against my naked chest. *Taste.* I dropped a kiss to her shoulder. All fresh skin and Harper.

I would endure a thousand dreams like that one if it meant waking up with her in my arms.

"You okay?" she asked, her voice groggy as she rolled to her back.

"How are you so beautiful in the morning?" Her skin was flushed from sleeping, a line creasing her cheek from her pillow, and I fell right into those turquoise eyes. How had I lived without her for so long? I'd pretty much wasted the last seven years fighting what was between us.

"Hmm." She smiled, but her eyebrow quirked upward. "Sweet of you to say." Her fingers swept across my forehead. "You're all sticky. You had another nightmare?"

"Just a dream. Nothing to worry about." I propped my head up and leaned on my elbow.

"Seems like a nightmare to me." She cupped the side of my face, her thumb skimming over my cheekbone.

I shrugged. "When they're the status quo, they just become dreams. Nothing special." Nothing a few years of therapy hadn't helped me learn to deal with. That was the thing about a publicized, mass casualty event. The therapists came running. Sometimes I wondered what happened to the kids who suffered alone, whose personal tragedy wasn't posted on the front page of every newspaper for public consumption. How did they deal with their dreams?

Harper sighed and lifted her head to kiss me, soft and sweet.

"Keep that up and we're not leaving this bed." I shifted my weight over her, and she parted her thighs, where I settled on instinct. Damn, and she'd fallen asleep naked last night after I'd kept her up for most of it. There was nothing between us but skin.

"That's a scrumptious thought." Her face fell. "But we have to get up. Elliot is going to be here in an hour."

Any and all thoughts of sex deflated like a popped balloon.

It was visit day.

"Right." My jaw locked, and Harper ran her fingers through my hair, her fingernails lightly scraping my scalp in that way that made me want to purr like a cat.

"It will be okay, Knox," she promised, but her smile was fake as hell.

"Yeah." I nodded.

Okay for whom? I asked myself as we went through the motions of the morning. It didn't really matter that I was apprehensive. I was the adult here, and Liam's entire body seemed to hum with a nervous excitement as he devoured his breakfast. Guess he'd be okay, right? But James was double fisting Cheerios without a care in the world because he didn't know what was going on. He'd never even met his father.

Shit, would he be scared? Would he look around for us and feel betrayed when we weren't there?

"You haven't touched your coffee," Harper noted, her hand skimming my lower back as she walked by.

"I'm a little nauseous." I stared at the full mug that sat on the counter between my hands.

"Yeah, me too." She plopped the diaper bag on the granite, stuffing it full of Liam's favorite snacks and three spare bottles. "I keep reminding myself that it's supervised, so it's not like he can just take off with them."

"How long are they going for?" She was sending enough supplies to feed six of them.

"Four hours." She drummed her fingers nervously, then squeezed her hand into a fist. "I just want to make sure they have everything they need. Do you think they need more snacks? What if they get hungry?" Her brow furrowed, her lower lip trembled, and that look in her eyes? It was pure, unadulterated panic.

"The bag looks great." I rubbed my hand over her back.

"It's just four hours," she whispered.

"Just four hours." But would it turn into more?

She glanced over at the clock. It was seven twenty-five. "They should be home before lunch. You'll be here?"

I nodded. "I'll be here."

She nodded and pressed her lips in a firm line, her gaze darting to the edge of the island where both boys were finishing up breakfast. "And then you'll drop Liam at the school and—"

"And take James to Cherry's," I finished for her. "Don't worry. We've got this. You sure you don't need to get to the school?"

She shook her head. "I want to be here, and I don't teach the summer session. Megan does. And Clara opens up the building every day, so they won't miss me for the first hour."

"Do you think we can go to the park?" Liam asked between shovelfuls of cereal. "We used to go to the park when he lived here before. I bet he still knows where it is."

"I'm honestly not sure what you guys will be up to," Harper answered, her tone light but her eyes heavy. "But I bet he's going to be so excited to see you!"

Even the way he chewed was full of nervous energy. "He'll recognize me," he said with authority after swallowing. "I haven't grown too much. And I'll tell him who James is."

Right. Because the guy hadn't bothered to stick around to see his second son born.

I was saved from my assholeish thoughts by the doorbell.

"He's going to love James," Harper promised, her smile faltering for a fraction of a second. She'd been a ball of worry since I'd gotten home, unfocused and hovering over all of us, not that I blamed her.

She was terrified.

I chose anger. It was the safer emotion.

"I'll get it." I pressed a kiss to Harper's temple and strode for the door, opening it like the Grim Reaper was on the other side. "Elliot."

"Hey, Knox." She gave me a professional smile. "Are the boys ready?"

"I have a couple questions." I stood in the doorway, one hand on the door handle.

"Figured you would." She peered around me. "Why don't you step outside?"

"Excellent idea." I stepped out onto the porch and shut the door behind me.

She held a small, spiral notebook in her hand.

"What's that?" I pointed to it.

"It's for visit notes. Nolan or the supervisor will jot down anything significant so there's a clear line of communication." Her assessing gaze swept over me. "You look like crap."

"I look like someone who is wondering why the hell it took Nolan four months to come for his kids." I folded my arms across my chest.

"Three months, three weeks, and—" She sighed. "Fine, four months."

I raised my brows at her with expectation. Maybe I didn't deserve an explanation, but James and Liam did.

"Knox, I can't tell you everything about the parent's private life," her voice softened.

"Then what can you tell me?" I gestured toward the door. "I know those aren't my kids in there, but—"

"But they feel like they are," she finished, sympathy lacing her tone. "And I can't imagine how this must all feel after you guys said you were willing to adopt."

"Shit," I clarified for her. "It feels like shit. Watching Harper go through it? Even more shit. But that's not important." I shoved my hands into the pockets of my work pants. "What those boys feel? That's important, and Liam is in there bouncing off the walls with excitement, which would be a great thing if you could guarantee that this guy isn't about to up and disappear on him again."

"I can't promise that." She shook her head. "But I can tell you his mind changed sometime in the last month. It could have been that his father was lying, and Nolan really was interested in…"

"Parenting?" I filled in the blank.

"Yes. He said he called as soon as he heard Lisa died. He wants to be their father."

"He *is* their father," I snapped. "He was their father from the second Lisa conceived them. Is he going to start acting like it now? And why did it take two weeks for this visit to happen after he called you?"

Her sigh was a sign of slipping patience, but I just didn't care.

"Besides getting on Judge Stone's docket, it took Nolan time to move his things back here, rent a place, and get us out there to make sure that it's safe for kids."

"And it is?" The nausea in my stomach had turned to pure, acidic frustration.

"Knox, do you think I'd be here, ready to take them over there, if it wasn't?" Elliot rubbed the skin between her eyebrows.

"No," I admitted.

"Exactly. Look, the visit is supervised at his place, so nothing bad is going to happen to them."

"Today." I swallowed the knot in my throat. "Nothing bad will happen to them *today*. So, what about after today?" When was the boys' safety net removed?

"We see how this visit goes, finish all the legal checks, and then go back to court. If all goes well, the boys go home."

I pressed my lips together to keep from saying that *this* was their home.

"And we keep them on our radar for about six months,"

Elliot finished. "So if anything suspicious happens, we're on the lookout for it. Knox, he deserves a chance to try."

"Again," I muttered. Because he royally fucked it up the first time.

"Again," she conceded. "Now, let's get the kids loaded up."

I nodded because that was all I could do. Elliot couldn't see the future. She couldn't tell me if Nolan was going to bolt on the boys again.

Harper had the boys pretty much ready to go by the time I'd finished venting my frustrations on poor Elliot.

"...and maybe the ice cream shop," Liam said as he grabbed his Legacy hat, which was just a smaller version of mine.

"Maybe," Harper agreed with a practiced smile and apprehension in her eyes, James on her hip.

She was so damn good at this, at making everything go as smoothly as possible for the kids.

Elliot held out her hand, and Liam took it without question as we walked to her car.

I took James and buckled him into the car seat Elliot brought with her, nodding with approval that it still faced backward.

Holy shit, I'd become the guy who knew babies needed to face backward.

A couple clicks and he was locked in, Liam beside him in a booster.

"He has sippy cups in there too," Harper explained as she handed over the diaper bag. "But he still refuses to drink formula out of anything but a bottle, so I packed those in the side pocket."

"Got it," Elliot said as she put the bag in her passenger seat. "See you guys around twelve fifteen."

Harper wrung her hands, and I moved to her side, tucking her under my arm as Elliot pulled out of the driveway with the boys.

The second they were out of sight, her composure slipped, and she sagged against me.

"It will be okay," I promised, kissing the top of her head.

"I just..." She sucked in a breath. "I just hope he lives up to Liam's expectations."

"That makes two of us."

CHAPTER TWENTY-ONE

arper

"THEY CAN'T SERIOUSLY BE CONSIDERING GIVING THIS GUY custody," Knox seethed as he read over the visit notes, pacing in front of the dining room table where I was sorting out a mountain of custom T-shirts. "He was a half hour late—*again*—which freaked Liam out that he wasn't going to show at all, still doesn't have a crib for James to nap in, let alone *sleep*, and gave him a cup full of milk. No wonder he puked all over everything. The kid is lactose intolerant."

I folded another Legacy Hotshot Crew T-shirt and put it in the right size pile. The bright orange and red phoenix stood out against the black fabric, and there was an exact replica of the patch on the shoulder. "You don't think it's bad luck to have these made three weeks before certification?" I asked.

Denial. That's where I liked to live when it came to the

whole Nolan situation, and he'd only been back in the boys' lives for two weeks.

Knox ceased pacing long enough to look over at me and shook his head. "Nope. Because there's no way we're going to fail certification."

"Hmmm." I kept folding, and he resumed pacing. There was no need to tell him I already knew how worried Emerson was—Knox knew Em and I didn't keep secrets. Taylor Rose had been busting her ass and gotten her mile down to where they needed it but was still struggling with chin-ups, and the certification team was doing a virtual in-brief to exchange records and evaluations next week.

Two weeks after that, the entire crew would be put to the test, and they'd either be certified as a hotshot crew, or I'd be tucking these shirts away into storage.

"He didn't even come to James's birthday party last weekend, and I know you invited him," Knox ranted.

I smiled at the memory of James smooshing his face into his little cake. How was he already one? He'd started walking yesterday morning too. "Even you can admit that he would have felt *really* awkward, considering he didn't know a single person here."

I lifted my brows at Knox and picked up another shirt, cocking my head when I thought I heard movement upstairs. The boys had been down for an hour, but Liam had been getting up more often, his sleep schedule unpredictable since visits had started. When there was only silence, I went back to folding and stacking. I hadn't had a good night's sleep since the call that Nolan was back. Hours would tick by while I laid awake, staring at the ceiling, dreading that the next call would be the one that took the boys, then hating how selfish that sounded in my own head.

My emotions were all over the freaking place.

"He can deal with awkward," Knox argued, tossing the spiral

pad into the diaper bag so we wouldn't forget it for the next visit. "It was James's birthday party."

"He got him a present." I had to defend Nolan. It was the only way I could convince myself the boys would be okay if that's where they ended up.

"You mean that choking hazard of an action figure?" Knox scoffed as he stood beside me, reaching for a shirt to fold.

"So, it was a poor choice of present, but he's...trying." I nearly choked on that last word. Trying to keep a constantly positive outlook on the whole thing was wearing me the hell down, but I had to balance out Knox's pessimism or we'd both be ripping this situation apart, and that was the last thing the boys needed.

It hurt. Everything *hurt*. Thinking of the day I'd wake up and the boys would be gone? Pain. Packing them for every visit while picturing the very real possibility I would eventually do it for a last time? Pain. Imagining Liam's face if Nolan backed out and ran again? Pain. Seeing the conflict in Liam's enormous brown eyes when things weren't as picture perfect as his five-year-old mind imagined they would be? Excruciating pain.

Everything...sucked. It was like living with a vise around my chest. Every time I adapted and got used to breathing with a little less air, it wound tighter, stealing away more of my oxygen.

"And the milk?" Knox challenged.

I grimaced. "That was..." Okay, fine, that had been atrocious, and hadn't exactly given me much faith Nolan would step up and learn about the boys and what they needed.

"Shitty parenting?"

"Unfortunate." I hip-checked him and kept folding. "He said he didn't realize that James is intolerant."

"Trust me, I wrote it down that first day in the notebook, and I guess Sir Pukes-A-Lot had no problem reminding him." He smirked.

"Stop rooting for him to fail." I shot him a look.

"Stop acting like he's the best choice." A twinge of hurt rang through his tone.

I set the shirt down and put my hand on his arm. "If it was a choice—some kind of battle between us and him—then yeah, I would agree. But it's not. And if he fails, then the boys get hurt."

Knox's gaze fell from mine. "We can't even fight for them. We have no legal standing. No right. Nothing."

"And if we could fight, then I would go to war for them," I whispered, that vise in my chest cranking a little tighter. There was nothing I wouldn't do for them, but we were totally and completely powerless, and that was the worst feeling of all. We were bystanders when it came to the future of our family. "But we can't. He's their father. And he's not perfect. Yeah, he ran away, and I can't even begin to sort through the feelings I have about that—the feelings Liam has about that." Anger didn't begin to do the emotion justice, but this was never about justice. "But there's no history of abuse, and I've read the studies, Knox. The trauma kids go through in these kinds of situations is unbelievable." I stroked his arm, and he looked down at me, the same conflict I felt raging in his eyes. "If this was some kind of competition where the better parenting skills won out, then I think we'd smoke him."

"We'd blast him away," Knox muttered.

Hell yes, we would. The thought was immediately followed by a wave of guilt.

"But the losers in that kind of scenario are Liam and James. Long term, what's best for them is Nolan stepping up, no matter how much it hurts for us to think of them leaving." I couldn't even picture it. The boys had become such a fixture in our lives the last four and a half months that I couldn't picture a future where they weren't here. My throat went tight, and I forced a deep breath through my lungs.

As if sensing how close I was to the breaking point, Knox

turned his attention back to the shirts. "You know what the rules are with these, right?" he teased.

My brow puckered. "The rules about T-shirts?"

"Yep." He picked up an extra-large and held it against his chest. "You only get to wear them if you're a hotshot."

"Oh really?" I cocked my eyebrow, looking over the dozens of them that littered the table. This was the last time I agreed to help Emerson with anything like this. *Liar.*

"There's one other exception." He gave me a heated look that made my breath catch and my knees wobble. Then he put the T-shirt across my chest. The fabric hit me mid-thigh.

"And what's that?"

He gripped my hips and tugged me against him. "If you belong to a hotshot."

I wound my arms around his neck, the shirt pressed between us. "Are you saying I belong to you?"

"Absolutely, Mrs. Daniels." He nodded, biting his lower lip as his hands slid to my ass. "But I belong to you too. So it's even."

My heart somersaulted as he lowered his head and kissed me. My lips parted and he deepened the kiss, his tongue stroking against mine, lighting up every nerve ending in my body.

Mrs. Daniels. I wasn't yet, not really, but Mom had forged ahead with her plans, and everything was set for the third week in October. All it would take was a simple form, and maybe I really would be Mrs. Daniels.

"I bought a white dress," I said against Knox's mouth.

I felt his smile. "Did you now?"

"It's at my mom's house."

"I put the deposit on the caterer you like," he admitted.

Now we were both smiling like fools.

The sound of little footsteps had us breaking apart, and Liam popped into view.

"I'm thirsty."

"I can help you," I said, already moving toward the kitchen.

"Sometimes I wonder how people have more than one kid," Knox teased, continuing to fold shirts.

I turned and walked backward for a second. "Laundry rooms."

"So soon?" I asked Elliot, balancing the phone between my ear and shoulder. My hands paused over the keyboard, where I'd been typing the newsletter I sent out every month to the parents of my preschool kids.

"Judge Stone has an opening and we took it," she answered.

"Three days," I repeated her timeline and looked at the calendar on my office wall, my vision blurring. My stomach fell to the floor and my heartbeat stuttered as the pressure in my chest imploded. Three days? I wanted to throw the boys in the car and drive as fast and as far as my car would carry us. I wanted to yell at Elliot that they hadn't vetted Nolan well enough to be certain he wouldn't abandon them again. I wanted to scream that biology didn't matter, not when I loved them so much they'd become a part of me. I wanted to keep my boys.

Bu they weren't *mine*. Not in the only way that mattered.

The edges of my vision went dark.

You have to breathe.

How was I supposed to breathe without air?

"Three days," she repeated. "September first. And this is the hearing where we'll want you to be there. Are you free that day?"

September first. The date was just shy of having the boys five months. Almost half a year.

"Harper?" Elliot asked.

I blinked rapidly and sucked in a breath, getting control of myself. "I can be there, but Knox is gone. The crew left two days ago for that fire on the front range."

"Oh." There was a pause. "That's okay, we only need one of you there, and we have you down as their primary foster parent anyway."

"From that first interview," I said slowly. God, it seemed so long ago.

"Right. So, September first, ten thirty a.m. sound okay?"

No, it wasn't okay. None of it was okay.

I switched my grip on the phone as I stared at the framed picture of the boys and Knox on my desk. That was supposed to be our family, but in three days, what if it wasn't anymore? How were any of us supposed to function? "Elliot…"

"Yeah?" Her tone quieted.

"Is he ready for this? Nolan?" I leaned back in my chair. "Because there's a little boy across the hall in class right now who really needs him to be."

There was a pause, so at least I knew she was thinking about my question.

"I'm not sure any parent is ever *ready*," she said. "But he bought a playpen for James. The apartment is safe. He's employed and there's food in the kitchen. There's no reason to keep them separated if we don't have to."

"Right. Of course." I cleared my throat. "And the boys' guardian ad litem agrees?" This felt wrong on so many levels, but maybe it was just because I loved them so much.

"She thinks that stability is what's best for the boys, and Nolan's shown every intent on staying here and providing that stability. They weren't placed in care because of Nolan's actions, Harper, but because Lisa died and he couldn't be found."

"But he said he didn't want them," I whispered, finally giving a voice to the thoughts in my head. "Who in their right mind would ever say they didn't want their children?" And how the hell was that person *ever* worthy of getting their children back?

It was so unfair to them, asking them to risk their hearts, their trust, for someone who had already proven themselves unworthy.

Another heartbeat passed.

"That's what Nolan's father said," Elliot said softly. "Legally, I have to go by what Nolan said, and his first communication with us was at the end of July, saying he'd learned of Lisa's passing and was coming to get his kids."

"Right." I nodded, as if she could see me or something. "It just feels so...sudden."

"I know. And I'm so sorry, Harper. I know how attached you and Knox are, and how attached the boys are to you. But it's been a month since Judge Stone ordered visitation, and it's gone as smoothly as we could ask for. It's time."

"Three days," I barely recognized my own voice.

"Three days," she repeated.

"You're not going to make Liam choose, are you?" My grip tightened on the phone as panic crept into my throat. "You're not going to put him in that position in court?" He'd asked me after last night's meeting with his guardian ad litem if his dad being back meant choosing, and it had just about broken my heart. That was way too much pressure to put on a kid.

"Absolutely not. Faith got all the info she needed without putting that kind of verbiage on it."

"Good. I just don't want him to feel torn."

We hung up and I sat at my desk, listening to the seconds tick by as the tiny hand of the clock made its rotation.

How fast would three days fly by? God, if I even blinked, it would already be the first.

My fingers trembled as I opened the phone and dialed Knox. As usual, they were in the middle of the land of no service, but I could at least leave him a voicemail and try to get a message to him through Emerson.

"This is Knox. Leave a message."

So quick and to the point like always.

"Hey, it's me." My throat went tight and my voice cracked. "I know you don't have any service, and I know how bad it is out there right now. But Elliot just called, and they moved the boys' court date up a week, so it's on the first at ten thirty, and they're going to petition for the boys to be sent back to Nolan." I couldn't make myself say home, not when I equated that with our house. "I know that fire is still at zero containment, and I even know there's little to no chance of them sending you home, but I just wanted you to know. I love you, Knoxville. Stay safe."

Three days.

CHAPTER TWENTY-TWO

arper

"HEY, IT'S ME AGAIN. I DON'T EVEN KNOW WHY I'M LEAVING YOU messages like this since I know you aren't in service. Guess I just miss talking to you. Do you realize that we've had James forty percent of his life? I was doing the math earlier because... Well, I guess it doesn't really matter why. They had another visit today, and Nolan was late again, but Elliot said it had something to do with his job.

"Liam came home crying, mad at his father because he couldn't get James to stop crying. Then Liam got mad at me because James quit crying when they got home, and it took about twenty minutes to even get that out of him. Such big emotions in such little bodies, you know? Anyway, I was thinking that if Richard—Judge Stone, whatever—orders them to go back to Nolan's that maybe we should send James's crib. He only has a playpen and, honestly, I'm not sure I could bare looking at those teeth marks he put in it without crying if he's not here, you know? I better go before the voicemail cuts me off. I love you. Stay safe."

CHAPTER TWENTY-THREE

arper

"HEY, IT'S ME. EMERSON SAID SHE GOT A MESSAGE THROUGH TO Spencer, but that part of the certification team is out there with you, so they can't send you home since you're a squad leader. I get it. I just wish you were here. Court is tomorrow, and I don't even know how to feel. That night when I said I'd take the boys, I never saw this coming, Knox. I never saw any of it coming. Not you. Not us. Not the way I feel about them. This is *hard*. I love you so much, and I just wish you could hug me. I saw that the fire is at eighteen percent containment and that's great. Please stay safe, Knoxville. I love you."

CHAPTER TWENTY-FOUR

arper

I STOOD OUTSIDE THE COURTHOUSE, GATHERED MY HAIR IN ONE hand so the wind stopped blowing it all over the place, and tried Knox one last time.

It went to voicemail.

"Hey, it's me. I'm headed into court. I'll let you know what happens when we get out. I love you." I hung up and took a deep breath. Then I walked in.

How different this place looked from the last time I'd been here, or maybe that was because I'd been marrying Knox. Now it felt…efficient. Cold.

Elliot saw me and waved, walking over with a kind smile. "Good morning."

"Hey." I gripped my phone so tight I thought it might bend.

"So, we're up next. Just wait right here"—she motioned to a

set of serviceable wooden benches—"and I'll grab you when it's time."

I nodded, taking a seat.

The wide hallways were mostly empty, which wasn't uncommon given how small our town was.

A flash of pink caught my eye as Knox's grams walked in, dressed in simple slacks and a cardigan. My mouth dropped slightly. I'd never seen her in anything that wasn't her diner shirt or just plain outlandish.

"You didn't think I'd let you sit through this alone, did you?" she asked, plopping down on the seat beside me and shifting her electric-green purse to her lap.

"Thank you." I drew in a shaky breath.

"Knox loves those boys." She shoulder-bumped me, reminding me of her grandson. "He loves you too."

I didn't bother to correct her.

"I bet he's spitting nails at Spencer for not letting him off the fire," she continued.

"How did you know?"

She waved me off. "Emerson told her mom, and Marla came into the diner this morning. That's how I knew you were here to begin with." She leveled a stare at me. "You should have called me, Harper."

"I didn't want to worry you. Lame excuse, I know." Plus, the more people I told, the more real it made this all feel.

"I always worry. That's my job title."

My phone buzzed, the notification startling me.

Knox: Just got back into service.

Knox: I'll be a few hours late, but I'm on my way.

My shoulders felt like ten thousand pounds had been lifted off them. I could get through whatever the next hour brought me as long as he was coming home.

Harper: Thank God. Can't wait to see you.

KNOX: CATCHING A FLIGHT TO GUNNISON. I'LL TEXT WHEN WE LAND.

"Harper?" Elliot came over. "It's time to go in."

"Of course." I stood, smoothing out the lines of my skirt in nervous habit.

"Oh, you're going to want to turn that off before we get in there. Judge Stone is a real ass when it comes to phones, remember." Elliot motioned to my phone.

"He's an ass about a lot of things," Grams remarked. "And I'm coming with her."

I typed out a quick text to Knox.

HARPER: HEADED INTO COURT. I LOVE YOU.

Then I switched my phone off and stuffed it into my purse. My lips turned up at the edges when I spotted Liam's favorite Hot Wheel. It was the fire truck, of course, and I'd had to confiscate it right before he walked into school this morning.

"Ready?" Grams asked.

"Nope," I replied with a smile and shake of my head. "But we're going to do it anyway."

Elliot walked us in and sat us in the row of seats behind the DSS lawyer for the county, Evan Baxter. Elliot took the seat beside him, and Faith, the boys' guardian ad litem, took the table behind theirs.

The proceedings began in a blur. My attention was solely focused on Nolan Clark.

He had a medium build, and his dark hair curled a little at the ends, just like Liam's. They had the same nose too, and maybe the same line of their chin, but I could only see his profile from this angle. It had been years since we'd crossed paths, and the gangly frame I remembered had filled out some. He looked healthy. That was a good sign, right?

Richard said something from the bench, and Nolan stood, leaving his chair out as he made his way to the stand. He was sworn in and took his seat, stating his name when asked to do so.

"And just for record, can you identify the minor children we're about to discuss by their names and birthdates?" Evan asked.

Nolan leaned into the microphone. "Yes. Liam Nolan Clark's birthday is January sixteenth, and James…Theo…Clark…" His forehead furrowed. "I think James's birthday is the first of August?"

My heart plummeted, and I must have made a face, because Grams's hand was quickly on mine, squeezing in support.

That wasn't James's birthday.

Evan tilted his head but didn't correct Nolan. "Can you tell us what you've done in preparation to take full custody of your sons?"

How the actual hell did he not know James's birthday? Anger and disbelief warred for control of my emotions.

"Sure." He shifted in his seat and tugged at the collar of his plaid button-down. "I've leased an apartment for three years, since I figured that keeping the boys in their usual surroundings was good for them."

There was a nod of assent from the tables in front of us.

"I've got a job on one of Ryan Coulter's construction crews. Pays good money, and he said he'd work with me on hours if I need to pick up the kids or anything." His gaze flicked toward mine and dropped away quickly.

How could two people love the same kids with such ferocity and still be complete strangers?

"I've got the apartment set up, and I know the boys' schedules."

But he didn't even know James's birthday. Knox would be furious.

Why are you so hung up on that?

"So you feel as though you're fully prepared and committed to the care of both the minor children?" Evan asked.

"I do." Nolan nodded his head enthusiastically.

"And what kept you from coming right after the death of the children's biological mother?"

My question exactly.

Nolan swallowed and glanced nervously at Richard, then me. "I..." He cleared his throat and tried again. "I left Lisa—their mother—in a bind. I know that. I'm not proud of it either. And when I found out she'd died..." He shook his head. "I guess I didn't know if I could be what the boys needed, you know? There was a part of me that thought maybe they were better off where they were."

Grams squeezed my hand, and I realized I was white-knuckling hers and eased up a little.

I was ashamed to admit it, but part of *me* thought the boys were better off where they were too. Maybe not at first, but after five months? They were adjusted. They were loved. They were stable. They were happy—

They aren't yours.

"But I realized that they needed me. I'm their father. I didn't want them thinking that something was wrong with them, or that I didn't want them. That screws a kid up. And it's not like I haven't screwed up a lot in my life, because I have, but I don't want to mess *them* up. Lisa's gone, so I'm all they have. And I'm not perfect, but I won't let them down. Not again." He raised his chin, and I saw it then—a steely determination in his posture, his eyes, that gave me a shred of hope that maybe he would do his best by them.

He answered a few more procedural questions from both Evan and his own lawyer, then stepped down and took his seat.

"Harper?" Evan said gently, motioning toward the stand. "Do you mind answering a few questions for us?"

"Sure." My knees shook a little as I stood. I followed his lead, walking between the rows of tables toward the stand. *Don't trip. Don't trip. Don't trip.*

Tommy Schreiner swore me in, and I stepped up onto the little, railed dais and sat, smoothing out my skirt.

Richard offered me a polite but tense smile. *Think of him as the judge, not your ex.*

"Can you state your full name for the record?" Evan asked.

"Harper Evelyn Anders." The amplified sound of my voice through the speakers threw me off for a second.

Evan's eyebrows shot up. "I'm sorry, I thought it was Daniels?"

My stomach hit the floor. Then the basement. Then the center of the earth itself. My gaze flew to Grams, whose eyes had widened, but she gave me an encouraging smile. I licked my suddenly dry lips. Was there actual cotton in my mouth, or was I about to have a nervous breakdown?

"I'm married to Knox Daniels, but I kept my name," I finally managed to say. Out of reflex, I looked up at Richard, who quickly masked his look of surprise. "It's kind of antiquated to assume a woman would take her husband's name, don't you think?"

"Right. Yes. Of course." Evan blinked. "Okay, so you and your husband are the registered foster parents for James and Liam Clark?"

"Yes."

"And you're also Liam's preschool teacher?" Evan must have seen the confusion on my face—it's not like he didn't know that already since his daughter had been in my class last year, because he quickly clarified the question. "This is just for the record."

"Yes, I'm Liam's teacher, and as of last year, I also own Little Legacies—the preschool. I've had Liam for two years now, and he'll be moving on to kindergarten this fall." Oh, good God, I was babbling. *Calm down. You're not on trial here.*

"And your husband is unable to join us today?"

I nodded. "Knox is on a fire and couldn't make it back in time." I would have given anything to see his face out there, his brown eyes holding me steady through this.

"And we wish him a safe return." Evan flipped a sheet on his clipboard. "How has Liam handled the transition of his father coming home?"

I glanced at Nolan and momentarily froze. His face was pale and a twinge greenish, and that look in his eyes? The one he directed at me? It was fear. He was just as nervous as I was. Was this the part where I was supposed to find a way to rip him apart? Find something to say that would make Richard think the boys weren't ready to go home yet?

Who would that help? Certainly not the boys.

"It's had both its challenges and its rewards," I answered honestly.

"Can you elaborate?"

"Liam has struggled a little with sleeping since Mr. Clark began visitations, but I think it's more due to feeling unsettled than his father's return." The light caught the diamond on my engagement ring and my chest burned. I wanted Knox to be here with me. He needed to be *here*. "He's always really excited to go to visits."

"And James?"

"James is one," I said with a little shrug. "He gets a little fussy after visits, but I do think that's because they can get scheduled during nap time, and again, being unsettled is a little hard for kids. He's getting to know Mr. Clark, and I think Mr. Clark is getting to know him."

Nolan nodded.

Evan asked another series of questions about the boys' day-to-day life, and then Nolan's attorney stood, buttoning his blazer.

"Mrs. Anders, I can tell how much you care for the boys." His smile was forced, polite.

"Thank you. Both Knox and I care deeply for them." *If we didn't, it wouldn't have hurt this much.*

"In fact, you agreed to be a pre-adoptive home for them, isn't that correct?"

"We did." I flinched. "We are. I mean, yes, when Elliot asked if we would be willing to adopt them, we said yes." *Don't say the wrong thing.*

"So it's fair to say that you only want what's best for them?"

"Absolutely."

"Last question. If you could give Liam and James one thing, what would it be? What are they lacking in their lives right now?"

A billion answers flitted through my brain.

"Right at this very minute," he pressed. "Not thinking of the future, but just today."

"Stability," I answered. "They're missing stability. Liam wants to know where he's putting his head down at night, and more importantly to him—where James is. He wants to know what time dinner will be and what the plan is for tomorrow. He just wants stability." Which he had until Nolan decided to come back. Which he'd only have again if Nolan stuck around or left for good.

They let me step down, and I made it back to my seat next to Grams, my heart thundering.

Faith gave her opinion as the boys' lawyer, seconding my own opinion that they needed stability.

Then Richard's eyes met mine across the courtroom and the breath froze in my lungs. He'd never looked at me that way before, even in all the time we'd dated. He was *sorry.* I knew what his verdict would be.

⁓

Four hours. That's all I'd been given to pack up five months of James's and Liam's life. *Immediate* meant there would be no last bedtime or dinner. No last story or trip to the park.

I'd picked them up early from school and daycare, so at least I had these precious moments as I filled suitcases and duffel bags with clothes and toys.

Liam colored at the kitchen island and James toddled happily in his playpen as I took the sippy cups and bottles from the cupboards and placed them in boxes.

Numb. I was totally and completely numb. It was almost like this was happening to someone else. Like I'd stumbled into someone's story and couldn't quite connect with the character. My hands moved, but I didn't recall directing them to. I was on autopilot. I breathed and my heart beat, but that was only because my body chose survival.

This was shock, right? I was careful not to examine my lack of emotions too closely for fear that one would slip from its cage and devour me whole.

The only sounds came from the few toys I'd left out for James to play with, and Liam's narration of how his day had gone.

I'd turned away Grams's offers to help. Everything about these hours was sacred. Private. I only wanted Knox, and since he hadn't texted, I could only assume he was still in the air.

"And he said we only have to share a room for a little while," Liam said from his stool, his brow furrowed in concentration over his picture. He'd taken the news with the same stoicism he took everything else—too old for his actual age.

"That's awesome," I replied automatically.

"And I told him I like sharing with James. It's okay." He shrugged and kept coloring.

"James is lucky to have you." I took the stack of bibs from the island drawer and packed them.

"So, I guess we live there now?" He stopped coloring and looked at me with solemn brown eyes. "With my dad?"

I'd already told him, and he'd asked at least three additional times. Not that I could blame the kid for feeling like the answer might change.

"You do," I answered, forcing a smile. "And I'll still see you at school—"

"I start kindergarten soon."

"Isn't that going to be fun?" I was absolutely *not* thinking about the fact I'd only have him in class for another few days as I ruffled my hand through his hair and glanced at the clock.

I only had five more minutes? How the hell had five months of our lives come down to five fucking minutes? And where the hell was Knox?

Ice-cold panic squeezed my throat, and I shoved it down, forcing it into the box where all my other inconvenient emotions were stashed.

"And we don't come back here?" Liam asked, eyeing the pile of luggage at the base of the steps.

"Nope." I tried so hard to sound chipper and failed miserably. "But I'll see you bright and early at school tomorrow, and you can tell me all about how your first night went. Okay?"

He seemed to ponder this for a moment before slowly nodding.

The doorbell rang.

I debated not answering it, but I opened the door.

Elliot's face was full of some emotion...maybe sympathy... before she transformed it into a grin as we walked back into the kitchen. "Are you excited to be going home, Liam?"

"Home." He took his time with the word, like he was testing out the taste of it.

"I'll start loading up your stuff. Harper?" Elliot motioned to me, and I followed her to the pile of the boys' belongings. "I figured I'd give you a minute to say your goodbyes."

"How thoughtful."

She drew back slightly. "Harper—"

"Don't," I whispered. "They've never even spent a night under his roof."

"Judge Stone—"

"Yeah. I was there," I interrupted. "But we did the classes. Aren't you supposed to transition them to weekends or overnights?"

"I get that this is difficult for you," she said softly, her eyes full of some soft emotion that turned my stomach sour.

"You have no *idea* what this is for me," I kept my voice low. There were no words for what this was. Hell didn't even begin to touch on it. "You're not even giving Knox a chance to say goodbye."

She blinked. "It's not goodbye, Harper. Not in a town this tiny. You'll see Liam at school tomorrow. And I really wish you could see how well you're doing, how much good you did for these two. Without you, they would have been separated into different homes over the last five months. You kept them together. You're helping put their family back together."

You're ripping us apart. Because at some point it had stopped being about *them*, and they'd simply blended into *us*.

"I really hope you and Knox decide to foster again if the need arises."

My gaze whipped to hers. "I'm sorry?"

"Not for Liam and James. I honestly think they'll be okay, or I wouldn't send them home. I mean, in case another family needs—"

"You should pack them up." I turned away before she could finish and left her to carry their stuff outside. I couldn't see past the next two minutes, and Elliot was already thinking about other kids? I wanted *my* kids, and she was taking them.

Liam stood next to James, patting his brother's head. "He's nervous."

I knew he was nothing of the sort, but I played along. "It's okay to be nervous, especially when there are big changes." The words clogged my throat.

"He's worried he won't see you again." Liam's lower lip quivered.

"He will," I promised him through watery eyes, lifting James out of the playpen and holding him close. He still smelled like the baby shampoo I'd secured in the Ziploc bag so it wouldn't spill on the ride to Nolan's.

"But he's happy too," Liam whispered.

I dropped down so I was at his eye level. "I hope he's super happy. That is all I want for him. For both of you." I wasn't going to survive the next few minutes. It wasn't physically possible to survive the misery that threatened to flood every chamber of my heart. *Hold it together for them.*

Liam's lips pursed and his eyes welled, making my own prickle.

"It's okay to have big emotions, Liam. You can be happy and nervous at the same time. You get to feel however you want. Do you understand?" I brushed a tear off his cheek with my thumb.

"Did we make you mad?" he cried.

"What?" The shock of his words cracked open that little box I'd shoved my emotions into, and I teetered between the calm numbness that had gripped me since court this morning and pure, ugly, raw chaos.

"Is that why we're never coming back here?"

"No." I snatched him forward, yanking him into a hug, holding them both so tight it was a wonder any of us could breathe. "No, Liam. I'm not mad. I'll always be here for you if you need me. You guys are the luckiest little boys because so many people love you. I love you. Knox loves you. Your dad loves you, and he's waiting at his place—at home—to show you just how much. You're not being punished, honey. All of this is a good thing. It's what you wanted, remember? You said your dad would come, and he did. He's waiting for you."

"I didn't choose." He sniffled in my ear. "I promise I didn't choose."

"Oh, honey." I rocked them both, feeling my composure cracking, preparing to break away in an avalanche. "I know, and I'm glad you didn't have to. The best thing about being little is that you don't have to make the big choices, and the worst thing is knowing you don't get to. And I know you won't understand that until you're older, but just know that everyone around you has tried their hardest to make the best choices *for* you."

He pulled back and wiped his nose on the shoulder of his sleeve.

For once, I didn't correct him. That wasn't my job anymore.

"I love you," he said. "That's okay, right?"

"Absolutely." I smiled, even though he wavered in my vision. "You can never have too many people who love you."

He nodded, and I stashed the rest of James's toys into his diaper bag before handing it to Elliot as I walked the boys to the edge of the porch.

"This is as far as I go," I told them, kissing James's forehead. "I love you, little guy. Try not to puke on everyone, okay?" Air ceased to exist as I handed him over to Elliot's waiting arms.

"Let's get you buckled in," she said, walking away.

"I'll take care of James," Liam promised.

I dropped down to his level. "You won't have to." I brushed his hair out of his eyes. "Your dad is going to take care of you both." *Please, Nolan, don't fail them.*

He launched himself into my arms, and I clutched him tight.

"I'm so happy for you, Liam," I choked out.

"I'll see you tomorrow." He let go, and I forced my arms to go limp. "And I left you a picture on the island!" He waved as he raced down the sidewalk toward where Elliot waited.

She buckled Liam in as I watched from the porch, then

headed back up the sidewalk. "I just wanted to thank you again for everything you—"

I put my hand up, palm toward her, stopping her before she got any closer. "Not today." Turning around, I walked into the house and shut the door behind me, listening until she pulled out of the driveway.

Then there was silence.

There was nothing.

No toys. No laughter. No hugs. Not even Knox. I was completely, utterly alone.

I stumbled toward the kitchen. I needed Knox, even if it was just to hear his voice through the phone. He had to have landed by now, right? Why hadn't he called?

Wrenching open my purse, I reached in and—*No.*

My fingers wrapped around Liam's favorite fire truck. I pulled it from my bag and the dam on my emotions burst. Agony sunk its claws into my chest and tore me open.

With the fire truck in hand, I slid down the edge of the cabinet until my butt hit hardwood, and then I heard the sound of a wailing wounded animal fill the room and echo off the walls.

Where was the happiness that they were reunited? Where was the satisfaction that we'd done what we'd set out to do? Why was it buried underneath mountains of immovable pain? It hurt so much I couldn't breathe, couldn't force my lungs to suck the air past my raw, aching throat. I couldn't stop crying, my sobs ripping through me with such force that I shook.

I should have reached for my phone and called Emerson or Avery, but they couldn't help, and they wouldn't understand.

The only person I wanted—the only one who could truly feel this with me—wasn't here.

He was never fucking here.

For the first time in my life, there was a part of me that hated Knox Daniels.

CHAPTER TWENTY-FIVE

K nox

IT WAS JUST AFTER FIVE BY THE TIME I PULLED INTO LEGACY, AND the vehicle the crew had left at the tiny airport in Gunnison was on fumes. Damn it, I was going to have to stop for gas. I'd only bothered showering at the airport because I had time before the flight, and I still smelled like ash and soot—it was permanently branded into my clothes.

Harper wasn't answering her phone. It had gone to voice-mail thirty-seven times, and all Grams would tell me was that I needed to go home, so I'd driven up the pass like a bat out of hell.

I pulled into the gas station on the edge of town and slammed my credit card into the reader like it was the source of all my frustration.

Harper's voicemails had been on repeat for the hour it had taken me to drive, and for the first time since Dad died, I fucking hated fires. I should have been here. Should have been holding her hand walking into that courtroom just like I was the day we walked out of it, married and fighting to keep the boys together.

The boys. Hopefully they'd still be awake by the time I got home.

They'd be at home. They had to be. There was no way Harper would let DSS yank the boys out of our home before they'd even spent the night at Nolan's. I was prepared for visitation to go to weekends, honestly. I just didn't know how many weekends it would take for Nolan to show his true colors and abandon the boys when the novelty of fatherhood wore off.

I jammed the gas nozzle into the tank and started filling. And why the hell was she even thinking of giving James's crib away? If Nolan Clark wanted a crib at his house, he could damn well buy one, just like we had.

"He better have fucking bought one," I muttered, leaning back against the mud-splattered SUV and tapping my foot like I needed to keep rhythm with a marching band on speed.

"Knox?"

I pivoted and saw Richard Stone filling up his Mercedes.

"I thought that was you." He rubbed the back of his neck. "Look, I want you to know that it had nothing to do with her name."

"What the hell are you talking about?" My eyes narrowed.

"Harper. The Clark boys." He raised his eyebrows at me, and I stared right back, putting it together. He would know what had happened because he was *there*. He'd been on the bench. "It wasn't that I didn't think you weren't a stable couple or anything."

"Explain." I pushed off the vehicle.

He looked at me like I was clueless, and at this moment, I couldn't argue with him. "I didn't rule to reunite the Clark family because Harper didn't take your name. It didn't play into my thinking at all, and I didn't want you thinking it was. Or that it was prejudice against Harper—"

"You fucking *what?*" I snapped, lunging toward him only to be stopped by the gas hose.

He put his hands up and retreated two steps, then cocked his head to the side. "Oh shit. You don't know, do you? You haven't talked to Harper?"

"You gave my kids back to *him?*" I was yelling, and I didn't fucking care.

"They weren't your kids, Knox." He shook his head. "And I don't owe you an explanation beyond the one I've already given, but there was no legal reason to keep them separated, and I chose what I thought would be best for the boys' long-term stability."

"You. Gave. Away. My. Kids?" I yanked the nozzle out of the tank and shoved it back into its holster at the pump. It was far less violent than the thoughts I had racing through my head of putting my fist through Richard's face.

I didn't wait for him to answer. Instead, I got behind the wheel, cranked the ignition, and put the car in drive, giving exactly two shits that the tank was barely half full. I didn't even swing by the clubhouse to get my truck. I went straight home.

He had to be fucking with me, right? There was zero chance I was going home to find James and Liam gone. Richard was being true to his dickish nickname and getting in a jab because I'd managed to do the one thing he hadn't—put a ring on Harper's finger.

Harper didn't take your name.

He didn't know what the hell he was talking about.

I broke the speed limit in a few places, but I shaved five minutes off the drive by the time I pulled into the driveway and parked.

I left my line pack in the back seat and got out, punching the garage code into the panel and waiting for the door to rise.

Everything looked the same. Liam's bike was in the corner, and I peered into Harper's car to see two car seats still installed.

Then I barreled through the mudroom door. "Harper!"

She wasn't in the living room or kitchen.

"Harper!" I called out again, striding toward the stairs.

"You're home."

I spun to see her coming out of the laundry room, her head down and a basket full of clothes in her hands. She walked right past me and into the kitchen, setting the basket on the island between us.

"What the hell happened?" I trudged after her. "And why the hell haven't you answered your phone today?" My voice rose.

"Hell is a great word for today." She took out one of my shirts and folded it. "And I didn't answer because you didn't call." There was no anger, no grief, no emotion whatsoever in her tone.

I ripped my phone out of my back pocket and showed her the call log. "I've called you thirty-seven times!"

"Did you?" She looked up at me, and my chest caved in. Her eyes were swollen and red, mascara leaving long black streaks down her cheeks. She moved robotically to her purse and took out her phone. "Huh. Guess I forgot to turn it back on after court." She pressed the side of the device and it lit up, turning on.

"You didn't turn it on." I repeated the phrase just to see if it sounded as ridiculous when I said it. It did.

She turned her head slowly, and there was fire in her eyes. "Sorry, Knox. I was a little busy packing up everything James and Liam own!"

I jerked my eyes from hers and took quick stock of the space. "Where's the high chair? And the playpen?"

"I put them in the basement because I couldn't stand to look at them." She set her phone on the island.

Gravity pitched sideways. Had Richard been telling the truth? "Harper, where are the boys?"

"They're home. At Nolan's."

"You let them take our kids?" I blurted.

She reared back like I'd struck her. "Let them? You think I *let* them?"

"Fuck," I muttered. "That came out wrong." All of this, every part of it was wrong.

"You think?" she fired back.

"They're really gone?" I stared across the kitchen at the empty space at the end of the dining room table where James's high chair was supposed to be. "Just like that?"

"Just like that." She folded another shirt.

"I didn't even get to say goodbye!" I ripped my hands over my hair. "How the fuck is that fair?"

"None of this is fair!" Harper shouted, throwing a pair of my shorts onto the island. "I begged Elliot for more time when we were at the courthouse, but immediate reunification is just that —immediate."

"At least you got to say goodbye to them." Misery and rage colored my vision red. How could they just be...gone?

"Yes, Knox. I'm the one who had to assure Liam that he hadn't done anything wrong, that everyone in this situation loved him. I'm the one who had to pack up every single thing while holding myself together! I'm the one who had to testify, had to look Nolan in the face, had to listen to Richard rule. *Me.* Not you, because you weren't here! You're never here!" She swung her arms out, gesturing to the empty space of the house.

She may as well have gone for the jugular. "Are you telling me that this happened because I wasn't here? That I could have somehow stopped it?" Maybe I could have. Maybe if we'd presented a united front—

"It had nothing to do with us! It never did!" She swiped at

her cheeks, wiping away tears that cut me to the quick. "We were never their parents. They were never ours."

I stepped back. "They asked us if we'd be willing to adopt them, and we said yes! We made plans. We rearranged our entire lives to be their parents. We prioritized them. We love them. We got married for them!"

She flinched. "Yeah." She nodded her head, her face tenser than I'd ever seen it. "And it was a beautiful, chaotic dream, wasn't it? We risked our hearts because that's what they deserved and let ourselves fall in love with them, but the reality is that they were never ours to dream about, and it was never about us. I mean, let's face it. You're right. We did get married for them. Without them, you never would have even looked my direction, let alone let yourself feel something for me. It was all about them."

Wait. It wasn't *all* about them, not for me. Maybe the boys had been the catalyst, but I'd fallen for Harper all on my own.

Harper didn't take your name. Bile rose in my throat.

"I've been calling you Mrs. Daniels since April," I managed to say.

Harper looked away.

"It's true, isn't it?" I scoffed. "You didn't take my name, did you?"

She shook her head.

"Wow." How fucking stupid could I have been to think that Harper Anders, the belle of the Legacy ball, would have wanted my name.

"Knox, it was because—"

"Save it. It's not even that you didn't take it. I'm not that chauvinistic. But to let me believe the lie that you did for all these months? That's low." My heart broke in a whole other way. Losing the boys had fractured it, but never having actually had Harper? The shards crumbled to powder.

"I'm sorry," she whispered, taking a step in my direction. "Look, maybe we both need to take a second and breathe here."

I moved back, keeping space between us, and she halted. "Breathing isn't going to help." This felt like someone had taken an eraser to the chalkboard of my life's plan and wiped it all away with one swipe.

"You're right." Her shoulders squared. "Maybe I should spend the night at my apartment—"

The motor in my brain blew a gasket. "You still have your apartment?" Holy fucking shit, she'd had one foot out the door this entire time?

"Yes," she admitted. "I just thought—"

"Don't." I wasn't sure my heart could take the explanation. She'd always been planning to leave. Guess it was more than one dream ending tonight. "Maybe it's better this way."

"What do you mean?" Her eyes flew wide.

Whatever logic was left in my head screamed at me to stop, to pause, to think, but it was like throwing a bottle of water at a wildfire. If she'd always been planning to go, then I needed to let her leave. "We built everything around Liam and James, and now they're gone. There's nothing left holding us to this—to each other."

Her lips parted.

"We're both free." Without another word, I walked out, leaving her standing in my kitchen.

The engine was still warm when I pulled out of the driveway, my nerves scraped raw and my chest heavy. Where the hell was I going to go? All of my friends were still at the fire, and I wasn't ready to see Grams or hear her account of what happened today.

I went to the only other home I had, parking in the lot of the clubhouse. Everyone's cars were still here, lined up like we'd just dropped them off last week.

Last week everything had been...perfect, and now life was utter shit.

I shouldered my pack and locked the vehicle, heading for my truck. Maybe tomorrow I'd see about getting a flight back out to the crew, but not tonight. The truck beeped as I hit the unlock button, and I threw my pack in the back seat—and froze.

Their car seats were still here, like they were waiting for me to pick up the boys. Another wave of pain...of grief threatened to pull me under.

I needed a drink.

It took exactly nineteen minutes to get to Wicked, Legacy's only bar, and another ninety seconds to park my ass on a stool and lift my hand.

"I wondered when we'd see you around here, Daniels," Bobby Atwell said with a grin, leaning on the other side of the bar. "I was starting to think you'd actually turned over a new suburban husband leaf."

"Ha." I wasn't in the mood for his shit, even if we'd gone to high school together. "Fat Tire, please."

"You got it." He turned and poured it from the tap.

The usual crowd was in for a Thursday night, at least who I remembered the usual crowd to be. Ryan Coulter was even in the corner, sipping on a beer and a blonde that wasn't his wife. I used to frequent Wicked every time I came into town, but I'd lived here five months, and this was the first time I'd stopped in.

I spun the gold ring on my left hand. Suburban husband, indeed.

I was a husband without a wife, and a dad without kids.

At least when my mom had walked out, my dad still had me.

"Thanks," I muttered as Bobby slid the beer in between my hands, then I stared at the bubbles rising to the top, the words Harper and I had thrown at each other echoing around my head like a game of pinball.

You let them take our kids?

You weren't here! You're never here!
You didn't take my name, did you?
I should spend the night at my apartment.
There's nothing left holding us to this—to each other.
The beer grew warm.

My eyes shut as a wave of shame swept over me, overpowering the anger. I'd said some horrible shit. The worst of it was that I wasn't even angry with her. Fine, I was pissed as hell she hadn't just come out and told me she'd kept her name, but the rest of it—that wasn't her fault. She loved Liam and James just as much as I did.

But had they been the only reason she'd loved me? She'd kept her apartment this whole time, like she knew we'd fail. She knew she'd need a backup plan because I'd let her down.

"You're looking pretty lonely," a redhead said from my left, sliding onto the barstool and turning in my direction.

"Looking pretty married." I held up my left hand, showing her my band.

"I won't tell if you don't."

"Seriously?" My eyebrows hit the sky as my head whipped toward her.

She gave me a coy smile and shrugged. "Never hurts to ask."

The guy I'd been six months ago would have taken her up on the blatant offer. But that guy hadn't known Harper's touch—Harper's love. He hadn't known that sex was simply physical gratification, like eating or drinking, without the emotional connection I'd come to crave, come to depend on.

Harper would have lost her absolute shit on this woman if she'd been here.

But she wasn't.

She was at home, alone again.

What the actual fuck was *I* doing here? I didn't need a drink. I needed Harper.

Slipping a twenty from my wallet, I gave Bobby the nod.

"Thanks." Then I set the money on the bar and got the hell out of there.

That fight between Harper and I had been just that—a fight. It was nothing we couldn't fix or talk out. Cooler heads just needed to prevail, and today had been ruled by emotion. At least that's what I told myself as I drove home.

I was already practicing my apology as I pulled into the garage.

My stomach sank. Her car was gone.

"Shit," I muttered to myself as I got out of the truck and walked into the house. She'd probably gone to Emerson's to blow off some steam.

I flicked on the kitchen lights and grabbed an electrolyte drink from the fridge, leaning against the island as I unscrewed the top.

My hands froze and my heart stopped beating.

"No, Harper," I whispered as I stared across the island. I didn't need to check the dresser drawers or the closet to know they'd be empty. Not when Harper had left her rings and her house key on the counter.

She'd left me.

CHAPTER TWENTY-SIX

arper

"And I understand your frustration, Mrs. Daniels—" the caterer said, his voice pinched with annoyance.

"Anders," I corrected him. It was too early on a Tuesday morning for this kind of shit, especially when my Labor Day weekend had been nothing but crying into a vat of ice cream.

"Sorry, Ms. Anders, but since it was Mr. Daniels who put the deposit down, I can't cancel the date without him calling. I'm sure you understand."

"As long as *you* understand that there won't be any wedding, so all you're doing is denying yourself the opportunity to book another client that day." I rubbed the bridge of my nose and leaned my elbows on my desk. This was it, the last call I had to make to cancel the wedding that never should have been.

The first call—the one to my mother—had been brutal, and

the worst part was that she'd remained so Zen about the whole thing. My whole life was disintegrating around me, and she was calm as could be.

She thinks this is just a spat that will blow over.

Maybe once I got this block checked, my own equilibrium would return. After all, it wasn't like I hadn't lived twenty-six years of my life without Knox, right? My gaze flickered to the framed picture of us and the boys on the corner of my desk. I reached out and flipped it facedown.

The problem with having Knox for those five glorious months is I'd seen what my life looked like in radiant color, and now it was back to black and white.

"That may be, but I still need Mr. Daniels to call."

After agreeing to disagree, I hung up with the caterer and let my head fall into my hands. I hadn't even seen Liam yet this morning, and it was already nine fifteen.

"You should have taken today off," Clara lectured from my doorway, sympathy dripping from her eyes. She held a bottle of water in her hands.

"And done what? Stayed home and felt sorry for myself?" At least the apartment was fully furnished, but it still felt empty and wrong, like I'd somehow become an anachronism in my own home.

Because it isn't home anymore.

Clara clicked her tongue. "Fine then. If you insist on being here, then at least hydrate. You look like crap." She set the water on my desk and walked away.

"I own this place, remember?" I called after her.

"That may be, but I'm the one who keeps it running," she retorted, already back at her desk.

I couldn't argue that point, so I cracked open the bottle and drained half of it, soothing my parched, sob-sore throat. Then I took out my iPad and opened the doc we kept for inventory. Fall session was beginning, and the new materials we'd ordered had been delivered, so at least I could make myself useful and inventory everything.

I walked out into the hallway at the same moment Ryker walked in.

"Hey, Harpy."

My posture sagged as relief rushed through me.

His eyes widened slightly before his strides ate up the distance between us, and then I was against his chest, his arms closing around me, his chin resting on the top of my head.

I let loose a little self-deprecating laugh. "I don't look that bad, do I?"

"I'm so sorry." He rocked us slightly, like we were kids again. "About the boys. About Knox. All of it."

My eyes popped open. "How did you know?" I hadn't called him, hadn't wanted to worry or distract him with so much on the line regarding their certification. The scent of ash filled my lungs—he must have come straight from the fire. It was almost funny how I'd once associated that sharp, smoky fragrance with misery, and now it was...home.

"I knew Knox was leaving the site—we split his squad between mine and Bash's, which told me something was up with the boys. By the time we were on the way home, Avery had told River, and Emerson had told Bash, who—"

"Told you," I finished for him.

He nodded, the motion catching the scruff of his beard in my hair. "I wish there was something I could do. Some way I could make it better. I could fucking kill him for this."

"Please don't be mad at Knox," I whispered. "A lot of this is my fault, and I'll never forgive myself if I'm the reason you lose your best friend."

He sighed. "Shit is complicated, Harpy. He's my friend, but you're my sister."

God love him, the words *I told you so* never left his lips.

The door opened behind us, and we broke apart, turning to

see Nolan ushering Liam through the door. They both seemed frazzled, but Nolan looked downright drained.

My gaze swept over Liam, and I took my first full breath since I'd said goodbye to him after class on Friday. His clothes were a little rumpled but clean, but his lips were pursed, his brows drawn tight under his Legacy Wildland Firefighting hat as he focused on where he was walking.

"Hey there," I croaked.

Liam's head snapped up and he smiled, breaking into a run for the fifteen feet that separated us.

I dropped down as low as my skirt would let me and opened my arms, hugging him tight. He smelled like the shampoo I'd sent home with him. "How's your morning?" I asked, making myself let him go.

"I'm late." The frown reappeared as I pulled back, my hands on his shoulders.

"Yep." I grinned with a shrug. "It happens to the best of us."

Liam's attention snapped upward, and his eyes lit up. "Ryker!"

"Hey, little man." Ryker tapped the bill of Liam's hat. "Nice hat."

"Thanks! Knox gave it to me!"

My heart missed a few beats.

"I figured. Looks good on you."

Liam beamed at the compliment.

"Why don't you hang up your stuff?" I suggested. "I bet Miss Megan will be excited that you made it!"

Liam nodded and headed a few feet away to his cubby, wiggling out of his backpack and hanging it on the hook. "I'll see you later, Harper. Bye, Ryker!" He waved at Nolan. "Bye, Dad!"

"Bye!" Nolan's smile came out a little contorted with tension, but he waved as Liam slipped through the door to his classroom.

Nolan looked at me.

I stared at him.

"And this would be my cue to exit this awkward moment and wait in your office." Ryker gave my back a pat and left me standing in the empty hallway with Liam's dad.

"Hi." Nolan rubbed the back of his neck and sucked in a breath, his gaze dropping away from mine. His eyes were a little red and sported giant purple half-moons under them, and he ran his hand through his unwashed hair nervously. He was dressed for work, but his shirt was on inside-out.

"Hi," I answered. Ryker was right. This was awkward as hell.

"I'm sorry he's late." He stuffed his hands in his pockets. "James threw up as we were getting ready to walk out the door, and I had to toss him in the bathtub. Then I realized I didn't have enough diapers in the bag, so we had to stop at the store, and it all kind of fell into chaos." He shot me a guilty look.

Like I had some kind of right to judge him.

But I'd been exactly where he was that first month with the boys. Instead of anger over Liam's tardiness, I felt...empathy. He wasn't neglecting the boys or packing his car to vanish in the night. The guy was trying.

I parted my lips to speak.

"And I know what you're going to say," he rushed. "That I'm not doing a good enough job. That I should have this all figured out. That they would have been better off with you, and honestly, it's nothing I haven't said to myself this weekend."

"I wasn't going to say that."

"But James isn't sleeping, which means Liam won't sleep. So they've both been up all night. Every night. And the super called me with a noise complaint because Jamie wouldn't stop crying. Like, what was I supposed to do? Gag him? And Liam...he's so mad at me. It's like he doesn't trust me—like he's the adult, and I'm failing. I don't feed Jamie right. I don't cut his sandwiches right. I can't find his fire truck. I don't have a laser tag set like

Knox. I don't brush his hair the same way you do. I don't know that he's supposed to get lotion after his bath."

His eyes flared. "I can't even remember the last time *I* took a shower because I'm too busy trying to keep Jamie's fingers out of the kitchen drawers or cleaning up the mess just in case Elliot stops by on a surprise visit and thinks I can't do this, and I'm so damned tired that I could probably sleep standing up in this hallway." He muttered something and his shoulders fell. "And now I've just admitted my complete incompetence to the enemy."

"I'm not your enemy." I shook my head and walked forward so there were only a few feet between us. He looked so much like Liam, and though Jamie was just a toddler, I could see Nolan in the shape of his eyes and stubborn set of his chin.

"You wanted to adopt the boys, and I ruined that." His shoulders rose and fell. "I'd say that puts us on separate sides."

I thought about Liam's smile on that first visit day, and how certain he'd been at the start of this that his father would come for him. "I'm on the boys' side," I finally said. "And what they need is you."

He blinked and shifted his weight.

"I'm not your enemy, Nolan," I repeated. "And I have been just as flustered as you are right now, but it was easier on me because I had Knox after that first night." And sure, he'd been gone a lot this summer, but he'd been there when it most mattered, while we'd gotten our feet under us. Nolan just needed to get his feet on that same, sturdy ground. "Give everyone a few weeks to settle into your new normal. It's a lot of change for all three of you."

"And until then?" Something flashed through his eyes. A plea?

I folded my arms across my chest and thought. "Until then, Liam needs to feel like James is secure. That's always his first thought, even as young as he is. If you have questions about

Jamie, just ask Liam. It will make Liam feel useful, and he'll start to trust you once he sees that Jamie is taken care of."

"Okay." He nodded. "What else?"

I thought back over his list of preferences. "Liam likes his sandwiches cut diagonally. James throws up every time he has lactose, or sometimes when he's just overly gassy. There are some good videos on YouTube to help you with that." My brows furrowed. "The fire truck got left at Knox's house. I'll see what I can do about that." The idea of calling Knox, of being the first to reach out nauseated me. "Have him show you how he likes his hair brushed. Lotion after baths helps calm them both, plus it's Colorado, so their skin dries out really fast. As for sleep, James probably misses his crib—"

"I can't afford one. Not until next paycheck." His jaw ticked. "I drained everything I had moving back here and getting the apartment set up."

"Let me see what I can do about that." I forced a smile. "The sleep will come. And shower as soon as they close their eyes. No matter how exhausted you are, you'll feel better if you can tune out the world for five minutes. You're going to be all right." I sucked in a deep breath. "And James…his birthday is the fourteenth of August."

"I know." He flinched. "Well, I know now. I wasn't here when he was born, and that's my fault, but I'm learning as fast as I can. Thank you. Really. I don't know how else to say it." His shoulders rolled forward.

"If you need something, let me know. I can always pick up Liam from school if you're running late, or take Jamie early if you need help before Cherry opens. Try not to think of me as the opposition. I'm here to help." The words were sharp and sour on my tongue but true.

His forehead crinkled. "Really?"

"Really." I nodded.

"But why?"

I blinked back the sting in my eyes. "Because I love Liam and James. I will always love them." I swallowed past the knot of emotion clogging my throat. "And more than anything, I want them to be happy. I want you to be successful. You *have* to be successful."

He swallowed and nodded. "I'd better get going. I'm already late. Thanks again."

"You're welcome." I stood in the hallway as he left, my shoulders relaxing when the door closed behind him.

I heard footsteps behind me and didn't need to turn around to know who it was.

"You are a way better person than I am," Ryker said, coming to stand beside me. "I'm still furious that he left those boys in the first place, and I know Knox is too."

"Knox is furious about a lot of things." *Mostly my actions.* "And I'm still mad," I admitted. "But there's nothing Nolan can do about the past. No way to go back and make it right. All the guy can do is move forward and show up for the boys. If we can help him do that, then the boys win. It's that simple." And that complicated.

"You need anything from me?" Ryker asked, wrapping his arm around my shoulder. "My place is always open to you."

I leaned into him. "No, I'm back at my apartment."

"So, no vacation rental?"

I shook my head.

"Need me to beat the shit out of Knox? Because that option is always open to you too," he offered like he was extending an invite to lunch.

"Don't even think about it." I narrowed my eyes at him.

He blinked with feigned innocence. "What? It's not like I didn't warn him. He hurt you, now I hurt him."

"Guy logic astounds me," I muttered. "I'm the one who left, Ryker. Not Knox. He may have prompted the move, but I didn't exactly give him a chance to talk me out of it."

Ryker's brow knit. "But you love him."

I shrugged. "Yeah, but I'm not sure he loves me." My heart crumpled all over again. "And even as immature as it was, there was some part of me that spent the weekend staring at my phone, at my door, hoping Knox would come after me. But you know Knox. He doesn't go after anyone."

Ryker grumbled.

I glanced through the window into Liam's classroom and smiled at the sight of him chatting it up with the girl who sat next to him. He'd come such a long way in such a short time, and I was willing to do anything to keep that progress moving forward.

I had to keep moving forward too.

"You know," I said to my brother. "There is something you can help me with."

CHAPTER TWENTY-SEVEN

K nox

THE SCENT OF COFFEE FILLED THE KITCHEN AS I TIED MY BOOTS, and my fingers froze. *Harper.* I'd been the one to push brew a couple of minutes ago, but she'd ordered the coffee for me. The bottom fell out of my world for the millionth time since Thursday, and my stomach reeled like it was my body in freefall and not just my heart.

Fuck, it was hard to breathe without her. Everything reminded me of Harper. My bodywash reminded me of kissing her in the shower. My sheets reminded me of her skin. Memories of her in my truck made it hard to drive. She was every room in this house. It was more hers than mine when I thought about it. Until this weekend, I'd never spent a night here without her. If I was being honest, I never wanted to sleep here without her again.

I loathed nighttime and the hours I spent tossing and turning, reaching for her in the slivers of hours I managed to find sleep.

She'd forgotten a lone bottle of perfume in the bathroom, and I'd tortured myself last night by spraying it on her pillow. I'd made the jump from miserable to absolutely pathetic.

So, pick up the fucking phone.

And say what? That I was sorry I hadn't been here when shit had gone down? Of course I was sorry, but part of apologizing meant changing, and I couldn't promise her it wouldn't happen again because it would. I would leave her over and over when the call came. And as much as we'd both known the score before jumping into this game, neither of us had been prepared for the actual price.

I stood, only to be met with the little fire truck that had been perched at the end of the island since Thursday. A whole, fresh jolt of pain singed my nerves. This was wrong. All of it. I should have been getting the boys ready with Harper and helping her buckle them in this morning. There should have been a hundred different sounds coming from every direction—toys singing, kids laughing, alarms going off to remind us it was time to go. Instead, it was silent.

I was going to have to sell this fucking house.

Everything was off, including me. I was four hours late for work, and I knew it didn't matter because the guys had barely gotten back this morning. No one else would be there except Emerson, and I wasn't exactly looking forward to anything she had to say about what had gone down between Harper and me.

The doorbell rang and my head snapped toward the entry hall. *Harper.* My feet moved without instruction, and I practically flew to open it.

My face fell when I found Ryker on the other side.

"You look like shit." He looked me up and down, then pushed his way past me, walking into the house.

"Come on in," I said sarcastically, shutting the door a little harder than necessary.

"Let me guess." He turned and folded his arms across his chest. "You were hoping I was a different Anders."

I winced. "If you're here to punch me in the face, just get it over with." I threw my arms out at my sides.

Ryker narrowed his eyes. "Tempting as that might be, I'll take a rain check. I'm just here for a fire truck."

Now I was the one glaring. "What the hell do you want with Liam's fire truck?" It was the last piece of him I had—besides the bike in the garage, and I wasn't forking it over to Ryker.

"I need it to complete my matchbox collection." Ryker rolled his eyes. "What do you think? Liam wants it." He flinched. "Turns out, the boys are having a hard time adjusting."

"And how do you know that?" My chest clenched.

"Because Nolan told Harper this morning." He cocked his head to the side. "You do remember Harper, right? Your wife? The one you let walk out?"

"You mean the one who kept her apartment the whole time as some kind of fallback plan because she didn't trust me to see us through?" Just saying it hurt.

His eyebrows hit the ceiling. "You think she kept the apartment as a plan B?"

I gritted my teeth and counted to five for patience. "You really want to have this conversation right now?"

"Nope. I'm afraid that I won't stop hitting you if I start, and my sister asked me to keep my hands to myself, so here we are." A muscle popped in his jaw. "I'm just here for the fire truck."

Ryker knew more than I did about what was going on with the boys, and the ugly green monster of jealousy reared up for a second before logic beat it back down. *Ryker knows what's going on.*

"Tell me what happened."

Seven hours later, I knocked on apartment one twelve's door and held my breath. This was such a bad idea. There was no guarantee I'd be able to hold my temper or soften my words and every chance that I was about to make this a whole lot worse.

The door opened, and Nolan Clark's eyes flew wide when he saw me.

"You know who I am." It was a statement, not a question.

He nodded. The guy was a handful of inches shorter than I was, with a leaner build and wary eyes. Eyes that looked too much like Liam and James for me to hate him on sight.

"Take a walk out to my truck with me." It wasn't an offer. "It will only take a couple minutes."

"Give me a second to put Jamie in the playpen?"

"Sure." I respected that.

He shut the door, and I leaned back against the opposite wall of the tight hallway. There was no finding fault with the apartment building. Pretty much everything in Legacy was new construction, so it wasn't like it was old or dingy.

It was just hard knowing James and Liam were right behind that door and I didn't have a single right to even so much as say hi to them. It was excruciating to go from being a pivotal part of their world to not even having spectator status.

Nolan opened the door and shut it quickly behind him, denying me even a glimpse of the boys.

I walked out and he followed, the fresh evening air doing nothing to relieve the tension between us.

"Look, if you're here to yell at me, or threaten me, then let's just get it over with," he said as we reached the truck, a healthy dose of trepidation on his face.

I snorted back a laugh.

He looked at me like I'd lost my mind.

"Sorry. That's just really similar to something I said to my best friend this morning." I'd backed the truck in, and my hand hovered on the tailgate latch. Was I actually about to do this?

Absolutely, because it was something Harper would have done. When Ryker told me why Nolan needed the fire truck, I knew that wasn't all he needed.

"I can already guess what I did that pissed you off. What did you do to your best friend?" he asked, folding his arms over the Coulter Construction logo on his T-shirt.

"Broke his little sister's heart." The truth of the words cut me like a thousand little blades.

"Ouch." Nolan grimaced.

"Yeah, but I'm not here so we can bond over our mutual fuckups."

"Why *are* you here?"

Because I'm trying to be the person Harper deserves.

"Because it's the right thing to do." I lowered the tailgate, revealing the disassembled parts of Jamie's crib and Liam's bike. "Because hating you isn't going to help Liam or Jamie, and I love them more than I'm pissed at you."

"I don't understand." Nolan swallowed, glancing from the crib to me and back again.

"You can't afford a crib. Now you have one. All the bedding is inside the cab." I nodded toward the back of the truck.

"You loathe me," he said slowly.

"I loathe what you did," I corrected.

He looked away, but to his credit brought his eyes back to mine. "Because I didn't come back immediately."

"Because you walked out in the first place." My fist clenched. "They didn't deserve that."

"No," he admitted quietly. "They didn't. I'm man enough to know that I fucked up."

"Are you man enough to stick around this time?" I snapped.

"No bullshit. No lawyers. No DSS workers. No judges. Just you and me, right here on this sidewalk. Tell me the truth. Are you going to bail on them again?"

"Never." His chin rose in the air.

I stared at him long and hard, trying to get a read on this guy. Judging character was something I was usually pretty good at, and I wanted to be right about this guy for the boys' sake. He didn't flinch. Didn't flush. Didn't look away. After a few tense moments, I nodded. "Okay then."

He visibly relaxed.

"All the nuts and bolts are there, so it should be pretty easy to assemble. You have a tool kit?" I hauled the largest pieces forward and out of the bed.

He shook his head. "All my tools are at the job site."

"All dads need a tool set at home." I shook my head and handed the first pieces to him. "A tool set and a shitload of double A batteries. Their toys eat them up like candy. I have a bag in the cab. You can borrow mine."

"Really?" He took the two, longer sides of the crib and laid them in the grass next to the sidewalk.

"Really." I handed over the shorter ends, then the mattress. "James deserves to sleep tonight, and so do you." Besides, this was all I had to give them.

I unloaded the bike, Liam's helmet, and the crib bedding set, then reached into the front seat. My hand curled around the tiny fire truck as I shut the door. "And this is for Liam." I held it out for Nolan to take.

His forehead wrinkled, and he looked up at my hat. "Liam has that same hat."

I nodded.

"Won't take it off, even for bed."

"It's our hotshot crew." I breathed into the ache that seemed to live in my chest now. "Well, not exactly. We're in the middle of getting certified, but we should be hotshots again by next week."

"Yeah, I know. He talks about you constantly." A corner of his mouth lifted in a sad half smile. "It's kind of hard to compete with one of the Legacy hotshots. That was always my problem with their mother. I never quite measured up to her first husband."

"Then measure up now." I held out the fire truck a little farther.

He reached, then pulled his hand back. "Why don't you come inside and give it to him yourself?"

My jaw slackened and my heart tripped over its own beats. "You mean that?"

He nodded slowly at first, then faster as he smiled. "Yeah. They'd love to see you." He glanced at the crib. "And honestly, I could use some help putting that together."

My answer was instant.

"No problem."

AN HOUR. THAT WAS ALL I'D GOTTEN WITH LIAM AND SIR PUKES-A-Lot before the call had gone out. There was a fire three hours north of Legacy, and we'd been called in, not as a Type 2.

It was time.

No field simulations for us, it seemed. The certification crew was in the vehicle just ahead of us as we drove into a tiny town that reminded me way too much of Legacy. The sky was pitch black, except for the ominous orange glow that outlined the ridge to the west. This fire would make or break us.

There was a palpable hum of both anxiety and excitement in our minibus. The crew was split in two, half in our bus and half in the other, with Bishop and Spencer taking point in the pickup at the head of our caravan. Lucky for us, the certification crew was in a whole other vehicle, so our nervousness couldn't be held against us.

The seat next to me was empty and Ryker sat across the aisle, casually glaring my way. He looked calm and collected, but the way he chewed that gum told me he was dealing with his own nerves.

I twisted the platinum band on my left hand around my finger and debated texting Harper again. I'd fought off the urge at least once every thirty seconds on the drive up. She'd know about the fire from Ryker. She'd already be worried.

And the things that needed to be said between us weren't the kind of words you texted. There was too much ambiguity in the tone, too many ways to be misunderstood. But the caterer calling me this afternoon, telling me Harper was canceling our October wedding date? That spoke volumes.

We parked outside the community center that was acting as our command center, and we all shuffled off the buses, stretching the stiffness out of our limbs. The Legacy logo was painted on the side of each of our brand-new vehicles, but the certification crew had slapped a "trainee" magnet right beneath it, reminding me what was at stake.

"Trainee," Bishop muttered as he unfolded himself from the truck.

Guess I wasn't the only one being served the reminder.

"Circle up," Spencer ordered, and we did so, putting our supe in the center.

I knew they were a few feet away, but it felt like the certification crew was breathing down our necks.

"I'm headed in with Bishop to get the latest situation report," Spencer said. "There are two other Type One crews on the way that we know of, and a few Type Two's, when I last heard about an hour ago. The 8:00 p.m. flyover showed it burned twelve hundred acres from when it started this afternoon."

The wind whipped through the parking lot, and we all grabbed our hats.

"And that, my people, is what we're up against. Forecast isn't helping us out tomorrow. Squad leaders, get your people fed and set up camp in that gym." Spencer pointed across the road. "I'll find you once we have our plans for the morning."

I spotted my five and gestured for them to follow as Bash and Ryker did the same.

"Feeling a little antsy?" Cameron Patel asked, a corner of his mouth rising in a smirk.

"Shouldn't you be with Cohen?" I asked as we walked across the road to the gym.

"Nope. We have guys with them. I asked for the honor of sticking with your squad for eval." He sounded positively giddy.

I muttered a curse word.

"Your chickens are coming home to roost, and I can't wait to watch," Cameron warned.

"Who the hell even says that anymore?" Ryker came up on my left, pushing his way between us. "Are you eighty?"

"I'm the one evaluating you," Cameron snapped. "Well, evaluating Daniels, here."

"Awesome," Ryker said as Bash opened the gym doors ahead of us. "Then unless you're evaluating how Knox zips up his sleeping bag—or you're interested in zipping it up with him—how about you back off? The fun doesn't start until tomorrow morning, and you've made your point."

Cameron put up his hands like he was under arrest but gave us a shit-eating grin as he walked off toward the other evaluators.

"I had him handled," I said, crossing the threshold into the gym. There were already fifty people in here, all lining up their sleeping bags and hitting the long line of tables that looked to be stocked with food and drinks.

"Fuck off and get your squad situated." Gone was the cool

and collected facade he'd shown Cameron, the one he'd perfected through years of high-pressure scenarios. Nope, I got blasted with full-on side-eye as he trudged forward.

"So, I'm guessing he's still pissed," Bash remarked, coming up to my side.

"That feels like a safe bet." I directed my squad where to lay their bags out and shook my head at Chance when he started to set up next to Taylor. That was *so* not happening on my watch.

"But you've talked about it, right?" Bash leveled his no-bull-shit stare at me.

"If, by talking, you mean him telling me that he wasn't sure he'd be able to stop hitting me if he started, then briefly discussing what's going on with the boys, then sure, we've talked." I laid out my bedroll and bag with quick, practiced motions.

"So there's no tension to worry about there." Bash set up at my side, eyeing Ryker's position a few rows over.

I winced.

"Fucking awesome," he quipped sarcastically.

Spencer came back with the situation report, and it hadn't changed much since the last one. "Get some sleep," he ordered. "We're hiking in as soon as the sun is up."

Bash called Emerson.

Ryker called Harper.

I called no one and told myself it was a decision made to protect my battery life, since there were more firefighters in here than outlets.

When I fell asleep, I dreamed about Harper for what felt like all of ten minutes before I was being shaken awake.

"Is it five already?" I mumbled, blinking up at Bash. Ryker stood behind him, his jaw locked.

"Four thirty," Bash whispered. "Get dressed quietly. We have a meeting outside."

I threw on what few clothes I'd taken off—I'd long since

perfected sleeping fully outfitted—and laced up my boots, swiping the sleep out of my eyes as I followed Bash and Ryker through the rows of sleeping firefighters out of the gym.

The predawn air was cool but carried the heavy scent of smoke. That smell was more effective than a cup of coffee at waking me up. That smell meant death for people caught sleeping.

We walked through the parking lot and onto a playground that was illuminated from the streetlights above.

I glanced at our surroundings and found Ryker doing the same, but Bash simply turned to face us both. "Where is everyone?"

"This is everyone," Bash answered.

"I thought you said we had a meeting?" Ryker finished buttoning up his shirt.

"We are the meeting." Bash pointed to both of us. "The three of us."

"I'm going back to bed," Ryker snapped, turning toward the gym.

"Consider it a board meeting of Legacy, LLC," Bash countered.

"You're actually serious," I muttered, raking my fingers over my sleep-mussed hair.

"We don't have a board, jackass." Ryker pivoted back to us, his arms crossed. "We're managing members."

"I don't give a shit what we are. You two are going to talk," Bash ordered.

I glanced at Ryker. He glared back.

"Good morning, Knox," Ryker said with a sarcastic smile before looking at Bash. "There, we're talking. Happy?"

"This isn't a joke!" Bash's voice rose. "Today is our only shot at this!" He gestured toward the orange glow from the ridgeline that made it look like the sun was rising from the west. "Every-thing that we've been working for, the years and the money we've dumped into this, it all comes down to today, and you two are going to fuck it up for everyone if you don't hash out your shit."

"No one knows—" Ryker started.

"Everyone fucking knows!" Bash interrupted. "I'm surprised the town council didn't put out a press briefing when Harper moved her shit out of your house, Knox."

I spun the platinum ring on my finger.

"And everyone is watching us. From the council waiting for us to fail, to the town who expects us to represent, to the eval crew who is watching for every misstep. And the crew in there —" He gestured to the gym. "The one we fought tooth and nail to assemble, they're all looking to *you* to work together and lead your squads."

Guilt and responsibility settled on my shoulders.

"Do you two really think our fathers want to look down on us and see you two like this?" Bash raised his eyebrows like he'd delivered the death blow.

"I think my father would kick his ass for what's happened with Harper," Ryker commented, shrugging his shoulders.

"For fuck's sake." I spun, facing my oldest friend. "We should have dealt with this yesterday."

He narrowed his eyes. "Dealt with you blaming her for the boys going back to Nolan?"

I flinched. "Not my finest moment."

"Obviously."

"She left *me*, Ryker. She packed her stuff and left before I even had a chance to process what had happened in court that day. I left for that fire with a wife and two kids and came home to *nothing*."

"You pushed her out," he accused.

"I know!" I shouted, my hands balling into fists. "Don't you fucking think I know that? Don't you think I regret every single word that left my mouth that night?" I shook my head, struggling to explain, to put words to the misery of the past few days. "When push came to shove, she never trusted me to stay, and hell, with my track record, I can't exactly blame her. She never gave up the lease on her apartment. What do you want me to do, Ry?"

"Stop proving her right, dumbass." He rubbed his hands over his face. "This is exactly what I *didn't* want to happen—"

"I know, you put her name on the list—"

"Fuck the list!" he snapped. "I didn't want to become some kind of intermediary between the two of you, but you're both so damned self-righteous. She wasn't keeping a back door open for your inevitable fuckup, Knox. She was working to sublet the space for a vacation rental to make some extra money on the side."

"She what?" All of the indignation left my body.

"If you'd ever taken the time to ask her, she would have told you."

I opened and shut my mouth a few times, trying to come up with something that didn't make me out to be the jackass.

Ryker arched an eyebrow.

"I didn't ask, because I didn't want to know," I finally admitted. "She was already spooked about the second wedding, and everything just seemed too perfect to be real. I didn't want to chance popping that bubble."

"It popped."

"No shit." I threw out my hands. "I didn't plan any of this, Ryker. Not finding her in my house, not falling for those boys, and definitely not hurting her."

"Yeah, I know."

"If I could take it—" I paused. "You what?"

"I know." He shrugged. "I don't think you hurt her on purpose, Knox. I think you ran your mouth, and kindergarteners could teach you a thing or two about communication and feelings, but I never thought you did it on purpose."

"Kindergarteners," I repeated, ignoring Bash's smothered scoff.

"Yeah." Ryker nodded. "I think when the shit hit the fan, you two went *at* each other instead of going through it together. She didn't give you a chance to process it, and she felt abandoned. You looked at her and subconsciously saw your mom walking out on you."

Bash and I both stared at him.

"That's...some impressive analysis for someone who avoids relationships like an STD," Bash remarked slowly, his eyebrows rising.

Ryker looked between us and rolled his eyes. "Oh, fuck off. It's Psych 101. And just because I prefer *not* to be in a relationship doesn't mean I'm incapable. It's a full-time job watching you two tie yourselves into knots over women."

The light in the park shifted into a predawn glow. It was almost time get the rest of the crew moving. "I don't know what to do about Harper, Ry. She made her choice, and I can't promise her to be around the next time something goes wrong. Neither of us can."

He stared at my left hand for a moment. "Did it ever occur to you that maybe she wanted you to go after her?"

My brow puckered. "No."

Now Bash was gawking at me. "Seriously?"

"Seriously." I nodded once. "She's never been one to play games, and besides, what could I possibly say to make this all better?"

Ryker blinked at me. "Oh, I don't know, maybe take a few notes from every other man in history who's ever had to actually fight for his girl?"

I looked to the only guy I knew in a relationship—Bash.

Bash stared back for a second, then laughed. "Oh my God, you're not kidding, are you? Start by apologizing. No flowers, otherwise she'll think you only bring flowers when you've fucked up."

"You might want to write this down," Ryker stage-whispered.

"Shut up," I retorted.

"Tell her you screwed up. Tell her it will never happen again —and follow through." Bash pointed at me. "They're big on that part. Grovel. Finish up by swearing you'll love her until your dying day, and then await judgment."

"Tell her that I lo—" I barely stopped myself from saying the words.

"You. Love. Her," Bash repeated. "Shit, maybe you do need a pen."

Ryker's eyes narrowed. "You do love her, right? Because she sure as fuck loves you."

Of course I loved her. I'd just never *told* her. "Even if I did, I think she deserves to hear those words before you."

Ryker's jaw hit the ground. "You've never told her you love her?" His eyes widened. "Is that why you said you fell for the boys, but you didn't say you fell for her?" Rage rose in his eyes.

"I didn't have to fall for her this summer, asshole. That happened seven years ago."

"You have to tell her, man." Ryker clapped his hand on my shoulder. "You have to tell her, and then you have to trust her to love you back. You don't always have to step out onto the ledge by yourself. That's the advantage of being with someone."

I nodded, and we fell silent as the sun began to rise.

"Should we group hug?" Bash offered.

"Fuck no," I blurted.

Forty-five minutes later, we'd packed up and driven to the highest point the road could take us into the national forest.

"Circle up," Spencer ordered as I tightened the straps on my line pack.

Bishop held a map against the rough surface of a nearby

boulder, and we gathered around him as the wind tugged at the edges. River stepped up and held the other side so the damn thing didn't blow away.

"She chewed through another thousand acres last night with these winds," Spencer told us. "And we've got two likely hours to get this done. Then the winds are picking up again until tonight, and the forecast is seventy-mile-an-hour gusts."

"Ninety degrees. Dry timber. Seventy-mile-an-hour winds," Ryker said with a shrug. "What could possibly go wrong?"

A dry chuckle went up.

The evaluation crew didn't look amused.

"We're going to cut a line right here." Spencer pointed to a steep ridgeline on the map. "Squad one, you'll hike in from here and cut here." Spencer looked at Bash, who nodded. "Squad two, you'll split off here and hike down to start cutting here."

Ryker nodded.

"Squad three." Spencer looked at me. "You'll hike in from the bottom and cut to join squad two."

I leaned in to look at the map. "Supe, wouldn't it make more sense to use the creek right there?"

Spencer shook his head. "If the wind shifts, you can't get out. You're trapped. And it's not on the topographical, but there's an old quarry right here." He pointed to an area just beneath where he wanted us to start cutting. "If we can get line cut to the south of that quarry and burn it before she crests that hill, we can save the town. The quarry gives us an advantage."

"And if she sweeps north? Right along that ridge?" I asked. Afternoon winds were a bitch to predict around here. Cutting a line there might stop the march.

"Then she'll eat up some acreage, but the town is still safe."

I nodded, still looking at that creek. Sure, it made for some sketchy terrain, but if we were fast enough—

"Keep your radios on. I'll be with squad one, and Bishop's going with squad two." He looked at me. "You got this, Daniels?"

"I got this," I assured him.

We were handed maps as we split up, each taking the worn but craggy hiking trails we'd been assigned. Ryker and Bash headed up with their squads, and I took mine down the trail that led toward the quarry. Lawson carried the chain saw just behind me, and when I looked back, I breathed a sigh of relief that while River brought up the rear, Taylor was more than keeping up as we headed down the path. Braxton would be proud.

An hour into the hike, we started uphill, sweat streamed down my back, soaking my shirt. "Stay hydrated!" I yelled back as we continued through the forest. It would all be ash by night-fall if we didn't get this done—as long as Spencer had chosen the right tactic.

"I can see the wheels turning in your head," Cameron said, pushing past Lawson to hike behind me.

"You can't even see my face. You don't see shit," I threw over my shoulder.

"You're thinking that you know better than Cohen," he continued. "That creek seems like a mighty fine natural barrier, especially if the winds don't give you those precious hours you need to burn."

"I thought your role was to observe."

"I thought your role was to lead your squad." He raised his eyebrows in question.

The terrain grew steeper, and the trail curved abruptly to the right, toward the stream, and I stopped, taking in my surroundings. The smoke plume rose above us, still moving west, but without eyes on the fire, I couldn't tell if she was shifting north or not.

"What are you going to do?" Cameron asked.

I checked my map. This was where the trail ended for us if we followed the plan.

"Are you going to lead with your gut? Or follow your orders?" Cameron pushed.

River raised his eyebrow at me.

"Is she going to sweep north?" I asked him. "Or is she barreling down this hillside as that front pushes through this afternoon?" Second to me, he had the most experience on our squad.

He studied the smoke and held out the wind meter, taking a reading. Then he shook his head. "It's too soon to even guess."

"What's it going to be, Daniels?" Cameron asked again.

"We're heading up here. Watch your footing." I started up the hillside, leaving the path behind.

"You're going for the quarry," Cameron commented. "Against your gut?"

"Shut up and observe."

"If you say so." He fell back.

"I fucking say so," I muttered and climbed. We gained altitude, my legs burning as we continued up.

"This is squad one. We've reached our location and we're starting to cut," Bash said over the radio.

"Roger that, squad one. This is squad two, estimating we're five minutes out." Ryker's voice filled my handheld.

I unclipped my radio and pushed the button. "Roger. This is squad three. Estimating five minutes."

Five minutes later, we made it to the edge of the quarry, sweaty and breathing heavily. I glanced over the squad and looked up the ridge, where I could see Ryker's squad already cutting line. The winds had given us a break, just like Cohen predicted.

"Take two minutes and hydrate," I ordered. "Then we cut."

Minutes later, the sound of the chainsaw filled the air as Lawson cut away the brush. The rest of us had our Pulaskis in hand, silent as our concentration and sweat went into cutting, working our way up the ridgeline toward Ryker.

Cameron had his fucking stopwatch out, timing us as we completed chain after chain.

My heart pounded with exertion and my muscles burned with complaint as we moved steadily across the rugged terrain.

Not a single one of us complained. We were efficient. We were quick. We were *good*.

It felt like hours, but we met up with Ryker's line as the fire licked over the top of the hillside above us. We had an hour. Maybe. Less if the winds picked up sooner than forecasted.

The lookout reported in over the radio. Winds were holding. We'd hit our window perfectly.

Once the line was complete, Spencer gave the order to set the fires.

We lit it up, and then we got the fuck out of there, hiking down toward the road as quickly and safely as possible.

"It's holding," River said, catching up with me. "There's a pretty black line right where Spencer wanted it, and the flames are climbing to meet the approaching front."

I glanced over my shoulder to see for myself and nodded. "Good."

We met up with the other squads, and the mood was already lighter, although exhaustion beat at us. Even if we'd simply shaped the path of the fire, we'd led her away from the town.

"Interesting choice you made out there," Cameron noted as I finished off a portion of my water. Winds had picked up again, bringing the blaze down the ridge. It was time to get out of here. "I always thought you were the kind to trust your gut instincts."

I glanced over at Spencer, who was already back at the map with Bishop, talking on the radio. "I choose to trust my superintendent."

Cameron lifted his brows. "I guess we'll know soon if he made the right call."

"Guess so."

"Load up!" Spencer ordered, and we started toward the vehicles.

"Hey, Cameron," I called out.

He turned back in question.

"You still owe us twenty bucks." I flashed him a grin, then climbed aboard the bus.

Our part of the evaluation was done.

Now all we could do was wait.

CHAPTER TWENTY-EIGHT

arper

ALMOST EVERY TABLE WAS TAKEN AT THE CHATTERBOX AS WE finished up a late lunch. My hamburger tasted like sawdust, but I knew it wasn't the cooking—it was my nerves, which weren't getting any better, thanks to Ryker checking his phone every five minutes.

"They already told us they'll make the call at the end of the business day." Emerson reached over the small table and snatched his phone. "You're going to drive me crazy if you keep looking."

"And they're calling Spence," Bash added, though I noticed his phone was on the table face up in case a message came in.

They'd spent one day on the fire that would determine their rating, and then they'd been sent home yesterday to wait for the verdict.

"You're sure they were meeting today?" Ryker asked Emerson, his fries all but untouched.

"Yes!" She responded at the same time Bash did.

"Excuse me if I'm a little nervous," Ryker muttered.

"What time are we supposed to be there?" Em asked Bash.

"Four," he answered, glancing at his phone.

"Be where?" I asked, dipping my fry in ranch before taking a bite.

"Knox's house," Ryker answered, lifting his brows at me like I was supposed to know this.

I dropped the rest of my fry. "I'm sorry?"

"Um. The…celebration." Emerson had the grace to blush as she glanced between all three of us. "We're all meeting at Knox's house to wait for the phone call, remember?"

"No." I shook my head. "I think I would remember agreeing to something like that." There was no chance I could see Knox. Not yet, not while I still felt this raw, this vulnerable, and especially not on a day like today. Every emotion was heightened. This is what they'd worked *years* for.

There was every chance I'd lose my mind and throw myself at him.

"Well, then agree now." Ryker shrugged.

"Since when are you on Knox's side?" I shot him a glare.

He shot one right back. "Since when is *everything* about Knox? That's my crew too, Harpy, and if we get the green light to put Dad's patch on, then I would think you'd want to be there. Not for him, but for *me*."

Well shit, now I felt about two inches tall.

Grams came out through the swinging door and waved at me, her smile bright as always.

I waved back and looked away quickly. I'd half expected her to throw me out on my ass when I'd come in, but she treated me like nothing had happened. Like I hadn't packed all my clothes

in record time and left her grandson—and her wedding rings
—behind.

"You have to be there," Ryker urged, and the blatant plea in
his eyes was more than I could stand.

"Who says he'll even let me in?"

They all looked at me like that was the lamest thing I'd ever
said—ever.

"He'll let you in," Emerson said, just in case I'd misinter-
preted their expressions.

Both Ryker and Bash nodded.

"I'm just..." I sighed. "I'm not ready to deal with that whole
situation, okay?" I wasn't ready to hear him apologize and
politely walk away. I wasn't ready for the closure I so obviously
needed. I liked my little slice of denial. I was happy there.

Fine, I was miserable, but still. Talking to Knox meant it was
really, truly over.

"Then don't talk to him." Ryker shrugged again.

"You honestly think it's that easy." I tilted my head at my
brother.

"I think you're an adult capable of making decisions without
me weighing in." He crammed a fry in his mouth.

"Well, that's a first."

Bash and Emerson shared a look.

Of course everything was easy for them. They'd carved their
names on the freaking wall two tables away, for all of Legacy to
see. They were freaking destined for each other.

"Please, Harpy?" Ryker asked.

I sighed, then flagged down our waitress. "Can I please get a
margarita?" I asked.

"Sure!" she answered, perky and happy and not at all heart-
broken like I was. "Frozen or on the rocks?"

"What are you doing?" Emerson whispered, like everyone at
the table couldn't hear her.

"I don't care as long as it comes with tequila," I told the wait-ress. "A *lot* of tequila."

"Coming right up!" She bounced away.

The three of them were staring at me.

"What?" I challenged.

"You never drink at two in the afternoon," Emerson said slowly.

I waved her off. "Well, it's not like I'm a mom anymore, right? I have zero responsibilities today, and if I'm going to be in the same room—scratch that—the same *house* as Knox, then there's no chance in hell that I'm going to be sober." I wasn't sure there was enough alcohol in the world to get me through this evening.

"So that means you'll come?" Ryker asked, a note of hope in his tone.

"That means I'll come," I agreed.

I drank three of the salty-sweet treats before we left.

With any luck, this would be Ryker's big night, and with a little more luck, I wouldn't remember any of it.

CHAPTER TWENTY-NINE

K nox

THE HOUSE QUICKLY FILLED AS IT APPROACHED FOUR O'CLOCK. I left the front door open as the crew filed in, single guys and families alike. I got the hell out of the caterer's way as they put the finishing touches on the mountain of food in the dining room.

I'm not sure what had me more nervous, the impending phone call from the certification crew or the rings in my pocket.

That was a lie. It was the rings. Those little suckers were putting my stomach into full somersault mode.

She'd be here any minute. Ryker, Bash, and Emerson swore they'd convince her to show.

"Thanks for having this here, Knox," Spencer said, shaking my hand as he came through the door. "It feels a little more family-oriented than getting the news at the clubhouse."

"No problem." I didn't mention that this had been the only

idea I'd been able to come up with to get her here. Could I have shown up at her apartment? Absolutely. Stormed the preschool? Sure. But this house…this is where everything happened, where we became *us*, so I figured that this was the best place to remind her of exactly how good we were together.

"Want to show me to your office?" he asked.

"Absolutely." I led him through the house and down the hallway to the office. "We'll keep everyone out of here so it's quiet for the phone call. Then you can come out and give us the good news when you're ready."

Spencer gave me a stressed smile. "As long as it's good news."

"It will be," I said with way more confidence than I felt. "There's no way that everything we've done, everything we've worked for, was in vain. It'll be good news." That fire was already at thirty percent containment and a lot of that was due to Spencer's strategy yesterday. He'd made the right call.

I'd made the right call by following him, even if Cameron didn't agree.

Spencer's attention snagged on a photo of the original Legacy crew, and his jaw flexed a couple of times. "Your dad would be proud of who you've become, Knox. Not just the firefighter but the man you are."

"Thanks." I managed to choke the word out. It didn't matter how many years it had been, the grief of losing Dad had never really lessened. It had become my shadow of sorts, elongating at certain times and hovering close at others, but never fully leaving. "I'll send Bishop in when he gets here."

I left the office and headed back to the gathering, which had yet to become a party. The clock struck four, and by a quick glance toward the living room and through the windows to the deck on my left, I could estimate that most of us were here.

Emerson stepped into my path at end of the hallway. Her lips were pressed together, and the emotion running through her eyes was pure apology.

"She didn't come." My chest deflated.

Emerson grimaced. "Oh, no. She came, all right."

"She's here?" I looked over the petite brunette and scanned the room for my wife, coming up empty.

"Yep." She nodded slowly.

"What are you not telling me?"

"She, well, um…." Her face scrunched for a second. "She kind of pre-gamed."

"Pre-gamed," I repeated like a parrot.

"You know." Emerson shrugged. "Like when you're going out for the night, but you have a few drinks before you head out."

"Em, I know what pre-gaming is." I scanned the room again, and still didn't see her.

"Right. Well, she pre-gamed pretty hard."

"Are you trying to tell me my wife is drunk?" I asked slowly.

"Maybe a little." She held up her thumb and forefinger, making a pinching motion, then widened the space. "Or a lot. I mean, if she were a bigger person…say an NFL linebacker, then it wouldn't really be that much, but she's kinda small, so—"

"So she's plastered," I guessed.

"I'm really sorry. If it makes you feel better, she only did it so she'd have the liquid courage to see you." Her nose wrinkled.

My jaw slackened. "That *doesn't* make me feel better, Em." In fact, it pretty much threw this evening's plan right out the fucking window.

Then Harper waltzed into my view, a giant smile on her gorgeous face. She had on the world's tiniest shorts and an oversize, off-the-shoulder sweater that ended at her hips, and her hair was loose down her back. My tongue swelled, she looked that damn good.

Then she swayed slightly, and Ryker's arm swept out to steady her.

"Plastered," I repeated.

"It was the only way she'd come."

I sighed, but a smile tugged at my lips. I couldn't even remember the last time I'd seen Harper let loose. Her timing was shit but kind of fitting in a way, since that's how it always went with us.

"Do me a favor," I said to Em as I slid past her. "Send Bishop into the office when he gets here? That's where Spence is taking the phone call."

"You got it." She gave me a thumbs-up. "And good luck"—she motioned toward Harper—"with all that."

I was going to need it.

The sound of Harper's laugh was an electric shock to my heart, throwing it out of whack, the rhythm skyrocketing before settling into a steady beat as I crossed the floor to get to her.

"Hey, Knox." Someone stopped me. "Where are the shirts? We want to be prepped."

The voice alone told me it was River.

"Boxed by size under the dining room table," I answered without taking my eyes off Harper, closing in on her.

Ryker glanced my way, then sent me the same apologetic look Emerson had given me as Harper laughed again…at something Chance had said, go figure.

"Does anyone know where the plastic cups are?" Avery called out from the kitchen.

"Top pantry shelf!" Harper answered, turning slightly.

Our gazes collided and held. This woman was worth the fight, even if I had to wait to plead my case, even if waiting meant pleading it over and over.

"Harper," I said quietly.

"Knox." Her smile slipped. "Ryker said that I don't have to talk to you if I don't want to." Her eyes widened, and she slapped her hand over her mouth. "Oh, that was loud, wasn't it?"

"It's fine." Considering that nearly every head in the living room had turned our way, yes, it had been loud, but I didn't care.

"But Ryker also thinks it would be a good idea if you heard him out," Ryker added, supporting her when she swayed again. Thank God she was in Vans. Heels would have done her in.

Harper's head swung toward her brother with exaggeration. "Traitor."

"Just giving you my honest opinion."

Harper looked back at me, and it took everything I had not to throw her over my shoulder and carry her out of here so I could make her listen to reason. There were a thousand emotions in her eyes, but the one I couldn't stand was the hurt, because I knew I'd caused it.

She stepped out of Ryker's reach and pressed her finger against my chest, glowering up at me. "I told myself that I wasn't going to talk to you. Because..." She shook her head. "Because of a lot of things. But you know what? Maybe I will. I haven't decided yet."

"Can we at least do this talking in private?" I didn't need the rest of the crew witnessing this.

Her gaze narrowed. "Fine. After the call comes in. But you have to keep your hands to yourself, Knoxville, because I can't think when you touch me."

I fought off a grin. There was something to be said for a drunk, filterless Harper.

"Please, God, have this conversation in private." Ryker groaned.

"Bishop just got here," Bash said, sliding through the crowd with Emerson tucked to his side. "He went back to the office."

"Now we wait." Ryker glanced at his watch as Harper retreated to his side.

We were going to talk.

A nervous hum filled the air and built as minutes passed.

The guys and Em did their best to fill our little circle with small talk, but I barely noticed what they were saying, not when Harper and I were locked into an emotional staring contest.

"It's four thirty," Bash muttered, shifting his weight nervously.

"They'll call," Emerson said, giving her most supportive smile to her fiancé.

"You know the town council is shitting bricks right now." Ryker slung his arm over Harper's shoulder, anchoring her when she swayed again.

Damn it, that was *my* job.

"They pretty much did everything they could to set you guys up to fail." Emerson's smile faded.

"We're not going to." I kept my eyes on Harper. "Failure has never been an option."

She flinched, and my chest went tight with fear that our talk might not go my way. Winning an emotional staring contest had never felt so shitty.

"Heads up!" Bishop's booming voice filled the house and silenced the crowd. "Get everybody in here."

"It's time," Bash said quietly.

Lawson motioned to everyone out on the deck, and they piled in, cramming the first floor of my house to its max occupancy.

I closed my eyes and took a deep breath. There was nothing that could be done now, so why was my stomach in knots? Either they'd decided to certify us, or they hadn't. The decision had already been made. It was out of our hands.

There were at least forty people in here, and silence reigned.

"I got the call from the certification team." Spencer stood at the edge of the kitchen where everyone could see him.

I stopped breathing.

A slow, proud smile stretched across his face. "Welcome back, Legacy, you're all certified hotshots!"

Holy shit.

The roar was deafening as we cheered.

My heart thundered and emotion overwhelmed every

logical thought as Ryker, Bash, and I grabbed for each other, our arms around backs, our heads pressed together as we shouted our joy.

The work. The sacrifice. The begging we'd had to do in front of the town council. The moves and the money. The sleepless nights we'd spent tracking down every living legacy. The training and the doubts...it had all been worth it.

We were our father's sons, and we had brought back their patch.

Every person in this room had played a part, but it had been the three of us from the beginning.

"We did it." Bash spoke first.

"Hell yeah, we did!" Ryker shouted.

"They'd be proud of us." My voice was strained, the boulder in my throat growing with every passing second and every blink of my aching eyes.

They both nodded, and we broke apart.

I was grabbed into another hug by someone—River—and he slapped my back before releasing me. Everyone around us was jumping, hugging, exchanging high-fives, and grinning like they'd won the lottery.

Bash had Emerson in his arms.

Ryker hugged Harper, lifting her feet off the ground.

The joy cracked in my chest. That was my wife. She was the only woman I loved—would ever love—and all of this meant nothing if I didn't have her to come home to.

"Maldonado!" Spencer called out.

"Here!" River and Bishop both shouted, making everyone laugh.

Shirts flew into the waiting hands of the crew.

"Daniels!"

I held up my hand and Bishop sent a shirt sailing over the living room. I caught it.

Around us, crewmembers were stripping off whatever they'd worn to the party, leaving their tops discarded on the floor.

"Well, today just got interesting," Emerson said with open appreciation as Bash stripped down.

Rolling my eyes, I did the same, tugging on the Legacy Hotshot Crew shirt. It slid into place, and I glanced down at the patch just beneath my shoulder. *Just like Dad.*

I turned, and a mass of blond hair was in my arms. *Harper.* Her arms were around my neck, her scent in my lungs, her body pressed against mine as I clamped my arms around her and lifted her off the ground. "Now it's perfect," I said against her temple.

"I'm so proud of you." She squeezed tighter.

If I could have frozen any moment and lived there for an eternity, this would have been it.

"I love you." The words fell out of my mouth with no preamble, no grace, with none of the practiced, pretty speeches I'd gone over in my head all day.

She jerked her head back, her eyes wide and drunkenly glazed. "Knox. Don't."

"I love you," I repeated, shocked that the world hadn't exploded into flames and quicksand by simply uttering those words.

She shook her head and shoved at my chest.

I let her go.

We stared at each other for what felt like an eternity but was probably only the length of a heartbeat. Champagne popped somewhere. Beers were handed around.

Harper arched a brow and turned, heading for the steps.

"Good luck," Ryker called out.

I was going to need it. *Eyes off her ass*, I told myself as I followed her up the stairs, but damn, it was right there. My palms itched with the need to hold her, and when she slipped, I bracketed her hips, holding her steady.

"Hey." She waggled a finger at me. "I said hands off."

"Would you rather I let you fall?"

Her forehead puckered, and she shook her head before scurrying up the last few steps.

She looked to the right—into our bedroom—then turned left, and pushing through that door instead.

I wasn't prepared for her little gasp, or the stab of pain that sliced me to the quick.

This was their room—Liam and Jamie's.

"It feels all wrong," she said, shaking her head as she sat on the lonely twin bed. "The room is still here, but they've been peeled away." Nothing personal of theirs remained. It was just a shell.

"Yeah, it does." I sat beside her, far enough that I kept my hands to myself as promised but close enough to reach her if she fell.

"You know what happens when you get all responsible for five months?"

I looked at her but didn't answer her rhetorical question.

"Your tolerance for alcohol disappears," she whispered. Her brow furrowed as she swung her gaze to mine. "I've had too much tequila to watch what I say to you."

"Then don't." That also meant she'd probably had too much tequila for me to hold her accountable for anything she actually *did* say.

She blew a strand of hair out of her face and then blinked as she stared across the room. "Where is Jamie's crib?" There were still divots in the carpet from where it had been.

"I gave it to Nolan."

Her head whipped toward mine, and it must have thrown off her equilibrium, because she grabbed ahold of my arm. "You gave it to Nolan?"

"It was Jamie's crib." I turned toward her and tucked her hair behind her ear. "I listened to every voicemail you left, Harper, and you were right. The best thing for the boys was to give it to Nolan." My chest went tight, thinking about all that had gone down the night she'd left. I didn't even know where to start with my apology, or if she'd even remember it tomorrow. "I was so mad that night when I got home and found out they were gone."

She drew back.

"And I was so stupid to let my emotions rule. So stupid to lash out at you the way I did."

She glanced around the room, then surged to her feet. "I can't do this in here."

"Harper," I started, but she was already out of the room.

I went after her, following her through our room and into our bathroom. She turned on the faucet and splashed cold water on her face.

I held out a hand towel and she took it, drying her face as she leaned back against the counter.

"I didn't take your name," she said, slowly bringing her gaze up to meet mine.

"Yeah. That sucked."

"And it wasn't because I don't love you." She twisted the towel in her hands. "That's the problem with us, Knox. I've never *not* loved you."

I moved toward her, and she put up her hand, stopping me.

"Just let me get this out, because God knows I'm going to regret it all in the morning."

It killed me, but I stepped back.

"And I knew, even when we rushed through that ceremony, that I was getting everything I'd ever wanted, but you weren't." She held up her finger, and my mouth snapped shut. "You were marrying me because you saw yourself in the boys, and you were willing to do anything, including chaining yourself to me, to keep them safe. And it was all temporary. We knew that."

My jaw clenched, but I kept silent.

"You've always said you weren't capable of falling in love.

And sure, I knew you were damaged. We all are. I'm not naïve, Knox. I've known you your whole life." Her eyes drifted shut for a second, and she pressed the towel to her cheek. "I knew once you met the right woman, the one you couldn't live without, you'd find a way to heal, and you'd fall in love." A smile ghosted her lips. "Because you have *so* much love to give. And I also knew, as much as it hurt, that it wasn't me." Her face crumpled and took my heart with it.

"Harper—"

"No." She shook her head even as she swiped the towel over her cheeks. "So when I went to sign the marriage license, I had a choice to make between grabbing ahold of everything I could from you and throwing myself into this...dream, or thinking about the pain it would cause when I inevitably had to change it back to Anders. Thinking about the woman you would one day *want* to give that name to, not just because you wanted to stand up for the boys but because you wanted her to have everything —your heart, your soul, and your name. And how unfair would it be to you that I'd taken it when you'd already given me so much?" Then she smiled—a real, full, genuine one—and my whole body clenched. "And then you called me Mrs. Daniels, and I loved it so much that I didn't have the heart to tell you the truth. I never thought we'd be married six weeks let alone five months."

"I understand." I didn't like it, but I got it.

"And as for my apartment—"

"I already know." I shrugged. "Ryker told me. I'm so sorry that I jumped to conclusions."

She nodded. "I'm so sorry I let you marry me."

"Fuck no. Harper, no." I closed the space between us and took her face in my hands. "Please don't regret that. I don't."

"We took it too far. I took it too far. And you were right, that night when you said there was nothing else holding us together but them."

"I was an idiot," I whispered.

"Admit it," she demanded. "Just once, tell the truth. If not for the boys, we never would have been together. You never would have kissed me—"

"I kissed you way before the boys were a factor." Just looking at her lips now made me want to sink right back into her.

"And look how that turned out," she whispered. "There really is nothing like kissing you, Knox. The whole world disappears when your mouth is on mine."

I groaned and rested my forehead on hers.

"It's kind of fitting to be here, isn't it?" The towel fluttered to the floor as she raised her hands to my chest. "You following me into a bathroom?" She raised her face and brushed her lips across mine.

"You're drunk." I felt the caress in every nerve ending.

"I prefer the term slightly overserved." Another graze of her mouth.

"And that means we can't—"

She rose up, tunneled her fingers through my hair, and kissed me, darting her tongue along the seam of my lips.

"Fuck." My hands fell to her hips, and I lifted her to the counter.

"Kiss me, Knox." She nipped at my bottom lip. "Even if it's one last time."

"It's not the last time. Didn't you hear me say that I love—"

She slammed her mouth into mine.

I failed the self-control test and kissed her back. My tongue sank deep, swirling over hers, tasting tequila and citrus and home. One hit of her and every good intention I had flew out the window.

Our mouths melded, the kiss deepened, and for a moment I forgot.

I forgot that she'd left me.

I forgot that I needed to win her back.

I forgot that she was too drunk to say yes.

She broke away long enough to pull her sweater off, and then came right back to me. I was high off endorphins and Harper, taking her mouth over and over. She wrapped her legs around my waist and rocked her hips against me.

"Fuck, you feel good."

"I want you," she whispered, her words slurred.

And I wanted nothing more than to strip her down and use my body to remind her what it felt like to belong to each other, but that wasn't happening. Not tonight. My dick didn't make decisions for me, not when it came to Harper.

"I want you too," I promised her, somehow finding the discipline to raise my head. "But you, my love, are drunk."

"I'm saying yes." She fisted my shirt.

"Say it tomorrow morning, and we'll do something about it." Like hell was I going to be something she regretted in the morning.

"Everything is spinning." She blinked rapidly, then dropped her head to my shoulder.

I grimaced. "Need me to hold your hair?"

She shook her head, then cringed, hunching her shoulders up. "Stop twirling."

"Yeah. It's bedtime for you." Her ankles were still locked around my waist, so I braced one hand on her back and the other under her incredible ass. "Hold on."

She whimpered, and I turned around slowly before carrying her to our bed.

I put her right where she belonged, then took off her shoes and socks.

"I've always loved your bed," she murmured, shimmying out of her shorts before I could stop her.

"I hate it without you in it." *Shit.* Those long, silky legs were going to be the death of me. I looked away as she slid under the covers.

Her bra landed on the floor.

I deserved fucking sainthood, because I kept my eyes to myself and stripped out of my shirt. "Sit up."

She worked her way up, and I put my shirt on her, helping her get her arms through the holes. That was better. Nice and covered up.

She threw her leg out from under the covers, putting one foot on the floor. "You should get back to the party. It's your big night."

I brushed her hair out of her face. "Believe me, Harper. There is nowhere I would rather be right now. I wasn't here when you needed me, and I know there will be times it will happen again, but tonight, I'm here."

"I'm stupidly drunk, Knox. Not dying. You can go downstairs. I'm so sorry if this is ruining your night." Each word came out a little more slurred.

"Honestly, getting you back in our bed was the best-case scenario for the night, so I think I'm doing pretty damn well." I smiled at her, but she didn't see me.

She was asleep.

CHAPTER THIRTY

arper

THE BEST HANGOVER FOOD IN THE WORLD WERE THE WAFFLES AT the Chatterbox, and I had a heaping stack of chocolate chip in front of me.

"You seriously snuck out on him like that?" Emerson asked, her mouth slightly agape.

"I folded his shirt," I said, as if it made it any better. "I was an absolute idiot last night, Em. I remember spilling my guts to him, and then trying to jump him." My belly twisted in mortification, or maybe that was leftover queasiness from last night. I'd showered as soon as I got home this morning, but I swore I could still feel tequila oozing out of my pores.

Turns out that doing six shots after five months of abstaining wasn't such a good idea.

"You did?" Her eyebrows shot up.

I nodded. "And he turned me down." I still couldn't decide if that was a good thing or not. "My memory goes kind of hazy once we got to the bathroom, but I remember that."

I love you.

Now that, I was pretty sure I'd imagined in my intoxicated state.

The world had started spinning, and he'd put me to bed. "Em, I think I ruined his night."

Emerson scoffed. "Trust me, you didn't. He came down once you were out and spent a couple hours with us before heading back up to you. And I'm pretty sure every other crewmember over twenty-one was way more wasted than you before the night was over. I've never seen so many shots in so many different colors. Turns out Indie can mix a mean drink."

"You don't look hungover."

"Spencer and I were the designated drivers, and Knox kept everyone hydrated while we delivered the drunken packages to their houses." She grinned. "You may have been the first to fall, but you were certainly not the last, Harper."

That made me feel a little better. God, it was bright in here. The waitress had been super sweet and sat us back along the wall, away from the windows, but even the overhead lighting sent shooting pains through my temples. I deserved every single ounce of the misery.

"I cannot believe I threw myself at him like that." I shoved the waffles in my mouth and groaned at my own stupidity, glad that Grams was over by the counter so she couldn't hear what an idiot I'd made of myself.

"He's a good guy," Em said, digging into her pancakes. "I know how badly he wanted to get you back last night."

"What?" My fork froze halfway to my mouth. "I mean...we talked some stuff out." My brow puckered, trying to remember exactly what was said. "But I thought he was going for closure." I shook my head.

"Eh." She cocked her head to the side. "From what Bash told me, the guys had it out right before the evaluation, and Knox made it pretty clear that he was fighting for you."

"You mean fighting *with* me."

"Nope. I mean what I said." A smile played across her mouth. "The guys gossip worse than we do, I swear. Plus, he was a man on a mission last night, and that mission was you."

I chewed my food thoroughly.

Emerson's eyes widened as she looked over my shoulder. "I think he's still on the mission."

"What are you talking—" My words stalled as I looked behind me and saw Knox stalking across the diner, his folded shirt in his hand. "Oh, he looks pissed."

"I think that's a pretty accurate description." She flashed a smile at Knox as he reached our table, glowering down at me. "Can we interest you in some breakfast?"

I swallowed, the intensity in his eyes stealing my breath.

"Enough." He bit out the word like it had personally offended him.

"Enough what?" I set my fork down.

"Enough of this." He motioned between him and me.

"I don't follow." Holy shit, was he about to dump me publicly? He'd never been one to let his softer emotions show in public, but his anger? He had a track record there.

"Enough of this bullshit where you run away from me."

People were staring.

Heat flooded my face. "I didn't run away from you this morning," I whispered, hoping he got the hint that the implosion of our relationship wasn't a spectator sport.

"When I wake up to an empty bed and a folded shirt on your pillow, I'd say that qualifies as you sneaking out and running away." He lifted said shirt, like he'd needed to bring evidence to this public hearing.

"Would you have rather I stolen your shirt?" I lifted a brow.

"Yes!" he shouted.

Every head turned.

Kill me now.

"That's your hotshot shirt." I stated the obvious and hoped he caught on.

"And your point is?" He lifted the offending shirt. "I put it on you last night."

"And I know the rules in this town," I hissed, shifting in my seat. "Only hotshots—"

"And the people who *belong* to hotshots," he interrupted, "wear them."

"Exactly." My cheeks burned, and I knew if I looked in the mirror, I'd be the shade of a cherry tomato.

"Okay, how can I make this any clearer?" He leaned into my space. "Let's do a visual demonstration. Arms up."

My jaw went slack.

"Arms. Up," he repeated, and the heat in his eyes had me raising my arms.

There was a distinct wave of muttering in the diner.

He put the shirt over my head, then tugged it down over the blouse I was wearing, taking the time to gently lift my hair free of the neck. "There. Get it?"

I slowly lowered my arms, speechless.

"Harper, I'm in love with you." His jaw ticked.

"You really said that last night?"

He nodded curtly.

"Well, you don't look too happy about it," I whispered.

He laughed in disbelief. "I was plenty happy about it before I woke up to find you gone. But I get it. If you need me to chase after you, then here I am." He flung his arms out wide. "If you need to see that I wasn't with you because you were convenient, or because of the boys, or because of whatever excuse you told yourself when you crept out of our bed this morning, here. I. Am." He rotated in a circle like the diner was center ring and he was going for the belt.

"What are you doing?" I was pretty sure Amy Donahue had her phone out.

He leaned down into my space and cradled my cheek with his hand, blocking out the rest of the room so there was only him and me. "I'm fighting for you. And I get that it's a new concept, so you might not recognize it, but this is what it looks like. You did all the talking last night, and now it's my turn."

My lips parted and my heart took off at a gallop.

"I'm not perfect. I make mistakes, and I've made more than my share when it comes to us. But you've seen me at my best and my worst, and you somehow manage to love me either way."

I sucked in a breath because it was true. There was nothing Knox could do that would stop my foolish little heart from loving him.

"You still do," he told me. "You've loved me since we were kids, and that's not going away because we got into a fight on what was possibly one of the worst days of our lives. You don't stop loving me because we took our anger out on each other instead of working through it together. You don't walk away from history like ours. I know. I tried to deny it for *years*. You don't give up on something like this. What we have, it's worth the fight." He lowered himself until we were at eye level. "So let's fight."

"Knox—"

"I fucked up when I said that we were only together for the boys, and I said it because I was pissed, and to set you free. The boys were never the reason we were together. They were the excuse I needed because I was too scared of losing you to ever try to have you.

"I fucked up when I walked out after the fight, because it

gave you the chance to doubt this—to doubt us. It gave you the opportunity to run, and damn, did you take it."

I flinched at his words, but his touch was soft.

"I fucked up when I didn't go after you that night, when I didn't haul you back to our house so we could hash it out.

"But the worst mistake of my life was not telling Ryker to shove his list up his ass the night I first kissed you. I knew then that you were the only woman I was ever going want—ever going to *love*. And yeah, Harper, *love*. I might not have known what it was then—or I was too scared to admit it—but I know now, and I'm trusting you with those words the way you trusted me with yours."

I bit my lower lip to keep it from trembling.

"I can't promise you that I'll always be here when you need me." His voice dropped to a whisper. "But I promise that no matter where I am, I'll be yours."

Before I could respond, he stood and pulled a knife from his pocket, turning toward the wall in one smooth motion.

Emerson gawked at him as his hand moved with quick, efficient strokes.

I couldn't think, couldn't breathe. I was only capable of staring up at him while my heart pounded out a reckless beat that had always belonged to him.

When he stepped away, his carving was front and center on the wall for the whole world to see. KNOX LOVES HARPER.

My vision wobbled as he dropped down in front of me, going to one knee. He reached into his pocket and pulled out his grandmother's ring—my ring.

"Knox," I whispered.

"The last time I put this ring on your finger, it was because I was scared. Scared that we'd lose the boys. Scared that they'd be separated. Scared that you'd walk out of my house and never look back if I didn't have a reason to keep you there." He lifted the ring to my left hand, sliding it just over the tip of my ring finger. "But I'm not afraid anymore. The worst has already happened to us, and we're still standing. You and me, we've been through it all. This whole town burned down around us, and we rebuilt and came back stronger. You and I always will. This time I want this ring on your finger because I'm certain there's no one else in the world who can love you like I do, and I'm ready to spend the rest of my life proving it to you. Fight with me, Harper. Marry me." His smile blew me away. "Again. Let's do this for all the right reasons."

There was no question in his eyes. No nerves. No trembling fingers.

This man knew exactly what he wanted, and it was me.

I leaned forward and kissed him, pouring everything I felt into it as the diner cheered around us.

"Is that a yes?" he asked against my mouth.

"That's a yes, Knoxville." A wholehearted, hell yes. Yes to the fighting and the work, to the love and the losses as they came.

He grinned and slid the ring home.

EPILOGUE

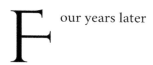our years later

HARPER

"HAPPY BIRTHDAY TO YOU," WE FINISHED SINGING, CROWDED around the picnic table in the park.

"Make a wish!" Liam said excitedly.

James leaned forward and huffed out five candles.

We all clapped, and he sat back on the bench, grinning at the praise. Nolan moved in, tugging out the still-smoking candles as a dozen eager preschoolers began clamoring for cake.

"It's hard to believe he's starting kindergarten next month," Knox said, wrapping his arms around me from behind and resting his head on my shoulder.

"Right?" I leaned back into him. "I feel like he just showed up for his first preschool class last week."

Knox snorted. "I still feel like he's only a handful about to puke down my back."

"He doesn't do that anymore." I rolled my eyes.

"Thank God. He wasn't going to score a lot of ladies with that habit." He gestured toward Liam, who was handing out cake. "That one is going to be a heartbreaker. He already knows the way to a woman's heart is through baked goods."

I shifted on my sore feet, and Knox's hands slid down my waist and over my stomach.

"Why don't we get you off your feet for a minute?"

I cocked an eyebrow at him. "Getting me off my feet for a minute is what got me here seven months ago." We hadn't even been trying, seeing that Ivy had only been a year old.

I glanced over at the nearest pine tree and smiled at the sight of Ryker holding his niece in the shade.

"I can't help that I find you irresistible." Knox kissed my neck, dipped, and lifted me into his arms like I weighed nothing. "And let's be honest, I never said you had to be off your feet. As I recall, I had you bent—"

"Knoxville!" I hushed him with a hand over his mouth.

He just grinned and nipped at my fingers.

He carried me to the next picnic table and sat me down on the bench, elevating my feet onto his thighs as he sat perpendicular to me. Then he rubbed the arch of my foot through my sandals, and I groaned in pure pleasure.

I soaked in the sight of him, knowing that having him home for even a week this time of year was something to be savored. We made the most of every moment we had together, and no matter how many times he was called away, I was always waiting for him with open arms.

"Hey, Knox, want to throw the football around?" Liam asked, already holding a red and black Nerf ball as he approached. His newest Legacy Hotshot hat was already dirty and torn in a few places, which made me laugh. That kid went through hats like nobody's business.

Knox shot me a look and I nodded. "Go have fun."

He carefully untangled himself as my footrest.

"Is this one a girl too?" Liam asked me, glancing down at my belly.

"Yep, she sure is," I answered.

"Did you want a boy?" he asked Knox, his brow furrowed.

"I wanted whoever was coming," Knox answered, flicking the brim of Liam's hat. "Besides, I can't think of anything better than being constantly surrounded by pretty girls."

Liam seemed to consider that, then leaned down until he was inches away from my belly button. "Hi, little girl. I'm Liam. Your parents are cool, so don't stress."

Knox laughed, and I couldn't help but smile as the two walked off a ways and started tossing the ball back and forth. It was all a little too picturesque, the kids running around with icing smeared on their faces, and all the more perfect for it.

I memorized everything about the moment so I could recall the memory on a night when Knox wasn't home, when the hard days fought to outnumber the good.

Knox slipped his phone from his pocket and answered it, holding it between his cheek and shoulder as he tossed the ball back to Liam. My chest tightened. Were they being called out? I whipped my gaze to Ryker, but he was still leaned back against the tree as Ivy napped on his chest.

Knox held up his finger to Liam, then walked toward me, the phone still perched at his ear.

"Is it a fire?" I asked.

He shook his head and set the phone on the table, pressing the speakerphone button. "Go ahead, Elliot. Harper is right here."

Oh, it was *that* kind of call.

"Hey, Harper."

"Hey, Elliot. You need a little help?" I swung my feet down and sat up straight while Knox swung his leg over next to me, straddling the bench.

"I have two siblings. Boy and girl. Ages seven and three. We're looking at respite care, nothing long term, but I'll know more on Monday when we have court."

Knox and I looked at each other. When the Pendridges had officially retired as our town's only foster parents four years ago, Knox and I had stepped up and taken over. Including Liam and James, twelve kiddos had come and gone through our doors in the past five years, though none had ever stayed as long the boys.

"Is this like last time when respite care turned into three months?" Knox asked, his tone teasing. "Or more like the time before when it was a week?"

"I honestly won't know until Monday," she answered.

"Give us a second," I said.

Knox hit the mute button.

"You feeling up for it?" Worry entered his gaze. "I can't guarantee I'll even be here Monday, and you're…" He gestured at our newest daughter.

"I'm pregnant, Knox, not dying." I rolled my eyes.

"Right. Just checking." He hit the unmute button. "We'll take them."

"Figured you would. Thanks, guys. I'll have them there in a couple of hours."

"Sounds good." Knox hung up and kissed me gently. "Here we go again?"

I smiled into the kiss. "Here we go again."

∾

THANK YOU SO VERY MUCH FOR READING! WANT TO KNOW WHAT happens when a rockstar takes up residence in Legacy? Muses and Melodies is available now!

IN THE MOOD FOR AN EMOTIONAL ROMANCE? READ WHAT happens when December Howard falls for Josh Walker, the hockey star next door in Full Measures, available now!

WANT TO SEE WHAT HAPPENS WHEN GRUMPY HELI-SKIING PILOT Weston Madigan accidentally becomes roommates with single mom Callie Thorne? Preorder A Little Too Close now!

DON'T MISS OUT ON THE NEXT RELEASE IN THE LEGACY WORLD! Sign up for my newsletter to be the first to get all the details!

ACKNOWLEDGMENTS

First and foremost, thank you to my Heavenly Father for blessing me beyond my wildest dreams.

Thank you to my husband, Jason, for your endless love, support, and chips and queso deliveries straight to my desk. Thank you to my children, who teach me about unconditional love every day. To our youngest daughter Audrey-Grace, who taught me what it takes to be a foster parent, and for the unbridled joy you bring to our house as a Yarros girl years later. To my son, Aidan, for inspiring me daily with your wholehearted devotion to your little sister, both in the years we fostered her and every day after. To my best friend, Emily, who never bats an eye when it takes me three days to respond to a text message while on deadline. To our social worker, Kristy, who fought for our daughter to have permanency.

Thank you to my editor, Karen Grove, for always understanding the weirdness that is my brain. To Jenn Wood, for dropping everything to copy edit, and to RBA Designs for the phenomenal cover. To my phenomenal agent, Louise Fury, who has a miraculous way of making my dreams come true.

Thank you to my wifeys, our unholy trinity, Gina Maxwell and Cindi Madsen, who always pick up the phone. To Shelby and Cassie for putting up with my unicorn brain. Thank you to Linda Russell for chasing the squirrels, bringing the bobby pins, and holding me together on days I'm ready to fall apart. To every blogger and reader who has taken a chance on me over the years. To my reader group, The Flygirls, for giving me a safe space on the internet.

Lastly, because you're my beginning and end, thank you again to my Jason. There's a little bit of you in every book boyfriend.

ABOUT THE AUTHOR

Rebecca Yarros is the *Wall Street Journal* and *USA Today* bestselling author of over fifteen novels, including *The Things We Leave Unfinished* and *The Last Letter*. "A gifted storyteller" (Kirkus), she is also the recipient of the Colorado Romance Writer's Award of Excellence for *Eyes Turned Skyward* from her *Flight and Glory* series.

Rebecca loves military heroes and has been blissfully married to hers for almost twenty years. She's the mother of six children and is currently surviving the teenage years with her four hockey-playing sons. When she's not writing, you can find her at the hockey rink or sneaking in some guitar time while guzzling coffee. She and her family live in Colorado with their stubborn English bulldogs, two feisty chinchillas, and a Maine Coon cat named Artemis, who rules them all.

Having fostered then adopted their youngest daughter, Rebecca is passionate about helping children in the foster system through her nonprofit, One October, which she co-founded with her husband in 2019. To learn more about their mission to better the lives of kids in foster care, visit www.oneoctober.org.

To catch up on Rebecca's latest releases and upcoming novels, including *A Little Too Close*, visit www.RebeccaYarros.com.

ALSO BY REBECCA YARROS

Standalones

The Last Letter

Great and Precious Things

The Things We Leave Unfinished

Muses and Melodies

The Flight & Glory Series

Full Measures

Eyes Turned Skyward

Beyond What is Given

Hallowed Ground

The Reality of Everything

The Legacy Series

Point of Origin

Ignite

Reason to Believe

The Renegades Series

Wilder

Nova

Rebel

Coming Fall 2022

A Little Too Close